Hope in Oakland

Rebekah Lee Jenkins

Hope in Oakland

By: Rebekah Lee Jenkins

Cover Design: Josephine Blake of Covers and Cupcakes

Chapter Header Design: Josephine Blake of Covers and Cupcakes

Editor and Interior designer: Alex McGilvery

ISBN: 978-0-9959793-2-1

Dedication

Hope in Oakland is dedicated to my grandparents Art and Reta Cowan.

In addition to my grandparents, hope is dedicated to my hometown, Souris, Manitoba including surrounding area. Your support of my writing warms my heart. I can't thank you enough.

Also, for my sisters on the sandbar, I love you all.

Chapter One

Toronto, Canada, 1904.

Canada's first female lawyer, Cora Rood, knew that anyone who dared represent Eli Pitman's wife in divorce court would face brutal and depraved retaliation from his hitman.

File in hand, trembling with anxiety, Cora knocked on Mr. Roth's office door. She chose him because of all the partners she worked for she believed he hated her the least. She tried to pull a mask of indifference over her face, because fear, like any other emotion, was not permissible in a lawyer.

"Come in." His voice sounded like ice on iron.

"There must be some mistake." Cora willed her hands to stop shaking while she presented the file for him to review.

Mr. Roth pulled his spectacles down onto the bridge of his nose and ignored the file in her hand. His eyes hardened." What do you want, Miss Rood?"

"I think I have been handed this divorce case by accident, Mr. Roth. The Pitman divorce...I am sure you intended that for one of the other lawyers. A more experienced lawyer." Cora's voice sounded shrill in her ears.

"You wanted family law — we are giving you what you want." Mr. Roth leaned back into his chair.

You enjoy this. Seeing my fear, you're like all the others.

"Eli Pitman is the biggest crime boss in Toronto." Cora's voice shook with fear. "No one who goes up against him survives. This is career suicide at best, but I fear for my life..."

"Then you better be clever." Mr. Roth looked down his nose at her and held her gaze with his own. "If you want a man to take this case, maybe it's time you came to the realization that women aren't cut out for the practice of law. No shame in giving up. You fought hard for what, five years? Screaming and shouting about equality? Only the suffragettes support you. Decent women think you are incurable. Hand that file in and admit defeat, give up on being a barrister, and go to work as a clerk."

Cora didn't reply. This was an all too familiar rant she had heard too many times. She let the words slide off her.

"I have a suggestion for you." Mr. Roth put down his pencil and looked at her hard. "Get married, Miss Rood, have some children, let the men practice law. There is a reason you are the only woman standing here, asking for a lighter case load. The intellectual powers of women are inferior to men. You do not possess the intelligence or strength of will to be a lawyer. Women are emotional, not logical, and the law is all about logic."

There was a time I would have fought you, but I lost my will to fight in a jail cell. You know as well as I do that I have to put up with your hatred and contempt for two more months until I finish my term so I can be sworn in as a barrister. I have no choices here, I can't turn this down.

"It sounds like the decision is final." She hated the defeat in her voice.

"I'm a busy man, Miss Rood. If you can't handle this, if you're too *delicate* for this, maybe we should reassign all your cases. We had no idea when we assigned this petition to you that your case load was so *taxing.*" He sneered at her. "None of the men are complaining about their work."

"I can handle the case load." She straightened her narrow shoulders and tried to sound hard, like him.

"We'll see." Mr. Roth looked back down at his paperwork, effectively dismissing her.

Cora crept back to her office. She closed the door and took a deep breath. Her mind raced as she thought about how she would talk Mrs. Adeline Pitman out of filing for divorce before she showed up for her two o'clock appointment.

She frowned at herself in the mirror. Her reflection revealed a broken woman — unruly chestnut hair, a drab olive green dress, and worn shoes. Her green eyes at one time gleamed with brilliance and excitement at the cases assigned to her. Now, disillusioned by her failures, her eyes had long ago lost their sparkle.

I'm tired of losing.

She shook her head at her sad appearance and turned around in time to see Mrs. Pitman standing at the entrance to the law office.

Mrs. Pitman checked her watch and tapped her foot while the front desk clerk, Jonathan, scampered around his desk to lead the way to Cora's office.

Adeline Pitman was a beautiful woman, in her mid-forties, with masses of dark copper hair piled high on her head and topped with an outrageous hat. She looked regal, refined, and determined. Sweeping by men who salivated at the sight of her, she made eye contact with no one. Mrs. Pitman wore a wool creation the colour of amber with contrast piping of jet black. Her left eye was hidden by the brim of her hat. Cora didn't have the first clue about ornithology, so she had no idea what poor bird had died and given up its feathers so that Mrs. Pitman could sweep in here, half cat, half bird, one hundred percent predator on the prowl.

Cora felt like a mud hen about to interview a peacock.

Mrs. Pitman swept into Cora's office, and they locked eyes. Cora was first to look away. "I am the lawyer assigned to your case," she said. "How can I help you?"

Mrs. Pitman cut straight to the point. "I need a divorce immediately." She pulled her gloves off and adjusted herself in the chair across from Cora.

"I looked over your petition, Mrs. Pitman. Have you spoken to another lawyer?" She settled in her chair across from Mrs. Pitman.

"I'm here for a second opinion. I disagreed with the first one. What can you do with this?" Mrs. Pitman gestured to the file marked "Pitman Petition."

"Very little," Cora responded cautiously.

"Oh?" Mrs. Pitman's eyes narrowed in disapproval.

"The law in Canada is very clear, Mrs. Pitman." Cora tried to head off a temper tantrum. "A party must be at fault. Men can divorce their wives on the grounds of adultery alone. For women, you cannot legally petition for divorce unless he has committed adultery *and* you can prove he is cruel. You have evidence of adultery, but this file does not meet the burden of proof for cruelty. I have to advise you to drop this petition. You won't win."

"I have to win." Mrs. Pitman's teeth clenched in anger. "I won't stop until I win."

"Adultery is not enough." Cora spoke sternly.

Mrs. Pitman's hands clenched into fists, her lips thinned. "This is an outrage. This is a double standard."

"I agree, and I sympathize." Cora leaned away from the petition as if it might burn her. "Outrage or not, it's the law. I can't change the law."

"My husband has been paying for an apartment in the upper west side." Mrs. Pitman held her chin high. "I was confused about why. Imagine my surprise when I went to that apartment to see for myself what exactly was going on. I watched him with binoculars. He exited her apartment bold as brass. Mirabel Salter, a daughter of a friend of mine, kissed him goodbye in her... well... unmentionables."

Cora shifted uncomfortably at the blatant pain on Mrs. Pitman's face.

"An apartment?" Cora moved closer to the petition.

"Yes. He's had this apartment for a while."

"How long?" Cora pulled the petition back in front of her and picked up a pencil to jot down the length of time Eli had maintained a separate residence.

"More than a year." Mrs. Pitman adjusted her gloves on her skirt.

Cora wrote down Mrs. Pitman's statement. "Is he cruel to you? Has he ever hit you?"

Cora couldn't imagine in her wildest dreams any man laying a hand on Mrs. Pitman. She carried herself like a queen. She would never permit it.

"Eli has never hit me." Mrs. Pitman frowned in confusion.

I have been hit by a man, and it's terrible. You will feel it for the rest of your life.

"Has he ever denied you money for basic essentials?" Cora grasped at this last straw.

"No." Mrs. Pitman's tone was cold.

"Mrs. Pitman, I am not unsympathetic. I understand the pain of adultery is very difficult. Even with a separate residence, though, I have to advise you to turn a blind eye and try to..."

"You, a woman, are advising me to turn a blind eye to adultery?" Mrs. Pitman interrupted as her voice escalated with anger. "I expected better from you!"

Cora wished fervently that she could crawl under her desk. Mrs. Pitman was not about to back down. This divorce was going to be filed, and Cora was going to have to argue it.

Conceding, Cora gathered her thoughts and tried to buy some time to come up with some sort of plan. "I just received this case today. Can you give me a day to research and try to think up some way to assist you? Would you mind coming back tomorrow afternoon?"

"Certainly! I am not unreasonable, Miss Rood." Mrs. Pitman hovered on the verge of a temper tantrum.

Mrs. Pitman wouldn't stop until she got her way; Cora had a day to come up with a miracle.

Chapter Two

Mrs. Pitman swept back into the law office the following afternoon. She didn't wait on Jonathan, the clerk, this time. She strode purposely to Cora's office, knocked on the door, and let herself in.

"What have you come up with?" Mrs. Pitman's face was granite hard, battle ready.

A sleepless night for Cora, searching through precedent, had presented one slim hope for Mrs. Pitman.

"I *might* be able to argue abandonment." Cora cringed. Abandonment was a long shot; she stood the distinct possibility of being laughed out of court.

Mrs. Pitman's eyes gleamed with triumph.

"Might!" Cora quickly tried to crush the hope in her eyes. "Listen carefully. This loop hole of which I speak is subject to opinion, and it will depend on the judge. It is rumoured your husband owns every judge in the land. Meanwhile, even though he is cavorting with Miss Salter, he is paying your bills. It's the longest shot in the history of long shots."

Mrs. Pitman smiled at Cora in anticipation. Cora suspected in her mind the case was already won.

"At first, I was outraged that they are assigning this case to a woman lawyer." Mrs. Pitman changed the subject. "The first woman lawyer in Canada, no less. I thought, how is she going to handle this? But then, while you were searching precedent, I looked into your background."

Cora took a deep breath and sat very still.

"Only real estate law, disappointing, but then it occurred to me. If he's bested by a woman, he will be so embarrassed he'll leave you alone so as not to look ridiculous to his associates."

"Mrs. Pitman." Cora held her hands out in supplication. "Men who are bested by women set out to destroy them. They do not ignore that sort of slight to their pride."

"Eli Pitman would destroy any man that stood up to him, but he won't take you seriously. You are like a secret weapon." Mrs. Pitman's eyes raked over Cora. "You took the top marks on the bar exam. Beat everyone by a landslide. I'm sure your brain will come up with something. The legal brain is typically more devious than the average person. You can see opportunities others can't." Mrs. Pitman leaned forward with excitement.

Cora settled back in her chair, refusing to be offended.

Devious indeed!

"I will try my best, but I must warn you Mrs. Pitman. There is no equality for women under the current statutes surrounding family law."

"We've established that, but I have every confidence that you will figure this out." Mrs. Pitman flashed her a smile. The smile told Cora that Mrs. Pitman was accustomed to using charm to get what she wants.

There is no charm in a court of law.

"I can't talk you out of proceeding?" Cora took one last stab.

"Absolutely not. Mirabel Salter is twenty years old. Twenty. She is younger than our oldest son. This is not his first mistress — it is his third. I had children at home. My parents were still alive, and the scandal would have killed them. I plastered a smile on my face and pretended there was nothing wrong. I have pretended for twenty long years. I'm done pretending."

"What do you think you will need?" Cora picked up a pencil and started to write down Mrs. Pitman's list of demands.

"I need my entire trust as well as $50,000. This last mistress was the last straw."

"Fifty thousand dollars in addition to a trust?" Cora gripped her pencil so hard it snapped in two.

"I saw the ring he gave his last mistress." Mrs. Pitman's eyes hardened.

Cora took a deep breath, found another pencil, and let her breath out slowly.

"How do you think you'll get your hands on $50,000 of Eli Pitman's money?" Cora could barely force the words past her throat as it clenched in fear.

Mrs. Pitman shrugged. "You'll think of something."

Cora opened her mouth to speak and then closed it.

"I know you have what it takes. I saw you at the rally for the suffragettes."

Cora stiffened at the memories of the rally.

"You were there in the front line with Dr. Harriet Stowe. You were arrested with her, weren't you?"

"Yes. I was arrested," Cora said hoarsely.

Arrested. My hands still tremble when I think of it. You don't take on the biggest bullies in Canada and get away without paying a price.

"I remember you standing up to the oppression like a soldier." Mrs. Pitman's eyes widened at the memory. "I knew I needed you, but I didn't realize you were a lawyer. I thought you were a doctor."

"Not a doctor, although the Dominion Women's Enfranchisement Association wanted me to work in that field. I had my reasons for choosing the law." Cora didn't elaborate. Mrs. Pitman wasn't interested.

The Dominion Women's Enfranchisement Association and the Women's Christian Temperance Union will dance down the streets with the news that I have landed this case. Win or lose — a trial involving this high-profile couple will expose the double standard for women in the law. Once they hear about this, I'll have no peace.

Cora shook away the thoughts of the pressure that would come from those women as she soldiered on. "I've searched precedent — there is very little. Divorce is so unheard of that we're breaking new ground here. As I see it, from what you have told me, you will need a bank account to deposit the trust into. As a married woman, you cannot open a bank account without your husband's permission, and that includes his signature."

"This is outrageous!" Mrs. Pitman hissed. She jumped to her feet, hands on her hips; she towered over Cora.

"Mrs. Pitman, it's all outrageous." Cora's voice hardened with warning. "All of it. No need wasting energy on being upset and angry with the law. The law fails women. That is a given. If I cannot talk you out of this, the plan you have to execute is going to need cool detachment and cunning like you have never had to have in your life. So, sit down and take notes. It's complicated."

Mrs. Pitman locked eyes with Cora again. Cora's hard, battle weary gaze clashed with Mrs. Pitman's spoiled, haughty eyes. "I knew I came to the right person." She sat down.

You have not come to the right person. I would have turned you down flat.

Cora's mind raced with possibilities to make this spoiled child of a woman, a client she reminded herself, happy. "A charity would be a legitimate reason to require a bank account. A charity that would necessitate the purchase of real estate would be ideal. It will be easy to ask him for large sums of money where part of the money goes to the charity and the other part goes to you. Unless you can think of another reason for Mr. Pitman to open an account for you."

"All right, a charity." Mrs. Pitman wrinkled her nose at the thought, as if charity work might smell unpleasant. "What kind do you suggest?"

"Whichever kind you want." Cora's jaw clenched with the effort of being professional.

"What would you pick?"

"Mrs. Pitman, I have no idea. Everything needs to change. I don't even know where to start. Maybe an orphanage? You will have to come up with the idea on your own."

"All right. How does one start a charity?" Mrs. Pitman sighed, resigned.

"You throw a lavish dinner party where you are going to ask your closest friends, neighbors, and business contacts for money for your new charity. Mr. Pitman needs to see that you are committed to the orphans or whatever. You need to make sure he wants to back this scheme financially. You'll need to be... uh... friendly with him."

"How will I be friendly with him when I want to rake his eyes out?" Mrs. Pitman's hands clenched into fists.

"I don't know. Drink a lot before... uh... well before you are... um... just drink a lot."

"I'm going to have to start now. What you are suggesting is basically prostituting myself for a bank account." Mrs. Pitman swallowed hard.

"Unfortunately, Mrs. Pitman, a lot of what you will have to do before you are rid of him is a form of prostitution. It's the only way." Cora reached into her desk drawer to pull out a bottle of brandy and two tea cups, no saucers. She poured a generous helping into both.

Mrs. Pitman took a big gulp; Cora took a delicate sip. "Two bank accounts, Mrs. Pitman. One that is a legitimate charity. Once he's in the bank, you'll ask his opinion. Nicely."

Mrs. Pitman's eyes narrowed.

"You will say, 'Do you think I should have a second account in case I need money to purchase things without the board's approval?' What does he think?"

Cora's mind raced to create a plan that would placate Mrs. Pitman and set her up for life in the event that Mr. Pitman didn't have them both killed. "You'll wait for him to formulate an answer. The bank account he opens for you with *your* name on it, not the charity, is the account for you to deposit your trust into and any money from him that is a *personal gift*. You cannot use money from the charity to line your pockets. You can, however, ask Eli for money for the charity and put it in that separate account as long as there is *no paper trail*. I need to be very clear. Absolutely no paper trail! When you have the money you need and you face him in divorce court, you'll have to be above board. They will check all the paper involved in the charity. The charity bank account is just to get him in the bank, to open the personal account. I don't see you taking notes." Cora frowned.

"So. Two accounts." Mrs. Pitman scrambled for a pencil and paper. "One for charity and one for personal use?"

"Yes."

"When he asks why a charity?" Mrs. Pitman's hand was poised to write down a reason.

Use your imagination!

"Have you ever considered using your wealth and your time to assist those less fortunate?" Cora tried and failed to keep the contempt out of her voice.

Mrs. Pitman squinted in confusion.

Cora sighed; this was going to be up hill all the way. "You'll tell him with the children grown up and gone you need a cause to support. You're bored. You're wondering if he doesn't permit you to start a charity, maybe there is something you can do in his offices."

Mrs. Pitman scratched down the reasons she was offering.

"You could suggest that maybe you should work for him. That will cause him to panic."

"This is all very devious." Mrs. Pitman's eyebrows raised.

"Mrs. Pitman, if you aren't up for this..." Cora warned.

"No, I am up for this. Continue!" Mrs. Pitman kept jotting ideas down.

"Turn on your charm with Mr. Pitman, and get that bank account. We can't proceed without it." Cora took a sip of brandy.

"Dear God, you are... you are..." Mrs. Pitman sputtered as she wrote down the words 'seduce Eli.'

"Determined to see you retain your trust regardless of how he reacts to this petition?" Cora filled in cautiously.

"I was going to say unconscionable." Mrs. Pitman huffed.

Cora shrugged and took a deeper sip of brandy. Mrs. Pitman tried her patience.

"What if I can't get him interested enough to be... friendly... with me." Mrs. Pitman's eyes glittered with tears. She shifted in her seat.

Cora's eyes softened with sympathy.

"Mirabel Salter is twenty years younger. I can't compete with that. I... don't know if I can get him to... be... with...uh...me in the manner you are suggesting."

It was hard, very hard for a woman like Mrs. Pitman to admit this to anyone. Cora's heart went out to her. The toll of a loveless marriage had to be heavy.

"Just try your best." Cora, whom the entire legal profession called an ancient spinster, took a bigger swig of the brandy and refilled their cups.

Gracious, there is no section on this in law school!

"You need to bring me the legal documents concerning your trust." Cora nodded at Mrs. Pitman to jot that down. "I need to look at the legalities of you accessing it. There will be more to this plan, but I do not want to overwhelm you. You have a dinner party to plan..."

"Oh, that is taken care of. This Saturday, we are hosting a huge gala event at our home. Randall, my son, is dating Miss Scott... yes, *those* Scotts. We have money, of course, but not *old* money. Eli is eager to see this marriage take place, no expense spared. We are announcing their engagement to our family and friends. The worst part of our arrangement is that he lives with Mirabel, but I am to host all the boring dinner parties and lavish balls in our ballroom. He seems to believe that I am slated for his public life. We present the appearance of the perfect couple and then he goes home to her." Mrs. Pitman's tone hardened as she spoke.

"Oh." Cora frowned. "I'm sorry."

Mrs. Pitman shrugged. "I've been putting up with it for twenty years. You'll get me divorced, and this craziness will all stop. My only fear is if I am with him in the manner you suggest, can we still petition for abandonment?"

"He hasn't lived with you for over a year, and he maintains a separate residence with a mistress. According to the precedent I read, that can be ruled as abandonment. However, in that particular case, the husband did not continue to provide for his wife. She was left destitute."

Mrs. Pitman shuddered as if that were a fate worse than death.

"The entire thing is a long shot." Cora rubbed her eyebrow to relieve some tension. "He provides for you financially, there is no guarantee the judge will rule in favour of abandonment. After Eli approves your charity, your next step is to request his permission to have a personal bank account. Once those two accounts are open, you need to start a board with women you can trust. I suggest Jean King of the Dominion Women's Enfranchisement Association. She's tough and she's well connected. I can personally vouch for her. She assisted me in my fight to practice law in Canada. You might want to involve the Women's Christian Temperance Union. They have a good grasp of what the women of Toronto need. I can guarantee these are women Eli hasn't...uh... been friendly with. Where should we meet from now on?"

"Why?" Mrs. Pitman's forehead furrowed.

"Until your orphan fund or whatever is established, he might get suspicious that you are meeting with a lawyer. If he knows you are filing for divorce, you will never get those bank accounts."

"I see." Mrs. Pitman nodded.

"The lawyer you already spoke to? Is he in any way connected to Mr. Pitman?" Cora's voice sounded shrill.

"I'm not sure. I just saw an office and walked in."

Cora took another deep sip of brandy to try to steady her nerves.

"Anyway, I have a doctor's appointment next week. It's a woman's complaint, so he won't ask anything about it." Mrs. Pitman opened her handbag. "Meet me there."

"That will work perfectly."

Mrs. Pitman tucked her notes away and handed Cora a card with the address of the doctor's office.

Now that the plan was in motion, raw anxiety created a headache at the base of Cora's skull. Mrs. Pitman was going to strike at Eli in a court of law. An arena where the odds were against them. Court was the only place that Adeline could be set free and the only place that she could just as easily be utterly destroyed. It was the ultimate gamble. Mrs. Pitman was prepared to throw the dice, and Cora steeled herself to support her.

"I should warn you, Mrs. Pitman, women who don't turn a blind eye to adultery pay a heavy price. You could lose in court *and* lose your friends. I've seen it."

"The suffragettes will take me in. I hesitated to join an order because Eli disapproved, but today I will join..." Mrs. Pitman stood up and pulled her gloves back on as if she were a boxer going into a ring.

"No, you will not," Cora said with such authority Mrs. Pitman's head snapped up. "You are to be the model wife. Everything he wants, you will do it."

Mrs. Pitman's eyes flashed with confusion and then pain as she slumped back down into her chair.

Cora wished fervently there was an easier way. From what she had seen as a suffragette on the front line of the battle for equal rights... in the jail cells... the world of equality would never exist. There would never be a time an Adeline could go up against an Eli and not pay a terrible price.

"Everything," Cora repeated ominously.

They looked at each other as the full weight of that word hung between them.

"You are walking out this door a submissive wife. You will conduct yourself with perfect wifely obedience. Whatever he wants, he gets, and you smile as you do it. This is the only way you can hope to win. You have to take him completely off guard."

My life depends on it.

Mrs. Pitman's hand clutched at her throat. "What on earth is perfect wifely obedience?"

"I expect exactly like it sounds." Cora pointedly poured more brandy into her cup.

Mrs. Pitman took another gulp of liquid courage. Finally, they shuddered and then visibly braced themselves.

"Mrs. Pitman, you are going to war, and you are denied any weapons. This is a game, and you are the only game piece who knows she is playing. That is the only power you have. Those who have no rights under the law must be clever and cautious." Cora's voice lowered in warning.

"You mean manipulative and cunning." A hint of disapproval in Mrs. Pitman's tone made Cora's back stiffen.

"Well, cautious as a serpent, innocent as a dove or something to that effect." Cora put her tea cup down.

Mrs. Pitman clenched the armrests of her chair. "It must be bad if you are quoting scripture."

"It is every bit as bad." Their eyes met. "You must bide your time, be obedient, give him everything he wants while you build your nest, and then you betray him. Provoke him. Destroy him. Pray your judge has a sympathetic bone in his body for women's rights."

"This is humiliating." Mrs. Pitman leaped to her feet again and paced to the window. "Perfect wifely obedience. Mercy! That might cause suspicion all on its own. He'll be wary."

"You might be surprised." Cora squeezed the back of her neck, trying to ease the tension. "Men like Eli feel that women have no brains and no purpose other than to cater to their every whim, so he'll just accept this change in you as if it were his due. Believe me, he won't raise an eyebrow."

"For a *Miss*, you seem to know a lot about men." Mrs. Pitman accused Cora.

"I despise the lot of them." Cora gave up on her neck. With one sweep of her arm she gestured at the entire office she worked in. "Pigs. All of them. All I deal with day in and day out is men. I am weary of their contempt."

Cora watched as Mrs. Pitman's eyes glazed over. Cora could tell if the conversation wasn't about her, she wasn't interested.

"I'll meet you at the doctor's office in a week." Mrs. Pitman straightened her shoulders. She went to the door and as she opened it, she turned.

"One last thing to think about. You'll need some insurance. Approach Mirabel and bring her on your committee."

Mrs. Pitman's eyes flashed with fury.

"Absolutely not." Her lips thinned.

"Mrs. Pitman, he'll back a charity his mistress is part of." Cora tidied up the file in front of her.

Mrs. Pitman's eyes appeared tortured. She shut the door and turned to Cora.

Cora stood up and came around her desk to face Mrs. Pitman straight on. "You have to take your emotions out of this. It's the only way. Stop feeling and start thinking," Cora admonished her. Conflicting emotions rolled over Mrs. Pitman's face. First fury, then resignation, finally acceptance.

"You are right. I will send a telegram to Mirabel today." Mrs. Pitman opened the door of Cora's office.

"Thank you, Miss Rood." Mrs. Pitman raised her voice so that some of the men looked up. "I am delighted to have your council on this upcoming charity. I wish to extend thanks for your generous donation."

So, it begins.

Cora watched Mrs. Pitman swirl to send one last wave back to her. Now every eye was on her.

"I appreciate all *your* hard work." Cora played along as she walked a little way with her through the thick gloom of smoke from the men working on legal briefs. "I know that this charity will be a boon to the city of Toronto."

"Good day, Miss Rood." Mrs. Pitman walked through the smoke toward the lobby of the building.

Cora swept her eyes over the rest of the men.

Two more months. I will walk away from you, be sworn in as a barrister, and I will never look back.

Cora returned to her office and closed the door; she shut her eyes for a brief moment.

Have I really just advised Mrs. Pitman to embezzle money from the most powerful mob boss in Toronto? Did I really just do that? Do I have no ethics whatsoever? Am I really going to justify the inequality in the law to explain what just took place here today? Fired at the end of this or not, I'm as good as dead anyway, so it won't matter.

Cora locked her office door and sat down at her desk. She ignored the pounding pain at the base of her skull and set straight to work making sure Mrs. Pitman had the documents necessary to start a charity. A real one. Run by a woman who was about to tackle Eli Pitman in divorce court.

Heaven help us.

As Cora went to the bookcase to find a book on trusts, she saw something move out of the corner of her eye. A man stood across the street watching her through the window in her office. Even with an entire street between them, she shuddered at his size. Well over six feet tall, his shoulders were broad, and his hands were the size of dinner plates. He dropped his cigar on the road and looked straight at her as he ground it out with his boot. She held his gaze until Mrs. Pitman swept out the front door and he turned his attention to her.

Is that Eli's bodyguard, Royce? Does Eli already suspect something? Oh heavens, Mrs. Pitman... we're in over our heads and we haven't started yet!

There was no way she was going to come out of this alive. A shiver of fear raced down Cora's back.

Chapter Three

Adeline Pitman was in just the perfect state of undress to seduce or be completely humiliated.

Eli's eyes lit up in appreciation as she sashayed through their bedroom. "To what do I owe this honour?" Distracted, Eli lost his place tying his tie.

"I'm sorry, Eli." Adeline stretched, arching her back. His eyes flicked over her as she hoped they would. She pulled a dress off a hanger, and he gestured that she should not get dressed.

"I've just been so distracted getting the boys settled, and I've been just, I don't know how to explain it. I haven't been myself." Adeline held the dress up as if she were thinking of a different one. She put it down and faced him; she gritted her teeth as she smiled.

"I know the boys were a handful before we sent them off." Eli was quick to lay the blame on the boys.

"Now that they are gone, I feel rather... well..." Adeline paused as Eli pounced on her from across the room. "Adrift."

"Oh?" Eli wasn't listening. He was busy nuzzling her neck. Adeline's body responded to him; it made her furious.

Traitorous body.

"I was thinking maybe I should come to work for you," she whispered.

"Whatever you want," he agreed, as he turned her and fought with the lacing on her corset.

"Perfect," she said brightly. "Would you like me to start in accounting? Maybe your front desk?"

"Wait, what?" Eli pulled back and looked at her, confused.

"I said, I want to work for you. The days are long here. I am certain you are swamped. You just agreed to whatever I want." Her eyes searched his.

16

"Darling, the world I work in, it's not for you. You would hate it. Ledgers, numbers, and finances. That's for men, my dear. It's not for a beautiful woman like you."

"You don't think I could do it?" Adeline pouted as she picked up her dress and made a move to put it on.

"I'm not saying that at all!" Eli took the dress from her and put it out of her reach. "I'm sure you would be an amazing clerk. The best... certainly the most beautiful. I'm just saying you don't *want* to do it. Leave that to men. It's boring."

"I need something, though. You didn't want me to participate with the suffragettes." Adeline let her pout deepen.

"Protesting and screaming about equal rights. So vulgar." Eli's hard hands caressed her face as he kissed her pout. "I can't have my wife at the helm of all that unpleasantness. They might arrest you! I will not allow that. Besides, what do you want? Name one thing I don't provide for you. Look at this house, your clothes — the boys have the best education. You don't have to lift a finger. I have never once denied you a penny. You are throwing the most lavish parties in Toronto for all your friends... I mean all *our* friends. What are you missing out on that you feel you need to protest for?" Eli looked genuinely perplexed.

"Equal rights, Eli. I think women should have..."

"You don't need to worry about that." Eli cut her off. He slid the strap of her chemise down. "You are provided for. Your children are provided for. That's my job, Adeline. I worry about all that for both of us. Your job is to be beautiful and charming and show off our money to our friends." He smiled as if this were the answer to life. "Every woman I know would love to have your life. What do you want?"

A man that is faithful to me. A man that wouldn't give Mirabel Salter a second look because he's got me at home.

"You're exactly right." Adeline swallowed down the venomous statements trying to crawl up her throat. She pulled her chemise strap back up, then reached around him and picked up the dress the designer had specially made for tonight. She stepped into her gown and pulled it up. "Would you fasten the back of my dress?"

"I'd rather rip this off you and forget we have a hundred of our closest friends in the ballroom," Eli growled in her ear.

Adeline tried and failed to ignore the sweep of desire that pulsed through her at his words.

"Let's show off our money, shall we?" she teased, even as her heart hollowed in disappointment. This was lust that he felt for her. Not love. It had never been love between them.

"But later..." He finished buttoning the back of her dress that left quite a bit of her back showing. His knuckles were hard against the soft skin of her back.

"Later." Adeline turned to face him and ran her hands over his shoulders and down his arms. For a man who ran huge corporations and spent a lot of time behind a desk, there was nothing soft about Eli Pitman. "Later, maybe we can figure out what I need to do to feel fulfilled. If I shouldn't work for you, maybe a charity?"

"A charity sounds great." Eli grabbed onto that solution like a man drowning.

"I've been thinking of starting a charity for the battered and abused women of Toronto, Eli. I spoke to a lawyer about it. I can't sleep thinking of the suffering of these women and children in our city."

"Sounds wonderful, darling. You should start that immediately." Eli's eyes fixated on her décolletage. Clearly, abused women were of no interest to him.

"There's just one little sticky point." Adeline moved her hands back up his arms and twined her fingers in his hair.

Thank goodness, I'm still attracted to him. I couldn't fake this. He would see straight through it.

"I would need some sort of... I don't know how you would call it." Adeline tilted her head in confusion. "An account of some sort? My lawyer said I need something I can write bank notes on? Is that what it is? Could you manage that? I just find the whole thing so complicated."

"That's no problem." Eli smiled. "We can open an account for the charity. I can set that up tomorrow."

"Would you?" Adeline answered breathlessly.

"Of course. I'll put the first donation into your account."

"Would I go with you then to set it up?" Adeline was careful to keep her voice sounding confused. Like a strumpet, she slid her tongue around her lips to wet them, knowing it would distract him.

"Yes. You'll need signing authority, it's called." Eli answered but didn't take his eyes off her lips.

"I'm so glad I have you, Eli. You just so easily solved every problem." Adeline tried not to gag on the syrupy sweet words as they left her mouth.

"All that matters is that you are happy." Eli moved to kiss her, and she let him. This mouth that kissed Mirabel Salter was kissing her now.

There was a knock at the door just as he pressed her back against the wall.

"Our guests," Adeline reminded him.

"Right. Our guests," Eli groaned. He straightened up and pulled his suit jacket on.

Adeline straightened as well, and when Eli opened the door for her, he put a hand on her arm.

"Better for you, as my wife, to put your energy into a charity. I will allow that rather than to run with a group of angry, *single,* suffragettes."

"You're right, Eli." *Allow...* Adeline shook with anger.

Eli moved closer. "Darling, you're trembling." He smiled like a wolf about to devour a lamb.

He thinks I'm shaking with desire.

"With excitement," she lied smoothly.

Adeline leaned into Eli as the butler turned away discreetly. She put her hand on the hard plane of his cheek. She looked deeply into eyes that were such a light grey that they were the colour of ice and played her part. "I'm glad I spoke to you about joining the suffragettes. That would have been such a mistake. I would hate to think I brought any sort of reproach onto you. If you want me to run a charity, then I am happy to do whatever you want. Nothing makes me happier than seeing you find something you can be proud of in me." Adeline hated the lies that spilled out of her.

"We can set that account up tomorrow afternoon. You might be too tired after this evening to be up and at the bank first thing in the morning." Eli smiled like a predator. "In fact, Adeline, I guarantee you are going to be very, very tired tomorrow."

"Whatever you think is best," Adeline purred.

I'm prostituting myself for a bank account.

He held his arm out, and she linked her hand in his elbow. His bicep and forearm were powerful under her fingertips. She was playing with fire, double-crossing him like this.

What is he capable of?

Adeline heard he had a thug that made people disappear. Rodd, or Bob, or something. She shook the thought out of her head. He stopped and opened the door of the ballroom for her.

A fission of fear crossed her heart.

19

What about our sons? Could he turn them against me? If he feels betrayed, would he go that far? I need my boys.

She shook the thought out of her head. She needed to end the pain she had endured nonstop since his first mistress. She needed to move on in a way only divorce would allow. A clean break.

Perfect wifely obedience indeed! Cora was right — Eli Pitman didn't suspect a thing.

Chapter Four

Rodd Royce, Eli's right hand man, entered Eli's office and closed the door so the secretary wouldn't hear him. The office had floor-to-ceiling windows, so he could look out over his empire. There was very little Eli didn't own, and he loved to survey it from his high perch on Bathurst Street.

"I was doing surveillance on Luther Holmes. He's hired Roth for that land deal on the upper west side. Your wife though, she was in Roth and Levine meeting with a lawyer."

Eli put his pencil down and scratched his eyebrow.

"I understand she wants to start a charity." Eli picked up his coffee cup and took a sip.

"The lawyer she saw is different."

"What do you mean, different?" Eli gave Royce a hard look.

"Well, it's a woman lawyer or some such nonsense." Royce frowned in confusion. "I didn't believe it — I double checked at the front desk of the law office."

"Woman?" Eli tilted his head.

"Apparently, according to the front desk clerk, she is just entry level to complete her term as an articled apprentice. They are counting down the days to get rid of her. She is only given real estate work."

Eli didn't like assumptions.

"Follow her."

"Can I question her?" Royce raised his eyebrows, seeking permission to do much more than question.

"Find out where she lives and see if you can find paperwork with Adeline's name on it. If you do, be sure to take it. I will do the questioning."

"Can I...?" Royce leaned forward with anticipation.

"No."

Royce's face fell.

"Just surveillance." Eli went back to his papers. Royce shuffled in front of him. "Let me question her first, and if I'm not satisfied, you can question her later."

"By question... you mean... just to be sure..."

"By question, I mean gather information by whatever means necessary." Eli watched Royce's face break into a smile.

"I want to see her immediately. Hand deliver this to her law firm." Eli shouted for his secretary to take dictation.

"But, I can't..."

"No." Eli's eyes narrowed, and Royce wisely didn't ask again.

***

Cora let herself into the lobby of Dr. Martell's office. The lobby smelled like antiseptic and nervous sweat. A lavish silver tea service and an assortment of dainties were stationed near the desk where the nurse sat. The lights were dimmed in an attempt to calm nervous patients. Soft seating and gentle music proclaimed this a private clinic for the rich. Cora approached the nurse, and her eyes swept over the women sitting in the waiting room. No Mrs. Pitman.

"I'm here to lend support to a friend," Cora explained in hushed tones to the nurse before settling into a chair by the entrance. She pulled out some correspondence to proof before mailing it.

True to her word, Mrs. Pitman swept into the lobby at precisely 10:45 then took a seat beside Cora.

"I have the papers you requested." Mrs. Pitman took out a large envelope and handed it to Cora as if it were contraband.

"How have you been feeling?" Cora asked, to keep up the ruse that she was here to lend support to a sick friend.

Mrs. Pitman blinked at her.

"I am just so glad I could be here for you today. Hopefully the doctor has good news for you." Cora hoped Mrs. Pitman would play along.

"I'm glad you could be here, too. Less daunting, for sure." Mrs. Pitman patted Cora's arm.

"I'll peruse all these documents while you are examined, and then we can have lunch together?" Cora asked Mrs. Pitman.

"Perfect."

Mrs. Pitman was asked in immediately following their exchange. Marriage to the richest and most powerful man in Toronto apparently meant you did not sit around waiting for medical treatment.

Cora opened the trust documents and nearly gasped out loud. Mrs. Pitman had enough in trust to live comfortably supporting twenty of her closest friends until she was about six hundred years old.

Has she seen these documents? Why bother with a charity to take more? She could walk away today and not look back.

People were a mystery to Cora. Not for the first time, she reminded herself that she loved the law because it was simple. Easy. You could interpret it, but at the end of the day, it was predictable. People, on the other hand, were riddles wrapped in mystery.

After twenty minutes, Mrs. Pitman returned to the waiting room.

"Shall we?" She pulled on her gloves as Cora gathered her work together and stood up to follow her.

Together they walked to a restaurant. They were seated by the window; two huge palms on either side of their table gave them some privacy. Cora was struck by the opulence of the room. The sun lit up the rim of gold on the china in front of her. She ran her hand along the heavy, rich linen tablecloth. Mrs. Pitman ignored the menu, rattled off her preference, and turned her attention to Cora. Cora quickly ordered the same thing.

"Setting up that account was a breeze. I should have done that all years ago." Mrs. Pitman took a sip of water and smiled.

"He didn't suspect anything?" Cora spoke through a knot of fear in her throat. Before clapping eyes on these documents, she had thought Mrs. Pitman on the verge of being penniless.

What is Mrs. Pitman's game here?

"No. You were exactly right. Perfect wifely obedience seems to disarm a man faster than a hand gun! His guard is down, and he suspects nothing. When he opened my private account, he deposited $10,000. He has already donated enough to buy a building. Or so he thinks. This is all working famously."

"Mrs. Pitman, do you know how much money you have in trust?"

"No. I have no idea." Mrs. Pitman took another sip of water and smiled at Cora to continue.

How could she not know? How do you just stroll through life and not worry about money?

The waiter brought two hefty-looking gin and tonics to the table. Cora waited for him to step back before she opened the document and showed Mrs. Pitman the amount on the bottom line.

"What?" Mrs. Pitman took the trust documents from Cora. "I thought it would be more."

Cora blinked in amazement. "More?"

"Double, at least." Mrs. Pitman's eyes scanned the document twice, as if looking for a different number.

"How much money do you think you'll need?" Cora put her hand to her throat.

Heaven help me, I'm dealing with a maniac.

"Mrs. Pitman, you could live very comfortably on this for... well for as long as you live."

"Comfortably! Who wants that?" Mrs. Pitman squinted at Cora. "I am entitled to half of what Eli Pitman is worth, right? In a world where women had rights, that's what should be coming to me."

"We don't live in a world where women have rights." Cora wanted to shout at her.

At the rally, that you weren't a part of, we all protested, and we paid a huge price. You have no idea.

"Relax." Mrs. Pitman signaled to the waiter. "Another gin for my friend here."

The waiter scurried away. Cora longed for her drab law office where she wasn't helping a rich, spoiled woman take thousands of dollars from Eli Pitman on her way out the door.

"It's going to be just fine. You've done your job beautifully. I deserve this, Cora. I absolutely do." Mrs. Pitman's eyes were sharp on Cora's.

"You're playing with fire here." Cora warned her. They were pushing every boundary, and only one of them knew the stakes.

"Do you know what it feels like to spend twenty-three years with a man who is having affairs with women, sometimes as young as seventeen years old? Do you have any idea what it feels like to walk into a room of your peers and know that they are talking about the last woman your husband was seen with? Could you even hazard a guess as to what that kind of humiliation does to you?"

"No," Cora answered honestly. She took a gulp of gin and tonic and hissed as it hit the back of her throat.

"The day I gave birth to our third son, that rake dressed in a tux, kissed me and his newborn son good night, and went out dancing with Lucretia Lopez. She was a seventeen-year-old flamenco dancer from Spain, of all things. He had an affair with her until our newborn was a year old. He traded her in for another dancer. Burlesque this time. Do I need to go on?" Mrs. Pitman's eyes glittered with tears. She reached out and took a swig of the gin that had been brought for Cora. "You know what's really pathetic?"

"I couldn't even guess." Empathy for Mrs. Pitman made Cora reach out to put her hand on her forearm. She might be a spoiled brat, but no one deserved this sort of treatment.

"I loved him. I ached for him, and I still do. Isn't that the most pathetic thing you've ever heard? One touch from him..." Mrs. Pitman took a deep breath and let it out slowly. "Well, you know..."

Cora wished desperately that she did know. She had no idea. Her life had been law books and fighting to be a barrister, not just a solicitor. Then being treated with open contempt and disrespect. Men didn't know what to do with her. She had no idea what to do with them. This sort of passion didn't exist in Cora's world, and it nearly brought her to tears. Ancient spinster they called her, and sadly, she agreed with them.

"I'm so sorry." Cora took her hand back and passed Mrs. Pitman a handkerchief.

"Don't be." Mrs. Pitman pulled a mask of civility down over her face. Cora marveled to see it. The pain was carefully hidden. Order restored.

"I want to destroy him. Utterly. But I can't, so I will take what is my due, well, what I consider is my due and see what happens. What do you suggest is my next step?"

"Meet with your board." Cora sipped at the gin slowly. "Including Mirabel Salter."

Mrs. Pitman shuddered and took a deep sip. "I'm not sure I have the fortitude."

"You do," Cora said firmly. If they had been at the front lines of a rally, they would have linked arms. "You *absolutely* do, if you can pull off perfect wifely obedience. I can see that's taking a toll, by the way. Drink more of that gin."

Mrs. Pitman shifted in her chair. "How do you propose I do this?"

"Call a luncheon with your ladies and ask them to assist, then assign them duties. You would be president, of course."

"What roll would you suggest she play?" Mrs. Pitman struggled to form the words.

Cora looked around the room to gauge how many people would watch Mrs. Pitman lie on the floor and have a temper tantrum when she said the next two words. The restaurant was packed; Cora held her breath. "Vice president."

Mrs. Pitman closed her eyes, swilled more gin, and pressed her fingertips into her temples.

"Vice president. Dear Lord, that makes perfect wifely obedience look like a walk in the park on a spring day." Mrs. Pitman choked on her gin. The waiter hovered.

"With no access to the money. She can't see the books, ever, so you are president and treasurer. One more thing..." Cora buttered a bun that she couldn't eat if there were a gun to her head. Her stomach churned with fear that one of Eli's goons sat at the next table and her knee caps would be broken on the way back to the office.

"I am not sure I can hear any more of your plan. It's been gruesome already." Mrs. Pitman's face flushed with embarrassment.

"You will actually have to run an orphanage or whatever charity you chose. You cannot take money from people and claim to give it to charity and then line your pockets. You can't — it's fraud." Cora watched as Mrs. Pitman processed this.

"This has to be a functioning committee?" Mrs. Pitman sputtered.

"Yes."

"Dear Lord. This is spiraling into a nightmare." Mrs. Pitman rubbed her forehead.

"Not really." Cora bristled. "I'm not saying you have to dig a ditch. You have a meeting once a week, and delegate some work. I don't see the problem."

Mrs. Pitman slumped back into her chair. "That sounds like a lot."

"It's delegating." Cora heard the hardness in her own voice and tried to temper it. Mrs. Pitman was a client, after all. "Except the books. You have to actually physically do the books yourself. You have to make sure the money from Eli goes into your account, and the money donated by everyone else actually runs a charity. It's a grey area legally, but you might get away with it because, technically, he is giving this money to his wife, and he is doing it of his own free will. If you choose to use that money for yourself as his wife, unless he forbids it, you could get away with it. I can argue that it was a gift. You cannot, under any circumstances, use the money donated to this charity for your own needs."

Mrs. Pitman pushed quail around her plate and pouted. "This is all very tedious."

"Bookkeeping?"

"Bookkeeping seems like the dullest work on earth." Mrs. Pitman looked up mutinously.

Cora fought hard to hang onto her patience.

"Unless you have a friend you can trust to delegate? I must advise you, at this point, Mrs. Pitman, I wouldn't trust your cat. All the women in your life know your husband is with Mirabel, and they've said nothing, right?"

"Right." Mrs. Pitman took a delicate bite.

"So, I think it's fair to say that you're on your own."

"Unless you do the books." Mrs. Pitman brightened like sunshine on a stormy day.

"Mrs. Pitman, I work twelve-hour days as it is. I do not have time to take on the books. You are going to have to get your hands dirty, I'm afraid. This is barely legal. I'm a lawyer. I can't even know about this. You'll get away with it because he's your husband. He'll have me shot and dumped in the river."

"Oh, he would never do that to a woman."

No, what a man can do to woman is infinitely worse than getting shot and dumped in a river.

"Honestly, you can save yourself a lot of trouble. Abandon this. Live on your trust. Carry on with your life," Cora pleaded.

"Lucretia Lopez," Mrs. Pitman snapped at Cora. "For that little tart alone, I'm taking a big chunk of Eli's wealth with me when I go. It's the only way I can hurt him."

"This is about revenge then. Really? Revenge! Using a law that gives us no rights whatsoever, and you want revenge that way?" Cora's voice was shrill with anxiety.

"I want money. I want to be free of him. I can only get a divorce in a court of law, so to court we go." Mrs. Pitman tossed her head.

"Well then, I suggest you get cozy with Mirabel."

"Once I get that set up, what then?"

"I have to have some time to think, Mrs. Pitman. I'm not used to coming up with Machiavellian schemes on the fly." Cora gulped down the rest of her gin. The waiter produced another one almost instantly.

"I don't believe that for a minute. You have the entire scheme mapped out. I can tell. You are brilliant, Miss Rood." Mrs. Pitman's eyes widened in wonder.

"You can only handle so much at a time, and you cannot let anything slip. Best you are on a need-to-know basis."

"Well, next week — same time, same place?" Mrs. Pitman rummaged around in her hand bag to find enough cash for their lunch.

"Sure," Cora said as Mrs. Pitman got to her feet.

"Have a good day, Miss Rood," Mrs. Pitman said simply as she turned to leave.

She swept out of the restaurant. Her hat was so wide a waiter had to leap out of the way to save a tray of drinks from being dashed to the floor. Cora shook her head in amazement as another man leaped up to open the door for her. Cora marveled at her. She took men leaping to her aid as if it were her due.

Cora stood up; the room swam around her. She sat back down, ate half of the lunch that was in front of her. She drank three cups of tea with sugar and then tried standing up again.

Better.

She left the restaurant and started back to her office. The hair on the back of her neck stood up when she noticed a man following her. He was there and then he was gone, then there again. An appointment at 2:00 p.m. at her law office nagged at her. She zigzagged around her office, stopped and smelled flowers, stepped into a book store and bought some poetry. Desperate to look like an average housewife running some errands, she consulted a false list. Finally, she could put it off no longer. She slipped down a back alley and ran to the back entrance of Roth and Levine.

She plastered herself against the back door and tried to settle her ragged breath.

You are overreacting. Eli doesn't suspect anything. You are being paranoid.

Men she worked with walked by her and rolled their eyes or worse, gave themselves *knowing* glances.

"Hysterics." Cora could hear them murmur. "What do you expect when you employ women... no place in a law office."

Cora tried to ignore the murmuring as she dashed to her office. She closed the door on their contempt and gave herself a hard look in the mirror. She looked like a disaster. Her hair was all over the place from dashing around the city trying to lose the man that seemed to be following her. Who probably wasn't.

Looking down at her drab outfit, tears stung her eyes. The only thing that would cause a man to be in pursuit of her was if she had tangled with the wrong man. Or in this case, the wrong man and the wrong woman. Every inch of her screamed lonely, spinster lawyer. Throat aching with unshed tears, she refused to blink. She willed the tears to go away. Crying at work was not permitted. She had no respect here as it was; crying would confirm what all of them thought of women in a work place. Hysterical, fragile, not cut out for this work. She took a deep breath and went to her half-dead plant on her cluttered desk.

"You're withered, and you're neglected," Cora whispered to her plant; as she touched a leaf it snapped off. "I know exactly how you feel. I'm ready to snap, too."

Cora gave the plant some water and straightened up. "Mrs. Pitman is a spoiled brat, and I'm not sure I can protect her. What should I do?"

The plant didn't answer. She was alone, facing a law that oppressed women, representing a woman who seemed to think she could somehow get revenge in this arena; Cora shivered.

She took a deep, shaky breath, and prepared to meet her two o'clock appointment.

Chapter Five

Adeline put on her best pearls to match her ivory-coloured gloves. In the way women waged war, she was battle ready. The mirror didn't lie — skin flawless, hair piled high, jewelry shining, her tea gown a deep purple extravagance. The beauty of a tea gown was the opportunity to go without a corset. Not today. The corset was like a layer of armour, protection she needed to face her newly formed committee. She bristled with rage at the thought of being civil to Mirabel Salter.

The butler ushered the women into the formal drawing room. Adeline looked in at Mirabel Salter, adulteress. Hester Colton, wife of a judge, representing the Women's Christian Temperance Union, Toronto chapter. Jean King, widow of a prominent banker and politician, representing the Dominion Woman's Enfranchisement Association. Finally, Caroline Swan, wife of a stuffy, controlling barrister. Of the three women who were not currently committing adultery with Eli, Adeline really liked Caroline. She was a breath of fresh air in this group. Adeline had a tremendous respect for Hester Colton and Jean King. Unlike most women of their social standing, they were not gossips and cared about humanity.

Adeline's thoughts caused her to pause. If she went through with this, if she actually pulled this off, what would she be? Wife of business tycoon presently — what about when she divorced him? Would she be considered a divorced harpy? What were women called who refused to stand for a spouse's adultery, when society expected them to look the other way?

Adeline squared her shoulders as her eyes raked over Mirabel Salter. She was absolutely the last straw. Who cared what they called her? What would she call *him*? That's what mattered. Adeline plastered a smile on her face and entered the room.

"I am so excited to be invited to start a new charity!" Mrs. Swan clasped her hands together in excitement.

Mrs. Colton smiled warmly at Mrs. Swan. "This really is a great honour."

Fifteen years Adeline's senior, Mrs. Colton lent a certain maturity to the group. She had never slept with Eli either, too old for him.

"I wondered about the direction this charity should take." Mrs. King took a sip of tea.

There's always one in every group! Unhappy with the direction before you even know what direction you're headed in.

Adeline fumed silently as she picked up her tea cup.

"Please, tell us your suggestions." Adeline graciously invited her to speak.

"As you know, I am here to represent the Dominion Woman's Enfranchisement Association," Mrs. King began.

"I wanted to join your group, but Mr. Swan wouldn't allow it," Mrs. Swan said sadly. "I really think your association has good ideas for women."

Adeline refused to admit that Eli wouldn't allow it either. She appreciated Mrs. Swan's honesty.

"There is a branch of the Association that has a tricky situation." Mrs. King stood up, went to her hand bag, and rifled through it. "I brought the minutes from the last meeting. I wanted you to see just how desperate this is. They want to create an environment for prostitutes who want to change their life. There is a disturbing realization that there are young girls being kidnapped and brought to Toronto. Some of them have been branded. It's appalling! As they escape, or are arrested, there needs to be a place for rehabilitation."

Revulsion rolled across Mrs. Colton's face as she watched her friend, Mrs. King, speak. Her eyes narrowed at the crimes of humanity these girls were facing.

"These girls need help," Mrs. King said simply. "This would include health care, obviously, and education. If we can train these women for work that does not involve... well improper conduct... we could assist these girls to get off the street."

"Sounds like a worthy cause. Thank you for bringing the plight of the prostitutes to our attention," Mrs. Colton said politely.

Adeline took pride in the fact that she didn't allow her eyes to slide to Mirabel as the word *prostitute* was spoken.

Mrs. King nodded at Mrs. Colton. "We also really want to address the increase of domestic violence happening to women with small children living in abject poverty. If the abuse is so bad, there has to be somewhere for these women to go where their husbands can't find them. I can't stand the thought of these little children on the streets because the fathers and husbands have beaten their mothers — it's just the most dreadful situation you can imagine." Mrs. King took a sip of tea, and everyone waited for her to continue.

"Your husbands may not allow you to participate in suffragette activities, but they may allow you to change your focus from an orphanage to this current and pressing need. While orphanages are, of course, very important, we have them in Toronto. This house would be similar to the Magdalene House but without the religious connotations. Whatever you think, Mrs. Pitman, this is your charity, but the Association requested I present this to you in the hopes that you would see a need you might fill in some capacity."

"Mrs. King, it is so good to know what the D. W. E. A. recommends. I have heard of homes like this. We could take this opportunity to create a Canadian version of the Hull House that is currently running in Chicago," Mrs. Colton said as she picked up a sandwich.

Mrs. King leaned toward Mrs. Colton. "I have read about the Hull House and I believe that this would address a need broader than prostitution and white slavery. It is education that will elevate women. The conditions of working class women in Toronto is fearful. We can create that here... if we all agreed, of course."

"What does the group think of this?" Adeline asked the women.

"It sounds like a very important charity. I love the fact that I can assist the suffragettes even if I can't be one." Mrs. Swan's eyes softened at the thought of women and children on the streets due to drunken men.

"Miss Salter?" Adeline's teeth clenched with rage as she addressed her.

She's insurance, while you secure funds from Eli.

"I am not sure if I want to be known to assist prostitutes." Miss Salter grimaced at the women.

Because it hits too close to home?

"Perhaps we weren't clear, Miss Salter." Mrs. King turned to face her. "We would be assisting not only prostitutes but..."

"I really don't know if I have time in my schedule for charity work," Miss Salter interrupted as she examined the seam of her glove.

Seething anger overwhelmed Adeline; she commanded herself not to reach across the silver tea set and slap Mirabel Salter for disrespecting an older woman in her drawing room.

Mrs. King and Mrs. Colton looked at her with open disdain. Mrs. Swan frowned in confusion.

Of course, you don't have time for charity work. How would you fit that in with all the illicit intercourse you are having with my husband?

Adeline plastered a smile on her face, wished she could call Mirabel Salter out as the adulteress that she was, and order her out of her home. Instead, with great force of will, she tilted her head to invite her to continue.

Miss Salter simply shrugged and said nothing further.

"We will need the following..." Mrs. King took over as the tension in the room escalated. "We need an old hotel or something that has many rooms, so that these girls can have accommodations and are taken off the streets immediately. I'm not sure what sort of building we would be looking at."

"Maybe an old school," Mrs. Swan suggested.

"Miss Salter, are you at all good with real estate?" Adeline dragged Mirabel back into the conversation. "Could we assign you the task of finding a suitable venue with Mrs. Swan here?"

"I'm not really sure." Miss Salter yawned as she picked up a tiny egg salad sandwich.

Mrs. King and Mrs. Colton glanced at each other; their lips thinned in disapproval.

"Miss Salter, to be invited to start a charity, and such a worthy one, is really an honour," Mrs. King said with more than a hint of disapproval. "A prospective husband would be most intrigued by a young woman who is working with the poor of Toronto."

All eyes went to Mirabel. At twenty-two, she was a flaxen-haired, blue-eyed, beautiful girl. Everything about her, the way her skin was effortlessly glowing, the shine of her hair in the sun, the brightness of her eyes, spoke to youth. Her figure in the tea gown was perfectly proportioned. Adeline noticed Mirabel had gone without a corset.

The four other ladies sitting at the tea table had left that phase behind, and just the sight of her made it glaringly obvious they were in middle age. You could powder it, pouf it up, iron it out, cinch it in, but you could not go back to the beauty of twenty-two.

Adeline looked at Mrs. Colton and knew she grieved a son who had died of pneumonia at a very young age. Mrs. King struggled with the grief of losing a husband two years ago. Mrs. Swan was lovely, but her husband was an absolute tyrant, ran his house and her with an iron hand. How Mrs. Swan maintained any shred of positivity was a mystery to Adeline. Life had beaten these women, and despite what they had endured, they were ready to put their backs into a project to bring relief to the abused and suffering women of Toronto. Girls branded and sold into prostitution — Adeline shivered at the thought.

Adeline dragged her eyes back to Mirabel.

Why does this beautiful woman want to be with Eli? Twenty-five years her senior? Ah. Money and power. Eli is very powerful.

A diamond flashed on Mirabel's right hand and caught Adeline's eye. Her tea cup stopped between her saucer and her mouth. Fury made her hands shake so badly she had to put down her tea cup. Her heart pounded with the possibility of a confrontation with this tart. It was coming. Adeline welcomed the day she could destroy this woman. Humiliation was a storm that raged through her.

How much money has Eli given you? What is your monthly allowance? How much are you taking from me besides my husband?

Adeline couldn't take her eyes off the pearls that wrapped around Mirabel's perfect throat. A throat her husband likely had kissed that morning. She closed her eyes and tried to push away the thought. She couldn't. She knew exactly what Eli's lips felt like when he pressed them against her throat, just under her jaw.

Pull yourself together, Adeline. If it wasn't this girl, it would be another one.

The rage ate at her.

"Mrs. Swan, would you be interested in assisting Miss Salter with this?" Adeline sounded hoarse even to her own ears.

Adeline, under no circumstances, could shop for a venue with Mirabel Salter. Everyone had their limits, and she was confident that after one hour with Eli's lover she wouldn't be able to stop herself from raking her eyes out.

"I would love to assist Miss Salter in finding a suitable building." Mrs. Swan reached over and put her hand on Mirabel's arm. Mrs. Swan was a natural peacemaker.

"We should assign duties," Adeline suggested and pulled out a pen and paper. "Who would like to do what?"

"You should be president, of course," Mrs. King suggested.

"I always really enjoyed numbers," Adeline lied through her teeth. "Maybe, since we are such a small group, I should be treasurer and president. What about vice president?"

"That honour should go to Mrs. King. This is really all her idea."

"I thought perhaps Miss Salter would like to be vice president, since she is very likely looking for a prospective husband. This would really stand out to a man, Miss Salter." Adeline smiled sweetly and wished this meeting was over. She yearned to smash every vase in the room.

Mirabel looked at Adeline, and a small smirk touched the right side of her perfect mouth.

"I'm not in a rush to find a husband, actually. I really *enjoy* being single." Miss Salter leaned forward, and Adeline saw the swell of breast with prominent blue veining press against her tea gown. Adeline's breath caught in her throat.

Lord in heaven, she's pregnant.

Adeline tried to see through the red rage that pulled down over her eyes in a veil. A wash of heat rushed through her as humiliation followed the rage. She forced her lips to smile. "Well, since Miss Salter has declined being vice president, perhaps Mrs. King would fill that role?"

Mrs. King nodded her agreement.

"Mrs. Swan would you be in a position to be our secretary?" Adeline forced the words past the lump of salty tears in her throat.

"Certainly, I can do that for sure." Mrs. Swan beamed at Adeline. "I really have to be going, though. So sorry to have to leave, but Mr. Swan is expecting me home by 2:30. I don't want him to worry."

Or be enraged that he doesn't know where you are at every minute of every day. Good grief.

"Miss Salter, we'll put you in charge of real estate, and Mrs. Colton we'll put in charge of sourcing beds and linens. This way we have a general idea as to what pricing we can expect."

"That would work well for us, I think." Mrs. Colton looked at Mrs. King, who nodded her approval.

"All right, meeting adjourned."

Mrs. Swan quickly gathered her belongings and was out the door in seconds.

If Mrs. Colton and Mrs. King wondered why Miss Salter was invited to engage in such a serious opportunity as well bred and respectful women, they didn't comment on it. As the rest of the ladies took their leave, Adeline remained at the tea table. The fury and humiliation was now replaced with the root of all that emotion. Adeline's heart was so broken she couldn't stop the tears as they welled behind her eyes. There wasn't enough money in the world to stop the pain that sliced through her. Taking a deep breath, she realized all the money in the world wouldn't fix her heart, but it would hurt Eli. At this point, that's all she could do. Nothing mattered but striking back at Eli with everything she could. Adeline heard Cora's voice in her head.

Those with no rights under the law must be clever and cunning.

Chapter Six

Eli's breath caught in his throat as he watched Mirabel Salter sit in a shaft of early morning sunlight. She poured tea then opened the newspaper that was spread out with breakfast. In Eli's opinion, and his was the only opinion he cared about, she was the most beautiful girl in Toronto.

"Come back to bed," Eli growled from the bed.

Her eyes looked up from the newspaper; she regarded him coolly.

"Get me off this charity craziness with your wife, and I'll consider it."

"If I have to get up and drag you back to this bed, you will be a very sorry little girl."

"I'm not a little girl." Mirabel's perfect mouth pouted. She tossed the skein of hair back over her shoulder, giving Eli a clear view of her perfect décolletage.

"It won't hurt you to have a social conscience." Eli bunched up a pillow and put it behind his head.

"You want me to develop a conscience?" Mirabel tossed her hair back and laughed. "That sounds very counterproductive to what we're doing here, sir."

"A social conscience, not a moral one," Eli growled with impatience.

"I don't want to be in a charity with Adeline. She's hard. She's too tough. I don't like it. It's taking up too much time. Do you think she knows?" Mirabel frowned at him.

Eli was done talking. He didn't want to discuss Adeline and what she knew or didn't know. He didn't care. Adeline was slated for his public life. Dealing with politicians, dealing with endless dull dinner parties. She was the mother of his sons, and she was a good one. She had done her duty and done it well. He thought of her innocence as she requested her own private bank account to give gifts to her sons and gifts to him in addition to an account for her upcoming charity. Prostitutes and battered wives or some such vulgarity.

Who cared?

He had not intended to allow her to have a private account; however, she had pleaded and raised a valid point. She might need to purchase things without the approval of the board. Eli understood. On his rise to the top, he had been on enough boards to know that there was nothing more stifling than having to pass decisions before a board that couldn't agree. Now, with his great wealth and power, he refused to be on any boards of any sort. Time wasters, all of them.

He had allowed Adeline to have a "private" account but promptly made sure the bank would send a copy of her reconcile, both charity and private, straight to his office. They were uncomfortable with that. Technically, a private account was exactly that. Private. Eli reminded them that she only had an account with his permission and that the account remaining open was subject to his approval. He could reverse that decision at any point.

So, why not indulge her? What was the harm? A woman with a bank account, what could possibly go wrong? He had even put enough in there for her to buy the hotel she was bleating about. His accountants would keep a close eye on it.

Mirabel stood up and walked to the window where the sun could shine straight through her sheer gown. Thoughts of Adeline and Rothstein fled as Eli sat up straighter to get a better look at the girl who was going to be back in his bed immediately if she knew what was good for her.

She turned slightly and his eyes swept over her. His eyes narrowed when he noticed a very slight swell in her abdomen. A pregnant mistress was one more complication to sort out. He added that to his list of things he had to do today.

"Get me off this charity," Mirabel demanded.

"Get in this bed and do as you're told. You are going to do this charity with Adeline or you'll be on the street."

Mirabel's face paled as he knew it would. Unmarried, pregnant, and on the street, was a fate worse than death. No one, not even her family, would take her in due to the shame. She'd gambled, and Eli watched as she came to the slow realization that she had lost. She moved cautiously to the bed, as if she understood finally, for the first time, she was a very small fish swimming with a very powerful shark.

"You can't throw me onto the street. I'm pregnant." Her voice trembled.

"Is it mine?"

Mirabel's breath caught in fear. "Of course, the baby is yours!"

Eli shrugged.

What is the real reason my wife has a lawyer and a bank account? Does she know about this pregnant tart? Is she thinking of petitioning me for divorce? But she asked to work with Mirabel on this charity. If she knows she's my mistress, why would she want to work with her?

Eli had henchmen exactly for situations like this. Once they questioned this odd lawyer, he'd have Royce investigate further.

If Adeline thinks she's going to divorce me, she'll be sorely disappointed.

The scandal of divorce would hinder his sons in finding upstanding marriage mates. Randall needed to land Miss Scott. Her entire family came from old money, the only kind of money Eli was interested in. Old money came with a certain reputation you couldn't buy. The scandal of divorce would end the union between Randall and Laura. His entire empire needed his sons married to upstanding women who would give him grandsons. He couldn't grow his empire any further without men he could trust. This pregnancy would have to be dealt with sooner rather than later.

"If I have to drag you into this bed, you will be very, very sorry. There is a lineup of girls who would join me here. So, I'm not asking again." Eli's voice was icy.

Just as he knew she would, Mirabel obediently joined him in bed.

You should be scared of those streets, Mirabel. You wouldn't last a minute on them. I know because I own them.

***

Adeline's butler delivered tea and the daily correspondence to the drawing room. Her eyes quickly skimmed over all the requests. One for today.

Hmm.

Jean King.

Why would Jean King want to see me today? And why would she want to meet me at the police station?

Adeline frowned. Eli would have apoplexy at the thought of his wife at the police station, but Adeline was sitting alone in the drawing room. Eli hadn't lived at 224 Tuxedo Street in more than a year, so it was of no matter or consequence what Eli thought.

Adeline's carriage pulled up to the constabulary at exactly 2:00 p.m. She joined Mrs. King in front of the entrance.

"Mrs. King, what an odd place to meet." Adeline's eyes swept over her. She was tall and tough, her steel grey hair covered in a hat.

"I wanted to speak to you privately, without the committee." Mrs. King's lips pursed in disapproval. Adeline squirmed under her scrutiny.

Adeline knew she had failed in Mrs. King's eyes. Mrs. King wasn't fooled with all this charity folderol. She saw straight through Adeline. Too refined to admit it, Mrs. King had seen too much, been through too much; she had no time for fripperies like Adeline or worse, Mirabel. There was work to be done. It had to be done today.

"I appreciate you asking me to be part of this charity. I really do. Once Mr. King died, I needed something that would inspire me again."

Mrs. King was not a poetic person. This was hard for her. Adeline tilted her head to indicate she should continue.

"Have I placed my trust in a group that has no interest in starting an actual committee here? Or is this some sort of war to get back at Eli? His mistress and his wife on the same committee — it is highly unusual."

Adeline's face burned with shame.

"Mrs. King!" Adeline sputtered.

"Ah. I didn't say that to humiliate you, my dear. I wanted to know what was going on. I have to know. If you cannot alleviate the suffering of these prostitutes and these battered wives, I have to find someone with deep enough pockets to do so."

"Of course, I want to alleviate suffering..." Adeline's voice trailed off.

"I see." Mrs. King looked at Adeline with displeasure.

"Mrs. King, I assure you. I want to help these women."

"You don't even know who you are helping." Mrs. King's eyes narrowed as she squinted at her.

'You will actually have to run this committee,' Cora's words came back to haunt Adeline as she looked at Mrs. King and blinked.

"That's true," Adeline admitted meekly.

"There is a lot of foot dragging over the purchase of the hotel. I am not sure what is holding things up." Mrs. King changed tactics.

"I've been busy."

"Busy doing what?" Mrs. King spoke sharply.

"I have been remiss." Adeline apologized as if she were in a principal's office and in desperate trouble.

"Yes. You have. Let's go and see how we can help these girls who have recently been brought in."

"Why?"

"Mrs. Pitman, if we had a house, we could take them off the streets today and start rehabilitating. As it stands, you've been busy. So, no house." Mrs. King's disappointment seeped into her tone.

Mrs. King was right, so Adeline didn't defend herself. Properly chastised, she followed Mrs. King into the station. Three prostitutes were lined up against the side of the lobby. Two were holding onto each other in fear. They were no more than sixteen years old.

Adeline's heart ached at their naked vulnerability. One had bruises on her throat; one had a black eye. The youngest girl wept softly as the older girl held her.

Is she fifteen? Hot and cold guilt plagued her for dragging her feet about this charity. *Where will these girls sleep tonight?*

Despite being filthy, they had enough pride left to be ashamed of their filth. The oldest one was seventeen at the most; Adeline's eyes met her gaze. The eyes looking back at her were flat and hopeless. This wasn't her first time here. The girl forced into prostitution dropped her gaze; her face was beautiful, despite the bruising. Her hair could have been a bright sunny blond; it was instead dirty and greasy. Adeline's heart broke apart as she looked at them. They were going back to the street because she was playing at taking her husband for half of what he was worth. She was responsible for wasting Mrs. King's time and energy. Mrs. King, who wanted to do the right thing for these girls. Mrs. King, who looked at her to do the right thing.

It occurred to Adeline, right there in that moment, she didn't have to be Adeline, wife of business tycoon Eli Pitman. This was an opportunity to be Adeline Pitman, President of Hope House. A home that would be more than a safe haven. A home that would restore self-worth and confidence, provide medical attention and guidance. The entire plan for the house unfolded in front of her. These girls needed to be fed, educated, and able to work in other avenues. To do that, they needed a hand up and hope in their hearts.

"I know your husband is sleeping with anything in a skirt," Mrs. King whispered in her ear. Adeline's eyes filled with tears. "I know he's living with Mirabel Salter. This charity won't fix that; however, I'm saying, you had a good idea starting a charity. So, let's run a charity."

Adeline pressed her gloved fist against her mouth to stifle a sob at the thought of these three little girls going back to the streets because she hadn't bought a hotel to make into a halfway house for them. Shame roared through her. She had let these girls down. It wouldn't happen again.

"There is only so much tea you can drink with other spoiled rich women, Mrs. Pitman. At some point, you need a reason to get out of bed in the morning. I'm giving you that reason." Mrs. King straightened up.

"How did you know?"

"Oh, my darling," Mrs. King said softly as she took Adeline's hand in hers. "It's all right. It happens to the best of us."

"Really?"

"Mr. King had three mistresses. They say it's just men being men. Hurts anyway."

Adeline shook her head and willed herself to stop crying.

"The best thing you can do in this life is try not to let the pain obliterate you. Give something back to those who have nothing, and they will remind you that what you have isn't so terrible. A broken heart is like a broken crayon. You can still colour with it. So, let's start colouring, shall we? These girls need a place to live, to learn, to grow. You have the means to provide it. So, let's get on with it."

"My husband's mistress is pregnant." Adeline looked at Mrs. King and hoped she had something profound to say.

"Eventually, every woman needs some insurance," Mrs. King said wisely. "Looks like little Mirabel isn't as naïve as we thought."

"What will I do?"

"You will start this charity and make it real. Put your heart into it. Bring hope to the hopeless. Let's alleviate suffering where we can."

"Does it help?" Adeline asked pitifully.

"No. But it distracts you enough that you don't mind the hurt so much." Mrs. King spoke with sincerity and wisdom. "When you line up all your hurts and suffering against theirs, you will see where you have so much in life."

Adeline opened her mouth to object.

"I'm not saying what happened to you isn't terrible. It is. What I am saying to you is that it pales in comparison to what these girls are facing. We're women, Mrs. Pitman, not little girls. Women stand together and they alleviate suffering where they can."

"I'll buy the hotel today. Would you come with me to negotiate terms?"

"Of course."

"Perfect." Adeline squared her shoulders and lifted her chin. "What we've discussed here today. Uh. I would prefer..."

"Mrs. Pitman, your personal life is none of anyone's business. Please, don't feel like anything you have said here today will go any further."

"Thank you."

"Come on, let's buy a hotel." Mrs. King had a gleam in her eye as they left the constabulary and went back out onto the street.

As they walked to the site to meet the estate agent and the lawyers, Mrs. King took Adeline through the tenements and slums of Toronto.

Adeline had never in her life looked at the poverty of the immigrants and families with too many children and not enough money. With every step, she understood the huge magnitude of the social programs that needed to be started. Finally, when she couldn't bear to see any more, she stopped and took Mrs. King by the arm.

"How do you work in this? How do we fix all this?" Adeline's eyes glittered with unshed tears.

"We can't," Mrs. King said simply.

The tears spilled down Adeline's cheeks as she watched children playing in rags, faces drawn in hunger.

"Then what is next?" she whispered.

"We believe, at the D. W. E. A., that if you elevate women, you will elevate society. It's our duty, as those with means, to try to fix what is right in front of us. We do our best with what we have. We need a name for the house we are going to run. The Hull House was based on the original owner. What would you like to call this home?"

"I think we should call it Hope House. I think these people need hope desperately." Adeline couldn't tear her eyes away from a little boy that looked like Randall at the age of four.

"I like that." Mrs. King nodded her approval.

"I'll have my legal counsel look into naming it and checking over the legalities." Adeline mentally added that to her list of things to do.

"Oh? Who is your legal counsel?" Mrs. King tilted her head.

"Miss Cora Rood. She works at Roth and Levine."

"Ah. I know Cora very well. The female lawyer, the one who takes her hat off in court and rides a bicycle." Mrs. King chuckled.

"You've heard of her?"

"Of course, Cora challenged the entire legal system! Everyone has heard of her if their husband is, or was in politics. The D. W. E. A. was behind her every step of the way. She was a dynamo."

"Was?" Adeline's eyebrow arched.

"Yes. Unfortunately, she ran into some trouble," Mrs. King said softly.

"What sort?"

"By the time Cora got out of jail, she was completely devastated." Mrs. King's lips were thin as if holding back information.

"I knew she had been arrested. I saw her at that rally with Lady Bronwyn and Dr. Stowe."

Mrs. King shot a hard look at Mrs. Pitman. "She was much more than arrested. She's a suffragette, Mrs. Pitman. They are on the front line of the battle for equal rights. She was in jail. They all were. They were brutalized. The fallout of that night tied up the courts for weeks."

Adeline swallowed hard. She had thought Cora Rood was a mouse. She had been wrong. "I thought she was arrested and released."

"Lady Bronwyn and Dr. Stowe were both released immediately. Their husbands were there to drag them out within minutes of arrest. Miss Rood didn't have a husband to come in and... get her."

"That sounds very ominous." Adeline shivered.

"The women who survived that night in jail... they say the warden didn't stop the guards from showing the women how they felt about women in politics, about women protesting. They say the beatings, and whatever else, went on for hours, until the morning shift came in and stopped it. The men who instigated the beatings got nothing more than a slap on the wrist." Mrs. King's lips pursed with fury. "Cora Rood was badly hurt."

"Hurt how?" Adeline hesitated to ask.

Mrs. King shook her head. "She doesn't talk about it. She left the public view for a few months to recover. Whatever happened in that jail cell... I can't even imagine."

"I don't want to sound insensitive because I really like Cora, and I care about her. However, do you think she has what it takes to stand up to Eli in court?" Adeline asked softly.

"Cora Rood from a year ago? Yes. If there was a way, she would find it and she would argue it with every fibre of her being. Without a doubt. Cora Rood today? It's anyone's guess. They say she can barely drink tea without it sloshing over the rim of the cup." Mrs. King took a handkerchief out of her bag and pressed it to her mouth, sympathy for Cora evident in her eyes.

"Gracious."

"It's a terrible battle these women have been fighting, Mrs. Pitman. Don't play with her. If there is a possibility that you can turn a blind eye to Mr. Pitman and his indiscretions, you should decide if the risk is worth it. She'll pay a price, Mrs. Pitman. Not you."

"What price?" Adeline whispered.

"She won't practice law again, likely. You must have heard how dangerous your husband is. He won't take it out on you. Too obvious, but she will not get out of it unscathed."

"Why did she agree to this?" Adeline frowned.

Mrs. King laughed; Adeline heard a sharp edge of bitterness. "Do you really think she had a choice? She's a woman lawyer. The first one in Canada and Britain. She has no choices *at all*. Her firm wants her destroyed. This petition landed in their laps. Perfect. She can fail against Eli Pitman, and he'll get rid of her. Easy. They'll dust their hands and say good riddance. They won't give her another look."

"Why is she working there then?" Adeline held her hands out in supplication, trying to understand why Cora would work anywhere she didn't want to.

"You really don't understand at all how the world works, do you?" Mrs. King shook her head. Adeline bristled visibly. "Mr. Roth owed Lord Bronwyn a favour. A big one. So, he took her on to article, and she has a little more than two months left. How clever of them to make sure she fails. Epically. She won't work in Toronto after this. If Mr. Pitman lets her live with this slight to his pride, I'll be shocked."

Adeline looked at Mrs. King as the blood drained from her face. "Eli wouldn't."

Mrs. King shook her head further. "Eli Pitman is a mob boss, Mrs. Pitman. No one who stands up to him lives to tell the tale. He owns this city and all the police, judges, everyone. Time to wake up, Mrs. Pitman."

"We're in too far to stop now. I can't... I had no idea." Adeline wrung her hands in fear.

"Pity," Mrs. King said quietly.

"I can't stop the divorce proceedings. I can't bear this life with Eli anymore." Adeline shook her head sadly. "I'll get this purchased today, once Cora gives me the go ahead with the terms."

"Good." Mrs. King smiled at her. "I will have the beds, linens, and food purchased as soon as I get your telegram regarding the possession date."

"I'll ask Miss Rood to look over these documents. Is there anything else you suggest I do for her?"

"She's going up against Eli Pitman and his henchmen. Get that girl a bodyguard. The biggest, meanest one you can find. I suggest you do it fast."

Mrs. Pitman looked at Mrs. King with fear in her eyes.

"Do you have any suggestions? For bodyguards, I mean?" Adeline's voice sounded small.

"Lord Bronwyn has always used Sol Stein. I saw him once — he's terrifying. If Vikings still exist, well, he's a Viking. He's six-feet-two-inches of angry, vicious, beat-someone-and-ask-questions-later boxer from Iceland. Doesn't talk, doesn't smile — he fights and he sleeps. Apparently, he lost his wife when they first got to Canada. She was mugged and stabbed or something, all very traumatic. According to Lady Bronwyn, he has no emotion whatsoever. If he's good enough for the Bronwyns, he's good enough for Miss Rood."

"I'll hire him today." Adeline jotted his name down. "Where can I find him?"

"He fights at a boxing ring in the lower east side."

"I've never been down there." Adeline's eyes widened at the thought of the lower east side.

"Of course, you haven't," Mrs. King responded dryly. "I'll telegram you his address. I suggest you don't wait."

"I'll do it right away. All of it."

Mrs. King's eyes softened as she looked at the younger woman. "You've done well here today."

Adeline held onto that praise like she was sinking and it was a life raft.

As Mrs. King moved to walk away, Adeline said sincerely, "I know you think I'm a silly woman."

Mrs. King turned around to face Mrs. Pitman.

"No matter what, I don't care what it takes. I can't handle the humiliation anymore, Mrs. King. I need to be free of him. I can't bear it."

"I know," Mrs. King said. She came back to Mrs. Pitman and pulled her into an embrace. "I wish you all the best. I look forward to building Hope House with you, Mrs. Pitman. You are going to do great things for the women of this city."

Adeline held onto her with both arms.

Chapter Seven

"Couple of things." Eli looked at Royce to be sure he was paying attention. "Track Cora Rood closer — search her apartment. Don't make it obvious. Find out if it's just a charity or if she knows about Mirabel. I'm going to invite her to have a discussion — I'll know if she lies to me. This Cora, I don't know her, and I don't know if she can be bought or not."

"Why bother with that?" Royce asked.

"Big names behind her, Royce. Very big names — Lord Bronwyn, Oliver Moat to name a few."

Eli stretched his arms out in front of him as Royce stood up to get to work.

"If she comes in while I'm searching?"

"Well, you'd have to defend yourself, wouldn't you?" Eli and Royce chuckled together at the thought of a man as huge and brutal as Royce needing to defend himself against a woman. "Remember, Royce, keep your hands off her. They don't care about street walkers, but a woman who has the backing this one does... no. They won't turn their eye to a woman lawyer who gets hurt. Too big a gamble. I'll never get you acquitted."

"Her word against mine." Royce shrugged and rolled his shoulders in anticipation.

"Your choice. Just wanted to let you know it's a risk. She's in Detective Asher Grayson's jurisdiction. So, if you lay a hand on her, you might want to be sure to be *out* of his jurisdiction. Drag her to the docks. Just a word of advice. Take it or leave it. Grayson is fast becoming a problem that needs to be solved."

"I can get rid of him."

"No, you can't. He's straight. No way to pay him off. No bribes work. He cares about prostitutes, of all things." Eli shook his head in disbelief. "Be careful in his jurisdiction. I've sent worse than you after him, and they end up in the morgue. We have to work around him."

Royce looked crestfallen

"A woman lawyer." Eli picked up his coffee cup, rolled his eyes, and took a deep swig. "What next?"

Royce shook his head, went back to the door and set off to do as he was instructed.

***

Adeline settled into the chair in front of Cora's desk as Cora tore open an envelope and pulled out a note. The sight of Eli Pitman's letterhead on heavy cardstock made Cora's hands shake with fear. She fumbled to open the letter while her palms and the back of her neck slicked in anxious sweat.

Miss Rood,

We request your presence on Thursday at 2:00 p.m. at the
Pitman offices to discuss Mrs. Pitman's charity.

Regards,
Eli Pitman

Cora noticed, a copy of the request was sent to the partners of her law firm so they knew she would be excused at that time of day. Fervently, Cora wished to go back to the gentle, boring world of real estate law.

"I am to meet with Mr. Pitman on Thursday at 2:00 p.m. at his office." Cora was hoarse with stress.

Adeline bit her lip with worry at the possible confrontation.

"How much money has Eli given you?" Cora took a sip of water in an attempt to calm down.

"He gave me $10,000, so I am buying an old hotel with it right away. He doesn't need to know I got the hotel for $1,000. 00. I brought the documents for you to have a look at."

"So, at this point, no money from Eli has been taken and put in your charity account, only personal?" Cora pushed passed the fear of the answer; she had to ask it.

"No, of course not. I was waiting for your instruction."

"All right." Air finally rushed back into her lungs.

"Mrs. Pitman, if I go into his office, my life is in danger. I can feel it."

"I know." Adeline's eyes were wide with fear. "That is why I am here. I am hiring a bodyguard for you."

Cora let out a sigh of relief. "Thank you. I am being followed everywhere."

"I'll hire him today." Adeline bit her lip. "I had no idea until I spoke to Mrs. King, just what sort of danger I have put you in. I apologize. I... I just didn't know. I can't turn back now, I can't bear this loveless marriage anymore."

Mrs. Pitman opened her handbag and set a bundle of bills down on Cora's desk.

"What is this for?" Cora could barely get the words out; she was terrified of what could be coming at her next.

"That summons to meet with Eli — he wants to assess you. You can't meet Eli Pitman looking like this."

"Why?"

"He might take you seriously." Mrs. Pitman's eyebrows knitted together. She spoke as if a woman being taken seriously was a fate worse than death. "You have to go in there looking like a tart. Men like Eli don't take a woman who is dressed to attract attention seriously."

"Mrs. Pitman." Cora stood up in frustration. "I'm done playing games. I'm a lawyer. I don't dress for men. I don't play *games* with men. I deal with them using the law."

Mrs. Pitman stood up and rounded on her. "This is a man's world, Cora. We have no rights here. None. You think I'm silly, but I understand maybe better than you. We have to manipulate this entire situation."

"You know we won't win." Cora's eyes narrowed.

"I hope the courts will let me be free of him, but if they don't, well, I've had a change of heart." Mrs. Pitman smoothed her skirt as she appeared to gather her thoughts. "You know what I am seeing in this terrible charity you made me start?"

"I can't even imagine," Cora said weakly.

"I am seeing oppression and violence against women and girls. Cora... they are just girls." Mrs. Pitman's voice caught with emotion, and Cora met her gaze. Tears glittered in Mrs. Pitman's eyes. "Beaten, used as prostitutes, sold into white slavery, branded... my eyes have been opened by my committee... I am shocked at the state of the working-class women and children in this society. I am going to take Eli for everything I can get. I am going to pour his money back into the streets of Toronto, and *you* are going to help me. It will take strong women to stand up to the corruption we see. Women like us have to champion rights for everyone."

"Mrs. Pitman..." Cora breathed in awe. "I had no idea you felt so strongly."

"It's Adeline. No more Mrs. Pitman, we're friends, I hope." Adeline bit her lip as if the invitation might be declined. "I didn't know." Adeline sat back down. "I had no idea what the state of the working-class women was, or the prostitutes, for that matter. Foolishly, I thought women chose that way of life. I had no idea how many children are forced to the streets. Mrs. King opened my eyes the other day. I have been a spoiled, rich brat. I have been remiss."

"How could you know?" Cora soothed her. Clearly, Adeline's conscience was bothering her.

"No excuse." Adeline ignored the sympathy. "I have put you in grave danger, Cora."

Cora shrugged. "I've been in danger before."

"Yes, and it broke you."

Cora met Adeline's eyes and saw sympathy there. "I'm still standing."

"You are a secret weapon, Cora. You just don't know it yet. A woman lawyer, a brilliant woman lawyer, no less. We present you to Eli as a tart with a diploma. He's gathering information on you with this meeting, but you can present a weak front to him. If you dress right." A smile tugged at Adeline's lip as her eyes swept over Cora. "One thing I do know is that you cannot champion women's rights in olive green and black, for heaven's sake. Would it kill you to add a sequin or a feather here or there?"

"I have to wear black in court," Cora said mutinously.

"You're not in court right now!" Adeline said triumphantly. "You look like a... you look exactly like a..."

"Lawyer?" Cora finished dryly.

Adeline and Cora burst out laughing. They laughed so hard they had to hold their sides and finally wipe tears from their eyes.

Cora sat back down and picked up the bundle of cash.

"I don't have any time to be running to designers." Cora warned.

"I'll have my designer stop by today, and he can use six of my dresses from last year. He can cut them to fit you. He won't have time to start from scratch. You need to look like you make your way in life having men fall all over you. Eli can't know you're brilliant. No more shirt waists and bicycles, my dear. Those days are done. Cheer up. You have to be strong."

"I used to be strong." Cora's sad eyes met Adeline's again.

Adeline smiled. "You're a lawyer about to take down Eli Pitman — of course you're strong. We have work to do! The house we are starting has to move forward — there is such a tremendous need. I will do everything I can to keep you safe. I need your legal counsel for Hope House."

"Hope House?" Cora tilted her head.

"Yes. It will be modeled after the Hull House in Chicago. We will try hard to get young girls off the streets, educate them, and help them lead meaningful lives. Give them some hope back."

"That sounds lovely." Cora beamed her approval at Adeline.

"Yes, wait until you see it." Adeline smiled right back at Cora.

A charity that started out as something fake is now transforming into something that might actually contribute to society. Something like Adeline herself.

"So, when I walk in there, to confront Eli and say that I am assisting you in running a charity and that is all, you swear to me, you have given him no reason to believe we are petitioning him for divorce?"

"None whatsoever."

"I still need to change my clothes?" Cora frowned.

"Dear Miss Rood, you change your clothes, and clothes will change your life. Let's get this sorted. My designer will be by today. You will meet with Eli tomorrow, and I will have the bodyguard stop by this afternoon after the designer."

"I have actual work to do today," Cora warned. New clothes sounded extravagant.

"Yes, but the work you've been doing is boring you to tears. Chin up, dear. This is going to be fun."

"I'm trying to keep you out of jail. I can't do that wearing sequins and feathers and anything else you can dream up."

"Bah. Never mind that. Eli will not have me thrown in jail. Gracious. What a thought! I'll go sort out the bodyguard and make sure you get the sorts of dresses that will represent me and the Hope House appropriately."

"No two-foot-wide hats," Cora warned.

"No promises. Stop looking like that! This is going to be fun!"

"Mrs. Pitman, the law is not supposed to be fun. It's is supposed to be dry and stringent. That's why lawyers dress like this. They dress drab so they will be taken seriously."

"Have you been taken seriously?" Adeline challenged Cora bluntly.

Cora glared at her mutinously.

"That's what I thought. In this case, darling girl, if he doesn't take you seriously, you have an advantage."

"Mrs. Pitman, when would you like to meet about these real estate papers?" Cora wanted to bring the matter back in hand. Less about dresses and bodyguards, back to familiar ground, dry as dust, boring-to-the-point-of-tears real estate law.

"Come by the house after you see Eli tomorrow. You can drop the papers off and fill me in on how your meeting went. I want to know how it goes."

"If I'm still standing," Cora said ominously.

"It's going to be fine. I'll get that bodyguard sorted today."

A knot of fear tightened in Cora's throat at the thought of going up against Eli in whatever frippery Adeline would dream up.

Chapter Eight

Sol Stein swiftly read the telegram asking if he would take a job protecting a lawyer from Eli Pitman. Just the name Eli Pitman would strike fear into the heart of many bodyguards, but Sol was not going to be in Toronto forever. The price of the job for this particular lawyer was enormous. Mrs. Pitman was either in love with this lawyer or what she was up against was going to be so dangerous she was willing to pay this price.

No matter what her reasons, and they did not matter to Sol, it was enough money for him to finally move on to the Icelandic settlement in Gimli, Manitoba. He desperately wanted to start his life over, on a farm, far from this atrocious city.

Without Isold.

He twisted the wedding ring on the fourth finger of his left hand and tried not to feel pain in his heart. Isold, who would not see the new land she had dreamed of.

He met with Mrs. Pitman at the gym where he trained as a boxer. A woman had never hired him before, and he looked around the gym feeling like he should have picked a better place to meet. Men didn't care; they would meet in an outhouse if they had to, but women were particular and fussy.

When she tapped on the door, his eyes narrowed. A wealthy, spoiled woman was all he could see as she swept into the room to meet him. Her nose curled up at the smell of sweat and blood that permeated the boxing ring and never went away. He should have met her at a restaurant or somewhere other than here. Anyway, too late now. She was beautiful, dressed extravagantly, and looked him over as if he were a slave at an auction.

Rich, spoiled women like her were emotional and dramatic. A woman like this, wearing a hat that could barely fit through the door jamb, could throw a proper fit. Exhaustion gnawed at him just looking at her.

I despise hysterics and drama. A lot of things would just go smoother if people could just get all these emotions under control.

He sighed and offered her a chair. He perched on the desk for two reasons: there was only one chair in the room, and he didn't want her to get too comfortable. Women loved talking, and Sol enjoyed silence.

"Thank you for agreeing to meet with me." Adeline smiled at him.

Sol nodded. He noticed it made her uncomfortable that he didn't speak.

Good, let's get this over with.

"I think the job will basically be full time. I'm not really sure how all this works — I have never hired a bodyguard before." She tinkled a laugh that immediately grated on his nerves.

"The lawyer needs to give me an itinerary. I escort him to and from work and to anywhere he feels unsafe."

"Oh, Mr. Stein. Not a he. This is a she."

"She?" Sol's head snapped up.

"Yes. I'm hiring you to protect a woman lawyer."

"A woman?" Sol's eyebrows raised in confusion.

"Miss Cora Rood. She is my legal counsel."

"Two women against Eli Pitman?"

"That is correct." Her head tilted a little to the side. She likely couldn't hold it up under the weight of the hat. "You know of Eli?"

"Yes. You should stop immediately," Sol growled.

"Well, that's why we need you." She ignored his comment. "We think his men are following Miss Rood."

"Of course, his men are following Miss Rood. You need a different bodyguard." Sol stood to indicate the meeting was adjourned.

Female lawyer! Who has ever heard of anything so ridiculous?

He dreamed of a farm in Gimli where the rest of his extended family had relocated. No time for women who were deranged enough to come up against Eli and think they could win. No. This was no good. This would not do at all. Sol's life was simple. He trained every morning at 6:00 a.m. sharp. He did surveillance in the afternoon if he was guarding someone. He fought and he slept. That was life. No needless talking. He had just finished up with a client who talked nonstop until Sol was sure his ears were bleeding. A woman client would be worse. He needed to prep for a fight, and he needed silence to do it. Not women with problems, dilemmas, and hysterics.

"We really are in a bit of a bind." Adeline's face creased into a perfect pout.

Inwardly he rolled his eyes. This type of thing didn't work on him. He was immune to women because no one held a candle to Isold. Ever. This one was already trying his patience.

"I can't help you. I don't work for women," he said curtly.

"But, don't women need your services more than men? Are not women more vulnerable?" She had the audacity to purr, thinking it would sway him.

"Normal women don't need bodyguards. They have husbands." Sol spoke through gritted teeth. He sat back down on the desk. "Listen." He gathered his small reserves of patience. "I do not work for women. It is too much of a time commitment. With men, I leave them at work and at home. A woman would require all day, every day attention. I am a boxer. It would interfere with my training and fighting routine."

"Could you try for a week and let us know?" Mrs. Pitman completely ignored his arguments.

"No."

Mrs. Pitman got to her feet. With him seated and her standing they were eye level with each other.

"We need you."

"Sorry." His teeth clenched hard.

"I fear for her life because... well... I have heard what he's capable of." Her eyes widened.

"I have seen what he is capable of with my own eyes. You're both insane. You should not be going up against him. I don't work for women."

Memories of Isold, cut down on the street by a deranged hobo, assaulted him. Isold, whose eyes were clear shiny blue, dull in death after she had fought to keep her meager wage. Fought and lost.

Where was I? Big man. Sick in bed with a fever that raged for days. So sick I couldn't stand up while my precious wife worked and was killed... here in this terrible city.

The women had told him later. Isold had turned down the sexual advances of her boss that day and lost her job. She was afraid to come home and tell him. Not because he would be upset with her. She was afraid he would kill her boss, Corbin. She was right to be afraid. Once he'd heard the news, he had been wild with rage at the thought of Corbin's hands on her. The women assured him she had gotten away; he hoped that was the truth. The thought of Corbin humiliating her, overpowering her, caused a vein to stand out on his forehead. His fists clenched now, all this time later, at the very thought of his beautiful Isold being hurt. Guilt washed over him still, all these years later.

She had run from Corbin on pay day. Alone, on the streets, there was no one to hear her screams when a hobo had grabbed her and held her at knifepoint for her wage. Shame roared through him as he thought about how she must have tried to fight back. Real pain, as if the knife had pierced him instead of her, sliced through him at the thought of the hobo attacking her. Isold died in the streets of Toronto over $2.84.

The other Icelandic men in their community didn't let him kill Corbin or the hobo. It took five men to hold him down in his grief and his anguish not to settle the score. Had Detective Grayson not gotten involved and made sure justice was served, he would have committed murder. Sol couldn't have another woman's blood on his hands. This woman was deranged enough to be a lawyer in this terrible city and go up against Eli. No, it could not end well.

"The answer is no."

"I'll double the salary." Adeline's voice hardened.

Sol sighed. He stood up and stalked over to the window. Double the salary meant no need to continue boxing. This was a *fortune*. He could get to Gimli a year earlier if he took this job. But a woman up against Eli-bloody-Pitman! He didn't want this job, but he wanted *out* of this city. He looked out at the docks. Docks that Eli Pitman ran. He looked up the street. At the refineries that Eli Pitman owned. He thought about double the salary.

"When is the trial?"

"Not sure yet."

"Estimate?"

"A month."

He'd be done with her in May. Perfect because he needed to be in Gimli by May if he was going to put a crop in.

She was handing him a fortune for a month of babysitting a woman lawyer. He would be foolish to turn it down. Sol was a lot of things, but never foolish. He remembered another woman that had changed his mind. When the majority of the village decided to immigrate, Sol had his mind made up not to come to Canada. Until Isold changed it. She had wanted to leave Iceland so badly he couldn't say no to her. A crying woman was blackmail if he didn't know for certain that she was guileless. This was the only time she had shed tears when she asked him for anything. The minute he saw her eyes well with tears, he became completely unhinged and whatever caused her pain had to be destroyed, fixed, changed. Whatever was in his power. So, when she turned her big blue suffering eyes to him when her parents died of typhus, one after the other, he fought it.

He fought and lost; he was powerless to her pain. He thought back to their home in Iceland. She went to their bed and curled into a weeping ball. He had reached out to her, and she had pushed his hands away.

"No. I can't. I'm too sad," she had wept.

"I just want to hold you while you cry. I am sorry about your parents, Isold."

"Not sorry enough to take me to Canada and away from the memories of them. I am alone now. I can't bear to be here anymore. Last year was terrible. I can't do another year. I need my sister and my brother. I have to go to them. Please... I can't stay here alone."

"Isold." Sol remembered trailing his fingertips through the white blond hair that fanned out behind her while her shoulders shook with the pain of being an orphan.

"Don't touch me. I can't."

"Isold, if that's what you want. We'll go. I just want you to be happy."

She had stopped crying then and turned to him. He didn't care if it was a trick. She was back in his arms, and all was right with the world. They sold everything and boarded the next boat to Canada.

A month. He sighed; he could stand a woman for a month. She was probably a hideous man hater. He'd keep his distance, keep her alive, and leave Toronto as soon as he could.

"I'll do it," he growled.

"Oh! That is wonderful!"

He turned to face Mrs. Pitman.

"But on my terms. What I say goes. I don't like a lot of chit chat. I do my work, she does hers. If I say no to something, it's no. I don't negotiate..." His warnings fell on deaf ears.

Sol could tell Adeline Pitman did not comprehend any part of the word no. She got her way. That was all.

"Oh! This is delightful!" She clapped her hands in glee. "I can't wait for you to meet her. She is lovely!"

This was far too much emotion for Sol, who wanted to crawl under the desk and away from words like delightful and lovely. He had no time for delightful and lovely. All he heard was some incurable woman, who was a lawyer of all things, was going to require his time and attention for a long month, and she would likely talk his ear off like this one. Already, from this conversation alone, he thought about drinking but promptly shook the thought away. When Isold died, he had crawled into a bottle, and when he finally dragged himself out of it, he started training as a boxer. No alcohol to dull his senses or his reflexes. He never touched a drop because he couldn't afford to let his guard down. However, Mrs. Pitman's tinkle of laugher alone was enough to have him yearning for the bottle once again.

"She has a big day tomorrow. She is meeting with Eli at his offices. It might be best if you come to meet her." Mrs. Pitman's eyes widened with fear.

"No need for us to meet. I can keep my eye on her with surveillance."

Mrs. Pitman frowned. "That won't do at all."

Sol sighed a sigh that started from his knees. "What time and where?"

Mrs. Pitman's brilliant smile irritated him. "You'll love her."

"I am not in the habit of loving the people I work for."

"It's an expression."

Sol didn't blink; his lips thinned.

Mrs. Pitman wrote down the date, time, and address on a slip of paper and handed it to him.

"You may enjoy working for women!" Mrs. Pitman smiled brightly.

"I will *never* enjoy working for women — they talk too much, and it's double the job. Besides, it's not her I'm worried about." He folded the paper and tucked it away.

"Cheer up! She doesn't bite," Mrs. Pitman admonished.

He looked at her in open disdain.

Try being an immigrant, living in a city that has robbed you of everything, literally fighting for a living, losing your wife here the first month off the boat. Cheer up indeed.

Chapter Nine

Just as Adeline promised, a dress designer entered the law firm of Roth and Levine and got to work. The law firm looked on in amazement as the blinds were drawn in Miss Rood's office and a small, slight man and Mrs. Pitman pulled the door closed behind them.

"Strip down," Adeline instructed.

"I. Will. Not." Cora clutched at her throat in mortification.

"Why ever not?"

"I cannot undress in this law firm during business hours in front of a... well a..." Cora grasped for words that eluded her.

"You're all right. I've seen everything," the dress designer, Mr. Crest, said. "I don't need you right down to your altogether. Just your corset."

Cora blushed sixteen shades of red and purple and instructed him to turn away so she could pull off the olive green she was wearing.

"This is the state of all her clothes. Olive green with a hint of black to cheer it up." Adeline rolled her eyes at Mr. Crest. He turned his back as he waited for Cora to be sufficiently disrobed.

"I am a lawyer," Cora protested weakly.

"Yes. A lawyer, but you need not be a spinster lawyer!" Mr. Crest's words shot pain through Cora's heart. She stopped protesting and stood, as dressed down as she could be without being completely indecent.

"You may turn around," Cora whispered. Tears burned behind her eyes. Spinster lawyer. That's what they thought when they looked at her. She swallowed hard to stop herself from crying.

Mr. Crest turned, ignoring her emotional distress as his eyes narrowed to thin slits.

"This is worse than I thought."

Cora hung her head.

"All of this needs to be completely reworked. Am I permitted to take your measurements?"

"Of course," Cora murmured.

Cora stood still as Mr. Crest took measurements of her entire figure and made notes. He shook his head over the state of her corset.

"Such beautiful clothing in the world, and you dress like this! Such a lovely figure and you may as well be wearing a sack. This corset does nothing for you. I can't work with these undergarments," Mr. Crest said to Adeline. "I need double the funds. I have to build her from the skin out."

Cora went pale. "Wait a minute! I ride a bicycle, and I prefer a shirtwaist. I don't want constricting corsets. I have work to do. I..."

"Oh, sweet mercy. Bicycle! Shirtwaists!" Mr. Crest nearly fainted at the suggestion. "I am not here to dress boys! You are a woman, Miss Rood. You must remember that. A beautiful woman is a powerful being. You must seize that opportunity. Put away your bicycle. We want you to make men stop thinking and start feeling. It's not easy to make a man feel when you're wheeling around Toronto like a fourteen-year-old boy. You must be a distraction to Mr. Pitman. Not his equal. Never his equal."

Cora looked from Mr. Crest to Adeline.

I've been listening to this my whole life. I am so sick of this. I can't fight this anymore.

"You only need to dress like this when you deal with Eli," Adeline suggested kindly. "Remember, you cannot allow him to think you are his equal. Dressing like this will distract him from your true purpose."

Cora knew when to pick battles, and this was not a battle to pick.

"You know him better than I do," Cora relented. "Do your worst." Cora turned to Mr. Crest.

"Mr. Crest, she needs to be completely outfitted by tomorrow at two." Adeline settled into a chair to watch.

Mr. Crest looked at Cora and sighed.

"Let's start with the dress you will be in for Eli's appointment. It has to be perfect." Mr. Crest helped her into a dress the colour of toffee, striped with cream. The piping was a contrasting rich red. Perfect for an almost spring day. The stripe of caramels and creams was pieced to make her waist look tiny, fragile, the red piping drawing attention to the cut of her figure. The dress was simple to set off a hat that Cora wished was only two feet wide. It was enormous, ridiculous. She caught sight of herself in the mirror. It was stunning. All at once, she got it. Why women dressed like this. No one could ignore a woman wearing a hat like this.

Cora knew the world of numbers but with sudden insight, began to understand the world of design. If you want something to look small or dainty, you put something big near it. This ridiculous hat made her naturally fine-boned body look tiny in contrast. By the end of the hour with Mr. Crest, she understood what Adeline wanted. A lawyer who looked like she was fragile; loaded with feathers and sequins to draw an eye away from the brilliance that shone out of her eyes.

When Mr. Crest was finally done with her, Cora had never felt so beautiful in her life. She watched Adeline hand over a huge sum of money.

"Miss Rood is legal counsel for Hope House, Mr. Crest. She will need a gown for fundraisers, please. The more outrageous the better. If the men we're asking for money take her seriously, we're all doomed. They need to think we're spoiled rich women playing with our husband's permission. It's a pretense, but only we can know that."

Mr. Crest looked from Cora to Adeline in grim determination.

"You're going into battle with Eli?" His face paled with fear.

"Yes, but we battle the way women do it. Cautiously, with a lot of feathers." Adeline gave him such a wide smile, Mr. Crest tentatively smiled back.

"I will be here at noon tomorrow to dress you to meet with Mr. Pitman. Does that suit you?"

"Noon will work." Cora wearily agreed. She pulled on the drab olive green ensemble that Mr. Crest shuddered at

"Lovely!" Adeline exclaimed after Mr. Crest left with armfuls of clothing.

Cora sat down feebly, worn out, and the day was only just beginning. She looked up as a man who had to be over six feet tall and recently stepped off a Viking ship, stalked into the law office. Her breath caught in her throat.

What now?

He prowled through the desks, eyes flicking over the men as they all watched him. Even without a Viking axe, his stance sent out a silent warning — he would pillage and burn this office to the ground if anyone got in his way. His hard, blue eyes darted around, assessing the room of men. He frowned at them as he marched inexorably forward to Cora's office.

"Oh good, he's here!" Adeline looked at Cora with a gleam in her eye.

"Oh, may the saints preserve us, what now?" Cora gasped. "Adeline, he's terrifying."

Blond hair clipped close, clean shaven, and immaculate, he raised his broad hand to knock on her open door. Cora tried to gather her few wits together. Really, a new wardrobe and a bodyguard on the same day — it was too much.

Adeline came to the rescue.

"Come on in." Adeline gestured for him to enter. "Please, close the door behind you."

Cora heard the law firm buzzing beyond the open door. Who was this man? Why are there all these men, *not clients*, in Cora's office? What is going on? Has she finally become hysterical and they could fire her and get on with the law?

All men. As it should be.

The Viking entered her office and pulled the door shut on the prying eyes of the male clerks.

Prying eyes indeed! There hadn't been this much commotion in Cora's offices since she was hired. Gone was the woman who was a little batty and, rumour had it, talked to her plant. What is Miss Rood up to? She could almost hear their minds working.

"Miss Rood, I want to introduce you to Mr. Sol Stein."

Cora leaped to her feet. She held out her slim hand and watched as it was engulfed by Sol's very large, very hard hand. Cora noticed his knuckles were raw; he'd recently been in a fight. He had a huge silver wedding ring on the fourth finger of his left hand.

Good, he's married, so there is no need to worry about any inappropriate behavior.

"Please, take a seat." Cora indicated he should sit in the chair beside Adeline and across the desk from her.

He remained standing until both Cora and Adeline were seated, then he sat.

A gentleman and a bodyguard.

Maybe. Any man can pretend to be a gentleman. How soon before you treat me with contempt like all the men in this office? Or worse.

Cora's eyes narrowed as she contemplated whether he would treat her with disrespect or not. His eyes narrowed right back.

"Mr. Stein has five years experience as a bodyguard." Adeline looked from Cora to Sol and then back to Cora. "He's the best in

Toronto. You are safe from whatever Eli can throw at us now." Adeline smiled at her as if all their problems were solved.

"Where are you from, Mr. Stein?" Cora asked politely.

"Iceland." His tone was flat and shut down any further conversation.

"I have a meeting with Mr. Pitman at 2:00 p.m. tomorrow. Would you accompany me to that meeting?" Cora's voice sounded small. "I'll have to leave here by 1:45."

Sol sat ramrod straight in his chair. He frowned with disapproval at the swamp of files and papers on Cora's desk.

"Do I go in with you or is surveillance sufficient?" He spoke in clipped tones. Cora noticed he had a hard time looking away from the clutter on her desk. She attempted to tidy things up, which made his frown deepen to disgust.

"I think you should go in with her," Adeline suggested.

"Have there been any attacks?"

"I thought someone was following me, but maybe I was mistaken. Since then, I'm not sure if my apartment was sort of rifled through."

"A simple yes or no is sufficient." Sol's lips thinned.

Cora bristled. He was blunt to the point of rude.

"No physical attack. So, no," Cora shot at him.

"I need to know when you go to work in the morning and home at night, so I can escort you between both those places."

"I am at work by 8:00 a.m., so I leave my apartment at 7:30 a.m. I leave here at 6:00 p.m."

"If there is a change in your schedule, I need to know a day in advance." He stood up to put an end to the meeting. Cora looked way up at his face. A boxer from Iceland in his prime. His height and the width of his shoulders made her nervous.

Gracious, what is a man this size capable of?

"Thank you for agreeing..." Cora swallowed hard.

"I didn't agree." He bent his head to meet her gaze. "I accepted payment for a job. Very different thing altogether. Let's get one thing clear. You're doing a very dangerous job. I think you are completely deranged. I will keep you alive, but you will not win against Eli Pitman. Another thing — I'm not your friend." His icy blue eyes froze her in her chair. "You should stop all this foolishness and get married and get a husband to look after you. This is insanity. I'm here for a paycheck, nothing else." Sol went to the door. "I'll be back to escort you home tonight. I am going to leave you to rethink whether you both want to take on Eli Pitman. You should reconsider this today before things get completely out of control and someone ends up hurt." He shot a pointed glance at Adeline before banging the door shut behind him.

Cora shot Adeline a pained look. "Well. He's very stern."

"He'll warm up." Adeline waved Cora's concerns away.

Cora rubbed her arms as if his icy words actually froze her. "I have a lot of work to do before I meet with Eli. I better get to it."

Adeline stood up. "See you tomorrow evening. Plan to come for dinner. I look forward to hearing how things went with Eli."

"I'll see you tomorrow." Terror knotted her stomach at the very thought.

Eli Pitman and a bodyguard with the personality of an iceberg, heaven help us.

Chapter Ten

C ora noticed Sol Stein out of the corner of her eye as she walked toward Eli Pitman's office. He tilted his hat to acknowledge her, then caught up quickly.

"Good afternoon," Cora said as her eyes flicked over him and then away.

"In the future, Miss Rood, you will wait for me to escort you out of your law firm."

Cora stopped and looked at him coolly. His tone got her back up.

"You were late."

"You said 1:45 p.m. It is currently 1:40." Sol checked his watch and looked at her with reproach.

"I like to be early."

"Fine, but be accurate." He spoke through gritted teeth.

"I'll keep that in mind."

"See that you do. I don't get paid if you get killed on my watch."

"Charming." Cora turned on her heel and stalked away from him.

He kept up with her easily. She hesitated at the door to the lobby of Eli's office. One of the men on the sidewalk jumped to attention and opened the door for her.

Maybe these clothes of Adeline's will pave the way for men to treat me with civility.

The man holding the door open let his gaze travel over the length of her; she shivered. The civility came with a price, obviously.

Cora stepped into Eli Pitman's world and tried to calm down. She took a deep breath to stop her heart from pounding out of her chest.

She looked around the lobby; the men at their desks looked at her as if she were a strumpet on patrol. She blinked back feelings of awkwardness, the painful self-awareness that she looked like a tart.

I'm a lawyer, not a tart!

She strode to the closest desk.

"I'm here to see Eli Pitman."

She purposefully didn't say Mr. Pitman.

Let them wonder what I'm doing in his office. Let them think the worst.

They didn't bat an eye. Probably used to strumpets strolling into his office and out.

"Follow me." A man old enough to be her father looked her up and down, then gestured she should follow.

Cora swallowed hard and followed up two flights of stairs. Sol's heavy footsteps behind her, the only insurance she had as she went inexorably forward into the very core of Eli's corrupt world. At the top of the stairs, she stopped to catch her breath.

Cursed corset.

Eli's office was huge. The entire floor. Windows, floor to ceiling, illuminated his work space. This was where decisions were made, fortunes were earned or taken. She looked around. Nowhere to sit. Looked like men came in here, reported, and left. Clearly, Eli didn't like anyone getting too cozy and taking his precious time.

She hesitated before she entered. Her eyes darted from Eli Pitman to his bodyguard. Outnumbered, all men downstairs on every floor. Only men. Men who answered to Eli.

Men who will not step in if I scream.

Memories of being taken from the front line of the rally and thrown in jail attacked her. Her hands trembled at the memory of the look on Lady Bronwyn's face as they dragged her away.

The hardness of a man's hand as it subdues you, the futility of fighting against all that strength. That's when the fight went out of me. That's when I lost my hope that I could effect change, that I was equal to the task in front of me... when he... took special pleasure in hitting me, hurting me, breaking me.

Cora shook her head. No more thoughts of that.

She had a job to do. That job had nothing to do with what she said but rather what she would *not* say in this office.

Typical, even now, in my profession I have to keep my mouth shut.

Eli's eyes skimmed over her and lit up on certain parts of her anatomy as she stood. His bodyguard dragged a chair out, and Mr. Pitman indicated she sit down.

Dear Lord, we all have bodyguards.

She watched the man stand back so she could sit and he would not get hit by her hat. For a big man, he dodged the brim nimbly.

His bodyguard is bigger than my bodyguard, but mine comes from a long line of Vikings and is permanently furious. Who knows what he is capable of?

Knowing Sol waited just outside the door made her calm down a little. If she didn't come out in a reasonable time, he would come in here and hopefully be able to take on two men at once. He was well within earshot if she started screaming.

"Good day, Miss Rood." Eli's eyes skimmed over her once again, and she felt as if she were exposed in the altogether.

"Good day, Mr. Pitman," Cora croaked. She cleared her throat.

Can I come up against you? Is it worth it? You have everything on your side, and I have nothing. Will you destroy me? Will you destroy Adeline? I can't go back to jail.

"We have a common interest." Mr. Pitman cut straight to the point.

"Do we?"

We have nothing in common. I have ethics, and you do not.

"You don't look like a lawyer, but you certainly sound like one. Let me guess. You're going to let me talk and see how you can ensnare me."

"Ensnare you?" Cora forced herself to chuckle. "You called this meeting, not me."

"So, you *are* a lawyer." He sat back and made a temple of his fingers as he contemplated her, like she was a unicorn that had landed on his desk. She could almost see his brain scroll through ideas of how to deal with her.

"I am." Cora's corset kept her ramrod straight in her chair.

"And Mrs. Pitman has retained you for what purpose?"

"I am her legal counsel, sir; I don't disclose what my clients have retained my services for." Cora wished desperately the corset would allow her to take a full breath; she cursed Adeline and Mr. Crest. New corsets indeed!

"If she retained you, I will be paying your bill, so you work for me. I want to know why she hired you."

"You have no choice but to pay her legal bills. *Smith v. Smith,* a husband is legally required to pay any and all legal bills incurred by his wife, no matter what the charges. She has a right to counsel, and she has a right to confidentiality. You have no right to ask me anything." She faced Eli Pitman straight on. Terrified but straight on nonetheless.

"Well, that's hardly fair!" Eli tilted his head to the side.

You dare complain about fairness! You have a mistress!

She met his gaze with silence.

"I think my wife hired you because she knows about Mirabel Salter," Mr. Pitman said so bluntly it caught Cora off guard.

Cora blinked, recovered, and said nothing. She waited.

"All this charity business... I think it's a complete ruse to drag money out of me so she can try to divorce me and walk away with half my fortune."

Silence from Cora's side of the desk.

"Why aren't you speaking?"

"I don't know what you want me to say." Cora longed for her olive green drab clothes to make him stop salivating over her. Even the bodyguard couldn't take his eyes off her figure. Unease crawled up her spine. To be in a room and looked at like a slab of meat, a striped slab of meat, no less, that could easily be devoured by these men caused fear to wash through her. A trickle of sweat gathered between her shoulder blades, and she cursed Adeline and Mr. Crest with renewed zeal.

Striped gowns indeed.

"She has a bank account with 10,000 of my dollars in it."

"Which you gave her," Cora replied coolly. "Husbands give their wives gifts of money all the time. She bought a hotel with it. If you didn't want her to have access to that money, why did you give it to her?"

Eli Pitman narrowed his cool icy grey eyes at her. His lips were as thin as his mustache. Revulsion crawled around her stomach; she hated a mustache like that.

"So, you won't talk about what my wife is using your services for." Eli made the statement sound dirty. Cora met his gaze unaffected. She didn't dare let what she thought of him show on her face.

"Let's talk about you then."

"I'll stop you right there." Cora stood up.

"Oh, come on, Miss Rood. Nothing in this file to be ashamed of. You are in the habit of pushing."

Cora took a step back.

"Are you going to try to push me?" he asked as he grinned. He looked at his bodyguard who chuckled with him. They were like big cats batting a mouse.

What would it be like to be a man and have the strength and the size to sink my fist into that insolent jaw?

Silence. She caught a look between them that made her palms slick with icy cold sweat.

"I think I'd enjoy that. I think you might, too," Eli said so suggestively fear kicked in her stomach.

Cora turned her back on him to walk away.

"They didn't want you to be a lawyer," Eli called out to her retreating back. She turned then to face him. "You had poor old Oliver Moat running around in circles to get you admitted to the bar. Was he sleeping with Lady Bronwyn behind Lord Bronwyn's back? Lady Bronwyn championed you, right? Is that what it was all about? Because, as I understand it, you are not a person under the law, so you had the law changed, and now, as a consequence, the Dominion Women's Enfranchisement Association owns you, right? You owe them for all the weight they threw around."

Cora stood stock still. "Is there a question here?"

"Ah, very much a lawyer." Eli leaned forward in his chair. "I believe you're used to getting your way."

Silence again.

"Still won't talk to me." Eli shook his head. "Should we see what my man Royce here can get out of you?" He chuckled at her as the blood drained from her face.

Terrified, Cora heard Sol clear his throat from the doorway. Mr. Pitman and Royce looked at Sol at the same time as Cora. Sol stood braced for battle. Her shoulders relaxed, knowing he was there, looking foreboding in the entrance. There would be no torturing information out of her with Sol in the room.

But, it would be two against one. *Is he capable of defending me against two men at the same time?*

Her eyes searched his for a very brief moment, and the look he gave her was enough to inspire confidence that he would take down this entire building if necessary. His paycheck depended on it. There was not a hint of worry in his eyes. He squared his shoulders, and his stance broadened as if he were ready to attack.

"No need for hysterics, Miss Rood. We're not animals."

Hysterics! Oh, how I hate that word!

Cora turned from Sol and looked at Mr. Pitman with utter contempt.

"Only an animal would suggest that." Cora heard the anger in her voice.

No anger. That won't work. That is an emotion. No emotion. Only logic. Stay calm. You can weep about this later.

He smiled. "Oh. You're talking. Why are you working for my wife? Why does she suddenly want to run a charity? Why try to involve Mirabel Salter?"

"She is running a charity with Mirabel Salter, Jean King, Hester Colton, and Caroline Swan." Cora purposely made her voice sound bored. "I checked over the documents for the hotel. All looks in order. As I understand it, they are going to take girls off the streets and educate them. It will be a huge undertaking, but they are working with the local chapter of the W. C. T. U. to accomplish this. Really, you are wasting my time and yours. These are all questions you could ask your wife."

"But why *you*? Why are *you* representing her as legal counsel? I have a tribe of lawyers."

"Maybe they aren't good enough." Cora met his eyes and didn't look away.

"Are you good, Miss Rood?" Mr. Pitman asked so suggestively Cora held onto the back of the chair to center herself.

Sol crossed the room to stand beside her, just back enough that he could intervene if necessary.

"You can call your dog off. I'm not going to lay a hand on you." Mr. Pitman's voice hardened as he looked at Sol and sized him up.

"He's not my dog."

Eli started to worm his way under her armor, trying to get her to feel, trying to make her weaken.

"Well, we know he's not your man. You don't have one of those, do you?" Mr. Pitman tilted his head to the side. He said it softly.

She rolled her eyes at him. "I'm a lawyer and a suffragette, Mr. Pitman. What on earth do I need a man for?"

Eli Pitman burst out laughing. "Maybe we should show you what you need a man for. Never mind. Call him off..."

Cora looked at Sol, who was ready to take down Eli with one nod from her. She shook her head no and turned back to Eli.

"Yes. A suffragette on the front line on the war for women's rights. Oh. Wait. You used to be on the front line. You abandoned that, didn't you? Did you lose your nerve?"

Cora said nothing, and Eli returned to the file.

"You earned a Bachelor of Arts in Mathematics at the age of sixteen. You are brilliant."

Silence. Cora refused to respond. She knew exactly where this was going. More flogging.

"Ancient spinster they call you." Eli flashed a quick smile at her, to see if she was saddened by the label. "No man, but an impressive group of women behind you. Harriet Stowe, Lady Bronwyn. What did they see in you, miss? Let's see if I can see it, the premier of Ontario, the Dominion Women's Enfranchisement Association... big names. Big stakes here." His voice lowered.

"I'm not sure what you want from me, Mr. Pitman. I'm not going to discuss any of this with you. I don't owe you any explanations. You have done your background check, as you say, there's nothing to hide. What is this all about?"

"You are used to petitions."

"Of course, I'm a lawyer." Cora stood straighter. "You have my transcripts there. You know what you are dealing with."

"You left Martell, Shine, and McFaul."

"I did."

"Why? Did they hurt your feelings?" Eli sneered.

"They made it impossible for me to practice law."

"How is it going at your current firm?"

"What do you want, Mr. Pitman?" Cora's tentative grasp on her anger started to weaken. She forced herself to sound bored, like he was trying her patience with trivialities. She needed this interview to be over. He wanted her to lose her composure and tell him everything. Give him an advantage.

"I want to hire you."

Cora's head snapped up at that announcement.

"You are the only lawyer that would work with my wife. Naturally, that makes me want you." He spoke so suggestively, Sol tensed beside her and moved near enough that she could feel his sleeve against her bare arm.

"I didn't choose to work with her. I was assigned. Charities aren't typically my field."

"My wife is no more running a charity than she's flying to the moon, or you're stupid. By the look of your life, you're not stupid."

"I was assigned this client. I..."

"Assigned," Eli interrupted. "So, you do as you're told?"

Cora remained silent.

Eli Pitman stood up, and Sol moved in front of her so his shoulder partially blocked her.

"I won't lay a hand on her." Eli grinned at Sol. Sol didn't move an inch. "Looks like your current firm doesn't like you much either."

"I don't really care, Mr. Pitman." Cora heard her voice shake and hated it.

"Anyone who comes up against me, well, they never do it again." He smiled.

"Are you threatening me?" Fear tightened her stomach into knots.

"I'm just making sure you know what you are up against. You won't practice law in this city if you come up against me. Just know that. So, I have an alternative for you."

"I'm not interested in an alternative." Cora took a step back. As much as Sol had been a trial to deal with, he moved with her, making sure he was partially between her and Eli. He would not let these two lay a hand on her. A surge of courage emboldened her, knowing she was physically protected with half of Sol's body in front of her. Mean and rude seemed like a liability yesterday; currently those qualities made him invaluable.

"Quit and work for me. I understand you live in almost slum conditions. I can make you a fortune."

"How do you know what sort of conditions I live in?" Cora could barely form the words.

"I own this city, Miss Rood."

Eli's haughty voice sparked a fury she thought had been extinguished in the bottom of a jail cell. Enraged, Cora placed her hand on Sol's arm to let him know he could stand down. He moved so she could face Eli straight on. Cora stepped toward Eli's desk and leaned over it just slightly.

"I don't have an ounce of respect for you," she hissed. "I need to respect the people I work for."

"If I find out you have lied to me here today..." Eli moved forward so they were nose-to-nose across the desk.

"You said yourself, I said nothing. How could I lie to you about anything?"

"Is my wife filing for divorce?" Eli demanded.

"A great question for you to ask her." Cora held his gaze and didn't look away. "Good day, Mr. Pitman."

She was halfway to the door when he called out to her, causing both Cora and Sol to turn.

"Young lady." Eli's voice was like velvet on iron. "If she files for divorce — and I suspect she is going to — if this is a scheme, you'll need more than him to protect you."

"No need to send for me again. We have nothing to discuss here," Cora said firmly. Sol stood back so she could exit the room before him.

***

They walked a block before the fury burning in Sol's gut made him take Cora by the upper arm and pull her down a back alley. She stiffened against him as he pulled her to a stop in front of him. He looked around the alley to be sure no one had followed them. Satisfied they were alone, he lost control of his anger and lit into her.

"That, what happened up there, is why women should *not* be lawyers, and they certainly shouldn't be going up against Eli-bloody-Pitman," he roared at her. "You and Mrs. Pitman are deranged, and you will pay the price. Not her."

He dropped her arm as her eyes widened with fear and then tears. Cursing under his breath, he took a step back so she would know she was not in physical danger from him.

"I'm not going to hurt you," he said, holding his hands out in a gesture of peace. She looked like she would start sobbing at any minute, and that was the last thing he wanted. With great difficulty, Sol forced his tone to be gentle and promised himself he would never work for women again. "We need to talk. Away from Adeline and away from your office. Do you have any idea what you are up against?"

Sol regretted taking this job more today than yesterday. He'd expected a drab, ugly lawyer. No. He was assigned a beautiful, brilliant woman who, dressed like she was today, would be impossible to keep safe. His careful routine for training was going to suffer because she couldn't be out of his sight for a second — nothing Sol hated more than his training routine suffering. He loved his day mapped out in front of him with no interruptions and no extra conversations.

Eli Pitman and Royce salivating over her bothered him. Then it bothered him that he was bothered. This was a job, he reminded himself, nothing more. He longed to return to the world of farming where he'd never have to deal with people. Certainly not complicated women like the one in front of him.

"You think women should not be lawyers?" Cora pulled her emotions under control. Her voice sounded ice cold.

"Were you not up there in that room? Did you not realize what could have easily happened?" Sol tried and failed to keep his temper under control.

"That is why Adeline hired you! What should I do then, Mr. Stein? What should my work be?" She crossed her arms over her chest.

"You should be married to a man and at home, having children like a normal woman. Women who get married and stay home don't typically need bodyguards," Sol said viciously.

"Unless their husbands beat them, and then they have no recourse in a court of law," she hissed at him.

Sol's mouth thinned. "Most husbands don't beat their wives."

"Really, you know that for sure? Most don't? Is *most* enough? You haven't worked in the environment I've worked in, obviously. Many, many husbands beat their wives. We hired you as bodyguard, not an advisor. You are welcome to keep your archaic, non-progressive opinions to yourself. I have a job to do." Cora narrowed her eyes at him.

Sol held his hands up in surrender. "Why not let a male lawyer handle this? I can work with him. We'll all be happy."

"No male lawyer would touch this petition," she shrieked at him.

Sol's eyes narrowed. "What is actually going on here?"

"Absolutely none of your business, sir. Just keep me alive and keep your opinions to yourself."

"It would help if I knew." His jaw clenched so tight he thought it would break.

"Mrs. Pitman is running a charity." Cora lifted her chin.

"Who is Mirabel Salter?" Sol cut straight to the point.

"Eli Pitman's mistress."

Sol threw his hands up in the air. "What?"

"Yes," Cora growled at him. "Some husbands are terrible, Mr. Stein. Some of them beat their wives, some have women tucked away in an apartment. The rumour is Mirabel Salter is pregnant. No law against it! Isn't that quaint? The law of Canada currently doesn't allow a woman to divorce if her husband commits adultery. We have to prove adultery *and* cruelty. So, a man like Eli Pitman can gallivant all over Toronto and sleep with whomever he pleases, and Adeline Pitman can't do a thing about it. He hasn't broken the law, and it is not grounds for divorce. So, it's not all roses in a garden when women get married. The law doesn't protect them. That's why I am a lawyer," Cora roared at him.

He watched her clamp her mouth shut with disapproval. She was a beautiful woman who had no idea she was beautiful. She didn't use it like a weapon to get what she wanted. Isold had been the same. Stunning, heartbreakingly beautiful, and she had no idea. If Isold had been here, listening to this, she would have frowned at him and demanded he keep her safe. Isold would have liked Cora Rood. Inwardly, Sol groaned. Marriage didn't guarantee a woman was safe — Isold had been cut down; he couldn't be with her every minute of every day.

"Tell her you quit. I mean it. You are... you can't... you have to quit this. Today." Sol resorted to begging.

"If I could get out of this, don't you think I would have by now?" Her green eyes flashed at him in fury. "I was up there. The way they looked at me..." Her voice caught with emotion, and she turned away from him. Guilt hit him in the stomach as her narrow shoulders trembled. She took a deep breath before turning back to him. "It's not *her* I would have to say no to."

Her eyes glittered with unshed tears.

Please don't cry. I can't handle it.

"I was assigned this case because the lawyers I work for want a reason to fire me. Preferably before my articling period is over so that I can't be sworn in as a barrister. It would be the ultimate devastation. To work this hard, five years of work, to come this far, to fight for this and then fail before I can swear in... They don't want to fire me. They want to destroy me. I have to do whatever they want until May 31." A tear escaped, but she dashed it away quickly. "So, they handed me this because they know I can't win it. Convenient for them they won't have to fire me. Eli will have me raped and killed by that terrible bodyguard, and that will get me out of their offices permanently. I don't have a choice. I have to represent her. If I had a choice, I would have said no. I'm not an idiot." Her voice broke; she turned her back on him again and rustled though her handbag, looking for a handkerchief.

Acid pooled in Sol's stomach at her words. Her situation was impossible, and he was making it worse. She didn't want to get married and have babies; she wanted to right wrongs that no one else was righting. Grudging respect started to replace the contempt he had originally felt for her.

"I see." Sol found a clean handkerchief and tapped her on the shoulder. She jumped and shrieked.

"It's just me," Sol said softly. Her nerves were on the brink, so with great effort, he kept his tone civil.

She snatched the handkerchief from him and with a hard glare she turned her back on him again.

She doesn't want to cry in front of me.

Sol said nothing as she tried to regain her composure. Finally, she turned around to face him.

"I have to see this through and hope for the best. If you want to quit, I will understand." She looked up at him. He couldn't help but see her vulnerability. Her pulse pounded in the hollow of her collar bones. "I will ask Adeline to find someone else. They were terrible up there." She gestured at the building they had just walked out of. "It would have been hard, right? One man against two. I was worried. I was really scared that you couldn't fight both of them."

"I could fight both of them with one hand tied behind my back." Sol sighed.

"Really?" She peered up from under the brim of her hat.

"Really," he replied dryly. "Back to your office?"

"Yes. Office first, and then home before we go to Adeline's. I need this hat off, and I need to get a few papers. This outfit is ridiculous. I need something drab. I can't even take myself seriously."

They began walking toward her law office. "If you are going to quit, can you let me know sooner rather than later?"

"I'm not going to quit. The money is too good."

He watched as she flinched at his words.

Stop hurting her. She's a victim here.

"I didn't mean it that way." Sol tried to repair the damage of his thoughtless comment.

Cora stiffened and then turned to face him. She dragged him down a back alley just like he had done to her only moments earlier. He let her.

She pulled her hat off and tossed her bag down as if she were going to fight him in hand-to-hand combat. His eyebrows raised.

"You don't like me. I am used to that, sir. I don't care. There are two sorts of men in this world, Mr. Stein. Two. Men who respect women, and men who don't. So far. You don't."

"I do," he protested.

"No," she roared at him. "You don't."

He said nothing because she was pulling pins out of her hair so she could drag her fingers through it. Once she scratched her scalp, her hair grew to be as big as a bush now that it wasn't under the hat and freed from the pins.

Is she having some sort of fit?

"Are you going to keep me alive, Mr. Stein? I need to know," she demanded.

"I told you I would." It was his turn to lose his patience and shout.

"All right then." She started twisting her hair into place. "What are you doing?" she asked as he picked up the pins she had thrown onto the sidewalk.

"You're throwing things everywhere. How do you live in this sort of chaos?"

She took a deep breath and let it out slowly. "That hat is so itchy. I couldn't stand it another minute. I feel ridiculous."

Silently, he handed the pins back to her. Delicately, she picked up a couple of pins from his outstretched hand.

He winced as she jabbed pins into her hair until it stayed in place.

"I'll keep you alive until May 31, then I leave this city, and I won't look back." He handed her the bag and the hat again. Sol mentally thought about hiring his brother-in-law to put his crop in, that way he would be able to stay until she was done her term of articling.

She nodded. "All right then."

She walked in front of him, and he took her by the arm again. She stiffened under his hand. "When I say, I'll keep you alive, I mean it." He dropped her arm. "You don't have to be afraid or scared of Eli or his bodyguard. You are safe with me."

"We'll see." Her voice sounded small as she turned from him and kept walking to the office.

Sol opened the door for her; she entered ahead of him. She went to her desk, and he heard her gasp as she looked at the pile of letters on her desk.

"What?"

"Can you close the door? I need a minute." Her eyes were swimming with tears.

She doesn't want to cry in front of anyone.

Sol pulled her door shut softly behind him. He waited as she pulled down the blinds so no one could see in. He looked around the law office helplessly, then sat down and waited.

You should walk away from her right now.

He heard her sobbing behind the door and knew with certainty he wasn't going anywhere.

Chapter Eleven

C ora's hands trembled as she picked up the letter. She tried to stop crying as she read the writing on the envelope. She had to change, she had to get to Adeline, but right now she needed the reassurance of this letter from this man. She tore it open, and her eyes devoured the words.

Dear Cora,
I haven't heard from you in months, I am starting to worry.
Are you all right?
I know you are done with your articling on the thirty first of May, I want you to come home.
Since Lucy's mother died, the cottage on our property has been empty. I will have it ready for you any time.
This is too much for anyone, Cora. You need to come home.
You said your nerves were bothering you. You need a sandbar and a summer of happiness.
Come home to Oakland.
Your brother,
Wil

Cora put the letter down, buried her face in her hands, and wept as silently as possible. The fear of facing Eli, the contempt from Sol, and now this kindness, was too much. She tried to stifle her sobs.

A sandbar and a summer of happiness. Oh, Wil, you have no idea.

If he knew about jail, he would have been on the next train. He didn't, and he couldn't. Finally, once the storm passed, Cora went to the mirror and carefully cleaned up her face. Her reflection didn't lie — she looked pale and tired. Her eyes and nose were so red, they clashed with her chestnut-coloured hair.

She quickly went back to her desk and dashed off a quick letter to Wil, letting him know she would be home as fast as the train could take her. She asked him to let Ada Bennett know she would be coming, and she wanted a visit as soon as she was able. Just the thought of Ada and Wil calmed Cora. She took a deep breath, straightened up, and opened the door to the office.

"We should be going," Cora said to Sol.

She handed her letter for Wil to the clerk. "See this is posted today."

The clerk ignored her.

Her eyes met Sol's, and his mouth was a thin line.

"Don't say anything," she snapped at him.

"I wasn't going to." He held his hands up in a sign of surrender.

Once at her apartment building, Cora picked her way through the dim hallway. Sol's silent presence reminded her that she was not safe in this grim, terrible building. She braced herself for the breakdown he would have from all the clutter behind her closed door. Embarrassed, she didn't want him to see just how poorly she lived.

"I'll just be a moment getting changed." She intended to slither through the door so he couldn't see inside.

"I'll wait here," he offered.

The key clicked in the lock, and she opened the door. She gasped and clutched her papers to her chest. Someone had slashed through the settee and upended every chair. They had ripped her few pictures from the walls. The contents of her cupboards were all strewn around her kitchen, glasses smashed. Everything she had worked for was broken. Her heart splintered at the destruction.

***

"I assume, from your gasp of surprise, it doesn't always look like this?" Sol pulled her out of the apartment.

Cora glared at him — icy green, red rimmed slits of rage knifed through him.

"Stay back." He checked up and down the hallway to be sure no one was lurking. "Let me go in first. In case they are still there."

Sol moved through her little apartment easily. Everything Cora owned had been smashed or ripped open. His eyes flicked over the sparseness of her apartment. She had only what she needed.

Isold had made his home beautiful. He hadn't known what he was missing until she filled it. He had come home to different flowers on the table each day, and she loved to paint, so her artwork was on every surface of his, their home, he corrected himself. When the house was full of her art, he started hanging it in the barn. The minute he had said *I do* to Isold, she owned him. No question.

He pushed thoughts of Isold and their home together out of his mind. No need to compare them. This was a job. Nothing more. If Cora wanted to live like a monk, it was none of his business. The window in her bedroom had been smashed. Thoughts of this happening when she was in that bed made him sick with nerves. She wouldn't be able to stay here tonight, or any night. The threat to her safety had already escalated.

He joined her back in the hallway.

Cora dashed tears from her eyes so he wouldn't see them. She turned her back to him, and guilt assaulted him. He shouldn't have said what he did about women getting married and having babies. It had hurt her feelings, and he didn't want to hurt her feelings. As he watched her fragile form shake with silent sobs, he realized he didn't want anyone else to hurt her feelings either. The men at her law office treated her with contempt; she had been afraid of Eli Pitman, who wanted to destroy her, and she came home to chaos. It was a lot for anyone.

Careful, Sol, this is a slippery slope.

"Ah... they are long gone," he said gruffly. "They came in through the window. It's been smashed, so you won't be able to stay here tonight."

Covering her face with her hands, she tried to stop crying. Awkwardly, he stood by her. This was the first woman he had been alone in a room with since Isold. If it had been Isold weeping, he would have... never mind. This is not Isold. Isold would never be in this dangerous of a predicament; he would never have allowed it. Although... she had been nearly raped by her boss and then knifed to death in broad daylight by a hobo. His hate for this city returned with renewed zeal.

"I have nowhere else to go." Her voice caught on a sob.

He tried not to be drawn in by the hurt in her eyes. His resolve to keep her at arm's length weakened as more tears splashed down her cheeks. "You are supposed to go to Mrs. Pitman's, so let's go and see what she suggests."

"I think Mrs. Pitman is so bent on revenge, I am scared to death to even imagine what she will suggest," Cora said openly and honestly. Gallantly, she wiped her tears away, trying to be strong.

Sol couldn't stop a grin from stretching across his face. Finally, after twenty-four hours of being in each other's company, they had something in common.

"I am pretty concerned about what she will come up with myself." The grin on Sol's face turned into a chuckle. Sol Stein, who hadn't laughed or chuckled since the death of Isold, stood in a trashed apartment and laughed. Cora's lip twitched.

"She really is fairly outrageous." Cora chuckled as the tension surrounding the day started to dissipate. Finally, she laughed with him. They laughed so hard, tears streamed down their faces. This was it. Both pitted against Eli Pitman, different reasons, same danger, and answering to a woman who was more bent on revenge by the day.

***

Together, they were ushered into Adeline's drawing room.

"It's simple," Adeline said to Cora as Sol stood back. She offered him a brandy, but he declined.

"You said so yourself, you need to be with her more than a normal client, so we'll say you eloped. I'll get you an apartment and have it furnished tomorrow. At end of day, you'll be settled."

"I can't live with him!" Cora's eyes widened with indignation.

Adeline stood up and poured more brandy into her glass.

"It makes perfect sense. Your apartment was disgraceful anyway. You needed to upgrade. I'll make sure there are two bedrooms." She looked from one to the other as if this were the only problem at hand. Like living together would not change their lives completely. "At the end of this trial you are going to Manitoba. Cora will say she was abandoned and get a 'divorce' from you. You go on with your lives."

Sol got up and marched to the sideboard and poured himself a glass of water. His hand twitched at the thought of blocking Adeline out with a brandy. He poured water into his glass and forced himself back into the conversation.

"Have you lost your mind?" Cora sputtered.

Sol wanted to cheer, and since Sol *never* wanted to cheer, this was concrete proof things were dire.

"Cora, I think this is the safest solution." Adeline's eyes widened as she looked from one to the other.

Sol put the glass down on the sideboard and crossed his arms over his chest.

"You said yourself, she needs more protection than the average client." Adeline's voice wheedled like a spoiled child.

Frustrated, Sol took a deep breath and let it out slowly. His gaze met Cora's. When he remained silent, she frowned at him.

"This has all gone too far," Cora finally said.

"She's right," Sol growled to add weight to Cora's protest, allies against Adeline.

"You are both adults. You can share a space and keep things professional," Adeline pleaded with Cora.

"Adeline, I'm not comfortable with this." Cora's jaw clenched so hard Sol worried her teeth would break. "I care about you, Adeline, not only professionally, I care about your charity too. I think it is very important, but I should tell you, when you find me an apartment, it will only be until the 31 of May because I need a break." Cora's voice broke. Sol shifted uncomfortably. "This has been a long fight and it's taken too much. I'm sorry. I just need you to know that I am returning to Oakland after I finish articling. So, just find an apartment until May 31."

"I know you've been through a lot," Adeline said as her eyes softened with sympathy.

Sol's eyebrows knit together; he straightened up.

"The D. W. E. A. sent this for you." Adeline handed her an expensive, heavy cardstock envelope.

Cora tensed as she skimmed the envelope; she opened it and read the correspondence swiftly; she took a deep sip of brandy.

Sol's eyebrows drew together in concern as Cora shook with fear. "I don't want it." Folding the letter, she placed it on the table by the settee. "I can't participate anymore. I told them that. The last rally... I can't face it." She held her hands up in defense, as if the letter was going to bite her.

What was in that letter? Who was it from? What happened at the last rally? Sol itched to take it from her and shield her from whatever that letter requested of her.

You are her bodyguard. Nothing else.

"I will agree to having an apartment beside hers." Sol dragged the conversation back to the matter at hand because Cora appeared to be on the verge of tears. He wanted the focus off whatever the letter was requesting of her.

"Do you know how hard that is going to be? To find two apartments side by side?" Adeline complained.

"Or across the hall." Sol deliberately misunderstood her. "We are not going to have Miss Rood's professional reputation damaged by a divorce scandal in her background. She is a professional woman — that would ruin her. If you'll remember, when you hired me, I said I don't negotiate, my word goes. I insist on this."

Sol towered over Adeline; he would not compromise. Adeline frowned and sipped her drink.

***

Cora marveled at him. What made Sol make such a huge change? In a day, he went from insisting women should not be lawyers, to now being worried about her professional reputation? For a man who seemed to plod relentlessly forward and seldom change his mind, he seemed more reasonable than ever.

"Fine." Adeline rolled her eyes. "I'll find you a new place tomorrow."

"What will Miss Rood do tonight?" Sol wasn't letting this drop.

"You can both stay here. I have scads of rooms."

"All right," Sol conceded, poured himself more water, and sat down.

Now that accommodations had been decided, Cora addressed Adeline.

"Eli asked me straight if you are petitioning for divorce. We are fast running out of time here, Adeline. Where are you in the process?"

"I almost have enough money. I requested thirty thousand dollars for startup fees for Hope House and personal expenses."

"Did you put that on your personal letter head or on the charity letterhead?"

"My personal letterhead. I made it clear that it was for my personal account. His accountants handed it over without a second glance. I asked the bank to put the trust in my account, and that will happen a week from today."

Cora shivered with worry at those words. Once the trust was empty, the divorce papers had to be filed immediately.

"We'll need a petition ready the day that money hits the account."

"I know," Adeline said. "It could be very soon at this rate."

"We'll draft it tonight." Cora put her drink down.

Chapter Twelve

It took two days for Adeline to find suitable accommodations for both
Cora and Sol. Cora's apartment was beautiful and extravagant,
exactly like Adeline Pitman. As Cora entered her apartment, she
shivered as a late spring storm raged against the high windows.

Saturday.

A day to catch up. A stack of petitions and real estate documents
had piled on her little writing desk because legal counsel for Adeline
meant no time for anyone else. Adeline was like the sun — everything
had to revolve around her. Cora stuck her tongue out at the stack of
work.

She needed one quiet day, no Adeline, no clients, no people. Just a
book and a cup of tea. As the spring storm beat against the window, she
snuggled down into a wool blanket.

Cora sipped her tea and opened her book, but her thoughts drifted
to Adeline. She had to admit, Adeline had changed. Every day she went
to work at Hope House her attitude evolved from spoiled brat to a
humanitarian, sympathetic to the world around her. As legal counsel,
Cora double checked all the paperwork and sat in on hiring a teacher
and a nurse. Adeline conferred with Cora over every employee they
added to the house.

Cora liked working with Adeline on Hope House. As she drafted
contracts for them, she was impressed that Adeline paid well. A few girls
were brought in by Detective Grayson and were given an opportunity
to learn. Mrs. King was particularly happy with how everything had
turned out, and Cora enjoyed working with her as well. A part of her
wanted to stay and build the house with the two women, but her heart
had to go home. She sipped her tea as the storm continued to rage. A
crash from the hallway interrupted her thoughts. Sol's voice came
through the door and immediately caught her attention.

She placed her book and tea on the tea service, and like a moth to a flame got up to investigate.

Sol stood in the hallway outside their apartments with a very upset and terrified family. The mother, baby, and little boy were all weeping. The father's eyes darted between Sol and Cora. The beautiful little boy with icy blond hair pulled at Cora's heart. The sight of him crying made her want to drop to her knees so she could gather him in her arms and kiss his tears away. She stood awkwardly by him; she had no experience with children, and in her line of work, she never would. Her heart ached with emptiness at the thought. She smiled at him and fished a candy out of her pocket. He asked his mother for permission in a foreign language. When the mother nodded that he could take it, Cora's heart melted further when she noticed an adorable little freckle on the edge of his eyelid. Cora reached into another pocket for a handkerchief, knelt down, and carefully wiped his tears away. The little boy wrapped his arms around her neck and wept into her shoulder. His little body, trembling against her, pulled a protective instinct out of her. She wrapped her arms around him and held him until the trembling subsided.

What is going on here?

"Everything all right?" Cora asked in concern.

Sol spoke to the family in Icelandic. He opened his door and Cora peeked into the immaculate conditions. Not a dust particle would dare to settle here. His apartment was neat as a pin. Once the mother and children were inside, Sol and the father remained in the hallway.

The men spoke in Icelandic, and Cora watched as greater worry flickered across Sol's face. Cora took a step toward him.

"They've been evicted, and they have nowhere to go." His tone was clipped with fury.

She held her hand out for the paper. "May I read the eviction notice?"

She quickly skimmed the document and then smiled brightly. "Tell them this is illegal. We can fight this. Well, I can fight this."

"They can't afford it. They will stay with me until we find something for them."

The man spoke rapidly in Icelandic.

"I will represent them for free," Cora insisted when the man was done speaking.

Sol tilted his head to the side and frowned. "Why would you do that?"

"Because they are your people. You care about them, so I care about them, too." Cora placed her hand on his forearm. "Tell them I will talk to the landlord tonight."

"It's dangerous." Sol took the paper back.

"According to this contract, they have to be given a month notice if they are being evicted, Sol. I can buy them a month." Cora begged him to see reason. "They can't be homeless, Sol. We have to fix this. I have to fix this."

The man twisted his hat in his hands and kept saying something to Sol.

"What is he saying?"

"He is saying they never missed a rent payment, that they are honest, and that they don't know what to do." Sol opened the door and ushered the father inside and then came back out.

"We'll go tonight. You and I, with him. How many families are on the street tonight because of this illegal document? Let's go."

Sol sighed. Something Cora was becoming vastly familiar with.

"Even if we can..."

"I can." Cora looked up at him in challenge. "Come on. Tell the father to come with us."

"Why are you insisting on this? Yes, they are my community, but that does not make them your community." Sol's eyes narrowed just a little, and Cora bristled with surprise.

"I know about community. It's important. Helping them is the right thing to do, Sol. I know the law, and this is not right. Let's go." She tugged at his arm.

"People treat immigrants badly. It's just the way it is, and it's appalling... I don't want you involved in this." He remained immovable.

Frustration made her eyes flash. "I know about it, so I'm involved. People treat women badly, too, so I know what it feels like. Come on. You've stepped in on my behalf, let me return the favour."

"I'm paid to step in on your behalf." His harsh tone sliced straight through her.

Her eyes narrowed as she looked up at him. He stood there, tall, broad, and arrogant. Residual anger from the injustice she'd suffered in a jail cell burned through her.

"You're mean," she hissed at him.

He looked at her in surprise, blinked, and then said nothing, which infuriated her further.

"I can't bear any more of this. I can't handle men who hurt women."

"I've never hurt a woman," Sol protested.

"You say mean things to me."

"I'm trying to protect you." Sol growled at her. "You are not going." His voice dropped dangerously low. "This is not your fight."

"I'm a lawyer, and this is against the law. It is absolutely my fight. I have a moral compass, you giant, ignorant... imbecile. So, I am going. Are you coming or not?" she roared at him.

"You are in enough danger," he shouted back at her. "You don't need any more!

"I didn't have a choice, just like they don't have a choice."

She turned on her heel. "I'm going to get my coat. I'll be back in two minutes. I am going to deal with this landlord, with or without you."

"Absolutely not. You tell me what to say, I'll go, and you can stay back with Inga and Silas." Sol spoke as if he had the last word.

She turned back to face him, so sick to death of being accused of fragility.

"Because I'm delicate? You think I can't handle this?" she spat at him.

"You are delicate." Sol crossed his arms across his very broad chest. "I know you can't handle this."

"I have the law on my side with this." Cora vibrated with fury. "This may very well be my last case, and I need a win. I seemed to have lost my will to fight in a jail cell. So, I am up against..."

His head snapped up at that. "Jail cell?"

"That is a story for another day." Cora tried to catch her breath. She hated it; she couldn't go up against this landlord without him. She was bluffing; going to a slumlord without him was suicide. He knew it; she knew it.

At this moment, in this hallway, she despised her own physical weakness. She knew what was right and couldn't enforce it without him. His strength and his power at his whim. She wanted to drag him to the front line of justice, and he was bleating on about safety.

"With Adeline, I don't have a legal leg to stand on. Somehow, I have to dig deep and find a shred of hope that there might be one person in power that will listen to the cries of inequality in the way the law treats men and women, and want to do something about it. As far as I can tell, the men in power don't care. So, let's go and let me fight this battle that I can win."

Because I haven't won in so long I've forgotten what it feels like.

***

Together, in the howling wind of a late spring Toronto blizzard, a furious Sol, a determined Cora, and a defeated Mr. Sigurdson battled the wind and the snow to get to the tenement building on the east end.

Real estate law was all about watching rich men get richer. It wasn't her calling, and she knew it. She thought about Silas and the freckle on the boy's eyelid, the way his arms tightened around her neck. She resolved to do what she could for this little one and straightened her shoulders. Finally, she was representing the oppressed instead of the oppressors.

She marched into the building where the owner lived and turned to Sol. It was infuriating to ask, but a message had to be sent before the door opened. Her timid knock wasn't going to strike fear into the landlord's heart.

"Would you... uh... pound on this door, please?" She requested politely. Sol made a fist and beat on the door. He stood beside her as they heard someone behind the door stirring around.

"What?" The man who opened the door was huge; great big belly, wearing a stained shirt, smoking a cigar, and his face was very greasy. Cora recoiled at his physical appearance.

She straightened up. "You have served the people of this tenement with an illegal document."

He went to slam the door shut, and Sol put himself in the threshold. The door bounced off his shoulder.

"The lady isn't done," he growled at the man.

"Get off my property." The landlord sneered at them.

"The people of this tenement are entitled to a month of notice. You have broken the law, sir." Cora spoke clearly.

"So? What are you going to do about it?" The landlord's eyes swept up and down her.

"You are coming with me to let them back into their homes," Cora demanded.

"You and whose army?" he chuckled.

"The constables of the police department. This is illegal. It's a terrible storm. You can't send this family to the street without proper documents."

The landlord rifled around in his desk and came back to the doorway. He handed her a notice.

"I filed this with the tenants a month ago. We are well within our rights to evict."

***

Sol watched Cora's brilliant green eyes quickly devour the document in her hands.

The landlord's eyes slid over her slender form. Revulsion churned in the pit of Sol's stomach. He moved to partially block her from the open look of predatory desire on the man's face.

"Did Mr. Sigurdson see this?" Cora's voice sounded defeated.

Sol asked him, and the answer was sadly yes, but he had no idea what it was, so he ignored it.

"Would you consider giving them a night to get new accommodations? It is a blizzard..."

"What are you prepared to do?" He ignored Sol and moved closer to her. Sol's body tensed; his hands clenched into fists.

"You give me a night, I give them a night?" The landlord licked his lips as he looked at her.

Fury roared through Sol as he braced himself to fight. Cora moved closer to him so his body completely shielded hers. She trembled against him, and he wanted to sink his fist into the landlord's fat jaw to make him take his eyes off her. He did none of those things. He stood still and let her use him as a human shield.

"Absolutely not," she replied. Sol heard the fury laced with fear in her voice.

You don't need to be afraid. I could kill this man and not break a sweat.

"Too bad. Get off my property." The man stepped back and slammed the door shut on Sol's face.

Sol guided Cora down the hall, away from the landlord's door. She shook in fear. She tripped, and he held onto her.

"You're trembling." He held her by her upper arms.

"If you hadn't been here... he would have..." Her eyes widened.

"I know. It's all right. You're safe." Sol let go of her and took a step back.

She took a deep breath.

Sol wondered if she would break down crying. Isold would have burst into tears and looked to him for a solution. Cora did neither. She tapped her finger against her lips, obviously thinking of the next step.

"They'll have to stay with you tonight until we can find accommodations tomorrow."

"No," Sol corrected her gently. Things had changed. She was trying her best. For him. For his friends. She didn't have to, and all the walls he had carefully built around his heart started to crumble. Why was he keeping her at a distance out of respect for a woman who was dead? Dead for five years. It was ridiculous. It wasn't her fault Isold died. She wasn't responsible for the city and its atrocities. "Thirty families."

Her face paled at that. "Thirty *families* are on the streets tonight in this storm!"

"Thirty families," Sol confirmed. "Between our two apartments we could shelter the women and children — we might have enough room. I'll stay on the street with the men; however, that would leave you unprotected."

"No, we can put them in Hope House but only for a few nights. That would get them off the street tonight." Cora pulled her gloves out of the pocket of her coat.

"Would Mrs. Pitman be all right with that?" Sol's eyebrows arched in surprise.

"Of course. Can you round these people up and we'll take them there tonight?"

Cora and Sol followed Mr. Sigurdson as he led them to the families huddled around burning barrels in a back alley. Cora gasped at the sight.

She reached out and put her hand on Sol's arm to get his attention.

"Tell them... tell them..." Cora's voice caught. "It's eight blocks to Hope House. Can they manage?"

"Of course." Sol adjusted her hood over her head to stop the snow from falling on her face and eyelashes.

"I don't know how to thank you." He reached forward and very gently brushed off the snow that had fallen on her face.

"Of course. I'm happy to help." Cora smiled at him. A genuine, happy smile amidst all this suffering.

"No. I mean it. I've been awful. I said all those terrible things. I was completely out of order."

"That's all right." She shrugged through the layers of clothes fast becoming soaked. "I'm used to it."

Sol saw the pain of that in her eyes — of all she had been denied and all she had lost due to her intelligence, her refusal to be ordinary.

Together, Sol and Cora rounded up the thirty displaced families to trek eight blocks through a terrible spring storm to Hope House. Sol watched Cora as she tried to explain to the women what was happening. The language barrier made her throw up her hands in frustration. She motioned for Sol to come over to assist her with a woman and her husband who held his wife as she wept by the side of the building.

"Tell her she has lodging tonight." Cora looked at him with tears in her own eyes. "Sol, she's terrified. Her husband doesn't understand. Tell her."

Sol spoke gently in Icelandic to both the woman and her husband.

"Is she all right?" Cora wrung her hands in anxiety.

"She had a baby two days ago." Sol cleared his throat. "She's..." He struggled to find words to describe the vulnerable state of the woman's physical symptoms.

"Oh, Sol, this is too terrible," Cora interrupted. The tears she tried to keep back spilled down her cheeks. "Where is the baby? I'll take the baby myself. I'm mostly dry."

Cora opened her coat and placed the newborn against her chest; she wrapped her scarf around the baby and then buttoned her coat to completely shield the newborn from the elements. She led a three-year-old by the hand, eight blocks through frozen ice and snow.

Sol marveled at the scene in front of him. The storm intensified as Cora led them forward. Thirty Icelandic families trailed behind her. Families who had given him solace. Sol wanted to kick himself from Toronto to Iceland and back for suggesting she should be married and having babies instead of wasting her time being a lawyer. She was single handedly making sure these little children didn't perish or become sick in this terrible spring blizzard. Once they reached Hope House, she opened the door to a surprised man hired to guard the residents from pimps.

I hate this city.

Sol juggled babies and toddlers and waited for Cora to convince the guard to let them in. Soon he would intervene, but he wanted to see what she could do.

"Wake up the cook — these people need a hot meal. We need thirty rooms made available and we need a telegram sent to..." Sol watched her fire orders at the staff. "Mrs. King and Mrs. Pitman both need to be aware of this situation. Please send those telegrams immediately."

"It's very late, miss." The guard frowned at the bedraggled group in the lobby.

"I realize that, but it is urgent." Her tone suggested the next time she spoke would be an order, not a request. Sol's respect for her ratcheted up another notch. She was fierce.

Where was this fighting spirit before?

She kept her composure as she led them into a dining hall.

"Can you tell the women to help me in the kitchen and we'll have a meal right away?" She nodded at him to translate. She unbuttoned her coat and moved to the cook stove while she held the baby against her. Sol spoke to the women in Icelandic and then followed Cora to the kitchen. He handed her an oversized tea towel.

"It's all we have that is dry," he apologized.

"It's better than nothing." Gently, she laid the newborn on the kitchen table. She very carefully swaddled the baby up against any chill. Warmth filled his chest as Cora pressed her lips to the newborn's cheek; she closed her eyes as she breathed in the smell of the baby. After cuddling the baby longer than necessary, she reluctantly handed her back to the father. Sol noticed she hesitated before pulling her hand away. Even though the baby was happy in her father's arms, Cora fussed and adjusted the tea towel around the baby's face. Sol watched helplessly as tears glittered in her eyes as the baby was taken from Cora and given to her mother. He stood near her and caught the look of yearning to hold the baby longer.

Cora gave him a tentative smile and blinked back tears. It was all he could do not to reach for her and hold her to try to alleviate the pain she obviously felt now that her arms were empty. She looked away, the moment gone. Cora led the women to the kitchen and pulled on an apron.

Sol followed right behind her.

Cora looked up at him in surprise. "What are you doing?"

"Helping you feed thirty families. Tell me what to do." Sol took his coat off and rolled up his sleeves.

***

Whatever task she or the other women assigned him, he did it without hesitation.

When Cora went to move the huge pot of soup to the dining room, he put his hand on her arm.

"I'll do it — it's too heavy for you." His voice low, near her ear, shot a kick of desire into the pit of her stomach. She tried to fight the desire for him. There was no place for this in her life. It made her feel weak and strong at the same time, but weakness was a luxury she could not afford. Weakness opened you up to hurt, and she had no capacity for hurt left.

Cora took a step back as he took the folded tea towel from her hands. The women murmured as he reached for the soup and turned around to frown at them. A few giggled as he spoke to them in Icelandic. Cora was desperate to know what they were saying.

"What are they saying?" Cora asked.

He frowned even deeper at her question.

"Come on. What?" Cora bit her lip in anticipation.

"They're saying I've gone soft for you." His eyes smoldered at her.

Cora blushed sixty-five shades of red.

"Have you?" Cora had the words out of her mouth before she could stop them. It was his turn to blush, which only made the tops of his ears red. The rest of him seemed unchanged. She noticed though, the tops of his ears looked like they were going to burst into flame. For the first time, an awakening of raw feminine power ripped through her. To make a man blush, to make a man feel anything other than contempt, was a new and heady experience.

"I..." Sol went to speak when one of the women who was watching this open declaration of feelings over a soup pot dropped a glass, making everyone jump. The moment was lost. Sol took the soup out, and Cora followed with the bread. Together, they served the group a warm meal of soup and bread. Once everyone was eating, Sol slipped away to retrieve Mr. Sigurdson's family.

An hour later, the families were given rooms. The women with little children went to settle them into bed, the women with grown children gathered to clean the kitchen, and Sol brought Cora her coat.

"I can help them," Cora protested as Sol held her coat open for her.

"They are saying they can handle it. You are exhausted, so it's time for you to go home. The horse and carriage are outside."

She pulled her coat on but didn't want to leave the kitchen. She hadn't worked with a group of women in a kitchen since her days in Oakland. Working with women was pleasant. They were such a tight unit. As they saw Sol hold her coat open and help her into it, they came to her, tears in their eyes, and they all said the same thing in Icelandic as they hugged her very hard.

"They are saying thank you and God bless you," Sol translated.

"Tell them I am happy to help, and we will try to get them permanent accommodations as soon as possible."

Once the last hugs were given, Sol helped her into the carriage. New tension sprang up between them. He respected her and approved of how she handled the situation. She wasn't sure what to do with this. A man, not related to her, who approved of her. This was uncharted territory. They said nothing for three blocks.

"Will Mrs. Pitman and Mrs. King be all right with all these people in their home?" Sol asked.

"I am certain all will be well. I sent telegrams so they would send more food." Cora shivered as ice and snow hammered against the window of the carriage.

"That was good of you." Sol pulled a lap robe across her knees.

"You would do the same." Her gaze met his; the intensity of the feelings between them was too much. She dropped her eyes to the lap robe.

Finally, they pulled up to the apartment building, and Sol helped her up to her apartment. While she took off her coat and boots and hung up her hat and scarf to dry, he stood awkwardly at the threshold.

"I have to take the horse and carriage back to Hope House, but I want to... I have to say this." Sol adjusted his cap on his head.

Cora looked up at him.

"I want to apologize for ever saying you should just be married and have children like a normal woman..."

"Don't worry about that." She waved her hand dismissively.

Sol placed his hands on her upper arms, and Cora swallowed hard.

"No. I mean it." He held her gaze and continued. "When my wife was killed, the hope went out of me, out of my life. It made me bitter and angry. I hated this city and everyone in it."

"Including me," Cora whispered.

"I was wrong," Sol said quietly. "I've been wrong since I met you, and I am sincerely apologizing. You are..."

She waited as his voice trailed off. He let go of her arms and took a step back.

"You are an inspiration, Cora. I was at the end of the group, watching you lead thirty families to shelter, and I was just... I don't even know what to say about that. You are a lawyer, and you should be. I want you to know that."

"Thank you." Praise washed through her; she blushed pink with pleasure.

"And, that slum lord who spoke to you..." Sol moved closer to her again. Her knees trembled and her heart hammered in her ears at his physical presence. "You were afraid of him?"

Cora nodded yes. Her eyes met his and then she dropped her gaze to examine a button on his coat. Very gently, he put his hand under her jaw to tilt her face up to him.

"I will *never* let anyone lay a hand on you." His voice, deep and strong, pierced straight into her heart. She bit her lip.

"You have nothing to worry about, Cora. No one is ever going to hurt you on my watch. Paid or otherwise." His eyes searched hers with such intensity her eyes widened. Sol stroked her jaw gently before dropping his hand.

Cora's knees buckled with desire.

"I better go." His voice was so low Cora had to lean in to hear him better.

"Miss!" a young man called from down the hallway.

"Miss! I have a telegram for you." The young man was out of breath. Cora tore her eyes from Sol's and took the note.

Her eyes flicked over the note quickly. Anxiety doused the flames of desire as she re-read the telegram.

"Thank goodness we have the horse and carriage still." Cora's voice hardened with fury. "We have to get to the jail. Immediately."

Chapter Thirteen

"Jail?" Sol exclaimed.

Cora's hands shook as she pulled on her coat and rooted around in the basket by the door for dry accessories. Scarves, mitts, and hats were flung all over the entrance as she looked for a suitable scarf.

"Any scarf will do." Sol couldn't help himself; he quickly tidied up after her.

"What are you doing?"

"I hate a mess. You know that." He folded her scarves.

"This is a crisis. Adeline is in jail," Cora reprimanded him.

"A crisis is compounded by clutter." Sol carefully stacked all her discarded mitts, hats, and scarves in the basket.

"Who are you?" She rolled her eyes.

"No eye rolling, Miss Rood. And no reckless disregard for tidiness. Adeline is in jail. There is nothing you can do for her tonight. First thing in the morning..."

"I'm not leaving her there tonight. It's terrifying. She'll be totally distraught. I have to go to her and stay with her."

"I really think..." Sol's protests landed on deaf ears.

"Come on. Let's go." Cora took him by the arm and sprinted down the hall in front of him.

Together, back out into the storm, they hurried into the carriage and raced to the jail.

"You're shaking." Sol put his hand on hers.

"I am terrified of jail."

His lips thinned at that statement.

"Did you break the law?" Sol asked.

"Yes," she responded — clear, direct, nothing to hide. Slight lift to her chin.

"What did you do?"

"I will tell you, but not just now." Cora straightened up and thought about where they were in the proceeds. Adeline had two bank accounts. Eli knew about it; he had to give permission for both. Adeline had money that was a gift from Eli in one bank account, the charity bank account was for the actual charity. He might wonder why the last thirty thousand was deposited into her personal account instead of her charity account. Hope House currently housed thirty Icelandic families and six former prostitutes. There was no paper trail demanding any money from Eli Pitman was to go to the charity. No receipts were given. The amount she had asked for was merely a suggestion. Cora had been firm about that. Nothing to trace that money to Hope House. So, why now? What happened that caused Eli to strike now?

Did the bank empty the trust and tip him off? Oh mercy... The bank must have deposited Adeline's trust and alerted him! Curses! I will have to file the divorce papers Monday morning at 7:00 a.m. I will have to hand deliver them.

Nerves tied her stomach in knots, and her palms slicked with nervous sweat as the carriage ground to a halt in front of the jail. Sol got out of the carriage first and held his hands out to Cora. She placed her hands on his shoulders as he lifted her out of the carriage and over a patch of ice. Once she was settled on the sidewalk, he didn't let go.

"You're afraid," he said gently.

"I am scared of jail." Cora stood at the doorway to the police station and hesitated with her hand on the door. She took her hand back. Sol stood behind her. Waiting.

She watched him put his hand on the door knob and move to open the door for her.

"Just a moment. I need a moment to gather my... uh... please, just don't open that door."

Cora took a step back as if the door would bite her. Sol waited patiently as icy rain fell around them. In her memories, she could hear the women screaming and begging. She closed her eyes and tried to think about the last place she felt safe — on the bank of the river in Oakland. She tried to conjure up the river in her mind, the way it flowed past the sandbar. Taking a deep breath, she let it out slowly. Just the thought of summer in Oakland made her neck start to loosen. If she lived, she would pack a picnic and sit by the rapids and listen to the sound of birds and water while the sun glittered off the surface of the river. Cora straightened her shoulders and nodded at Sol to open the door.

"I'm right beside you. Nothing to fear," Sol said softly as she walked by him. She gave him a nervous smile as she approached the front desk.

The constable behind the desk narrowed his eyes at her when she asked to see Mrs. Pitman. "This isn't a hospital. She doesn't get visiting hours."

"I'm her legal counsel," Cora insisted.

"You can't be."

"She is," Sol growled at the constable.

He took one look at Sol and jumped to attention. "I'll see what I can do."

Pacing and wringing her hands, Cora tried to calm down. "What do you think they've done to her?"

"Cora, she's fine. I'm sure." Sol put his hand on her shoulder in an attempt to calm her down.

She blinked up at him in fear. "She won't be fine. This would be terrifying."

"This way." The constable took them down to the jail cells in the basement. Adeline stood up and held onto the bars of her cell.

"Oh, Adeline!" Cora exclaimed.

"The bank emptied my trust a week early. They sent him a telegram to let him know. Isn't that nice of them? When I went there to speak to them about it, they said he had signing authority on my personal account. Everyone who has signing authority is alerted when sums that high are deposited. Under the law everything I own is his." Adeline's voice was clipped with rage. "Eli has gone completely insane. He had me arrested for fraud."

"I'm not leaving you here alone at night." Cora pulled her scarf off her head. "I'll deal with Eli first thing in the morning."

"Thank you." Adeline sat down on her bunk. "What is our next step?"

"I serve him with papers."

"You should go then. You'll need some rest." Adeline leaned against the wall, her head bowed with exhaustion.

"I'm not leaving you here." Cora and Sol, on the other side of the bars, sat with their backs against the wall. "It's around midnight Adeline. You should try to get some sleep."

Adeline lay down on her bunk. "I am so upset. I'm sure I'll never sleep. How far do you think he'll go? He wouldn't leave me in jail, would he? Could he?"

Adeline tossed and turned, unable to get comfortable, so she got back up off the bunk and paced around her cell.

Cora paced with her. "We'll get you out of here. He can't afford scandals in his family when his sons are looking for wives, right?"

Adeline's head snapped up. "That is genius. You are completely right. Randall is courting Laramie Scott's daughter — they come from very old money, and Eli needs that sort of backing to expand his shipping operations." Adeline took a deep breath and let it out. "I think I can sleep now. I am just going to rest my eyes for a minute."

Within minutes she was sleeping.

Cora slumped against the wall and rubbed her eyes. When she shivered, Sol took off his coat and wrapped her in it.

"You'll freeze," she protested.

"I'm from Iceland. It takes more than this to make me cold." He smiled at her as she snuggled into the coat that was way too big for her.

"I want to know about when you were in jail." Sol's voice was very quiet, so as not to disturb Adeline.

Cora scratched her eyebrow then moved so she was sitting on his coat because the cold permeated through the rock of the floor.

"I'm not so sure I can talk about it, Sol."

"I want to know why this is your biggest fear. Please." He leaned into her.

She turned to face him.

"What happened?"

"We have no time for that," Cora protested.

"We do have time for that. You hesitated before going in to see Adeline —you seemed traumatized. I want to know what happened to you in jail. You are too fragile for jail." He reached forward and adjusted her scarf so her neck would be warm.

"Do you know, I've heard that my whole life?" Cora said sadly. "You can't go into mathematics, miss. You are too fragile for mathematics. It is a profession for men. I fought them. When they said, you can't be a lawyer, miss. You are not a person under law, nice women don't want the vote. I fought very hard."

"I wasn't saying that to... uh... impose restrictions or anything."

"But those statements *do* impose restrictions, Sol! The same men who say we're too weak to be educated don't interfere with domestic abuse. It is the same men, in this country, who determine if a woman qualifies for contraception because we are too fragile to be educated but not too fragile to have twelve or thirteen babies. The laws say you can pay a woman half what you pay a man for the same work, which means we have to work twice as hard to support children. Children that men are not interested in supporting. Do you know the physical toll of that?"

Sol held his hands out in a gesture of surrender. "Men are supposed to..."

"Yes. Men are *supposed* to do a lot of things, but sometimes they don't," Cora pleaded with him to understand. "They just don't. Not all men are like you. Some are terrible."

"I meant no offense." He spoke with sincerity. "The thought of you in jail horrifies me."

"I never dreamed it could happen." Cora rubbed her eyes. "It was a peaceful demonstration until one woman lost her senses and threw a brick through a window."

"What were you demonstrating for?"

"Equal rights, voting, equal pay. We were demonstrating for everything."

"Why are you so passionate about the vote?" Sol tilted his head.

"The laws of this land treat women harshly. They do not allow us to have voice in how we are governed. Worse, the laws are particularly vicious when it comes to married women. Currently, a husband is considered the authority in his home. That means he can impose *punishments* on his wife that are not subject to court. I have seen so many beaten women, Sol. It breaks my heart — there is no recourse in a court of law. Legally, a married woman is not her own person. She cannot own land, retain rights to her children — she is the property of her husband, nothing more than chattel. To change the law, we need legislation. For that, we have to be in government. To be in government, we need the vote. That is what I wanted to change in that rally."

"Wanted to?"

"They took me to jail, and I realized the futility of this fight, what we are *really* up against. We will not win against these men, the ones with all the power, so I just went to work where they let me, and I gave up... I gave up. Tomorrow I have to stand up to Eli, and I don't have what it takes. They took it from me." Cora brushed tears away from her cheeks.

"What happened in jail?" Fear of the answer caused Sol's voice to dip lower.

Cora looked away quickly, and Sol leaned forward so his forearms rested on his thighs.

"Ah... it was terrible." Cora trembled beside him and looked away to gather her thoughts.

"Just tell me, what happened?" His voice was gentle.

"I was on the front line at the rally." She turned back to him; his eyes were full of sympathy. "The rally was supposed to be peaceful. As I said, a brick went through a window, and the police launched on us. They had been waiting for an excuse to use force. So, they did."

"They used force against women?" Sol sounded shocked.

Cora peeked at Adeline to be sure she was sleeping and then back to him. "They used *brutal* force against women. They *enjoyed* it." She shivered.

"What happened to you in that jail cell? What did they do?" Sol leaned in closer, his eyes intent on hers. He wanted the truth. He wanted to hear the whole thing.

Cora swallowed and dashed at a tear that had escaped.

"Did they rape you?" His voice was lower than before.

Two more tears escaped. Sol gently brushed them away.

"Did they?" Sol insisted on an answer.

"No," Cora whispered.

He visibly relaxed at the statement. "But they hurt you?"

"My jaw was fractured. It was unbearable pain," Cora admitted.

"Why? Did you fight back?" His eyes softened in sympathy.

Not for long.

"I tried." Two more tears slid down her cheek.

"Which side?" Sol's hard fingertips on her jaw caused her breath to stop. She slid her eyes shut and wanted to put this memory away to think about later for the rest of her lonely, spinster existence.

"Left side," she whispered.

He moved her face to see her jawline clearly. He traced his fingertips across it, and she couldn't help herself, she inhaled sharply. His touch along her jaw stole her breath.

"What then?" Sol brushed the tears off her cheekbone and reluctantly let her go.

"The warden said the guards could do anything they want. They broke me, Sol."

"How did they break you?" He pulled his coat around her tighter.

Cora scrambled to her feet to get away from the questions that opened up an ache of sadness inside her. She went to the window and looked out into the dark night. No moon. She had never spoken of this to anyone. She had buried it so deep; she tried to believe it never happened. Sol got to his feet and stood by her, keeping a careful distance. Waiting politely for her to gather her thoughts and continue.

"It took Lady Bronwyn too long to get me out." Cora's voice broke on a sob. "The guards let me see the futility of fighting. I saw up close that the guards hated what we were doing — they hated us. They didn't just want to incarcerate us for breaking the law. They intended to break our spirit. Some women, from a previous rally, were already in custody and they had been on a hunger strike before we got there. The guards did force feedings, they made me watch..."

She tried to turn away so he wouldn't see her tears.

"Why you?" Gently, he took her by the upper arms and turned her to face him.

"Because I was in the front line, and I was their biggest threat." Her face crumpled further as she recounted her worst nightmare.

"Why were *you* their biggest threat?" His voice deepened as he moved closer to her. He waited patiently for her answer.

"Sol." Dropping her forehead to his shoulder, she let his shirt soak up her tears. He pulled her against him. Finally, she composed herself enough to look up at him again. "I was the biggest threat because I was the most educated, and I was connected to the highest powers; Lady Bronwyn, Dr. Stowe, and Oliver Moat. Once Lady Bronwyn and Dr. Stowe were taken out of the jail, I remained and they considered me to have the most influence because of my connection to them. That night..." Cora stopped speaking. She pressed her forehead back into his shoulder, his arms tightened around her as she wept uncontrollably.

Once the storm of emotion passed she looked up at him. "That night, I saw what we were up against, and I could never face that kind of treatment again. I couldn't ask women to stand with me, knowing they would face... that violence." Cora's voice escalated with anxiety and trauma. "I couldn't help them." She put her hands over her face to hide her shame. "I heard them screaming and crying, and I could do nothing. I was powerless. I couldn't even defend myself."

She held her hands over her mouth to stop the sob that crawled out of her. Sol pulled her back into his arms. Cora trembled at the memories and then laid her cheek against his chest. His heart hammered under her ear; it calmed her.

"It makes me the worst failure. I can't go back to that jail. I left those women there, the women who had followed me into battle... but there was nothing I could do. I quit protesting after that because there was no hope left in me. I was defeated. I allowed them to bury me under real estate law. I allowed them to... well... steal my hope and silence my voice."

"The letter you got at Adeline's, was that a request for you to rally again?"

Cora pulled back a bit to look up at him. "They want me to lead a rally, and I can't do it." Her lips trembled. "They'll be upset. They pulled so many strings for me, they'll think I'm ungrateful, but I can't do it anymore. I still wake up in terror about what happened. I feel like such a failure." .

"But you are here with Adeline." His gentle reminder stopped her from crying.

"I had no choice."

"No. You are here in this cell with her."

"Anyone would."

"Oh really? Which lawyer do you work with that would willingly spend the night with Adeline Pitman in a jail cell?"

Cora let her eyes meet his. She blinked as she thought about that.

"Why did you become a lawyer in the first place?" He wiped her tears away with his sleeve.

"Women need lawyers who can understand what they are up against and fight for them within the law, not just dismiss them and send them home to abusive husbands. I don't think men fully understand the vulnerability of women. You can't understand this, Sol." Her eyes flicked over him. "You're huge and terrifying — you don't know what it feels like to be vulnerable."

"Really? You think that? Men love women, Cora. We are designed to protect them. I can tell you this — most men, the men I know anyway, would defend a woman at the risk of their own life. If a woman we love is hurt, it hurts us, too." Sol looked at her with such intensity, she tried to look away but couldn't.

Reaching up, Cora put her arms around his neck and hugged him hard.

"You didn't answer my question. Why are you a lawyer?" Sol asked; his chin rested on the top of her head and she felt his stubble on her scalp.

"I had my Bachelors of Mathematics at sixteen, and my father said I needed to use my mind to promote good in this world. That's all. I just wanted to help women and children. I saw someone beaten once — she was a victim of domestic violence — and it haunts me still. We have to have laws to protect those who cannot protect themselves. I gave up though, and I feel the worst about that." Cora pulled back to look at him.

"Or maybe you are just fighting in a different way," Sol suggested softly. Cora blinked. "What do you mean in a different way?"

"Maybe you are ready to fight again. You seemed to be, in that room facing Eli. The fight simmered just under the surface."

"It has to stay under the surface. If I show him my strength, he will delight in humiliating me. I know men like him. We're not going to win, and I'm not putting myself back in the ring. We will lose, and the stakes are too high."

It was Sol's turn to look out the window. She studied his profile.

"You don't know that."

"The law is against us, Sol."

"Then you will change the law." Sol looked back. Cora met his eyes, and she didn't look away. "You did it once before. You can do it again."

"I didn't. Oliver Moat and Lady Bronwyn did," Cora whispered.

"They saw something in you worth fighting for. Or was Mr. Moat in love with you?"

Cora chuckled at that. "No. We are not even friends. He's married to the head of the Dominion Woman's Enfranchisement Association, and she wouldn't allow him to back down when he desperately wanted to."

"She wouldn't allow *him*?" Sol's eyebrows were a full inch higher than usual.

"I know. It's a brand-new concept." Cora laughed at him. "He did it for her, not really me. Anyway. I've never... I haven't had any time for men, and it seems that men do not fall in love with smart women."

"Brilliant is the term I heard them use for you." His gaze burned into her.

"Doesn't matter now, does it? Even if I can get Adeline what she wants, her reputation will be destroyed. We are put in these boxes of

morality. We have to play by different rules than men. We won't win."
Cora shrugged.

"What do you hope for now?"

"I had hoped for equality, and we are further from that than ever before. I hope I can bully Eli, the biggest bully in the world, and get Adeline out of jail."

Sol looked back out the window.

"I have a confession to make, miss," Sol said in a tone that indicated he was changing the subject. Cora liked the lilt in his accent.

"I've never guarded a woman before. I've been a bodyguard in Toronto for five years, since I got here. Since I lost my wife. Since Isold, I have lived in the world of men. Not women."

Cora saw the pain in his eyes as he said that.

"We immigrated to follow her siblings here when her parents died. Immigrants do not live in the best of conditions. I got really sick. We both worked at whatever jobs we could to make enough. One night she was coming back from work. She had been paid that day, and a hobo mugged her. She fought back and she was beaten badly. He stabbed her. Isold died of infection from the knife wound. I was lying in bed with a terrible fever. I should have protected her. That was my job. As her husband, I let her down. The police ignored the whole thing, but one constable, Asher Grayson, tracked him down. He found him, and the court hung him, but the damage was done."

"I'm so sorry." Cora's eyes filled with tears listening to him speak. He was still in pain from losing his wife. "You must have loved her very much."

"She was everything. I..." Sol looked away from Cora. "I never let her walk in the city alone. She was so beautiful. When we were together, I saw how other men looked at her and I was worried, but I was so sick I couldn't even stand up. Anyway. I know a little about losing your heart, losing your direction in life. It's awful."

Cora leaned forward and put her hand on his forearm.

"She was knifed over two dollars and eighty-four cents. No one cared then, they certainly wouldn't now. I fell into a bottle of vodka after that. My community, you met them — those thirty families we still have to deal with once we get all this settled. Anyway, they kept me alive while I drank my pain away."

"That's why you don't drink now?"

"It was an ugly time of my life, and I made it uglier by losing control. So, one day I decided no more of that. Sig, my friend you met, he said that was enough. Time to get serious. He was kicking me out. Who could blame him? He told me to take my anger to the ring — I could make money boxing. I put down the bottle and started training. All I could think about was Isold's dream of having a farm in a new land. I could make that happen in her memory. So, when Adeline came up with this job, I took it. I already put a down payment on a farm in Gimli. So, that's the whole story."

The pain she heard in his voice connected to the ache in her heart. Loss, people, passion, love, hope, whatever was taken against your will, it was a knife in your soul.

"After this, you're going to Gimli?"

"Yes, what about you?"

"I sent a letter to my brother. I'll be in Manitoba, too, but in Oakland. My brother has a place for me to stay until all this dies down. I need out of this city. I need to go home. I miss the peace there."

"It sounds nice."

"I miss by brother and my community. I need to redirect after this. I need a break before I am called to the bar to be sworn in. Family law, not real estate after I get out of this terrible job. Only two more weeks. I can't win many battles, but I can keep the courts aware of the inequality women face by fighting the battles I can. Eventually something will change. Mostly, I just want some time off. I'm tired."

The night was quiet around them. They settled down together; Cora drew her knees up, and Sol turned toward her.

"Are you warm enough?"

"Not really." Her voice sounded small.

He opened his arms to her, and she hesitated. She looked up at him, her eyes wide.

"It's all right," he reassured her as she crawled into them. She rested her head on his shoulder like it had been there her whole life. She breathed in the scent of him — lemon cleaner. Probably the immigrant crisis interrupted him from dusting for the third time that day. Cora smiled at the thought.

"You're smiling." He smoothed her hair down so it wouldn't tickle his nose. "Are you warm enough?"

"Yes."

Sol didn't believe her. He picked her up and settled her onto his lap so that no part of her was on the cold floor. She naturally curled into him.

"Is that better?"

"Yes. The floor is so cold," she admitted as she drew her knees up.

"If you get cold in the night wake me up." He adjusted her against him so she was comfortable.

"All right." She burrowed into him. "Sol."

"Yes," he whispered against her hair.

"Thanks... thanks for being here in this mess."

"Of course, I'm here with you, I'm your bodyguard. Go to sleep, Cora. You have a big day tomorrow."

"Do you typically cradle your clients in your arms if they are cold?" she teased him.

"Always. That's why I'm the most sought after bodyguard in Toronto."

Cora heard him chuckle deep in his chest. She smiled at the mental image of him cradling Lord Bronwyn and laughed against him.

"Go to sleep, Cora. Tomorrow is going to be terrible."

"Right. Good night, Sol."

Cora felt safe for the first time in months, on the floor of a jail with Sol's arms wrapped tightly around her, smelling lemons — it was a taste of bliss.

***

Sol held Cora until she fell asleep on his chest. She was an adorable mess. Her hair had been wet from snow and steam from cooking. She was limp against him. He moved her to be a little more comfortable as he tucked his coat around her shoulders. In her sleep, she burrowed into him even tighter. He let his hand move up and down her back and thought about not going to Gimli for the first time in five years. He thought about the possibility that Cora was like a light in a very dark world. Sol Stein knew what it felt like to fall in love, and tonight in this jail, he gave his heart to this woman who rode a bicycle, wore a shirtwaist, tucked newborns into her coat, and planned to stand up to Eli Pitman.

***

Cora blinked in the early morning sun. Sol was sleeping, and she was almost right on top of him. The floor was cold, and her sleeping body was trying to stay warm.

Sure, let's blame the cold floor!

Wickedly, Cora snuggled closer. Today, they would take on Eli Pitman, and this was the last time she would be entwined with Sol Stein on the floor of a jail. Or anywhere for that matter. He was going to Gimli, and she was going to Oakland, and this was it.

She looked up, and her eyes locked with Adeline Pitman's.

"I bet you are rethinking my offer of getting you an apartment to share," she said smugly.

Cora said nothing. She buried her flaming face into Sol's shirt.

"I'm happy for you. You deserve a man that will care about you."

Cora peeked at Adeline. Sol stirred under her. He shifted so they were both sitting up. Cora moved away from him a little. She immediately missed his warmth. She shivered as he helped her up. Despite Adeline watching them like a cat that had got the cream, he wrapped his coat and then his arms around her.

"I'll take the divorce petition to Eli today." Cora rested her hands on Sol's forearms.

Adeline's eyes went wide.

"I'll get you out of here. We have the law on our side. He can't keep you in jail. There has been no fraud. I will handle it and have you out of here before lunch."

"What if you don't?"

"I will," Eli said from the doorway.

Chapter Fourteen

Every eye was on Eli as a guard opened the jail cell and let Adeline out.

No one spoke. Sol's arms tightened around Cora and then released her. This was her arena. Already, as in most things, Eli had an advantage. Cora hated that she faced him disheveled and weary from a night relocating Icelandic immigrants and keeping Adeline safe in jail. Cora knew, with sudden insight, this was Eli's way of flexing his muscle, causing Adeline and, indeed, Cora fear before he addressed the divorce he knew was coming.

"I think it's time we all sat down and put our cards on the table. Don't you agree?" Eli sneered at Cora.

Vibrating with either rage or fear, Adeline grabbed onto Cora's arm.

"Where and when?" Cora lifted her chin and spoke with such force, Eli smiled.

"Why not your office? It's closer," Eli suggested. "I think the partners at Roth and Levine will be very interested in knowing what you and Adeline have been up to."

"No. Let's settle this in court. Let's parade this in front of a judge." Cora called his bluff. He couldn't have a scandal if he wanted his sons to find proper wives.

"No, Miss Rood, let me show you my cards before you insist on court. I think you will agree, we settle this today. Out of court. You may lead the way."

Together, they made a strange sight. Three people who had spent the night in a jail and one man who looked like he'd stepped out of a barber shop. No one spoke. When they arrived, Eli Pitman opened the doors to the law office as if he owned it. Cora shivered in fear — he probably did.

Once Cora settled Adeline into a board room, Eli motioned for Sol to join him in the hallway. Sol looked at Cora, who nodded. She was safe here in her own offices.

Sol went to her and placed his hand on the back of her neck as he leaned down to speak into her ear. "I'll be right back," he reassured her.

"Sure," she agreed then watched the men leave the room and shut the door behind them.

***

Sol followed Eli into a room and they sized each other up. Sol knew he was bigger and probably faster due to endless hours in a ring. However, Eli was a threat nonetheless because he had an element of manipulation Sol detested.

"I'm going to make this very simple," Eli said as he walked to the window that looked over the city, putting distance between them.

"Thirty immigrant families are going to look for shelter today, and they won't have anywhere to live. There won't be a broom closet available to them. Cora is going to be arrested for fraud as soon as we finish our meeting. She's already lost her job. That I can't reverse. I own almost everything, but I don't own Roth and Levine. They came to the decision to fire Cora on their own. Unfortunate, two weeks before she finishes her mandatory articling. No call to the bar. Pity. Anyway, Adeline was already arrested for fraud, out on bail, so she will go to jail unless you agree to the following terms."

Fury roared through Sol as Eli turned to look at him. Sol immediately realized his mistake. He would never have let Eli put Cora in a room with him alone; he never dreamed that he was at risk of being threatened by Eli.

"You walk out the door and you leave Toronto. Right now. You go to Gimli. Your land is paid for. You start life all over and forget about Adeline. Forget about this nuisance, Cora. Forget all of it. I'll give Cora six hours to leave Toronto, and I guarantee she is safe from my men."

Sol's eyes narrowed in disbelief.

"Safe from your men. You expect me to believe that?"

"I guarantee her safety if you leave right now and she leaves in six hours. This is a train ticket. Paid for. Farm. Paid for. Your girl is safe from charges of fraud. This offer is good for thirty seconds and requires no thinking on your part." Eli attempted to tower over Sol.

Sol stood up and took Eli by the lapels; he lifted him off his feet and slammed him into the wall. Eli's eyes narrowed in rage.

"How will I know she's safe?" Sol demanded as he held Eli against the wall against his will.

"I give you my word," Eli hissed.

"What good is your word? You are a criminal," Sol growled at him.

"If one of my men lays a hand on her, she would prosecute. I can't have a slight on my reputation when Randall asks Laura Scott to marry him. You can trust that I need to look squeaky clean." Sol let go of Eli's lapels and took a step back. "Adeline goes home. She continues to be my wife. Cora leaves in either direction, East or West. All criminal charges are dropped. You start farming next week. Twenty seconds."

Cora, not the thirty families who were like family to him. Not Adeline, who was a pain in his neck but a pain he had started to care about. Cora. It came down to her being safe. Being protected. When had that changed? Last night in a jail cell? Is that it? That's all it took? To go from loving Isold to Cora? Ah. Isold. Cold in a grave and Cora warm, soft in his arms... pay attention, he's speaking.

"I guarantee she will be safe. I'll send a man with her. She won't see him. He'll see her safe wherever she lands. Eight seconds."

"I'll go." Sol took another step away from Eli. The full weight of how many lives depended on him walking away from Toronto and away from Cora made him sick to his stomach.

"Once she lands, a picture of her safe arrival will be sent to you," Eli said calmly. "Change your mind, I will throw those thirty families on the street and not think twice."

He couldn't get to Cora through her own connections. He got to Cora through me. What kind of man could do such a thing? Thirty innocent families.

"You're a monster," Sol said through gritted teeth. Sol could see the women weeping as they tried to shelter their babies and little children from the elements. Little Silas with the freckle on his eyelid jumped into Sol's memory. He could see the men, hopeless in the face of the storm and forces beyond their control. He couldn't have those women and children on the street again. He couldn't bear to have Cora facing fraud charges. Her worst fear of going back to jail would be realized. Her worst fear was now his own. She had huge enemies. Enemies he could no longer protect her from because if he didn't leave... the implications were gut wrenching and outrageous.

Was Adeline truly changed? What is she really capable of? She may have stolen every penny and was ready to hang them out to dry.

"Maybe I'm a monster. Maybe I just take what I need." Eli flashed him a smile with gleaming white teeth. "Just remember this. They are in Hope House, but who do you think really owns Hope House? Adeline is mine. Everything she has. Mine. I gave it to her, and I can take it away. I allowed her to own and operate Hope House. I did not allow her to be involved with the suffragettes, and they have filled her head with nonsense. Miss Rood, bleating on about equality, ridiculous."

Sol stared into the flat grey eyes of Eli Pitman and suddenly, with every fibre of his being, understood why Cora had been on the front line of the women's rights battle. How repressed Adeline must feel in her life. Owned, by a man like this. She had no recourse in a court of law. Eli could treat her any way he wanted, and there was nothing anyone could do. The thought that a husband could so easily impose such humiliating restrictions on a wife made him sick to his stomach. He had no idea women were subjected to this sort of degradation. Adeline would be devastated. She would return to a home where he didn't even live because he had a mistress, and Canadian law allowed for that. Right then, Sol wanted to throw his hat in the ring with Cora. He wanted to fight back at a law that brutalized women.

How had he not known of this before? Did he really believe that everyone had a marriage like he had with Isold?

His eyes narrowed at Eli.

It's not all roses in a garden when women get married. That's why I'm a lawyer... Cora's words raced back to him.

Cora has to keep working. She has to. This can't continue... She has to be sworn in as a barrister and continue, and I have to make sure she's safe from this animal while she does it.

"How do you sleep at night?" Sol's tone of voice hardened. The only way Cora had a hope of continuing as a lawyer was if he walked away without a backward glance. Eli, a master at presenting the most impossible situations and watching people bend to his will, smiled an icy smile. Sol's heart plummeted as he thought about leaving Cora here.

"Like a baby, on a pile of money, with Mirabel Salter. Time's up, Mr. Stein. You need to walk out of here right now, or let your woman face the consequences. How many judges do you think will care about her story when I present mine?"

"Let me say goodbye to her at least. Let me explain..."

"Mr. Stein. The time is up."

"I'll go." Sol wanted to beat the life out of Eli Pitman, and it took great force of will to hold himself back. "If I find out you touched a hair on her head, I am coming back for you, and this face will be the last face you will ever see."

"Mr. Stein. Your girl is safe, if you leave in ten seconds. You have a train to catch."

Sol stood up, took the train ticket, and left the room. His heart wrenched as he looked in at Cora comforting Adeline. He moved to the door, and Eli stepped between him and the door that led to Cora.

"Kindly turn your attention to the front desk. You'll notice two police officers ready to arrest Cora Rood if you so much as make eye contact with her."

Triumph gleamed in Eli's eyes as Sol saw the officers at the front door. He turned on his heel and walked out of Roth and Levine, walked to the train station, and didn't look back. He was breaking Cora's heart; he was breaking his own heart. But he saw no other way to keep Cora out of jail or Adeline and thirty Icelandic families safe.

***

Cora heard the door slam in the distance and put it out of her mind. She paced as Adeline sipped hot tea. They waited for Eli.

Finally, Eli reentered the room.

"A word, Miss Rood?"

"Where is Sol?" Cora's voice edged on panic.

"I can explain if you would just step into this room with me."

"He's my bodyguard." Cora refused to move.

"Well, the partners at Roth and Levine are coming in with us, so you are well protected. Let's step in here, please."

"Where is Mr. Stein?"

"This way, please. It will all become clear."

Cora looked at Adeline. She was grimy, dirty, exhausted, and on the verge of tears. Cora reluctantly walked into the room with the partners of Roth and Levine.

"Sol Stein just sold you out for a farm." Eli let that statement hit her heart and explode. She gasped. "I offered him a train ticket and a farm in Gimli if he would walk away today."

Cora's heart shriveled and died. She struggled to breathe.

"I will let Adeline rot in jail. I will drag this fight out in court until she is old and grey unless you walk away from this fight. You leave Adeline and go back to wherever you came from. The only reason Adeline would want to take 50,000 dollars from me, less the cost of the hotel, which never entered her charity account, and then empty her trust, is because she is going to file for divorce," Eli hissed in Cora's face. "That will never happen. I will not allow that scandal to befall our family. She goes back to being my wife. She can run Hope House but with no interference from the D. W. E. A., and the minute she steps out of line, I will close the doors and not a court in the land can stop me. It's time she remembered that she is to do as she is told. I've allowed far too much latitude, which I will correct right now. No charges of fraud to her or you, if you leave right now. If you stay, you will be arrested on charges of fraud. No one comes up against me and wins. No one. Certainly, not a woman."

"You can't prove fraud," Cora roared at him.

Eli moved closer so she could feel his breath on her cheek. His physical presence made her shake in fear. He was big, and she was not. "Of course, I can. Very easy, we found some documents."

She tilted her head in confusion.

"Do you know what the best thing is about being a man?" Eli laid the bait for her with his words. "I can have a beautiful mistress like Mirabel Salter and as long as I don't physically hurt Adeline, nothing and no one can touch me. Certainly, not you. You should go home to your little village, find a man that will marry you. You are a disgrace to women. When you try to come up against the big boys, we will slap you down."

Cora's face paled in fear as she stood up and put distance between them.

"Oh, that's right. You already know that. You have been slapped down already. I forgot. So, you know what you are up against, and you know that you have failed. You should find a husband and learn your place. That is my suggestion to you."

"You're bluffing. You have no evidence of fraud. You gifted Adeline money. I had nothing to do with it." Cora didn't care about her job. Not just now. She cared about her client. Her voice hardened even though her heart was broken.

Her eyes widened as Eli Pitman spread out falsified evidence of fraud in front of her. Her signature on Hope House letterhead requesting huge amounts of money.

Cora's eyes swept over the fabricated paper trails of fraud that would land her and Adeline in jail for most of their natural life. After reading everything, her eyes met Eli's.

"This is all false. You can't enter this... this is false."

This is a nightmare. Adeline is waiting to be exonerated.

A giant hand reached into Cora's heart and crushed it into oblivion as the partners stood up and spoke, "Mr. Pitman's evidence of fraud is enough for us. We have no reason to believe it is falsified outside of your word. And frankly, your word doesn't hold much value with us."

"This is false, I have not committed fraud, and neither has Mrs. Pitman. If Eli chose to give her 50,000 dollars, that was his choice." Cora tried to defend herself.

"We are not going to split hairs. We aren't going to fire you, but we are letting you quit because as much as this evidence looks incriminating, we have no interest in dealing with a backlash from Lord Bronwyn. So, we are letting you go with a document saying you ended your period of articling two weeks short of being called to the bar." Mr. Levine picked up a document, looked over it, and put it back down.

"You don't have what it takes to be a lawyer. You are too emotional. Take our advice and quit before you are humiliated."

Mr. Roth tossed her severance letter in front of her, and together, the partners walked out. Leaving her alone with Eli, a predator.

"This is false. You gave Adeline that money of your own free will." Cora's jaw clenched in fury.

Eli moved closer to her so that his lips were right against her ear. "Prove it," he whispered against her neck. She shook with revulsion, with fear. "In a court of law."

The will to fight shriveled as she looked hard into eyes that had no soul. He'd toss her in jail on false charges and forget about her in thirty seconds.

Prove it.

No way to prove it. He had the upper hand. She knew the power behind that hand. Her jaw ached in remembrance of what a man's hand could so easily do to a woman's jaw. No Sol to stop it. Sol, who sold her for a farm in Gimli. Just her facing down Eli. Alone. Vulnerable. Hot tears scalded her throat and behind her eyes as she willed herself not to cry.

You cannot give him the satisfaction.

"I guarantee my men won't lay a finger on you. You somehow sneak back here, I offer no protection from my men. Royce was very taken by you. I'm not sure what he would do if he met you on the streets of Toronto." Eli stroked his thin mustache.

"I'll go." Her voice was small, even to her own ears. "If it will keep Adeline out of jail, I will go."

"You have six hours of protection in this city, and then you're bait." Eli crossed his arms over his chest.

"How do I know you will keep your word regarding Adeline?" Cora hated that she was trembling in fear.

"You won't. This is not your concern. You are fired. Did you really think I was going to let Adeline divorce me? Do you think for a second I would allow it? She has a duty to me," he hissed at Cora. "The scandal surrounding this? Did you both think Randall's chances of marrying Laura Scott would be put in jeopardy and I wouldn't do something about it?" He shook his head. "We won't have a deranged mother in the background lessening their choices. She will do as she is told."

"I'll go," Cora said quietly. "I'll go. If you guarantee she will be safe."

"You'll go or you'll be in a jail cell for the rest of your life. Get out of here, and Miss Rood, I suggest you don't look back."

The full implication of the day settled around her. No Sol, no case with Adeline. No hope for a resolution. No call to the bar to be sworn in. No hope at all.

The firm and the determined face of Eli Pitman were not moved by her plight.

"I'll go." She stood up and hoped her legs wouldn't buckle from the fear.

She raced to her apartment building and banged on Sol's door. No response. She wept as she banged on his door harder. Why would he leave her there to face that alone?

Finally, her mind comprehended that he'd left her. Left her to Eli. Left her to face jail with Adeline. It was true. She was a paycheck to him and nothing more. Cora slid down the wall and buried her face in her hands. She wept until someone came down the hall. Was it one of Eli's men? She jumped up and scurried into her apartment. Trashed again.

Tears coursed down her face as she gathered up anything that wasn't destroyed. There was precious little Eli's thugs hadn't defaced, shredded, or broken. She put any clothes she could into a bag and took her savings from under a floor board.

As she left her apartment, she turned to look at Sol's door one last time. She wept as she pummeled his door until her hands hurt. Foolishness and humiliation washed over her. He was a liar.

I am a stupid coward.

Cora's shoulders bowed under the weight of despair. Even as she hated herself for running, she raced to the train station to get as far away from Eli as she could in the time allotted. As she handed her bags to the porter, she saw a man with close-cropped blond hair. Her heart soared with happiness. Of course, he didn't leave her! He was here. Right here! The man turned, and her heart fell to her feet. Not Sol. No. She was alone. No job, no call to the bar, two weeks short of finishing her articling. Adeline disgraced. Now, Cora was running from Toronto under threat of rape. Heartbroken. Devastated. Her eyes darted around, terrified that one of Eli's men was following her. A man who looked a lot like Royce stepped onto the train, a car behind hers.

Her hands shook with fear at the thought of Royce on the same train. What was he going to do to her? There was no other train to catch; she had to take her chances. She thought for a minute of lying down on the tracks — it would be less painful than what was facing her if Royce got his hands on her.

Cora stepped back off the train. Sure enough, the man that had been following her stepped off as well. Heart pounding in her ears, her eyes darted around, looking for protection from Royce.

Royce pounced on her. She gasped as his fingers bit into her arm and made her wince in pain.

"I'm here to make sure you get home safely." Royce pulled her forward, and when she tried to pull back, he swung her around to face him. "Give me a reason to restrain you." He pulled her against him then bent her over his arm as if they were lovers. He leaned in and spoke into her ear. "I beg you." His breath was hot on her neck. "Give me a reason to subdue you. Either you get on this train, or I get to force you. How do you want this to end?"

"I'll go." She struggled against him.

"Know this. I will follow you wherever you are going, and if you even think of trying to return to Toronto, I'll be right there to meet you. I guarantee it." Royce put his mouth against her ear. "I look forward to the day that you break your word with Eli because I get to make sure you *never* do it again."

Cora shook with fear as he dragged her onto the train, up the stairs, and pushed her down into a seat. His fingers bit into her upper arms as he held her in place until the train pulled away from the station. Trying to break free was useless; she sat silently and tried not to shake with terror. As soon as the train was moving, Royce stood up and left her alone.

Rubbing her arm, trying to erase the feeling of his fingers biting into her, she stifled a sob. She pressed her forehead against the cool glass of the window as rain started to fall. The grey around her matched her mood — lifeless, empty, and broken. She had been such a fool to think she could go up against Eli Pitman and help Adeline. To think she could expose injustice in the courts to a country that didn't care. Her chin lowered to her chest as her body slumped against the seat of the train. As the rain beat against the window, her tears became uncontrollable. Hopelessness weighed her down, gutted her, until she was hollowed out, empty except for anguish.

I give up. You win, Eli. You win, Toronto. I'll never fight again.

Chapter Fifteen

Oakland, Manitoba, May 1904

M rs. Daindridge placed a piping hot cherry pie on her freshly scrubbed windowsill. A cloud of dust caught her eye.

What in the world is causing all this dust? She squinted down the street. Why is the stagecoach on Lilac Street?

"Yoo hoo," Mrs. Carr called out as she came in through the back door.

"Are you expecting a visitor? The stagecoach is on our street." Mrs. Daindridge frowned at Mrs. Carr.

"The only people expecting visitors are the Roods." Mrs. Carr's eyebrows drew together. "Wilbur's sister, that Cora. Apparently, she's done shaking her fist at society and finally got her way. Working as a lawyer. Preposterous. What next? I hear she's expected in Oakland any day." Mrs. Carr's lips pursed in disapproval. "She's of an age she should be settled down with children."

"Cora Rood wouldn't be staying with the hermit Mrs. Charbonneau." Mrs. Daindridge's frown deepened as she dismissed Mrs. Carr's concerns about Cora Rood. "She's staying in the cottage behind their house where Mrs. Rood's mother stayed in the summers."

Their eyes met. A visitor they didn't know about? If they didn't know, no one knew. Quickly, they both fumbled for their spectacles in the front pockets of their aprons. They peered out the window through a break in the lilac bushes just as the stagecoach ground to a halt in front of Mrs. Charbonneau's house.

"Mrs. Charbonneau hasn't had a visitor since her husband dropped dead eighteen years ago!" Mrs. Carr helped Mrs. Daindridge crank the window up higher so they could see more clearly.

"Remember that scandal?" Mrs. Daindridge moved the pie out of the way so they wouldn't accidentally push it into the flower bed.

"Do I?" Mrs. Carr whispered as they watched Matt Hartwell adjust the reins and settle his precious horses down before turning his attention to the occupant of the stagecoach. "I've thought of little else since we watched that commotion!"

"Imagine sending your son, daughter-in-law, and granddaughter away the *day* of the funeral. I've never heard of such a thing in my life." Mrs. Daindridge's lips pursed with disapproval once again.

Mrs. Carr shook her head in agreement. "It's appalling is what it is. Matt Hartwell, unmarried at this age is a shame too. Look at him."

Both middle-aged married women looked at Matt Hartwell as if he were the last butter tart on a plate. Nearly six feet tall with sandy brown hair and blue eyes, he made their hearts flutter.

"Why he won't give Cissy a second look is beyond me." Mrs. Carr frowned as Matt opened the door to the carriage.

Because she is as dull as dishwater, Mrs. Daindridge thought but was careful not to say out loud.

They held their breath as the door to the coach opened.

Having ruled out Cora Rood, they were flummoxed.

"Who is that?" They both gasped at exactly the same time.

Their eyes widened as Matt carefully helped a young woman with masses of curly black hair out of the coach.

They watched as the mystery woman leaned against Matt as he held her up. Mrs. Daindridge scrambled to find binoculars to get a better look at the young woman.

"She's not able to stand." Mrs. Daindridge's mouth gaped open as she held the binoculars tight to her spectacles. The scandal in front of them escalated.

"Not able to stand?" Mrs. Carr sputtered. "My turn with those binoculars, please."

Reluctantly, Mrs. Daindridge passed them to her. Previously, the binoculars had been used by Mr. Daindridge as he tracked the native bird species in the area of Oakland. He loved to watch his precious mourning doves; he found them soothing. Until now, those binoculars had never landed on a bird like the woman in front of them.

"She's got a black eye!" Mrs. Carr exclaimed. "She's trying to cover it with that net veil, but that is a black eye!"

Mrs. Daindridge wanted to grab the binoculars out of Mrs. Carr's hands but didn't dare. She was a guest, after all. And Mrs. Daindridge didn't require binoculars to see Matt Hartwell simply scoop the young woman right up off her feet and into his arms. Neither of them needed binoculars to see her settle her head onto his shoulder as if she had been in his arms before.

Has she been in his arms before?

Mrs. Daindridge and Mrs. Carr clutched at each other. This type of romantic gesture was foreign to the residences of Lilac Street, Oakland, Manitoba, Canada.

Matt Hartwell and the mysterious black-haired woman disappeared behind the stagecoach.

"She must be a relation of Mrs. Charbonneau." Mrs. Daindridge strained to see through the window of the stagecoach.

"Is it her granddaughter?"

"Has to be." Mrs. Carr put the binoculars down.

"How much luggage does she have? That will indicate how long she plans to stay." Mrs. Daindridge finally got her hands back on the binoculars and craned out the window again to watch Matt unload the luggage.

Both held their breath as they waited in expectation.

Matt returned to the carriage, and after one last look at the Charbonneau's verandah, he slapped the reins down and was off.

"No luggage," they both said in unison.

***

Priscilla Markus woke early the next morning to the sounds of her grandmother making breakfast. She shivered with cold. Her nightgown clung to her due to the fevered sweat that drenched her. She closed her eyelids over eyes that ached from the sunshine spilling into the room. Cramping pain in her abdomen intensified and caused her to moan in agony as she curled into a ball, hoping it would go away.

Something is wrong.

The pain churned through her. Mrs. Charbonneau came to the bedroom door.

"It's time to be up. Your stagecoach will be here right away."

"I'm sick... I think I'm really sick." Priscilla twisted the sheets as the intensifying pain continued to twist through her.

"If you are away from your husband much longer, it will only be worse for you when you go back. Up you get and into that coach. I'll send your food with you."

Despite being barely able to stand, Priscilla pulled her clothes on over her sweaty, clammy skin. Her hands shook as she adjusted the veil to try to cover the black eye and bruises on her face.

She went downstairs on unsteady legs, and her grandmother handed her a cup of tea.

"I meant what I said." Mrs. Charbonneau silently counted out the exact amount of money needed to return Priscilla to her husband. "This is just a time of adjustment. Once you learn what makes him happy and what angers him, it will get easier. Your mother..."

"Yes?" Priscilla slumped onto the settee in pain. She wiped at the sweat soaking her forehead.

"Your mother raised you to believe you are the equal of a man. You have been misinformed. Once you know your place in life, things get easier." Mrs. Charbonneau's tone hardened.

"My mother was right, though," Priscilla protested weakly from the settee. She wasn't strong enough to hold her tea cup.

"Your mother was an immoral suffragette. She was never right about anything, and look at where it got her." Mrs. Charbonneau's lips thinned in anger.

She worked under the best dress designer in Montreal and then went on to open her own fashion house in Winnipeg where she met your son and was very happy.

Priscilla only thought the words that defended her mother. Instead, she said nothing. A year and a half of being beaten bloody by Richard Markus III had left her empty with no will to fight. She lay on the settee and closed her eyes as her grandmother recounted all the reasons she hated Honor Charbonneau. Immoral! She thought too highly of herself, no respect for her husband Jack. No respect for her in-laws. Refused to stay home like a normal woman and raise her daughter, and now look at the price she was paying. Took her daughter to work with her! Disgraceful. She raised a misfit who didn't know how to keep her marriage happy. Priscilla shriveled as the hate-filled rant washed over her.

"Tell me, did he beat you because you were immoral, too?" Mrs. Charbonneau's eyes gleamed with anticipation at Priscilla's response.

The fever raging through Priscilla made her eyes feel hot and dry. She struggled to focus on the woman who was supposed to be her grandmother. She should be outraged that her granddaughter was hurt by the man who had sworn to love her.

"He beat me because he loves the feel of my flesh bruising under his hands," Priscilla said with the last of her strength. "He craves submission and obedience through humiliation. He delights at the sounds of me whimpering in fear. That's why he beats me."

"You are just like your mother." Mrs. Charbonneau's face lit up as she let her words tear back into Priscilla. "You feel no responsibility for your actions. There has to be a reason — you must have provoked it somehow. Men don't beat women for no reason."

"They do, Grandmother Charbonneau. They absolutely do." Priscilla let her eyelids slide shut; her eyes felt like they were on fire.

"Take my advice: go home, learn what makes him unhappy, and stop doing those things. If you are a good wife, the beatings will stop."

"What if they don't?" Priscilla struggled to open her eyes.

"It's up to you to make it work." Mrs. Charbonneau's lips thinned with disapproval. "You made your bed. You have to lie in it."

"I have no intentions of..." A knock at the door interrupted Priscilla.

"He's here. Matt is always prompt."

Priscilla struggled to her feet; the cramping pain in her womb nearly brought her to her knees. "I am really feeling sick, Grandmother, I think I should see a..."

"Get in that stagecoach and get home to your husband and fulfill your duty." Grandmother Charbonneau's voice dripped with poison as she opened the door to Matt Hartwell. "I don't want to hear another word from you. You are a spoiled child. I'm surprised you weren't pregnant out of wedlock to entrap him."

Priscilla tried to take a few steps toward the door.

"I'll go." Priscilla wiped sweat off her brow. "I'll go, and you will never have to see me or hear from me again."

"That would be best. Your life is with Richard Markus III. Try to remember that."

Priscilla fought down bile that rose in her throat. *A few more steps.* Matt took a few steps toward Priscilla, indicating he would carry her again. Mrs. Charbonneau stopped him with an icy look. Priscilla took another step toward Matt and had nearly reached him when the cramping pain brought her to her knees. Matt ignored Mrs. Charbonneau's frosty glare, brushed past her, and went to Priscilla.

"Ensure that she gets to the train on time, Matt. We cannot delay her meeting with her *lawful* husband." Mrs. Charbonneau passed the train fare to him.

"You're all right," he said softly as he pressed his hand against Priscilla's forehead. "You have a high fever. I'll take you to a doctor."

"There is no time for a doctor, Mr. Hartwell. She needs to be on the train today. Things will only get worse for her if she delays any longer." Mrs. Charbonneau's shrill voice pierced Priscilla's brain.

Priscilla curled into Matt's outstretched arms and gasped in pain. Matt very gently picked her up off the floor. He adjusted her a bit in his arms and walked to the door.

Priscilla pressed her face into his lapel so she wouldn't have to look at the hatred on her grandmother's face.

She winced when Mrs. Charbonneau slammed the door shut on both of them. Tears of shame and pain built behind her eyelids. Her heart pounded from the confrontation or the fever; she wasn't sure which.

"Doctor or not, you and I both know that you are not, under any circumstances, going back to whoever did that to you." Matt carefully laid her down on the seat of the stagecoach.

"I am so scared." Priscilla's skin ached from the fever. She curled into a ball of agony under the lap robe Matt tucked around her.

"First, we get you well, and then we deal with everything else." Matt shut the door to the coach.

Despite the lap robe, Priscilla shook with cold.

Within minutes, the coach stopped and she heard Matt speak to someone. "She's in bad shape, Mrs. Bennett."

"Let me take a look," Mrs. Bennett requested in a low tone.

The stagecoach door opened, and Mrs. Bennett crawled in to place a cool hand on Priscilla's forehead. "Take her straight to Dr. Davies. This fever is too high. You were right to stop her from travelling. I'll go with her."

Within minutes, Matt carried Priscilla into Dr. Davies office and laid her down on an examination table.

"Matt..." Priscilla said softly against him.

"Yes."

"In case I die, and I feel like I will, thank you for your kindness."

"No one is dying. Dr. Davies is excellent. He'll get you all fixed up in no time." Matt frowned with concern.

Priscilla moaned; she clutched his arm to be sure he was listening. "Don't let anyone take my skirt."

"What?" Matt leaned forward so she could speak directly into his ear.

"Make sure my skirt stays safe."

"Your skirt? Did I hear you right?" Matt frowned.

"Don't let anyone take my skirt," Priscilla begged as her grip tightened on his arm.

"Your skirt is safe. I'll keep it for you. I won't let anything happen to it," Matt promised.

"When did this happen?" Dr. Davies directed the question to Priscilla, but she could only moan in pain.

"I picked her up from the train in Brandon yesterday." Matt's voice sounded as if he were very far off. "She had all those bruises then," Matt said quietly. "She didn't say anything to me, just that she was on her way to visit her grandmother. She was weakened from the pain, I think, so I offered to carry her from the stagecoach to the front door of Mrs. Charbonneau's home."

"Did she have this fever yesterday?" Dr. Davies asked Matt.

"No. When I carried her into the house she seemed a normal temperature."

"Thanks Matt, I will want to see you later today. When you're back from Brandon, please stop in, and we will try to get to the bottom of this situation. Someone has beaten this woman. It looks like a criminal investigation needs to take place, and I want a statement from you."

"Please, just... uh... be careful with her. I know you are a doctor and a midwife." Matt's eyes flicked up at Mrs. Bennett. "But she seems just unusually fragile. I will pay any bills on her behalf. I just want her to be all right."

"We'll do our best, Matt. You can rest assured! If we can help, we will. I'll see you tonight."

Matt left the room, shutting the door behind him gently.

***

Ada Bennett moved to the woman shivering on the bed. The fever ravaged her fragile frame. "When did the pains start?"

"This morning." Her jaw clenched in pain.

Mrs. Bennett signaled at Dr. Davies to give them some privacy. "I'll do an examination and let you know what's going on. If you would just give us a moment."

"Of course."

Mrs. Bennett helped Priscilla get undressed.

"Can you tell me what happened, dear?" Mrs. Bennett asked softly.

"My husband beat me." Priscilla slumped against Mrs. Bennett.

"I see that," Mrs. Bennett said very softly. "When was the last beating?"

"Monday. He was upset about a dinner party..."

"It doesn't matter what reason he gave you, my dear girl." Mrs. Bennett pulled Priscilla's corset off and then her shift. Her clothes were drenched in sweat. Mrs. Bennett stifled a gasp as she looked at Priscilla's back.

Whip marks? Is that possible? Is that what I'm looking at?

"A man is never justified in beating his wife." Mrs. Bennett managed to keep the fury out of her voice, even though the condition of Priscilla's back devastated her to the point she wanted to weep. "So, Monday he beat you. Then what happened?"

"I decided I had to leave."

"Did you leave on Monday, then?"

"No. I couldn't. I was... in the hospital. The butler took me to a doctor because the beating caused me to miscarry."

Mrs. Bennett saw the blood soaking her skirt at the same time as Priscilla.

"You're bleeding from a miscarriage, then? Not your typical time of menstruation?

"From the miscarriage, yes," Priscilla confirmed.

"Did you notice the bleeding increased?" Mrs. Bennett maintained a professional, calm tone, even though worry snaked through her.

"I don't know. I'm just in so much pain I can't stand it..." Priscilla moaned, and Mrs. Bennett helped her back onto the examination table.

"Don't leave me. Please, don't... leave..." Priscilla grabbed Mrs. Bennett's forearm.

"I'm not going anywhere. I'm just going to tell Dr. Davies what's wrong. Just a moment."

"Would you join us, sir? She has had a miscarriage. I believe she has retained part of the placenta," Mrs. Bennett said softly, so Priscilla wouldn't overhear.

Dr. Davies crushed his cigarette and came around the table. The hair on the back of Mrs. Bennett's neck stood up as she listened to the young woman recount the tale.

"He pushed me down the stairs, and the pains were terrible about four or five hours after that." Priscilla struggled to concentrate on the faces in front of her.

"What day was that, dear?" Mrs. Bennett forced her voice to sound calm despite the horror she felt looking at both fresh and faded bruises on her body. She held Priscilla's hand and stroked the hair back from her fever-soaked face. Mrs. Bennett noticed deep purple bruising on the top of her wrists. She tenderly turned Priscilla's hands over and noticed four perfect finger mark bruises under her wrists. The bruises were fresh, the same deep purple as those on the other side.

"Tuesday night." Mrs. Bennett snapped back to attention as she focused on Priscilla's statement. "The butler took me to the hospital. Don't tell anyone that." Dr. Davies and Mrs. Bennett heard the fear in her voice and their eyes met. "He saw that I was bleeding. I'm still bleeding."

Dr. Davies immediately set up his tray with instruments to perform a dilation and curettage. He started scrubbing with carbolic acid, and Mrs. Bennett's eyes met his once again.

Dr. Davies started administering chloroform. As Priscilla drifted into unconsciousness, Dr. Davies said, "Mrs. Bennett, this interview is over. This girl is dying of retained placenta, and she needs to be in surgery before the septicemia kills her outright."

"Of course," Mrs. Bennett agreed.

"There is every possibility she will not live to see the end of the week."

Mrs. Bennett scrubbed her hands and took her place beside Dr. Davies as she had many times before.

Once the surgery was completed, Dr. Davies straightened up and wiped sweat from his brow.

"Will she be able to have children?" Mrs. Bennett wiped Priscilla's brow with a cool cloth.

"I can't say for sure. I was very careful, but it is always difficult to know how much scar tissue will result. Her body has been through a lot. This is horrifying. I've never seen such brutality." Dr. Davies shook his head.

"I have."

Dr. Davies jaw dropped at that pronouncement. "Mrs. Bennett, who?"

"My neighbor, Mrs. Wheaton. It sickens me that there is nothing we can do. Domestic abuse is just so despicable, Dr. Davies."

"I worry for her as well. Fortunately, she has you as a neighbor — one of the best midwives in the country. However, a man who refuses medical treatment for his wife from a doctor concerns me."

"Me too," Mrs. Bennett agreed.

"We'll document this abuse. Every bruise, every lash mark. Can you help me? I will testify under oath that if this woman returns to her husband, I'm certain he will kill her. This miscarriage is the result of a fall. Is there evidence that she was pushed?"

"Let's start with the bruising on the top of her wrists and the finger marks on the undersides here. She says she was pushed down the stairs. Doesn't this marking indicate that he pulled her wrists up and *then* pushed her?" Mrs. Bennett placed Priscilla's arm against her side and pulled the blanket up over her shoulders.

Dr. Davies put a cigarette to his mouth, lit it, and took a long drag. "I'll put that bruising at the top of the list, along with the lashing. This is a terrible business, Mrs. Bennett."

"When she regains consciousness and you need a place for her to heal, I'll take care of her until she is well. She'll be safe out on my farm. I have a feeling whoever did this might try to track her down, and they won't find her all the way out at Bennett farm. It's about the safest place on the earth." Mrs. Bennett stroked the hair off Priscilla's cheek. "Poor little thing. She can't be much more than, what would you say, early twenties? To endure something this awful." Mrs. Bennett shook her head.

"Very generous of you. Maybe the Women's Christian Temperance Union will get that hospital up and running sooner rather than later. She will be a burden to you with seeding in full swing."

"The hospital is coming along nicely. We're very excited to participate in such a big project." Mrs. Bennett smiled warmly. "She is no burden at all. She needs to sleep, eat, and have some peace. Send her as soon as you can. Mr. Hartwell knows the way. He can bring her when it is convenient for both of you."

"Thank you for your assistance today, Mrs. Bennett." Dr. Davies held out his hand.

"It was my pleasure," Mrs. Bennett said as she shook his hand.

Chapter Sixteen

Matt Hartwell dashed into Brandon and was back in Oakland by 4:00 p.m. He dreaded going to see Dr. Davies almost as much as he dreaded going home. He went to the livery stable and made sure his horses were happy and tucked in for the night. Even though Matt was miserable, he gave them extra treats because someone should be happy today. He brushed them and then brushed them again.

"Matt, they won't have hair left if you don't put that brush down," Constable Cole McDougall said as he put his horse, King, away in his stall.

"I like my horses well groomed," Matt growled at his friend.

"There's groomed, there is well groomed, and there's obsessive behavior. You, Matt, are obsessed with these horses."

"Maybe," Matt conceded as he put away the brush and picked up a hoof pick. Cole rolled his eyes. He leaned against the stall as Matt carefully started checking each hoof on each horse.

"A little bird told me that you were seen cavorting with a woman this morning. How is Min going to take that?"

"Badly," Matt said as he put down a hoof and picked up the next one. "I wasn't cavorting. I took her to the doctor. She was supposed to go to Brandon to catch a train, and she got sick. I am to go to Dr. Davies in a bit to check on her."

"More women to take care of. Lucky you," Cole said dryly.

"I'm quite concerned about her, actually. She arrived in town with a black eye."

Cole immediately straightened and visibly shifted from friend to town constable. "Black eye! Any other injuries?"

"I'm not sure. I didn't ask, and she didn't say. She had a very high fever this morning. I think it was some sort of... well, I don't know but maybe... uh... woman trouble?"

"Matt, don't ask me. Women are a complete mystery," Cole groaned.

"Well, I think it was something to do with woman business," Matt said in a hushed tone. "Ada Bennett stayed with Dr. Davies to examine her. I'm to check in and see how she is."

"If you find out who hurt her, let me know so we can press charges. We will not have men beating women in this community." Cole scratched his eyebrow.

"Of course, but I think it happened in Winnipeg — that is where she came from."

"That figures," Cole said, as if all crime happened in Winnipeg and they should all be grateful they lived in a small town. "If you find out differently, if there is something I can do to help her, let me know."

"Of course."

"Back to Min," Cole pressed on.

Matt bristled.

"She can live without you, Matt."

"It would be great if someone told her that. Up to this point, it seems like she can't." Matt's back stiffened in anger as he braced himself to have this discussion with his oldest friend for the millionth time.

Matt kept his back to Cole and kept picking at a hoof that was so clean you could eat off it.

"How soon are your exams? I can look after your ladies while you go to sit them."

Matt put down the hoof and turned to look at his friend.

"May 29. Would you look after them?" Matt's eyes arched in surprise.

"Of course, I would." Cole handed Matt a curry comb.

Matt took it and turned away from the sympathy in Cole's eyes. Matt had been friends with Cole from the first day they met at school. He knew Cole had no idea what his life really was like. He wanted to ask for help but didn't know what to ask for. Cole wanted to help but had no idea what Matt needed. Being men, they carefully avoided discussing emotions or anything closely resembling an emotion.

"No matter what Min throws at you, Matt, you are sitting those exams." Cole's mouth thinned in determination.

"I really wish it were that simple." Matt scratched his temple and scowled at his friend.

"It is." Cole pumped more water for the horses. "You need to get Min in hand. You have to stand up to her. You also need to finish those exams this year. No ifs, ands, or buts. I mean it, Matt. If I have to move in with your mother and Min, I will. This year, Matt, everything is happening for you this year."

"Thanks, Cole." Matt heard the fury in Cole's words. Cole had no idea what Matt coped with, and Matt hoped he would never know the reality of life behind the closed door of 129 Glenwood Street. Matt finally put the grooming tools away, and they left the livery stable together.

"I will take you up on the offer to deal with mother and Min. Just let me figure it out. I just need a couple of weeks to make it work."

"Matt," Cole said quietly to Matt's back.

"Yes." Matt turned around to face Cole. He sounded defeated even in his own ears.

"I hear your lady friend is beautiful." Cole's face broke into a slow grin.

Matt rolled his eyes. "She is not my lady friend. I picked her up at a train station, took her to her grandmother's, and took her to a doctor. The end."

"I heard she needed some assistance getting into Mrs. Charbonneau's home and then back into the carriage this morning."

Matt sighed and hung his head.

"She was too weak to walk, so I did what any gentleman would do. I carried her. Honestly. Oh, I promised to protect her skirt. That's it. Isn't that the oddest thing you've ever heard of?"

"Matt, you are a good man, but your mother and sister really need to let you live your life."

"That is much easier said than done."

"It's not your fault your father died and your mother can't cope. It's not your fault your sister has been sick most of her life. They need to find ways to let you live your life while coping with their own problems. This can't continue. It really can't."

Matt sighed. "Who all knows about the lady in the stagecoach this morning?"

"Everyone." Cole's eyes lit up.

"Everyone, including Min, do you think?"

"Especially Min."

Matt stifled a groan. Despite being an invalid, his twin sister knew everything that happened in the community.

"If you need anything, let me know," Cole offered before turning towards the barracks.

Matt dragged his feet home. He split wood before entering the house.

Dark.

Always dark.

Matt yearned to tear down the heavy curtains that covered the south-facing windows. He wished, just once, he could come home to happy people. Instead, his mother sat in a rocking chair staring at the fire. She didn't look up when he came in the house. Min lay on the settee with a cool compress on her head. She had suffered from rheumatic fever as a child and had constant bouts of nerves and headaches. Matt tiptoed to the cook stove so as not to disturb her and started supper. He dropped a pan, and Min moaned in pain.

"Sorry, Min," he whispered and continued working. Matt whispered, and Min had two volumes. Whisper or scream. Min couldn't handle loud noises unless she was the one making them. Matt served supper to his mother and sister then gulped his own food down quickly so he could get back to the doctor's clinic.

"Where are you going?" Min demanded. Her eyes narrowed at him as she picked at her food.

"I have to meet with the doctor." Matt kept his tone casual so as not to set her off.

"Is it about that woman from this morning?" Min's voice dripped with poison.

"What woman?"

"The woman you were carrying all over town. Is that what it's about?"

Matt stood up and put his plate in the basin. He took a big gulp of water before turning to face his sister.

"Min, I have to go, and I don't have time to discuss it. I still have homework to do tonight. It would really help me if you would clean the kitchen," he suggested gently.

He handed his mother some hot tea. She needed to bathe, but she stared off at the wall. No use trying to see out the window — three layers of heavy drapery impeded the view. Min could not handle light.

"I have had a headache for two days — I can't clean a kitchen. I've been waiting for you to get home all day. You can't leave me here with her." The rant was all too familiar.

"I'll be back in an hour, Min. I would really appreciate it if you would please clean up these dishes before I get home so I can study for my upcoming exams."

Min's eyes filled with tears. "I just can't. You don't know how bad I feel, Matt. I can't." Min rubbed her temples and tried to brush her tears away with her fingertips.

Matt softened.

"Don't worry, Min. I'll look after everything when I get home. I'm sorry you are not well. I'll be back straight away."

"When? When will you be back?" Her lip trembled, and Matt wanted to stop her from crying. He didn't want to do or say anything that would escalate her anger.

"Soon." Matt fled out the door and went as fast as he could to Dr. Davies's office.

***

Matt waited for Dr. Davies in the lobby of his office, worrying about the young woman he had left there that morning.

Is she in pain?

He couldn't stand the thought of it. Matt could still feel how fragile she seemed in his arms.

"The doctor will see you now," Miss Ellis said. She smiled at him, and if she hadn't been so old, he would think she might be on the verge of flirting. He put that thought out of his mind. Miss Ellis had to be sixty! No way she'd be thinking anything of the sort.

Matt entered into Dr. Davies's examination room and sat down.

"Good afternoon, Matt." Dr. Davies entered the room and then sat across the desk from him.

"Hello, sir." Matt shifted on the hard chair, trying to get comfortable.

"I'm hoping you can shed some light on this situation?"

"Honestly, I don't know much. She is Mrs. Charbonneau's granddaughter. She had the black eye and bruises when I picked her up." Matt held his hands up in a gesture of innocence.

"Matt, I've known you for years, and I am not accusing you of putting those bruises on her."

Matt let out a sigh of relief. "I was a little concerned that you thought... well that maybe you thought..."

"Not for a second. Matt, you are the kindest man on two feet. You couldn't hurt a woman if your life depended on it."

Matt relaxed visibly.

"There is a matter of fees, though. I am not sure what to do about that. She is a married woman, but I don't think it would be in her best interests to send a bill to her husband."

"Very wise of you." Matt nodded in agreement.

"Is there any more information you can give me?"

"I'm sorry. I don't know anything else about this woman." Matt shook his head.

"She will require around-the-clock care. Mrs. Bennett has volunteered, and I was hoping you could take her out to the Bennett's in the stagecoach? Would that be all right?"

"Of course." Matt mentally added that to the list of things to do before he had to go to Winnipeg to sit his exams.

"In the matter of fees, I propose this. My brother is a doctor in Winnipeg. I will ask him to send a bill to her husband from his offices there. That way he won't be able to trace her here."

"Great idea," Matt agreed. "I'm not sure if this is inappropriate or not, but could I see her, just to be sure she is all right?"

"Of course, I was thinking you probably would like to see for yourself. She is sedated. Her fever is coming down. You saved her life, Matt. I wanted you to know that." Dr. Davies extended his hand, and Matt shook it.

"Thank you."

Together they went into the exam room where Priscilla lay on the bed.

"Dr. Davies, if she was running to Mrs. Charbonneau, she must have absolutely no other family." Matt tentatively placed his hand on Priscilla's forehead. She still felt fevered but nothing like the fever that raged that morning. He let his hand very gently caress the curve of her cheekbone. Her skin felt impossibly smooth and soft.

Stop. She's married.

Regretfully, he pulled his hand away.

"I think so." Dr. Davies frowned.

"I can sit with her for a while, if you want? While you finish up with your patients? Maybe Miss Ellis can eat her supper while I keep an eye on her," Matt offered.

"That would be great, Matt." Dr. Davies smiled and went to the door. "That would help us out a lot."

Dr. Davies closed the door behind him, and Matt pulled up a chair and sat across from Priscilla. She stirred a little in her sleep, so he took her small, fine-boned hand in his.

"I don't know if you can hear me, miss... well missus, I guess. Anyway, I know that your husband did this to you. That's all I know. I want you to rest easy because he will never hurt you again. I promise it." Gently, he brushed her hair back off her face. The bruises on her skin drew a protective fury out of him he had never felt before.

I have no business promising this. She is married, and I have to walk away. This is inappropriate.

A clock ticked on the desk by the door; he wanted to pitch it into the street in case it disturbed her rest. He watched her like a hawk for any sign of pain. His throat tightened with concern as Priscilla shivered from the fever. He pulled another blanket out of the cupboard by the window and very carefully tucked her in.

***

When Miss Ellis returned to take over, she stood back and watched Matt very tenderly wipe Priscilla's face with a cool cloth.

"I can handle things from here, Matt," Miss Ellis said softly, so as not to disturb their patient.

"Thanks, Miss Ellis." Matt moved the chair back to where he'd found it. "Please, take good care of her. I think she's been through a lot."

"She's in good hands," Miss Ellis assured him.

Matt Hartwell took one last look at the woman sleeping on the bed and then went home to face Min.

Chapter Seventeen

T he next day, Wilbur Rood offered to drive the stagecoach to Brandon because Matt's hands were full with Min, his mother, and now a stranger from Winnipeg, as if he didn't have enough on his already full plate. Cora's letter had been short, and Wilbur was worried. Something happened in Toronto. He could feel it. As a single woman, there was every possibility she had been hurt. In the back of his mind, he always worried about Cora, and as her brother, he knew he always would. If she were married and not alone in that huge terrible city, he might be able to calm down. He dragged Matt's horses to a halt in front of the platform. Wilbur's heart pounded in panic when his eyes landed on Cora.

A very large man spoke to her as they stood on the platform. Instinctively, Wilbur knew she was scared; he flew off the buckboard and went straight to her. The man walked away, and Cora dropped down onto a bench, covering her face with her hands.

"What is going on here?" Wilbur's eyes darted from Cora's devastated form to the retreating back of a man big enough to strike fear into the heart of anyone.

"That was my escort from Toronto. Is he gone?" Cora wept into her hands.

"He's gone." Wilbur crouched down and put his hands on Cora's upper arms. She flinched in fear. This sort of drama was unfamiliar to Wilbur Rood, owner of a mercantile shop in the sleepy village of Oakland.

"Cora, what's going on?" Wilbur repeated as he pulled her into a hard hug. Instead of answering, she buried her face in his shoulder and continued to weep.

"Where is all your luggage, Cora? Why were you escorted out of Toronto?" Fear for her safety started to coil tighter around Wilbur's heart. If that big man hurt her, he wanted to know and press charges immediately.

"Everything I own has been destroyed. This is all I've got." Cora wept piteously.

"Destroyed? Who is that man?" Wilbur demanded as fear edged into his tone.

"He works for Eli Pitman." Cora pulled away and tried to clean up her face with a handkerchief.

"Who in the world is Eli Pitman?" Perplexed, Wilbur pulled out another handkerchief in case she needed it.

Cora sobbed harder. Wilbur could do nothing but hug her closely and wait for her to calm down.

Finally, he decided this storm was not going to pass. "Never mind now." Wilbur pulled her up off the bench and picked up her one small bag. "It's you and me, four horses, and not a Pitman in sight. The man following you has left. He's gone. Did he... uh... hurt you, or just follow you? What is going on here, Cora?" Wilbur looked around once more to be sure she was indeed safe.

"He will report back that I left Toronto and I am in Brandon."

"Tell me what to do. Should we have him arrested?" Feeling helpless, Wilbur wasn't sure if he should run after the man or stay with her.

"No. No need. He's with Pitman. He's as slippery as an eel." Cora pulled herself together and let out a long sigh. "Terrifying me and seeing me all the way here is not illegal. I just want to get out of here. Please take me home, Wil."

"Of course. Come on. The missus packed you a lunch. Cora, you're all right. You're safe here. If Eli Pitman shows up in Oakland, we'll make short work of him."

"Oh, Wil. I'm so glad to see you." Cora wiped her face and tried to regain some semblance of composure. Wilbur watched her look around. Satisfied the man who had escorted her was truly gone, she took a deep breath. "I haven't felt safe for months. It's taken a terrible toll."

"The cottage is all ready for you. Lucy has aired every speck of it. You'll be happy there. Are you hungry?"

"No. I couldn't eat if my life depended on it."

"You're too thin. How long have you not been eating?" Wilbur's eyebrows lowered in concern.

"I can't handle an interrogation right now. Please, get me out of here with no one following me, and maybe I can keep something down." Cora bit her lip. "What did Lucy pack?"

"The best egg salad sandwiches in Manitoba and some bread and butter pickles. She remembered how much you loved her chocolate cake — I think there are two pieces for you."

Cora's eyes welled up with tears again.

"Cora..." Wilbur held his hands out to her. "Cora, why are you crying now?"

"Wil." She wept as she scrambled to find another fresh handkerchief. "No one has done anything nice for me for so long. I forgot what it feels like to be home."

"Well," Wilbur said gently, "you are home, and you and I both know there is no safer place on the earth than Oakland. Not much happens here, and that's how we like it. If this man shows up in Oakland, imagine the interrogation from Mrs. Daindridge and Mrs. Carr! He'd run screaming back to Toronto. You have nothing to worry about. Get in the coach and start eating. If he circles back and is following us, we'll know. Nowhere to hide on the prairie."

"That's true." Cora straightened up. "Thanks for coming to get me, Wil."

"Good thing I did!" He gave her one last hard hug before opening the door to the stagecoach.

Matt Hartwell can't handle anymore weeping females. He had his hands full.

***

Cora's eyes scanned the prairie as they pulled out of Brandon. She watched behind them for half an hour. Seeing grass and freshly planted fields in every direction delighted her. Tension eased out of her shoulders at the familiar landscape. The stagecoach ground to a halt in front of the Rood's where Lucy stood on the step to welcome her sister-in-law.

Together, the three of them went to the summer cottage. The whole cottage had a fresh coat of white paint inside and out. Nestled between lilac bushes and fruit trees, complete with flower boxes and shutters, the cottage looked like something from a story book. It was only mid-May, so no blossoms yet. Cora took a deep breath of warm, sun-soaked air and tried to calm down.

"Are there locks on these doors?" She tried to sound casual and failed. Lucy and Wilbur's eyebrows raised at such a ridiculous request.

Locks on doors?

"Ah. Cora, no one has a locked door in Oakland," Lucy sputtered with confusion.

"I need some locks, Wil. Please, I have to be able to lock everything." She tested the door and wrung her hands. "I won't sleep a wink with the doors wide open to any possible Pitman henchman."

Lucy Rood shot a worried look at her husband. He shrugged and shook his head in confusion.

Cora entered the cottage and searched through every closet and under the bed.

"Cora, you're going to have to calm down. There is no one here. It's all right." Wilbur frowned. "It's just us."

Lucy bit her lip with concern.

"Darling, no one is going to hurt you here." Lucy put her hand on Cora's arm. "Why don't you settle your things, and we'll have supper."

"I'm not hungry." Cora's eyes were wild with fear.

"Of course, you are." Wilbur took the situation in hand. "Come along. Get settled. Supper is ready in half an hour. We'll make a fresh pot of tea, and we'll talk about this, whatever is bothering you. Whatever you ran from, there is going to be a solution."

"There is no solution, Wil." Cora's voice heightened with anxiety. "It's all over. Everything I fought for, it's done. I'm here completely defeated — nothing is left for me."

"Come along, Cora, don't you think that's a bit dramatic?" Wilbur began losing his patience. They were in Oakland — land of the quiet and reserved.

Cora burst into tears, and Lucy frowned at Wilbur.

"You take all the time you need. I'll bring you a plate." Lucy put her arms around Cora and shook her head at Wilbur.

"I am all right." Cora pulled herself together. "I need to lie down for a bit, please."

"Of course. If you need anything at all, please don't hesitate to ask. We're glad you are here." Lucy hugged her hard and finally let her go.

Cora shut the door behind Lucy and Wilbur, then propped a chair up against the handle and curled up on the bed that smelled like summer sun and wept until she couldn't weep anymore.

Chapter Eighteen

Priscilla opened her eyes cautiously. She tested to see if the light would bring on an instant migraine. No migraine. Fevered sweat made her nightgown cling to her.

"Good morning," a soft, kind voice said.

"Hi," Priscilla croaked. Her mouth felt full of cotton.

"I'm Mrs. Bennett, but please, call me Ada. You've had a long battle, but you turned a corner last night."

Ada leaned forward with a glass of cool water.

"What is wrong with me?" Priscilla's eyes darted around the room in fear. "Where am I?"

"When you miscarried, the hospital didn't check to be sure the placenta completely delivered. That is what caused the fever you experienced at your grandmother's house. Dr. Davies did a procedure to make sure the last of the placenta was removed, but you still had a slight fever. The fever broke though, and I'm so glad you are all right. You are going to be just fine."

"Where am I though?" Priscilla's heart pounded in fear as she sipped the water.

"You are in Oakland still, but at my farm with my family. We know your grandmother probably wasn't able to lend assistance. Matt brought you to the clinic, but he couldn't take care of you, not appropriate for a man to... uh... deal with this sort of thing. He has his hands full as it is. At any rate, you are safe here at Bennett farm. I'll bring you some breakfast, and we'll get you all cleaned up. Your fever soaked through your gown. I'll strip the bed." Quickly and efficiently, Mrs. Bennett helped Priscilla change, remade the bed, and served breakfast.

"I don't know how I can repay you, Mrs. Bennett." Priscilla's eyes welled with tears; the kindness overwhelmed her.

"I don't expect to be repaid, my dear girl. You focus on getting well."

"The doctor though, he will expect something." The thought of the bill being sent to her husband, with its return address, made Priscilla shake with fear.

Mrs. Bennett pulled up a chair and took Priscilla's hand in her own.

"Listen, Matt reported that you were covered in bruises when he picked you up. He brought you to Dr. Davies and me. We saw the extent of the damage done to you, Priscilla. I don't know how you lived through the beatings."

Priscilla's eyes filled with tears. "If I had gotten out sooner, I could have saved my baby, though."

"It's clear to me that you did your best for your baby. You must not think like this." Mrs. Bennett gathered Priscilla into her arms and hugged her hard. "Dr. Davies sent a bill to your husband for all the costs incurred. He also padded the bill to look after any expense that you will have here. There is no expense, so I'm going to give you the money."

"He'll know where to find me then." Priscilla's voice broke on a sob.

"Priscilla, Dr. Davies thought of that." Mrs. Bennett pulled back so she could look at Priscilla as she spoke. Her voice was low and firm, like an anchor Priscilla held onto while her mind escalated with worried thoughts. "His brother has a practice in Winnipeg, and he is sending the bill from his brother's offices in the city. We've thought of everything. He won't find you, and he won't hurt you here. We won't allow it."

Priscilla let out a very deep sigh of relief. "How do I thank you for this?"

"You just did." Ada's eyes softened in sympathy. "You need to focus on getting well. If you feel up to it, you can take a book onto the verandah. I'm planting a garden today, and the children are at school, so you rest wherever you feel comfortable."

"I think I'll stay here in bed. I am feeling quite weak."

"Of course. You stay here. I'll leave you a book in case you want to read something. Rest well, Priscilla." Ada patted her on the forearm before leaving the room.

Priscilla closed her eyes and tried to block out the thought of Richard finding her here. She tried to stop the fear that caused her hands to shake at the very thought of him. What would he do to the

Bennetts for taking care of her? What if he traced her here? How would she stop him? Her hands trembled on the blankets.

She tried to let the simple and sparse beauty of the room calm her. The muslin curtain swept in with the early spring breeze. The bedside table had a collection of handkerchiefs cheerfully embroidered with yellow and purple pansies. Beside the handkerchiefs sat a kerosene lantern and a collection of books to choose from. The single bed was wrought iron painted white. The sheets Mrs. Bennett had made the bed with smelled like spring sunshine. The quilt was made of a pattern of tiny fans. She let her fingertips trace over the fans and wondered who had made this quilt. Was the woman who quilted this happy, or had she lived a life of despair?

The dressing table held a vase of pussy willows. Who picked them? Ada or her children? Or maybe Ada's husband was so thoughtful that he made sure to bring pussy willows home at the first site of them for his lovely wife, Ada.

The thought of flowers from a husband should have made Priscilla smile, but all she could think of was all the times Richard had brought flowers to her... it made her sick to think of it. Flowers followed attacks. The memories of his fists and his rage came back and assaulted her. She tried to stop her body from trembling in fear that Richard was going to find her here, and who knew what he was capable of. She had never tried to run away before. Every action she took had a brutal consequence. Priscilla lay in the tranquil room on the beautiful Bennett farm and shook with terror.

***

Matt Hartwell held the letter from the University of Manitoba in his hand. Apprehension gnawed in the pit of his stomach.

How am I going to leave Mother and Min for a week to sit my architect exams?

He thought about Cole taking on Min and Mother; he knew with every fibre of his being Cole was not up to the challenge. A good man in a crisis, Cole could deal with almost everything, except needy women. Matt walked slowly home, dragging his feet in the process. As he opened the door he tried to see his life through his friend's eyes. A mother who sat in the same chair day in and day out. On a good day, she could bathe herself, and that was it. On bad days, she didn't leave her bed. Min, Matt was embarrassed to admit, had started to become violent when she didn't get her way. Matt had bruises where he had been hit with a pan for disagreeing with her. Yes, he was twice her size. No question, he could snap her like a twig, but he couldn't hit a woman if his life depended on it. Just restraining her left her with bruises. Embarrassment made his face flame red; his life had spiraled down into tiptoeing around an invalid mother and an incurable sister.

Incurable. Is that right? Yes. She is. Absolutely, completely, lock her up and throw away the key incurable.

She depended on him and hated him at the same time. Surely, he was the only person on earth shackled with a twin that couldn't pick out clothes for the day without his input, couldn't feed herself, couldn't look after her basic needs, and yet if he asserted himself at all, she became violent. Lashing out at him with anything she could get her hands on. If Cole knew the extent of it, he would shake his head. Cole would have them all locked up. Including Matt. For the first time since all this started, Matt thought about being locked up, and it seemed like a dream. No dark drawing room, no whispering, just sleep. No looking after an incurable, two incurables. He hated thinking of his mother like that, but she hadn't uttered a word since his father had died ten years ago.

Matt opened the door to reveal Min in a rage and his mother keening in fear in the corner of the room.

"Where have you been all day? You've been with her, haven't you? That woman is all you think about. You've been with her!" Min picked up a pitcher and threw it at his head.

He ducked in time, and it smashed against the wall.

"I was working, Min." Matt struggled to keep his voice calm, hoping her anger wouldn't escalate further. Her rage consumed her. This had been simmering for days, ever since he'd picked up Priscilla from the train station.

"You are going to leave us for her!" Min threw a plate at his head, and he stepped out of the way.

"No one is saying anything of the kind. Calm down, Min."

This was where things got tricky. Matt couldn't leave his mother alone with Min in a rage, but he needed to walk out the door until she calmed down. Min attacked Matt. With her hands clawed, she tried to rake her fingers down his face. He grabbed her by the forearms and dragged her to the settee. He sat her down and then went to his mother. Carefully he pulled his mother's shaking, whimpering form off the floor. Min attacked again, beating her fists down on his back as he dragged his mother into her room.

"You are not leaving me here with her," Min screamed. "You are not going to leave here. I can't take it! You have to stay here. You have to stay with me. I hate you, Matt! I hate you! I hate you! Don't leave me!"

Min picked up a fire poker and came at him. Matt took the fire poker from her before she could beat him with it. He tried not to hurt her as he dragged her back to the settee. He went back to his mother's room, and shut the door. His mother whimpered and cried as Min threw herself against the door, over and over again, until finally she started crying.

"I'm sorry, Matt," she wept against the door. "I'm sorry, I love you, I love Mother... I'm so sorry."

This was his cue to come out, comfort her, tell her everything would be all right. This was the agreed upon pattern. Min flew into a rage. Everyone tiptoed until she calmed down, and then she wept and asked forgiveness, and all was right until the next rage. This time, though, his mother stopped whimpering and took off her robe. Her sleeveless nightgown showed purple bruises up and down her arms.

Bruises from Min.

Horrified, Matt got to his feet. If he left his mother in Min's care, she would kill her. If he left Min and his mother in Cole's care, he was pretty certain Cole would happily strangle Min to death. Cole had a great respect for women, but he had no patience for this kind of lunacy.

I won't be able to leave them for a week to sit my exams. There is no way around it.

Matt crawled through the window of his mother's room.

A grown man reduced to crawling through a window.

He straightened up on the other side of the glass, snuck out of the yard, and ran to Rood's Mercantile. He quickly purchased locks and screws and a screwdriver.

He returned home in minutes and crawled back in through the window. His mother watched with wide eyes as he put a lock on the inside of the door so she could lock herself in and Min out. He put another lock on her window to keep Min from crawling in to get to her.

"Mother," Matt said quietly as he finished putting the last screw in the lock. "Min has been hurting you."

His mother wept as he held her hands.

"I can't stay home with you, mother. I have to work, but if she goes crazy like she just did, you can come in here and lock her out. Do you know how these locks work?"

She nodded yes. Matt wondered what her voice sounded like; it had been so long since he had heard it.

"I have an exam in Winnipeg in a couple weeks, Mother. You need to make sure that you know how to get away from her. If she hurts you again, I need to know about it."

His mother nodded again. She crawled back into her bed and lay down. Matt sat on the floor against the door. With his mother crying on one side of the door and his sister wailing on the other, he didn't dare let himself break down. Matt knew if he started to weep, he would never stop.

Chapter Nineteen

"You're up bright and early." Ada Bennett smiled at Priscilla as she settled a crisp white tea towel on her rising cinnamon buns. Her baking was arranged on a long table in the spring sunshine to rise as she worked.

"I feel much better." Priscilla poured herself a cup of tea and sat down at the table. "Thank you so much for taking me in and looking after me. I really appreciate it."

"No trouble at all. We are happy to have you here." Ada placed a hot tea biscuit, butter, and jam in front of Priscilla.

"I am concerned about one thing, and you will think it odd. Do you know where my skirt went?" Priscilla tilted her head in question.

"Matt said you asked him to hang onto it. He assured me, he has put it in a safe place for you. He must have forgotten to bring it when he brought you here. John will be going in for the mail tomorrow, and I have a Women's Christian Temperance Union meeting, so why don't we swing by Matt's tomorrow, and we can pick it up then? Is it a special sort of skirt?"

Priscilla fidgeted with the handle of the tea cup. "I'm not proud of how things worked out between me and my husband. I hate to even tell you about the skirt." Shame spiraled through her.

"I understand that things were difficult for you." Ada spoke in soft tones, sympathy evident in her voice.

Priscilla took a sip of tea while she thought about how to explain the depth of depravity she had endured, and how she had been left with no other recourse. Would this lovely, honourable woman understand? How could she?

"If you want to talk about it, you might find you feel a little better." Ada filled her tea cup and sat down across from Priscilla.

"I'm so terrified he's going to find me here, in all this peace. He would destroy it." Priscilla's heart wrenched as she thought of Richard here, in this house with this lovely family.

Ada's eyes softened in sympathy as Priscilla broke down completely.

"Why don't you start from the beginning?" Ada passed her a handkerchief.

Priscilla pressed the handkerchief to her eyes. "It's so awful. I don't want to tell you everything... I can't speak of it."

"You miscarried, Priscilla, you were dying of retained placenta. The abuse you have suffered is evident in your physical condition. I am a midwife, and I assist Dr. Davies, so you can tell me anything, and it will go no further. You can't bear this burden on your own. It's too heavy for you, my dear." Ada refilled Priscilla's cup of tea.

Priscilla took a deep breath and let it out slowly.

"We disagreed. No, that's not entirely correct. He said something, and I kept my mouth shut. I knew by then that if I said anything, it would cause a fight. I said nothing. He kept screaming at me and trying to provoke me until finally, I tried to go upstairs to go to the guest room so I could lock him out..."

Ada listened sympathetically; she reached across the table and laid her hand on Priscilla's forearm.

"I tried to outrun him, and I stumbled... I righted myself by holding onto the banister. We have this... well *he* has this sweeping staircase. Anyway, I held onto the banister, and I thought he was going to help me."

Ada squeezed her forearm.

Priscilla shook visibly, took a deep breath, and spoke through her tears.

"The butler, Mr. Moore, stood there, and he didn't do anything. I kept thinking he'd step in, and he didn't. The last man that intervened was fired on the spot."

Silence permeated the kitchen as Priscilla took a deep breath and tried to formulate all the horror into a sentence that would make sense. "He was screaming — he called me terrible names. He couldn't be sure the baby was his. He kept shouting that he wasn't going to raise someone else's child. He was so enraged. I clung to the banister. It all happened so fast. He put his hands over my wrists, and he yanked my hands off the banister, and for a second he held me in front of him, and I thought he'd help me to the landing. He didn't. He threw me down the stairs."

"I'm so sorry this happened to you." Ada squeezed Priscilla's hand.

"I tried to protect my head and my baby —I catapulted down the stairs, and when I finally came to a stop at the bottom, the butler ran to assist me. But Richard..." Priscilla covered her face with her hands. "Richard said to leave me there. Richard said if the butler helped me, he'd be fired. The butler left me there."

Ada dashed tears out of her eyes as she got up and came around the table. She gathered Priscilla into her arms; they wept together.

"I'm so sorry," Ada said simply. She held Priscilla hard until she regained her composure. As the storm of emotion quieted, Priscilla pulled back and wiped her eyes. After taking a shaky sip of tea, she took a deep breath and then plunged into the rest of the story.

"Richard was almost drunk already, but the butler gave Richard a lot more to drink. He kept pouring until Richard passed out. He and the carriage driver picked me up off the floor. At that moment, somehow, I knew that if things were so bad that he would force the staff to leave me on the floor, I couldn't stay. I knew with certainty that my life was in danger. As they helped me into a carriage, I made them go back for my skirt. They took me and my skirt to the nearest hospital and left me there. I'm certain they would have been fired." Priscilla took a sip of tea.

"So, you left the hospital and went to your grandmother's?"

"When I was discharged, I ran to the only living family I had, my grandmother Charbonneau. I didn't know what else to do."

"The skirt?" Ada tilted her head to the side.

"Please don't think badly of me. There was no other option available. In my skirt, I sewed jewelry, spoons, any heirloom I could fit between two layers of wool. Any money Richard left lying around when he got drunk, got sewn into the lining of my skirt. He won't even miss it. My skirt is my ticket out of his life. I am certain I will have to keep running."

"You may choose to keep running, or you may choose to stay here and hold your ground." Ada leaned back in her chair.

"He told me if I ran, he'd find me and he'd never let me go. I have to stay a step ahead, so if I could get that skirt, I can be out of your hair right away. You don't think Matt would steal from me..."

Ada smiled at Priscilla. "Matt Hartwell is the most honourable and kindest man on the face of this earth. You have nothing to fear from Matt."

"I stole from my husband. Do you think badly of me?" Priscilla's eyes searched Ada's.

"Stole from your husband?" Ada stirred the sugar in her tea. "No. That's not how I see it. Once you are married, everything that is yours is his and vice versa."

Priscilla let out a long sigh. "I need a plan because my grandmother is going to tell him where I am. She has likely already sent him a message."

"Why would she do that?" Ada shook her head in disbelief.

"She believes I provoked him. She thinks I need to go back and fulfill my duty."

"What do you believe?"

Priscilla met Ada's gaze, her chin lifted. "If I go back, he'll kill me and none of his staff will step in. His rage killed our unborn child. I am going to protect myself from Richard no matter what that takes."

"The W. C. T. U. will help you do it." Ada squeezed her hand in solidarity.

"Maybe I should meet with them, too?" Priscilla offered.

"That would be a great start. We'll figure out some sort of solution."

"My dream is to own my own dress shop." Priscilla's eyes lit up at the thought.

"Dress shop?" Ada's eyebrows raised in amazement.

"My mother worked as a dress designer for Emmaline Prue. Maybe you have heard of her?"

"No, sorry."

"Well, she opened up a store for her in Winnipeg, which is where she met my father. As soon as I was old enough to hold a seam ripper, I worked with her. When I wasn't in school, I was on the design floor with her. She was amazing. I really miss dress design and sewing. I loved designing hats as well. To own a dress shop and have my own line of clothing would be a dream come true. I shouldn't even speak of it — it seems so impossible. I shouldn't get my hopes up."

"It sounds like you are very resourceful." Ada smiled.

Priscilla shrugged. "Doesn't matter now. I'm not sure how I can work and run from Richard at the same time."

"Let's get your skirt, then meet the ladies of the W. C. T. U., and we'll make a plan."

Priscilla let out a breath she had been holding. "You're suffragettes?"

"Not aggressive ones," Ada reassured her. "We want to see women and children have the protection they require. The majority of domestic abuse is rooted in alcohol, as you can attest! So, we fight that."

Priscilla settled back into her chair. A smile played on her lips. The first one in many months. "I have a feeling I'm in good hands."

"We'll see. You have to get past an inquisition from Mrs. Daindridge and Mrs. Carr." Ada rolled her eyes. "The rest of the women are reasonable. Put some jam on that tea biscuit — you are really too thin."

Hope bloomed in Priscilla's heart as she slathered raspberry jam on her hot tea biscuit. In the presence of Ada Bennett and her gentle kindness, it felt as though there might be a solution.

"Rest easy." Ada patted Priscilla's hand. "There is no rush. When you are ready to work, we'll figure out your next step. Somewhere safe, I guarantee it."

Chapter Twenty

W*ho's talking?*
Min opened her eyes, expecting dark and gloom. Somehow in the night, the heavy drapes opened a crack. The light flooding in made her moan in pain. The headache raged behind her eyes and made her feel sick to her stomach.

"I have to take the stagecoach to Brandon in half an hour. Mother needs to be bathed, Min." Matt spoke softly against her closed bedroom door.

His voice felt like needles stabbing into her brain.

"I can't," she moaned into her pillow.

Shut up. Leave me. But don't leave me with her. I can't handle it today. Please leave me... stay... stay, Matt. Stay... don't leave me. Min pressed her hands against her temples, trying to find a way to make her thoughts line up. Rage simmered in her and threatened to erupt. She struggled against it, but rage always won.

You don't understand, Matt. You don't understand me. I'm so afraid you'll go.

"I have to go. I ran the water, and I made her breakfast, but she must be bathed today, Min. Tell me you'll do it," Matt demanded.

"I'll do it," Min forced herself to say the words he wanted to hear so he would stop talking. Her mind couldn't process this. The thought of dragging herself out of bed to eat seemed overwhelming. Bathing an invalid mother was impossible.

"Min, we've been over this. I can't stay. I have to work to support us. You have to do your part."

The darkness inside her plummeted deeper than before. She was powerless against it. The darkness reigned over her and obliterated any other emotion. Only fury remained. Hot, dark anger roared up through her.

You're leaving us for Winnipeg. Her thoughts howled through her mind and took on a life of their own. You're leaving me here with her alone. I hate you! Don't leave me!

She heard Matt step away from her door.

Why do you love her? Why do you care about that invalid?

The vehemence of her thoughts shocked her.

She's my mother. Min tried to hang onto that rational thought. I should care about her, but I don't care. She is a burden I can't carry... he shouldn't leave me with her. It's not fair. I am sick, too. He only cares about her illness. Not mine. I hate him. Min's thoughts unraveled and screamed at her. Oh! I hate him, and if he leaves...what will happen to me if he leaves?

Min stirred around in her room. He was waiting on the other side of the door. Waiting for her to come downstairs and help their mother. Min tried to feel something other than hatred for the woman. Nothing. In the absence of rage, there were no emotions in her heart.

Min came out of her room and watched Matt brace himself.

Good. You should be afraid of me and what I'm capable of. You can't leave me. I'm sick. I'm sick. You don't believe me. You have no idea how sick I am. Why don't you love me? Why don't you care? You only care about Mother!

"I'm sick, Matt. I am so sick. Why don't you understand that?"

"I do understand," Matt soothed. "We all have jobs we have to do. I have to drive a stagecoach so I can put food on the table. I need you to help me."

Some days she could quiet the rage; other days it bent and destroyed everything and everyone in its path. Including her.

They both heard a gentle tap at the door at the same time. Matt stiffened.

Who is here? No one comes here.

Min's eyes narrowed to slits as Matt went to the door. His hand hesitated on the door handle.

He's ashamed of me. How dare he be embarrassed?

She hid behind the door of the kitchen. She watched him through the key hole. He opened the door for Mrs. Bennett and another woman. A very beautiful, delicate, black-haired woman. Matt stepped out and closed the door behind him. Min rushed to the window and peeked out at them.

Min's lips thinned with fury. Sweat soaked her body from the heat that flushed through her as she watched Matt speak to Mrs. Bennett and the mystery woman.

You are going to leave with the black-haired woman. She's going to steal you. I hate her! I hate you! Don't leave me! Matt, don't leave me! You have to look after me! You have to! You are my brother. You can't have her. I won't allow it.

Suddenly, he came back into the house. He took the stairs two at a time and returned with a skirt.

Min's mind immediately jumped to conclusions. *Has he seen her without a skirt? Here in this house? Why does he have her skirt?* Just as she stepped forward to question him about the skirt in his possession, the door slammed shut behind him.

"How dare you!" Min stifled a scream. She stalked across the parlour to watch them through the front window. "You can't leave me, Matt... I need you... I won't let you go," Min hissed against the window. "You can't leave me here! You can't leave with her!"

Min's eyes hardened as she watched Matt bend his head to listen to the black-haired woman. Min despised her on site. She hated her small and fragile figure. The delicateness of the dark-haired woman's body made Matt look like a giant in comparison. Min tried to see through a veil of red-hot jealousy as Matt smiled at her in a way Min had never seen Matt smile before. She could read him like a book. His smile said, 'I care about you. I'll protect you. I want to make you happy. I don't love Min. I love you.' Once that thought entered her head, she couldn't shake it out of her mind.

I don't love Min. I don't love Min. She pressed her fists against her temples, trying to silence the intrusive thought. The voice in her head got louder and louder until her brain screamed one sentence. *I don't love Min.*

She picked up a vase and hurled it at the wall in the kitchen. The glass splintering around her enraged her so much, she picked up another vase and hurled it against the sink. Her mother whimpered from her spot by the cook stove. Resentment reared up and roared through her as she flew back to the window in time to see Matt look at the woman with the black hair as if he were spellbound. He reached out to carry her skirt, and then he held his arm out to her. She watched as the black-haired woman tucked her small hand into the crook of his arm.

"You can't take him from me! I hate you! You won't get away with this!" Tears coursed down Min's face as she howled into the room, "I hate you! I hate you, Matt. Don't leave me!"

***

One look at Priscilla and hope sparked in Matt's heart. The sight of her made him think there were better things ahead. He noticed her dress didn't fit. It didn't matter; she was stunning and would have been beautiful in a flour sack tied with a rope.

She's married.

Priscilla smiled at him, and he couldn't stop his eyes from sweeping over her. She held onto him as if he were an anchor in a storm.

"Thank you for keeping my skirt safe, Mr. Hartwell."

"Oh, of course."

"Is your mother all right?" Mrs. Bennett asked. "I apologize for dropping in on you unannounced. We can't stay. I know your stagecoach has to run, so don't let us detain you."

Mrs. Bennett had a way of helping people retain their dignity when there was precious little left. Matt loved her for it on a regular day, but today, with beautiful Priscilla looking on, he could have wept with gratitude.

"My mother is fine," Matt lied through his teeth. He was thrilled to leave the house. To get away from the darkness and the defeat. "Your skirt, it's rather heavy. What is it made of?" Matt asked Priscilla.

"Double wool. I know it's too hot for this time of year." Priscilla smiled tentatively.

"I see." Matt didn't see, but it didn't matter. If she wanted to wear sixty-five layers of wool, that was up to her.

"Would I be able to take the coach into Brandon for supplies? I need some material for clothes, and I have an errand to run," Priscilla asked Matt shyly. Her eyes darted between Matt and Mrs. Bennett as if what she was asking was illegal and she could be carted off to jail at any minute.

"Of course you can." Matt's heart soared with anticipation.

"Mr. Bennett will be in town for a meeting with council at 3:00 p.m. Would you drop her at council chambers at 4:00 when the meeting is done?" Mrs. Bennett asked. "I hope that is not too much of an imposition? She can catch a ride home with Mr. Bennett that way."

"I would be happy to." Matt couldn't tear his eyes away from Priscilla.

Mrs. Bennett handed Priscilla a seam ripper. "You might need this."

A look passed between them that left Matt confused. He didn't mind. Priscilla smiling made his heart sing with happiness. She took the stitch ripper from Mrs. Bennett. "I will, indeed. See you this evening Mrs. Bennett."

"All set here?" Matt smiled at Priscilla as he held his arm out. She tucked her hand into his elbow and handed him her skirt when he offered to carry it.

Matt and Priscilla went to the livery stable, and she leaned against the stall while he worked to get his team ready.

"Can I help at all?" Priscilla offered.

"No, no, I'll do it." Matt smiled at her. "This tack is far too heavy for you."

"Can I pet one?" she asked shyly.

"Of course."

You can do anything you want, as long as you keep looking at me exactly like that.

Priscilla moved cautiously to the horse nearest her. Tentatively, she stretched out a hand and rubbed his nose timidly.

"It's all right. They won't hurt you. Go ahead." He put the harness on Lucky and smiled broader as he watched delight slip across her face as she slid her hand over Bud's neck. Matt watched in surprise as she put her arms around Bud's neck and hugged him.

"I think he's blushing," Matt teased her as he put the harness on Jake next.

She grinned. "What's his name?"

"Bud."

"No." Priscilla frowned at him.

"Yes, his name is Bud."

"That's terrible. He's so beautiful. He needs a beautiful name." Priscilla frowned at Matt.

"What name would you give him?"

Priscilla's eyes met Matt's, and she suddenly became serious. She went right in front of Bud and scratched his nose. Bud leaned in close and breathed against her neck. Matt had never been envious of a horse in his life until this moment.

"What do you think your name should be?" Priscilla asked Bud, as if he would answer back. "He says he hates the name Bud and has been wondering when someone would ask him his opinion on the matter."

Matt laughed outright. "We can't have Bud dissatisfied with his name. By all means, ask him what would make him happy."

Priscilla tilted her head to the side and then pressed her forehead to Bud's as if they were actually sharing thoughts. When she pulled away, her eyes met Matt's.

"Bud would really prefer to be called Freedom."

"I see, Freedom. Has he been dissatisfied for long or just recently?" Matt played along.

"Ever since you gave him that name in the first place, he was mortified."

"Well, thankfully he has you to intervene." Matt grinned at her and reminded himself yet again that she was married. "Whatever he wants. Are the rest similarly dissatisfied? I'm not sure we have time to interview three more horses."

Matt moved towards Priscilla with the harness for "Freedom." Priscilla skittered out of the way.

Is she scared of me?

He watched her pet Jake, who was completely unaffected by her slim hand moving over his neck. Matt's breath strangled in his throat watching her hand move along the neck of the horse.

Pull yourself together, man!

Finally, despite the distraction of Priscilla in the livery stable, Matt managed to get all the horses harnessed and hooked up to the coach. Finally, the entire operation was ready to move.

Matt opened the door to the coach and held his hand out in case Priscilla needed assistance with the steps up.

"Would it be all right to be up at the front with you? Is there enough room?" Priscilla tilted her head to the side.

"There is, but it's really dusty and dirty... I don't think you want to be up there."

"Please, Matt?" Priscilla took a step forward.

Matt's heart seized in his chest.

"I really want to be out soaking up this sunshine today. Look at this day! I can't be stuck in a coach when this day is so beautiful and so perfect. Please?"

Matt would have handed her his heart on a plate if she needed it. He sternly reminded himself that she was married. Not happily, but married nonetheless. Priscilla, enchantress of horses, eyes shining with happiness, asking him if she could sit beside him, had him so distracted he could barely form words.

"Whatever you want, Priscilla. I don't think you can crawl up there. Is it all right if I just lift you up?"

"Do you think you could?" Her eyes widened.

Does she have any idea what she is doing to me?

"Yes." Matt's voice was suddenly hoarse at the thought of putting his hands on her. "I can lift you... of course... only... uh... if you are comfortable with that."

"Certainly." She smiled brightly.

She moved closer to him; he could smell flowers and fresh air. Tentatively, she reached out and put her hands on his shoulders.

Matt put his hands on her waist, and his heart banged hard when she bit her bottom lip. Matt lifted her and settled her on the buckboard. He handed her skirt up next, and she smiled down at him.

"Thank you," she said cheerfully. Her smile lit up her face. He felt even more disarmed than before. He took longer than he needed to double check the harness before crawling up beside her.

"All set?" He peeked over at her.

Priscilla leaned back against the back of the buckboard and tilted her smiling face to the sun. Matt had never met a woman like her. His mother stared vacantly out a window covered in three layers of fabric and hadn't spoken in ten years. His sister alternated between loving him and hating him. On a bad day she threw vases at his head and screamed at him. Women who said please, smiled cheerfully, and celebrated every beautiful thing in the world around them were completely foreign to him. Tension from tip-toeing around his mother and sister dissolved.

Matt's shoulders lowered an inch. An overwhelming tenderness for this pretty, delicate creature beside him overtook him. He wanted to shield her from anything that might cause her to worry. To make sure her face always shone with this sort of happiness. Matt Hartwell, known to everyone in Oakland as kind, reserved, and peaceable, knew with every fibre of his being if Richard Markus III came after this angel sitting beside him, Richard would be leaving Oakland in a casket. The violence of the thought shocked him.

"Yes, Matt! I'm ready to go!" Priscilla turned and put her hand on his forearm. "I'm doing my favourite thing today. Fabric shopping! There is nothing better. I hope you won't be bored. You can drop me off. I don't expect you to stand around and wait. I need a lot of supplies."

"Oh, no. I'll stay with you. I don't think you should be alone in the city. I couldn't forgive myself if anything happened."

"Do you think something could happen?" Her eyes clouded with worry.

He knew right then, with every certainty, he wanted to spend his life making sure her eyes never clouded with worry again. The full weight of what he dealt with at home crushed down on him. He couldn't inflict his mother and Min on her. He shook off those thoughts.

A day like this with a woman like her is a gift.

"No, but I think we should stay together. I don't mind waiting. Really," Matt said. He cleared his throat. Priscilla brightened again.

"Do you ever think you would love to be a pagan so you could worship the sun?" Priscilla tilted her head back to soak in the spring sunshine. "Isn't it the best feeling after a long winter, to let the light sink down right into your eyes and straight into your soul?"

If I had to pick something to worship, it would be you.

"I hadn't thought of it," Matt said cautiously. This girl talked to horses and secretly worshipped the sun. Matt Hartwell, against the warnings in his head, fell head over heels in love with her.

She's married. I cannot fall head over heels in love with this woman. But her husband hurt her. He hurt her so badly she nearly died. He will never hurt her again!

***

Mrs. Daindridge and Mrs. Carr stepped out of the mercantile shop as the stagecoach slowly rumbled by them. Both ladies blinked in the early morning sunshine as if their eyes were deceiving them. The same beautiful woman with glossy black hair had her hand resting on Matt Hartwell's forearm.

"Do you see what I am seeing?" Mrs. Daindridge sputtered, watching Matt Hartwell looking at the woman beside him as if she hung the moon and all the stars.

Mrs. Carr scrambled to put on her spectacles to see exactly what scandalous behavior was unfolding in front of them on Crescent Street in Oakland.

"Who is sitting beside Matt Hartwell *on the buckboard?*" Mrs. Carr gasped at the scene.

"Looks suspiciously like that lady he was carrying around just the other day," Mrs. Daindridge said out of the side of her mouth. She didn't tear her eyes away so she wouldn't miss a speck of the action.

"We really need to get to the bottom of this." Mrs. Carr spoke as if they were the moral police of Oakland. "Women running around on *buckboards!* What next? The most unladylike thing I have ever seen. What sort of woman are we dealing with, do you think?"

"It's anyone's guess." Mrs. Daindridge's eyes narrowed as she shifted her package of baking powder and brown sugar in her arms. "I heard she's from the city."

"Well, that explains a lot. Women from the city think they can get away with anything." Mrs. Carr's eyebrows furrowed with disapproval. "When Hazel Harris moved to the city with her husband, she started putting on airs. She became most tiresome to deal with."

Mrs. Daindridge had heard about those "airs" every Thursday for the past twenty years and hoped Mrs. Carr would at some point just let all that go.

"She's going to get a reputation before we even know exactly who she is." Mrs. Daindridge shook her head with that dire prediction.

"We know one thing." Mrs. Carr readjusted her spectacles as she watched the stagecoach and occupants rumble to the end of Crescent Street. "She's nothing like her hermit grandmother."

"Indeed, she is not." Mrs. Daindridge's eyes squinted as she watched masses of glossy black hair tumble down the young woman's back when she threw her head back in laughter. Matt Hartwell smiled at her as if she were the only woman in the world. Mrs. Daindridge knew with certainty if Matt wasn't careful... this woman sitting on his buckboard was going to lead him astray, if he hadn't been led astray already.

Both women shook their heads with disapproval as the woman smiled at Matt, then laughed with him.

"Well. She's doomed. Flirting and cavorting in public. Nothing ruins a girl's reputation faster than that. You mark my words," Mrs. Carr said disapprovingly. Thoughts of her daughter Cissy with Matt crashed and burned all around her as she stood, clutching her bag of Robin Hood flour.

Mrs. Daindridge knew of Mrs. Carr's aspirations to have Cissy settled as Matt Hartwell's lawful wife, and her heart softened in sympathy. Other than the unrelenting retelling of Hazel Harris's list of offenses real and imagined, Mrs. Carr was a good old soul. A woman who wound her pin curls a little too tight and often forgot one in the back of her head, which Mrs. Daindridge would lovingly retrieve for her.

"Come on, Mrs. Carr." Mrs. Daindridge was determined to cheer up her friend. "I have some leftover butter tarts from last night. Let's be wild and have a cup of tea and a tart this morning..."

"I have bread to set, Mrs. Daindridge!" Mrs. Carr was unfamiliar with tea dates first thing in the morning. First thing in the morning was for setting bread, hanging fresh laundry, and getting your day organized.

"Mrs. Carr, girls are cavorting on buckboards. It's a whole new world, a world I disagree with mind you, but I think we can risk the scandal of having a butter tart before lunch."

Mrs. Daindridge and her familiar face smiling at her with a kind offer cheered Mrs. Carr right up.

"Cissy is going to find someone, Mrs. Carr. You mark my words. She's young yet anyway."

"Young! She's nearly twenty! She's planning to be educated! It's like a nightmare I can't wake up from," Mrs. Carr sputtered as they started walking towards their residences on Lilac Street.

Mrs. Daindridge was as concerned as Mrs. Carr. Twenty was certainly getting long in the tooth for a girl to be unmarried. If only Cissy could look... well... interesting! Mrs. Daindridge struggled to put her finger on the problem. As they turned onto Lilac Street, they stopped in their tracks again.

Mrs. Charbonneau was out on her front lawn. Women on buckboards and a sighting of a hermit!

What next?

Mrs. Charbonneau saw them coming and turned the other direction. Mrs. Daindridge and Mrs. Carr immediately settled their brown-paper-wrapped parcels on Mrs. Daindridge's front verandah and followed from a safe distance away.

"She's turning..." Mrs. Carr murmured.

"She's going down Fourth Avenue," Mrs. Daindridge confirmed.

"There is only one reason to be on Fourth Avenue," Mrs. Carr whispered.

"Post Office!" they both exclaimed at the same time.

Both of them went back to Mrs. Daindridge's residence and tore into some butter tarts and tea as they picked apart why Mrs. Charbonneau, after eighteen years of quiet seclusion, decided to risk life outside Lilac Street to take a letter to the post office.

What is in that letter? Both women could not and would not settle down until they found out.

Chapter Twenty-One

After a day of fabric shopping with attentive and kind Matt Hartwell, Priscilla told herself to put him out of her mind. She couldn't. Priscilla's hope for a better life here in Oakland sparkled like sunshine on the river as she wondered if he would have a part in it. Happiness bloomed inside her as she leaned back on the porch swing at the Bennett's, took a deep breath, and let it out slowly. No matter what, this place, this day was a dream come true. Tension eased away as she settled into life at Bennett farm.

How will I repay them for the gift of healing here?

The peace Richard had so violently ripped from her slowly settled back around her. For the first time since her parents died, Priscilla felt calm.

Now, no longer fevered or in pain, it was time to go. Her pulse beat hard with anticipation at the thought.

A new start, a fresh start, with the fabric she had bought in the city. Her fingers itched to cut patterns and start sewing.

She left the porch swing and joined Ada in the kitchen.

"Could we meet with the W. C. T. U., Ada? I think it's time to figure out my next step."

"Are you sure you're ready?" Ada's forehead creased in concern. "You've been through so much. You are still weak from your ordeal. I don't want you to feel pressured to go."

"Ada, you are a good friend, but I have to provide for myself. I have to start over somehow. I have some money, and it's time I got to work. I feel stronger every day." Priscilla straightened her shoulders.

"I'll set up a meeting with Lady Harper, Mrs. Rood, and Mrs. Holt. We don't need the entire W. C. T. U. to know your situation, Priscilla. We can keep the details of your escape away from the gossips. The less people know, the safer you are. I can set that up for Thursday."

"I can't thank you enough for what you have done for me."

"Priscilla, you are a delight." Ada smiled.

***

Hillcrest was a beautiful, castle-type home that sat proudly on the bank of the river. Priscilla marveled at the shiny stained glass as it gleamed in the sun. The property was surrounded by oak trees. The little foot bridge connecting one bank of the river to the other seemed fragile, but there were two townsfolk on the bridge. The carriage stopped, and Priscilla felt a ripple of apprehension at the people that must live here. Mr. Bennett helped them both down from the carriage, and together they walked up to the front door. Mrs. Bennett knocked firmly.

"Mrs. Bennett," a butler said as the big door opened.

"We're here to meet with the W. C. T. U., Jaffrey. How are you today?"

"I am fine, thank you. Please follow me."

Jaffrey led them to the drawing room. Mrs. Holt and Mrs. Rood were already there; Lady Harper hadn't joined them yet.

"Good morning." Mrs. Holt stood up to greet them.

"Good morning." Mrs. Bennett smiled at her two friends.

"Mrs. Daindridge and Mrs. Carr didn't see you sneaking over here, did they?" Mrs. Rood asked Mrs. Holt. She wrung her hands with fear.

"Mrs. Rood, we can't live in fear of Mrs. Daindridge and Mrs. Carr. We're well within our rights to meet without the entire group." Mrs. Holt grinned at Mrs. Rood and settled back in the settee.

"I'm sorry. I feel like my nerves are on the brink." Mrs. Rood pressed her handkerchief against her lips.

"You'll be all right. We'll speak later." Mrs. Bennett put her hand on Mrs. Rood's forearm.

Priscilla's heart warmed to see Mrs. Bennett calming her friend, Mrs. Rood. She missed her friends. Richard hadn't allowed her any friends. They had slowly faded away as time went on.

"Well, Mrs. Daindridge and Mrs. Carr aren't here now. This is a matter to be handled with great delicacy. We can't have it broadcasted all over the community. Priscilla, this is Mrs. Holt. She is the mayor's wife and the treasurer of the W. C. T. U. Mrs. Rood is the secretary, but today this will all be off the record. We will be presenting the bare minimum of your experience for the W. C. T. U. to vote on."

Lady Harper swept into the room and joined the gathered ladies. Priscilla stood up to shake her hand.

"Lady Harper, ladies, this is Mrs. Priscilla Markus," Mrs. Bennett introduced her to the group. "Lady Harper is the president of the W. C. T. U."

Priscilla bristled at being called Mrs. Markus and looked forward to changing her name back to Charbonneau as soon as she could. Legally or not.

"Mrs. Bennett is our vice president, and a very good one." Lady Harper smiled at Mrs. Bennett.

The faces of the ladies were smiling and kind. Priscilla's apprehension started to ease. No need to fear.

"Welcome to Oakland, Mrs. Markus." Lady Harper handed Priscilla a cup of tea.

"I called this meeting because Priscilla is in a bit of a predicament. She had to flee from an abusive husband."

Priscilla watched the eyes of the women soften with sympathy. Priscilla's heart pounded at the thought of sharing her story.

How much detail do I give them?

"How can we help?" Mrs. Holt's voice was soft.

"I don't know what to ask for because I don't know what to do," Priscilla started tentatively.

"Why don't you tell them what you feel comfortable sharing," Mrs. Bennett suggested quietly. She reached across and put her hand on Priscilla's.

"I was married for a year and a half before I ran away." Priscilla could hear the timidity in her voice and hated it. "When we were courting, he was wonderful. He swept me off my feet. I was working as a dress designer in Winnipeg for Emmaline Prue. Maybe you've heard of her?"

"I have." Lady Harper smiled at her to continue. "You must be very good if you are in her employ."

"My mother was very good." A flash of pain sliced through her heart as she referred to her mother. "I was trained by my mother to do dress design. Anyway, Emmaline sent me over to do some alterations on Richard's sister's wedding dress. That is where I met him. We were married, but within a month I started to see through his façade. He started controlling everything. Within a year and a half things escalated until the night I left. He threw me down a flight of stairs, and I miscarried our child that night. The butler and the carriage driver took me to the hospital once Richard passed out drunk."

"Oh, my dear," Mrs. Rood gasped.

Mrs. Holt's lips thinned with indignation.

"I went to my grandmother, Mrs. Charbonneau, and she sent me back. The day I was to return, I had a high fever — some of the placenta hadn't fully expelled, so Dr. Davies and Mrs. Bennett dealt with that. Now, I am not sure if I should keep running or what I should do. If he finds me here, he would drag me back."

"So sorry to hear of this. The loss of a baby is devastating." Lady Harper spoke gently. Her eyes shimmered with unshed tears.

Does she know the pain of losing a child?

"Do you have anywhere to go? Any other family that might take you in?"

"No, I am alone. My parents are both deceased, and I have no siblings. My grandmother is my only family." Priscilla took a deep breath and let it out slowly.

"The way I see it, if you are to stay, you need a place to live and a way to support yourself." Mrs. Holt got straight to the point.

"She'll need protection, too. If her husband comes looking for her, she will be unsafe," Mrs. Bennett added.

"How would he even find her here?" Mrs. Rood asked softly.

"He'll find me." Priscilla's voice sounded strangled in her own ears. "My grandmother will tell him I'm here. She insisted I return to him."

"Did she know about... well... everything?" Mrs. Holt's hand flew to her throat.

"She wondered if I provoked him." Priscilla blinked back tears that threatened to fall. "I don't believe men are entitled to treat their wives like that, even if I did provoke him."

"Mercy," Mrs. Rood said faintly.

"I have a carriage house that is available for you to move into today." Lady Harper reached out to Priscilla and patted her arm.

"I have some money." Priscilla's face flushed hot with embarrassment.

"You have a big battle ahead of you, so wherever we can help, we will. You should keep your resources for what you are up against," Mrs. Holt said.

The ladies all took a sip of tea as they nodded their agreement.

"We'll pack my sewing machine and dress form," Mrs. Bennett offered.

"What else do you need from us, other than a place to live?" Mrs. Holt asked.

Priscilla's heart warmed at the generosity of these women. "Obviously, I can't advertise my services. If you could tell your friends and family that I am working as a dress designer in Lady Harper's carriage house, that would help me tremendously."

"I need a new tea gown." Lady Harper brightened at the opportunity in front of her. "We'll introduce you as my personal dress designer who is taking new commissions."

Priscilla's eyes met Lady Harper's. "You would do that for me?"

"Of course."

"My sister-in-law showed up from Toronto with very little luggage. I'll send her to you for a new wardrobe," Mrs. Rood commented quietly.

"Is Cora settling in?" Mrs. Bennett's eyes were soft with sympathy.

"She's not well." Mrs. Rood shook her head at Mrs. Bennett. "Perhaps you would stop by on your way home, Mrs. Bennett? She has asked to see you when it is convenient."

"My bag is in the carriage. I'll come by before I head home. What sort of illness?" Mrs. Bennett got straight to the point.

"I don't know. She won't eat or bathe. She lies in bed and cries." Mrs. Rood twisted her handkerchief.

"Gracious, I don't know if I can fix that. You might need Dr. Davies."

"Well, a friendly face might go a long way," Mrs. Rood suggested.

"I'll drop by." Mrs. Bennett patted Mrs. Rood's arm and turned to smile at Priscilla.

"This is all so kind." Priscilla put her delicate tea cup and saucer down on the tea tray. "I expected you to look at me and think I was wrong somehow." Relief flooded through her as she searched their faces for evidence of harsh judgment, but found nothing but sympathy.

"Priscilla, a man who beats his wife never stops. We have a situation in our community exactly like what you are describing, and we have tried to help her leave to protect herself and her child. Unfortunately, in her situation, if she leaves her husband, he retains all the rights over her little girl. We were all very discouraged to hear that when we looked into helping Mrs. Wheaton escape from her abusive situation. You have left, but it is the laws of the land that you are up against. You will have no rights under the law, so you'll need all the support you can get." Mrs. Bennett squeezed Priscilla's forearm.

"If I had left earlier, I might have saved my baby, though." Priscilla's hands trembled.

"Mrs. Markus, I don't speak of this other than to these few women here, but I have suffered many miscarriages." Lady Harper wiped tears from her eyes. "It is so devastating for women. Please, move into my carriage house. I would love that. I have hired a midwife from England to assist on this pregnancy, but I haven't heard if she is coming yet. So, please move in and let us help you. If she can come, there are two rooms, so you can be roommates. It is not your fault that you lost that baby. Your husband is liable for this great injustice."

"Do you think my conscience will ever believe that?" Priscilla pressed a handkerchief to her eyes.

"Were you given a choice? Did someone offer you a chance to leave so you could protect the baby?" Mrs. Rood asked politely.

"No," Priscilla whispered.

"Then you did your best in the situation you were in. You are right, though. Not everyone will see it that way. Some will judge you, even among our own group here. So, it is best if we keep this under wraps. Remember, we must not answer for the actions of others. It is quite enough to answer for our own. Your husband vowed to love you. He broke that vow." Mrs. Holt put her tea cup down. For a woman who looked exceedingly fragile, she spoke simply. Her open and fair assessment was refreshing.

Priscilla sighed a long sigh of relief. A weight lifted off her she hadn't realized she had been carrying.

"I'll have Biddy make sure the carriage house is ready for you," Lady Harper said warmly. "You are safe here, Priscilla."

Priscilla nodded and spoke past a very hard, hot lump in her throat. "Lady Harper, I know with certainty, I am not safe anywhere."

Chapter Twenty-Two

Cora groaned into her pillow when she heard a tap on her door.

Go away.

The tapping continued.

"I'm not well," Cora called out. She hoped whomever was at her door would leave her alone.

"Cora, it's Ada."

Cora dragged her body out of bed and caught a glimpse of herself in the mirror. Her hair was a huge chestnut-coloured bush around her head. She grimaced at her pale face. She hadn't bathed since she landed in Oakland, and for the life of her, she couldn't make herself care. Her nightgown hung on her frail frame.

No wonder Sol ran the minute he had a chance.

Wearily, she opened the door to her longtime friend, Ada Bennett. Ada stood on the threshold, starched and ironed, not a brown hair out of place. Her brown eyes gleamed above a big smile. It faltered and fell as she took in Cora's appearance.

"Cora!" Ada gasped. "Dear Lord, what is going on here?"

"Did anyone follow you?" Cora rested her head on the door, too weak to hold it up.

Ada looked over Cora and tsked. "Who on earth would follow me in Oakland? Heavens, if someone showed up that we didn't know, Mrs. Daindridge and Mrs. Carr would contact Cole immediately and give him detailed instructions on the proper way to arrest any stranger they didn't approve of. They don't approve of anyone, so no need to worry about unfamiliar men in Oakland! All the citizens are here and accounted for. No one is following you."

"Someone did follow me from Toronto," Cora whispered.

"Did they crawl into the stagecoach with you? Did you see them on the prairie behind you? Have you seen anyone around here?" Ada's eyebrows raised in confusion.

"No, just me and the robins," Cora admitted.

"Cora... are you sick?"

"I can't stop crying." Cora's eyes welled with fresh tears.

"You sit down. I'll make the tea. What have you eaten today?" Ada swept past her into the tiny little kitchen.

"I don't eat. I can't keep food down." Cora sunk into the nearest chair.

Ada put wood in the firebox of the cook stove, then rummaged around and found tea and a tea pot. There were meals, untouched, on the counter.

"Are you in pain?" Ada asked Cora cautiously.

"My heart is broken. I didn't realize that was actual physical pain a person could feel."

"I see."

"Do you?" Cora dragged a lap robe over herself.

"Do you want to talk about it?"

Cora rocked back and forth as she looked out the window.

"I was fired and run out of Toronto. I was up against a man so powerful and dangerous, by the end I needed a bodyguard."

"Gracious!" Ada brought the tea and cups to the table.

"I thought the bodyguard was interested in me. I thought he loved me." Cora wiped tears from her eyes. "At the first sign of trouble, he sold me out for a farm in Gimli." Cora's eyes refilled with tears as she gazed out the window. "A farm, of all things! It's humiliating."

Ada poured the tea, sat down, and leaned forward, giving Cora her full attention.

"Can you imagine anything so awful? I was two weeks short of finishing my articling with the only law firm the Dominion Woman's Enfranchisement Association could strong arm and pull strings to get me in to work. I cannot be sworn in until the articling is done. So, no job, no man, no clothes. The woman I represented, I don't even know what happened to her. I am just sick, Ada. Absolutely sick about everything. I couldn't protect her under the law." Cora's voice quivered with anxiety. There was no need to be strong in front of Ada. She wasn't a law firm full of men wanting to destroy her. Cora opened her broken heart to her friend.

"Eli's henchmen destroyed everything." Cora's voice cracked with emotion. "For the last two months, I have been followed everywhere I go. My nerves are wound so tight that I can't sleep well. I can't keep food down."

"I can help with that. I'll put together a tincture," Ada offered.

Cora slumped down in her chair further. "I don't want to feel better. I want to lie here and hide."

"Too bad." Ada's face broke out into a smile. "I won't allow it, my dear girl. I am going to put a tonic together for you that will calm you down and help you eat. I am not leaving here until you eat a meal and have a bath. This won't do."

Cora moaned and put down her tea. "I can't be bothered."

Ada got up and rummaged in her doctor's bag.

She pulled out some bottles and mixed things together.

"Ada, it won't help," Cora protested weakly.

"Open your mouth or I'm calling Wilbur in to make you," Ada threatened.

Cora glared at her friend.

"Wil and Lucy are worried sick about you. Open your mouth and drink this."

Cora obediently took the spoonful of tincture. Immediately, her stomach settled.

"What is in this?"

"Never mind, I'm going to pour you a bath, and you are going to eat a meal."

Cora didn't bother to complain because Ada had an iron will and a hard look in her eye that meant she wasn't going to take no for an answer.

An hour later, a bathed Cora ate a bowl of soup under Ada's watchful gaze, took another spoonful of tincture, and lay down on a fresh bed.

"What makes you happy?" Ada asked quietly, as she moved around the room. She opened Cora's window to let the light and soft breeze in.

"Keep that window locked, Ada," Cora croaked from her bed.

Ada shot Cora a defiant look as she raised the window higher. Cora scowled at her.

"When was the last time you were happy? Really happy. No worries on your mind, just free and happy?"

"I used to feel free and happy when I rode my bike. I also remember feeling peaceful when I sat on the sandbar at your place. Is it still there? Sometimes the river moves them around."

"It's there but a bit too chilly to be sitting on sandbars. While we wait on the weather, tomorrow you need to take your bike and ride it to the bridge and back."

"I don't have a bike here."

"Wil has one outside your door. Ride that bike tomorrow. There is a dress designer in town. She will be waiting for you to stop by. I understand you need a new wardrobe, and she needs a client. She's in the Harper's carriage house. I'll be by to check your progress. How's the stomach?"

"Better."

"How's the heart?" Ada sat down on Cora's bed.

Cora put her hand on Ada's. Her eyes filled with tears.

"There's more to this story. This pain is not just from coming up against a terrible bully. What else happened in Toronto?" Ada probed gently.

Cora took a deep breath and trusted Ada with the truth. "I was arrested in a rally."

Ada sat still and waited for Cora to continue.

"They arrested all of us. I led that rally, Ada, it was me. I was responsible. One woman lost her head and threw a brick through a window, and the entire lot of us were thrown in jail. The women with husbands were bailed out. The rest of us were left there, and they beat us..." A sob tore out of Cora at the memories of the women begging for mercy.

Ada put her arms around Cora and hugged her very hard. "That sounds terrifying, Cora. I can't imagine how that would have felt."

Ada held her while she wept. "I'm so sorry that happened to you, my dear."

Cora pulled herself together and mopped her face with a handkerchief.

"You must put that behind you. You are a couple weeks from finishing up your term, and then you will be called to the bar to be sworn in. That's where you are. You're forgetting what you have accomplished so far." Ada patted Cora's shoulder.

"I can't do it," Cora replied mutinously.

"Of course, you can't do it when you are sniveling in a bed in Oakland."

"You think I can effect change, Ada?" Cora's eyes flashed at her friend. "I can't do anything. I have experienced the brute strength of a man who delights in destroying people. Do you know what that is like? They made me watch it..." Cora looked out the window to gain her composure. "What they did to the women. How they force fed the suffragettes. They made me watch because I led the women. It was me at the front of the rally. I fought them, Ada. I tried. The beating they gave me finally stopped when they fractured my jaw, and I passed out from the pain."

Ada's eyes filled with tears for her friend as she pulled Cora back into a hard hug. "I'm so sorry."

"I have come up against the wall of power that men wield in a jail cell and in court. It is merciless. The Canadian government is not going to hear the cries of the daughters of this land. So, I won't do it. I won't have their blood on my hands, Ada." Cora's voice caught on a sob.

"Oh, Cora." Ada pulled her closer.

Cora laid her head on Ada's narrow shoulder.

"Cora, you are discouraged. That is all this is. Compound that with fear and anxiety, no wonder you aren't sleeping or eating."

"I think I passed discouragement miles ago. I think I'm in despair," Cora moaned.

"I don't blame you." Ada cradled Cora's face in her hands. "You care about the women you represent and try to assist. You've been through a lot, Cora. Hope obliterates despair, and you will find hope here. I promise it." Ada smiled at Cora.

"How do you know that?" Cora wiped her face with a handkerchief.

"I have a tincture for it." Ada grinned at her devastated friend.

Cora smiled sadly. "There is no such thing."

"Cora, my darling, hope lives and flourishes anywhere there is love. You are home with your people, Cora. Maybe you have forgotten what small town, prairie community means now that you live in a big city. If that is the case, I'm here to remind you. You are ours, and we love you." Cora's eyes filled with tears as Ada spoke from her heart. "We have watched you stand up to oppression and keep fighting. Your success has encouraged us, and we have cheered for you all along." Ada reached out and wiped away the tears that fell down Cora's face. She took Cora's hands in her own. "There is hope in Oakland, Cora. Get ready to be surrounded in it. This community knows you are equal to everything you are up against. You just need to trust us until *you* believe it again. You need to find *your* way, your own unique voice, and use it."

"What if I can't?" Cora rubbed her temples with her fingertips.

"You are brilliant. You'll figure it out." Ada patted her sad friend on the shoulder. "I love you, Cora."

"I love you, too," Cora's voice caught with emotion.

"I'm coming back to check on you in a few days."

Cora nodded.

"One more day of this and then you get up tomorrow and ride your bike. I want your word," Ada demanded.

"You're terribly bossy, Ada Bennett."

Ada tucked her in and smoothed her hair back. "I know. If you're still in bed, I'm bringing Dr. Davies, and we'll do a full assessment."

Cora took Ada's hand and squeezed it.

"I will ride my bicycle tomorrow. I promise."

"Go see Priscilla and get some new 'drab spinster-wear' you are so fond of. You'll feel like yourself in no time." Ada laughed as she let herself out.

Chapter Twenty-Three

Priscilla settled into the carriage house and got to work. Her first dress was completed in three days for herself. She knew she would not be taken seriously as a dress designer if she wore cast offs. She smiled with excitement when there was a knock at her door. Her first client after Lady Harper.

"Good morning," Priscilla said as she opened the door.

"Good morning." Cora held out her hand, and Priscilla shook it. "I understand you are a dress designer?"

"Absolutely." Priscilla smiled brightly and let Cora into the house.

"I need an entirely new wardrobe. I need to be outfitted from the skin out."

"Are you Cora Rood? I heard you were coming and that your wardrobe was a little thin. I'm Priscilla. I just moved here from Winnipeg."

"Yes, Cora Rood, just here from Toronto."

"Toronto!" Priscilla went to her cook stove to make tea.

"My brother and sister-in-law are Wilbur and Lucy Rood."

"I met her a few days ago. She's with the W. C. T. U., right?" Priscilla took two tea cups down from the cupboard.

"Yes." Cora immediately felt welcome in Priscilla's home.

"Let's have a cup of tea, and then I'll take your measurements, and we can discuss what you need."

As Priscilla handed her a tea cup and saucer, her hands shook. The tea sloshed over the brim of the tea cup into the saucer. When Cora took the cup, her hands shook harder. Their eyes met over the cup, and they had a moment of immediate understanding.

"Are you all right, Miss Rood?" Priscilla bit her lip in worry.

"I thought I was," Cora admitted.

"Your hands are shaking." Priscilla's happy smile fled as she put her hand on Cora's forearm.

"So are yours."

They looked away from each other to try to gain some composure. Finally, they met each other's gaze again and took a deep breath.

"I'm running from a really terrible man," they both said at exactly the same time.

The tears fled as they started to laugh. Slowly at first. There was nothing funny about Richard Marcus III or Eli Pitman, but somehow, safe in this little carriage house in Oakland, the fact that they were both on the run seemed hilarious. Tears of fear and anxiety fled as they laughed so hard they had to hold onto their sides.

"Would you like to talk about it?" Cora asked sympathetically, when they finally got control of themselves.

"Miss Rood," Priscilla started.

"Please, call me Cora."

"Cora, I'm finding the less I talk, the better. We are going to have a fun morning designing dresses. If I talk about him, it steals my joy. I have learned that no one gets to steal my joy. Let's get to work." Priscilla put her tea cup down. "Unless you want to talk..."

"Heavens, all I've done is talk. Wilbur is hounding me day and night. Why are you sleeping so much? Why aren't you eating? You have to get out of this cottage... He's relentless." Cora rolled her eyes.

"It sounds like he loves you very much." Priscilla picked up her curly tape measure.

"He does. So does Lucy. I am not ready to tell him everything. It's too much. He'll be wild I didn't tell him before. Anyway, the first thing I need is a swimming costume."

"Swimming costume?" Priscilla's eyebrows raised in surprise.

"I'm going to need that first."

"I don't have material for that, I'm afraid, but I can certainly get it. Are you some sort of competitive swimmer?"

"No." Cora took a deep breath. "I used to be a lawyer."

"Lawyer!" Priscilla gasped.

"Not as glamorous as it sounds." Cora lifted her arms as Priscilla pulled the tape measure around her waist. "Ultimately, the government of Canada finally allowed me to take my training and then the "gentlemen" of Canada set out to destroy me. So, here I am. Destroyed. I need a swimming costume because the only thing I need right now is a sandbar and a big thermos of lemonade."

"Sandbar?" Priscilla's head tilted in confusion.

"They are a delight. These fingers of sand that show up in different spots every spring. There's a perfect one down the hill from Ada's house. I can't wait to get there."

"Swimming in a river?" Priscilla's nose wrinkled in disgust.

"I think it's the only way to survive what I've been through," Cora said gravely.

"If you say so." Priscilla shook her head. She jotted down the measurement on a note pad. "It sounds muddy and dreadful."

"Very muddy and absolutely delightful."

Priscilla laughed. "Well, let's get you measured, and we will start on that first. Anything else?"

"I need a corset that lets me breathe while I ride a bicycle."

"Bicycle!"

"I need these two things desperately."

Priscilla jotted down notes.

"Also, I don't like a lot of frills. I prefer a shirtwaist."

"I see." A smile tugged at Priscilla's lips.

"What do you see?" Cora frowned.

"I see that you are going to take some of the pressure off me." Priscilla laughed. "When they see you wheeling through Oakland in a shirtwaist and crying on a sandbar, suddenly I won't be the only thing Oakland is talking about."

"Are they talking about you?" Cora tilted her head to the side. There was a delicacy about Priscilla that Cora instantly responded to. Priscilla was a gentle soul. Somehow, the thought of someone hurting her seemed especially repellent. It was as if there were a light in her Cora didn't want to see extinguished.

"Ah, Cora, they have talked of little else. Why is she running away? Why isn't she doing her duty? You've made your bed — you have to lie in it. If you can think of a negative thing to say, it's been said."

"I'm sorry that you are facing that sort of criticism."

There was a movement in the front yard — a very tall, very broad man was near the woodpile.

Royce has found me here! Cora dove under the table.

Priscilla peeked under the table at her new friend in alarm.

"That is only Cole McDougall, the constable. You can come out from underneath the table." Priscilla spoke quietly.

"Are you quite certain?" Cora hissed in fear.

"Yes."

"Why... what is he doing in your yard?" Cora's heart calmed down enough that she could crawl back out from under the table.

"Matt met with the men once I was moved in here. They agreed to patrol around here in case Richard, my husband, comes to Oakland."

Cora dropped into a chair and tried to calm down.

"Goodness, I didn't recognize Cole in a uniform!" Cora's hand shook as she picked up her tea cup.

"He checks things while Matt drives the coach. Cora, even though my grandmother tried to send me back, coming here was the best thing I did. I feel safe here. I hope you start to feel safe very soon."

"There's been no sign of Eli's henchmen, so I am starting to calm down." Cora's hand trembled so hard she put down the tea cup.

"Looks like it." Priscilla scoffed. "I'm glad. Now, Cora, it's time to talk colours."

"I have no idea. You figure it out. I wear black and olive green."

"Oh, that won't do. Your complexion... black... no."

Cora remembered a similar conversation with Adeline, who insisted on making her look like a tart. She fervently hoped Priscilla would let her keep some dignity!

"I had to wear black as a lawyer. It is mandatory."

"Are you working as a lawyer here?" Priscilla challenged her new friend.

"No." Cora's voice hardened.

"Then let's take black off the table and leave it off." Priscilla shuddered.

Memories of Adeline complaining about her black gowns made Cora smile fondly, even as she worried about her.

"Terrible for your complexion." Priscilla's eyes raked over Cora as she assessed her hair and skin. "You need nice rich chocolate browns, caramels, and cream. You need some purple."

"Purple!"

"Trust me." Priscilla smiled. Cora had seen that sort of look before on Mr. Crest — it was the smile of a professional who knew what she was doing and didn't have to explain.

"I'm in your capable hands. Just make sure the bathing costume isn't purple! Oakland would never recover from that sort of scandal," Cora warned.

"We'll see." Priscilla grinned. After a few minutes, Cora's face broke into a smile, too.

"If the purple is almost black..." Cora relented.

Priscilla laughed and shook her head no.

***

Cora let herself into her cottage and smiled at Priscilla insisting on purple — she was as pushy as Adeline. Her eyes lit up at the bouquet of flowers and a small plate of sugar cookies on her small table. Lucy Rood was the world's greatest sister-in-law. Her smile faded as she saw a stack of correspondence beside the vase of flowers.

Four letters.

One from Mrs. King, one from Lady Bronwyn, one from the Upper Canada Law Society, and another from Gimli, Manitoba. Her breath caught as she picked up the letter from Sol. She ran her fingertips over his handwriting. Straightening her shoulders, she went to her cook stove, and with grim determination to protect her heart, she lit a fire and burned his letter.

Next, she opened the letter from the law society.

Dear Miss Rood,
It has come to our attention that you did not finish your term of articling at Roth and Levine.
In order to be sworn in on July 25 with the rest of your class, you need to complete another two weeks of articling before June 30, 1904.
Regards,
Malachi Marks
Upper Canada Law Society

Cora frowned and braced herself before she opened the letter from Mrs. King.

Dear Cora,
Please send me a telegram at your earliest convenience to inform me of your health and well-being. Mr. Pitman has suspended the initiative at Hope House until further notice. My fear is he has run you out of Toronto.
The D. W. E. A. is very concerned that you have not finished your term of articling with Roth and Levine. The law society has contacted the D. W. E. A. gloating over this fact, and we have given them your forwarding address.
Obviously, it is our hope that you will be sworn in as a barrister on July 25 with your class. The entire D. W. E. A. is shocked that you have run to Oakland. I know Eli is behind it. If I can assist you in any way, please know I am here for you and at your disposal.

Your humble servant,
Mrs. Jean King

Biting into a sugar cookie, Cora braced herself to open Lady Bronwyn's letter.

Dear Miss Rood,
I hope this correspondence finds you well.
It has come to the attention of the D. W. E. A. that you have not finished your term of articling at Roth and Levine...

Cora skimmed over the ranting and exhortation to return to Toronto at her earliest convenience. Cora's heart hardened further — the women's rights movement would have to find another champion. She put down the letter and pulled out her paper and pen to begin her return correspondence.

She wrote a similar letter to both Mrs. King and Lady Bronwyn. She started by apologizing and told them both that she was staying in Oakland until further notice. She agreed with them — it was a shame that she could not finish the articling — and at present had no plan in place to resolve that unfortunate situation.

Yes, the women's rights movement would have to plod along with a new champion. Cora wrote that her health and well-being had to take precedent in this matter. She ended both letters with the reassurance that if her circumstances changed, they would be the first to know. She knew Lady Bronwyn would shake with rage when she read it and would not take no for an answer. Cora shrugged. She was far from Toronto and a grown woman; she could do as she pleased. Lady Bronwyn had left her in a jail cell at the mercy of the guards; she didn't owe her anything.

Cora refused to return correspondence to Malachi Marks and the Upper Canada Law Society. He would gloat with the rest of the benchers. Malachi's words rang in her ears. "I told you a woman didn't have the mental tenacity to practice law. The courts are for men, not women. The fairer sex is too delicate, too hysterical — no logic in women, only emotion." Although remembering his hard statements irritated her, she didn't have the strength to go back and fight him.

In the war on women's rights, I give up. My heart is not in it.

Sol's correspondence burned to a crisp in her cook stove. She hardened her heart as she remembered how she felt when she faced Eli alone. Sol Stein could rot on his precious farm in Gimli; she wouldn't give him another thought.

***

As Cora returned correspondence, Priscilla got straight to work on the clothing Cora needed. After a few hours of work, the beauty of the spring day called her out of her carriage house. She grabbed her hand bag and set off for the post office. She walked down Crescent Street with a newfound happiness she clung to with both hands. Two clients gave her a tremendous bolstering of confidence. As she slipped down Crescent Street, she thought about a corset design that would allow for bicycling. The thought of designing a new corset was exciting. Priscilla had forgotten what it felt like to face a new design challenge. Her face broke into a smile as she drank in the beauty of a Manitoba day in May. The lilacs were almost blooming, and she found herself wondering how many vases the carriage house had because she planned to put lilacs in every nook and cranny of her new home.

She caught a reflection of herself in the window of the post office. On the outside, Priscilla looked like any other young lady. This outfit, in particular, was so cutting edge every eye in Oakland was riveted to her. Her hat dipped over her left eye. She had layered it with plumes from an ostrich, so it was outrageous... stunning. Emmaline Prue would have approved. Her dress was soft grey and plum. The deep plum accented her eyes. She glanced at herself in the window and felt beautiful and happy. In the reflection, she noticed a man coming toward her.

Immediately upon seeing him, Priscilla broke out into a cold sweat under her bodice. She heard her shoes clip on the boards of the sidewalk as she jogged toward the post office. Her fear escalated as he lengthened his steps. He didn't need to jog to catch up.

***

Matt sighed as he got his mail. He was weary already from dealing with Min. Thankfully, Cole drove the stagecoach for him because Mother was still too agitated to leave alone. Min had insisted on going to the mailbox with him.

Why is she suddenly insisting on checking the mail?

If she saw correspondence from the university it would set her off. She had started accusing him of sitting other exams. Townsfolk were kind to her but kept moving as they went to the post office. There was a look to her that made them nervous. He sifted through the mail and saw the letterhead for the University of Manitoba.

Min's eyes clamped down on it as he debated opening it and thought better of it. He tucked it under other correspondence and cursed himself for his cowardice. Just the thought of Min in full rage over a letter from the University of Manitoba made him tired. He was about to put the letter in his breast pocket when he saw a fairly outrageous hat scurry by the window. Immediately, worried it was Priscilla, he thrust the mail into Min's arms.

He bolted out of the post office as a man approached Priscilla. Matt's hands clenched to fists at his side as he saw her step back, away from the threat of the man in front of her. Matt's mind narrowed to one thought — Priscilla is in danger. He dashed down the block, just as the man tried to hand her an envelope. Matt's eyes were slits of anger as he watched her take another step away.

"You, there," Matt said in a voice that didn't sound like him.

The man turned to look at Matt.

"Mrs. Markus, are you all right?" Every muscle in Matt's body tensed, ready to defend her.

"I... I don't know..." Priscilla's eyes were wide. "He says he's a..."

"I'm here to give Mrs. Markus a choice." The man gave Matt a hard look and then returned his attention to Priscilla.

"You can come with me, and I can escort you back to your lawful husband, or I can give you these papers, and we will see what a court does with you." He spoke to her like a criminal who had escaped from jail.

Matt yearned to smash his fist right into the man's smug face, but he held himself back. The blood drained from Priscilla's face.

"She's not going anywhere with you," Matt growled. He moved in between them so his body blocked Priscilla's from any possible harm.

"Does he speak for you?" the man demanded.

Priscilla peeked around Matt's shoulder.

"Is this who you left Richard for?" The vulgarity of what he suggested was so flagrant Matt ached to beat him to a pulp for the implied insult to Priscilla.

Priscilla swallowed hard. "No."

"I was to give you an option to return before I served you with these papers. So, you won't return then?"

"You heard her." Matt spoke through gritted teeth. His patience was stretched on a good day, and Matt hadn't had a good day for over ten years.

"I will not return, now or ever." Priscilla's voice shook with fear.

The man reached around Matt and handed her the envelope. "He'll see you in court."

He turned on his heel and walked away.

Priscilla shook hard as she held on to the papers. Once the man was far enough away that Priscilla wasn't in physical danger, Matt turned to her. She pressed her hand to her forehead and swayed a bit. Immediately, he put his arm around her waist.

"It's all right," he murmured into her ear. "I'll take you home."

"Oh, you mustn't," Priscilla whispered back. "What would people say?"

"Can you stand up?" Matt's eyes clouded with worry.

It was tricky to see around the hat unless he held his head at a certain angle. Tears gathered in her eyes, and her body shook with fear.

"I'll take that as a no." Matt pulled a handkerchief out of his pocket and very carefully wiped the tears from her cheeks as they spilled down. "I'm going to walk you home."

"What about... what do you think... what will..." Priscilla was so distressed she couldn't form a sentence. Her body trembled against his.

"Mrs. Mark..." Matt stopped speaking as he watched pain flash across her face at being called by her married name.

"Please, please don't ever call me that again. I can't bear it."

"Priscilla, let me walk you home in case he follows you. You can barely stand up. I can't leave you here like this."

Priscilla dashed tears from her eyes and nodded her agreement.

As Matt and Priscilla made their way toward the back alley of Crescent Street, two sets of critical eyes followed them. Mrs. Daindridge and Mrs. Carr watched the spectacle of Matt with the dark-haired granddaughter of Mrs. Charbonneau. Their eyes widened as they watched them together, heads bent as they turned down the back alley.

"No good can come of this. They say she is a married woman on the run," Mrs. Carr hissed at Mrs. Daindridge.

"I heard he is so besotted with her, he might even postpone his exams! Can you imagine? A married woman has turned his head. What is he thinking?" Mrs. Daindridge shook her head. "The state of marriage is under attack, Mrs. Carr. Women like her leading men like Matt Hartwell astray — it's the beginning of the end."

Chapter Twenty-Four

M att opened the door to the carriage house and helped Priscilla to the settee. She took off her hat and placed it carefully on the table. Something filmy and lacy hung from a hanger. His eyes swept over it, and he immediately blushed as he realized what he was looking at. He found himself wondering what it looked like on a woman, a woman like Priscilla, and thought he better turn his attention elsewhere.

He went to the cook stove and put a kettle on for tea. He didn't want her opening the letter alone. His eyes swept around the room. She had a dress form with a dress partially pinned on it. Her work area was neat and tidy. The big dining room table was covered in material with a pattern pinned to it.

"I didn't tidy up for company." Priscilla wiped her eyes and looked up at him from the settee. He longed to reach out and brush those tears away for her. Instead he cleared his throat.

Matt took the kettle off the cook stove and made the tea. He looked out her kitchen window, his eyes scanning for the man who had served her with papers. He hoped Min had gone home. If she followed him here, who knew what sort of scene she would cause.

He poured Priscilla a cup of tea and came back to the settee with a tea cup and saucer. She tried to take the cup from him, but her hands were shaking so hard the tea sloshed over the edge of the cup.

"I'm sorry," she whispered.

"I'll set it down. It needs to cool a little bit anyway," Matt suggested.

Priscilla let her hands fall to her lap.

They sat together awkwardly as the clock ticked on the mantelpiece. Matt could have happily taken that clock and fired it from the bridge into the river to silence it. The escalating violence in his mind concerned him. Everything bothered him. Everything.

Priscilla straightened her shoulders and took a deep breath. She took the envelope and carefully, slowly opened it.

"Matt, I don't think I can do it. I don't think I can read it... I'm a coward. I'm so afraid of him. What do you think it will say?" Her eyes filled with tears.

Matt sat beside her and cursed Richard Markus III. He fought the desire to gather her into his arms.

"I don't know." Matt's jaw clenched in fury. Whatever it was, it wasn't good.

He saw so much suffering in her eyes; he didn't dare ask another question.

She put the papers down without opening them.

"Just open it, and then you'll know what you're dealing with, and we can face it... well... we can get... I will get help for you... just open it," Matt finished lamely.

"Can you read it?" Her eyes met his.

Matt would have happily stopped a bullet for her if it would take the pain out of her eyes.

"Of course. You drink your tea, and I'll read it."

She handed him the letter and picked up her tea.

Matt unfolded the paper and read through it. At first, as he read the petition for divorce, relief flooded through him. However, as he continued to read, he swallowed hard as the bile rose in his throat at what Richard Markus III demanded of Priscilla.

"Is it very bad?" Priscilla's voice shook. Matt reached out and took the tea cup and saucer from her and placed them back on the tea tray. He took her small trembling hands in his own and held them.

"Priscilla, it is a petition for divorce." His eyes searched hers, gauging her reaction.

"That's all right." She managed a bright smile. "That means he knows it isn't working. Maybe he feels bad about what happened. Maybe the butler told him about the miscarriage and he wants to let me go..."

"No, Priscilla." Matt's slim grip on propriety fled. "It's not all right. He's petitioning you for divorce on the grounds of...well... on...oh my goodness, I can't even say it... on the grounds..."

"Matt, how bad can it be?" Priscilla tilted her head and smiled at him. "If he is petitioning for divorce, this is good, right? We are both in agreement."

Matt didn't have the heart to read it to her. Hands shaking with horror, he handed her the paper and watched her face fall as she read the last paragraph.

She closed her eyes and opened them. The petition was still in front of her and still saying the same horrible thing.

"...that the said Priscilla Markus did on the 30 day of April A. D. 1904, withdraw from cohabitation with your petitioner and has kept and continued away from him without any just cause whatsoever and from thence hath refused and still refuses him conjugal rights.

Your petitioner therefore humbly prays that your Lordships will decree a restitution of conjugal rights to your petitioner from the said Priscilla Markus and that your petitioner have such other and further relief as to your Lordships seem meet." Priscilla's voice shook with horror as she read the petition out loud.

Restitution of conjugal rights!

***

Priscilla's heart galloped with terror. Any conjugal right she was forced to submit to was rape. The petition of divorce was no such thing. This petition was alerting the court to the fact that they were legally married and he needed the court to order her home to render conjugal rights. Her chest tightened in fear.

Surely there are laws to protect me.

"Can he... can he do that?" Priscilla pressed her hand against her lips.

"I don't know." The look Matt gave her was tortured.

"I'll have to run. I'll have to pack up tonight." She turned to face Matt; her eyes darted around the room. "Can you take me to the train tomorrow?"

"Where are you going to go? You can't run from this. We'll get you a lawyer. Immediately. There has to be a way to fight this. Surely the court can't order you back to... well to render... there has to be a way to fight this, Priscilla."

Priscilla's eyes filled with tears. The tentative grip on her sanity started to slip. Helplessness crushed down on her. She could run, but where and for how long before he found her there?

"But if a lawyer drafted the petition, surely he would know if the courts could order it or not." The peace she had carefully crafted and clung to splintered apart. "It seems to me that the courts can order it, Matt." She tried to blink back tears.

Matt leaned into her. "I'll speak to Lord Harper and see which lawyer he suggests, and then we will have this divorce petition looked at straight away."

"Would you?" Tears slid down her cheeks. He took the handkerchief from her hand and very gently wiped her tears away for the second time that day. From a cheek only recently healed from Richard Markus III's fist.

"Of course, I will," he whispered.

She put her hand over her mouth to stifle a sob.

"I'm sorry. I just can't seem to stop crying... Matt... what will happen if he comes here? If the courts *can* make me go back, what will happen to me?" She tried to blink the tears out of her eyes.

"No one can make you go back, Priscilla. I won't let him force you back. I promise. It's going to be all right. You're safe here. You're safe in Oakland. I'll talk to Cole, and we'll make sure you have more protection."

Priscilla's eyes widened. "Matt, he'll kill you. He's really big, and he's terrible — he never stops once he starts." She put her hand on his forearm. "You can't fight him — you won't win. Promise me you won't ever fight him. I mean it." Priscilla took her hand back so she could wring her hands in fear.

Matt covered her hands with his own. "Shhhh. It's all right."

"It's not all right," Priscilla wept. "He beat the carriage driver once."

"What?" Matt frowned.

"He was upset with me. A gentleman spoke to me at a fundraiser, and Richard hated that, and he always was upset with me for speaking to men! Anyway... we were coming home, and he started screaming at me in the carriage, and the carriage driver stopped the carriage."

She twisted her handkerchief in her hand.

"Richard went crazy," Priscilla whispered. "He got out of the carriage, and the driver got down to see what was going on. Richard wrestled the horse whip from him and beat him with it."

"This sounds harsh maybe, but better the carriage driver than you." Matt handed her a fresh handkerchief from his own pocket.

"Oh, Matt," she whispered. "When he was done with the carriage driver, it was my turn."

"With a horse whip?" Matt gasped.

Priscilla nodded her head yes.

Matt closed his eyes to regain his composure. When he opened them, she met his gaze.

"Priscilla, I want you to listen to me very carefully. Stop crying. Please. Just stop. I can't bear it. Listen. You need a lawyer. That's all. There has to be a way to fight this."

Priscilla trembled as she looked away.

"Look at me, please."

Priscilla's eyes met Matt's.

"Priscilla, I swear to you, I promise you right now, you are safe here, and I will not let anything happen to you. We are going to see a lawyer tomorrow, and we are going to get this all sorted out. I don't want you to be scared. You are going to be fine. But, as a precaution, we are going to move you to the basement of Hillcrest. There is a room in the basement, fully furnished, for when there are prairie storms. We'll settle you down there tonight, and then you will be in earshot of Jaffrey and Lord Harper. Let me just settle that with Lord Harper first, and then I'll move your things right away."

"I think that would be best. I didn't want to say anything, but I am really scared to stay here alone."

"Of course, you are," Matt agreed. "You pack up your things, and I will make the arrangements. Are you all right for a few minutes?"

Priscilla nodded.

Matt flew to Hillcrest and met with Lord Harper, who told Matt that the basement was empty and she was welcome to stay. Armed with that good news, Matt went back to the carriage house.

"We are going to move you under a cover of darkness. That man that delivered the petition might be hovering — better if he doesn't know where we have relocated you. You just take the afternoon to get packed up, and maybe you should lie down."

Priscilla swallowed hard. "I'm better, thank you. Matt, I couldn't sleep a wink. I would rather work. It will take my mind off things."

"Don't wear yourself out," Matt commanded. "I'll be back tonight."

Matt got up and put his hand on the handle of the door and turned back to look at Priscilla. She gave him a watery smile.

"I'll be fine, Matt. Thank you for bringing me home and arranging things for me to stay at Hillcrest. I really appreciate it."

"I'll be back at ten," Matt promised. Finally, he tore himself away from her to go home and face the wrath of Min.

***

A block from home, he heard screaming coming from Glenwood Street. He broke into a run and was third on the scene after Dr. Davies and Cole. Instinctively, Matt knew Min had gone too far if Dr. Davies and Cole were at the house. A familiar wave of hopelessness washed over him. He didn't want to admit that he was completely defeated by this woman, who was so out of control he couldn't bear another day. He hesitated as he placed his hand on the doorknob. For a second, Matt rested his forehead against the hard wood of the door. Tears built behind his eyes as he wondered how far she had gone this time.

What options are available for a man dealing with a deranged sister and fragile mother?

Matt straightened up and entered the house in time to see Cole handcuffing and restraining Min while Dr. Davies pushed a hypodermic needle into her upper arm. Amidst the chaos, she fought them like a wild animal.

"Dear Lord!" Matt exclaimed. The house was in utter shambles. She had shredded the heavy curtains with a knife, so they were in tatters; the pillows were stabbed through. She had tried to light the house on fire.

"How is Mother?" Matt's throat tightened in fear.

Cole held Min down and within seconds Min slumped across the settee. Both the restraints and the drugs swimming through her veins silenced her. Finally.

"Min assaulted your mother, Matt." Cole's face was neutral, professional, as if he walked in on daughters assaulting their mothers every day of the week. "Dr. Davies will document the extent of the damage for trial. I'm taking her to jail today."

Matt sat down heavily on a chair at the realization that Min was off his hands, and by the look of Cole's face, indefinitely. God forgive him, his spirit lightened at the thought of Cole dragging her away and incarcerating her. Close on the heels of that lightening of spirit was guilt. Guilt that made him feel hot and cold at the same time. His conscience beat him with waves of thoughts.

Could I have done something differently?

He pulled his hands over his face. Cole came to him and pulled up a chair.

"Dr. Davies is in your mother's room. The beating was brutal, Matt."

"Will she live?" Matt's eyes were hard; he watched Min's still form while he spoke.

"Her arm is broken. She has severe bruising, contusions... How long has this been going on, Matt?" Cole spoke gently.

Matt took a deep breath because he was ready to start crying or screaming or a combination of the two.

"Too long, Cole. I don't think I can look at the damage and not strangle Min to death," Matt said to Cole with such honesty Cole put his hand on Matt's shoulder.

"Your mother is distraught. I think it would calm her down to see you."

Matt scrubbed his hands over his face. "You must be appalled."

"Appalled? Why? This isn't your fault. None of it is your fault. It doesn't matter, Matt. It's over. Min is going to be tried for attempted murder, and it's obvious that she is an incurable. Dr. Davies will testify to that. She's going to be in some sort of facility for a very long time, so let's get your mother squared away, and then we'll figure out your next step. You've been putting up with far too much Matt. I wish I had known."

"Oh yes?" Matt asked as he stood up. "And just what would you have done, Cole? Why burden you with this?"

"I'm your friend, Matt," Cole said simply. "You're my best friend. Why didn't you tell me?"

Matt wiped at the tears that were forming in his eyes and looked away from Cole.

"When you deal with something like this, day in and day out... it's really hard to explain the shame that surrounds you. I felt ashamed and overwhelmed. Slowly, every single day, I lost a tiny bit more hope until finally, the hope was gone, and I was empty. I wanted to walk away. Then I felt guilty because these women are my responsibility. I should love them enough to bear it. It's hard to live a life without any hope for a better day."

"I did notice your temper flared easier, that you were having a hard time coping with..."

"Is it any wonder?" Matt shouted as he rounded on Cole. He didn't want to hear any criticism. He couldn't handle it.

How dare Cole speak to him about not coping!

Matt buckled under the weight of holding a family together for years. He yearned to snap but couldn't afford the luxury.

"Do you have any idea," Matt growled at his best friend, "what it is like to come home every day to darkness? Just utter darkness. No light, no joy, no hope. Never, ever any hope. If you feel any tiny slice of joy in your life, you hide it because it will be attacked. It's like living in a dark hole. Every day, I would leave for work and wonder what she would do in my absence. No one could help me, no one could fix it, and so I kept going and dreamed about a day when it would be over. Every day, the day starts and it's *worse*. Slowly, I realized the only thing that is going to change it would be so devastating that I couldn't even hope for it. Dealing with this, day in and day out, planted a bitter seed of anger in me. The anger grew until it was all I could see. I haven't felt hope that things would improve for so long, I don't even know what that feels like now."

Matt dashed at the tears as they coursed down his face.

"Matt, I'm so sorry. I had no idea."

"Of course, you didn't. You wonder why I'm angry? You dare to suggest I'm not coping? You couldn't cope with fifteen minutes in this hell, never mind ten years of it."

"You're right, Matt. I'm really sorry that this has been going on. I can't even tell you how sorry," Cole finished lamely.

Matt slumped in his chair and faced Cole with such a tortured look on his face, Cole immediately softened his tone.

"Matt, I don't know what you've been through. I don't. I can only guess... please, just listen. Please. Dr. Davies is going to help you. Tell him what you told me."

"What do you think is going to happen now? I can't bathe her. I can't be here to look after her. I don't have any... I just can't..."

"I don't know, Matt. If Dr. Davies can't figure out a solution, we'll run this by Ada Bennett. When Maggie died, I thought I would never be able to cope, but Ada was a rock. She helped me a lot. Matt, I don't know much about women or their ways, but I think the women, and Ada in particular, hold all the hope in Oakland. They can get to the bottom of a situation and come up with solutions men don't think of. Ada will know what to do." Cole turned from Matt for a brief moment. "When Maggie was dying and there was nothing else to be done, Ada was there, in the room, watching Maggie until she died. It was unbearable pain, and somehow Ada made me believe I could survive it."

A moment of silence passed while Cole pulled himself together.

"When it was over, she..." Cole stopped speaking for a moment and regained his composure. "I don't even know what to tell you about Ada Bennett except, she's a miracle. If anyone can step in here and sort out your mother, it's Ada."

Matt wiped his eyes on his sleeve. Min started stirring on the settee. Matt went to her and crouched down to look her in the eye.

She spat at him.

"Careful, Matt. She's restrained," Cole's voice was low and calm.

He wiped away her saliva and held her face between his hands so that she couldn't look away from him.

"Cole is taking you to jail tonight, Min," Matt said so softly Cole moved closer to hear him. Matt was certain Cole thought he would need to intervene. "You've beaten our mother, and for that, I will stand in a trial and make sure you get the maximum sentence. You are a horror of a woman. I will feel no sympathy and no regret when they haul you away and you never see the light of day again."

Min started screaming and raging against the restraints when Matt let go of her and turned his back on her. It was the ultimate insult to Min, who cursed him from the settee.

"Could you take her now? I can't stand to look at her."

"Of course, Matt." Cole took a step toward Matt. Matt held his hands up.

"I'm barely getting through this. I have to check on my mother, and Priscilla's husband has come back for her with a petition. I was worried about her safety staying on her own, so I am moving her into the basement of Hillcrest tonight."

"Matt, she's married. Why don't you let me..."

"I know she's married. You think I don't know that! She's been beaten — she's been defeated by her husband, and I know how it feels. She is the only speck of light, Cole..." Matt stopped before he sobbed. "She has no one. She can't face what she is up against alone. I'll stand by her."

"You're going to get hurt, Matt." Cole issued a warning Matt didn't want to hear. All he could see was Priscilla's head tipped back enjoying the sunshine. It was the first glimmer of joy, hope, and light Matt had experienced in ten years. He was going to hold onto her with both hands and deal with the hurt when it happened.

How will I survive if she has to run?

"You know something, Cole," Matt said through teeth that were gritted so hard his jaw ached. "There is no realm of hurt left for me. I'm not letting Richard Markus III put a hand on Priscilla again. I will not stand by and do nothing when Priscilla's in danger."

"No one is suggesting that, Matt. She is married, and your heart is already involved. Let me step in if need be. I won't let her get hurt, and you won't be getting involved with a married woman."

The sheer size of Cole would stop anyone from hurting Priscilla.

"You wouldn't let anyone step in if someone threatened Maggie."

"Maggie was my wife. It's different. I swore to protect her, and that was my privilege. This, however, is a *married* woman." Cole tried and failed to drop the warning tone. "Just think it through, Matt. As you said, you've been through enough."

Matt clamped his mouth shut and watched Cole drag Min off the settee and to the front door kicking and screaming.

"Please, get her out of my sight. That's the best thing you can do for me right now."

As Cole left the house Matt heard his mother moaning in the other room.

It took every ounce of willpower to go to her bedroom and gently knock on the door.

"Matt, is that you?" Dr. Davies asked. "Come in here, please."

Matt took a very deep breath and opened the door to the sight of his mother ravaged on the bed.

"I'm calling Miss Ellis to stay here tonight, so you will have to make alternate arrangements. Your mother will need a nurse, and you need a break. This has gone on far too long, Matt. I feel bad that I didn't know about it before. I could have sent Min to a facility years ago."

Hearing someone acknowledge how difficult this had been made Matt want to weep with relief. Dr. Davies finished putting a cast on his mother's arm and adjusted her pain medication. When both men were sure she was sleeping and not in pain, Dr. Davies followed Matt into the kitchen. Hot with shame, Matt brushed broken crockery off the chair so Dr. Davies could sit down.

"How are you doing, Matt?" Dr. Davies asked so gently Matt sat down across from him and put his head in his arms on the table and burst into tears.

Dr. Davies waited patiently for him to pull himself together. "When did this all start?"

"My father passed away when I was fifteen," Matt scrubbed his hands over his face. "My mother didn't get out of bed for days. After the funeral, she quit speaking. Min was always fragile. She was always really needy, but things started to sort of increase after the funeral."

"So, your mother stopped speaking, and your sister started acting out after that event?"

"I thought it was sadness from my father passing, but slowly the times that she couldn't handle light or sound and had to be catered to increased. The times that she could function seemed to shorten."

"When do you think Min could actually get through the day without your assistance?"

"I don't remember a time that Min could get through the day without me," Matt answered honestly. He watched Dr. Davies's eyes soften with sympathy.

"Matt, this has been too much for anyone. How are you holding up?"

"Not very good," Matt admitted.

"Here's what is going to happen, Matt." Dr. Davies jotted down notes as he spoke. "Your sister is facing criminal charges for what happened to your mother. No question, she's going to jail. Regardless of the outcome of the trial, I will recommend that she is put in a treatment facility for incurables. So, she is now out of your life indefinitely. We know very little about how the mind works, but she clearly has a mental problem that makes her a danger to herself and others. That's what is happening today. For sure. We are going to keep a close eye on your mother. If, with the absence of Min, she starts to come out of her deep sadness, meaning she starts to speak, I will consider leaving her in your care with a nurse to come in one day a week to give you some relief. She can bathe your mother, and you can have a day to take care of your own happiness."

Matt's jaw dropped open. "I didn't know that was an option."

"It is a pricey option. However, if your mother doesn't improve, Matt, I am going to recommend she is placed in a care home facility that specializes in cases where people can't cope with life. It is not ideal, but you're a man, and taking care of a woman in this capacity is inappropriate. So, we won't make that decision today, but I will be here every week to monitor her progress. You should think about the possibility that she very likely will not recover and she will need full time care at an institution, too. Don't worry about it yet. However, prepare yourself for that outcome."

"Thank you," Matt said so hoarsely Dr. Davies gave him a smile.

"You need to think about how you will fund that. I hate to put that on you today."

"It's all right. My father left a trust, and we have enough."

"How are you sleeping? How are you doing, Matt?"

Matt hadn't been asked that for ten years. His life revolved around others, worried about Min or his mother, and everyone just expected that Matt, as the strong one, would soldier on forever. Dr. Davies was the only person who acknowledged that being in a care-giving role for ten years with no end in sight took a terrible toll.

"I don't sleep well. I am exhausted, angry, bitter, and I feel like my entire life is tiptoeing around lunatics. I have no patience for anything. Little things that I should brush off make me angry because I just can't handle any more problems. Sometimes the violence of my thoughts scares me. Am I incurable, too? I wish I could sleep. I think that would help." Matt tried to speak around the lump of hot tears in his throat.

Dr. Davies scratched his eyebrow and took more notes.

"This has gone on too long. You are certainly not incurable." Dr. Davies managed a chuckle amidst all the horror.

"I think when you live with this sort of lunacy... it seems to warp you." Matt sounded defeated. Dr. Davies looked him square in the eye.

"You are not crazy. Matt, you obviously are the most well-adjusted person to deal with all of this and not strangle Min to death in a fit of rage. Not a court in the land would have convicted you. When are your exams?"

"May 29."

"I want to meet with you the day after tomorrow. I have to make some arrangements. Leave this with me. I can spare Miss Ellis for two days. So, can you move in with Cole at the barracks for two days?"

"I can, yes."

"You need to be in a better frame of mind before you sit your exams. I am giving you this laudanum. Twenty drops before bed. Every night until your exams are over."

"What about my mother?"

"Matt, I'm going to keep her very heavily sedated. You have no need to worry about your mother. You need to prepare yourself for the very real possibility that she cannot cope, even with the positive change of Min released from your care. Everything else, I am going to take to the W. C. T. U. We'll let them see if we can get some relief for you until we decide if your mother needs some permanent care. Pack a bag for tonight. Miss Ellis will be here in a few minutes."

Matt put some clothes together and when Miss Ellis showed up, Matt shook the doctor's hand and walked away from 129 Glenwood Street devastated and ashamed that his mother had been hurt and his sister was in a jail cell. Slowly though, a seed of hope took root in his heart and started to choke out the seed of despair. Every footstep that took him toward Priscilla and the basement of Hillcrest and away from the darkness of his home caused that hope to grow. His mother was in the capable hands of Miss Ellis, and Min was in the firm hand of the law.

For the first time in ten years, the crushing weight of responsibility eased enough so he could breathe.

He turned the corner to Hillcrest to find Jaffrey waiting for him to help him move Priscilla's things. Screams coming from within the carriage house shattered the calm of the evening. They both broke into a run. Fury crawled up Matt's neck and strangled the hope that had just started to grow.

Chapter Twenty-Five

T he door to the carriage house was locked.

"Please, don't..." Matt heard Priscilla scream; anger roared through him. Through the window, Matt saw a man, whom he assumed was Richard Markus III, standing over Priscilla. She cowered in a corner of the room.

"Priscilla!" Matt screamed through the window. His eyes met Richard's through the glass. Richard's teeth were bared as he brought his belt down on Priscilla's back.

"Get Cole," Matt growled at Jaffrey, as he threw himself against the locked door. The door burst open; Matt shook with fury as his eyes swept over the scene.

Richard turned from Priscilla to face Matt.

Matt Hartwell, devastated by the actions of his sister, whom he could not physically harm because she was a woman, stood before Richard Markus III and prepared to go to battle.

Fair fight.

Rage roared through Matt when he saw blood pouring out of Priscilla's nose. Though he was desperate to get to her, he had to battle through Richard first. A battle he wanted. Matt craved the feel of his fist connecting with Richard's jaw. The violence that erupted from him when he saw Priscilla cowering in the corner shocked him.

"You can turn yourself in for trespassing, assault, and battery right now, or I can do it for you," Matt taunted Richard.

"I'm here to take what's mine." Richard sneered at Matt.

"There's nothing here that belongs to you." Matt rolled his shoulders in anticipation as his fists clenched at his sides.

Richard chuckled. "That's my wife. She comes home with me today. I gave her a choice — she chose wrong. I'm trying to be reasonable."

"Reasonable?" Matt moved so he stood between Priscilla and Richard. Richard's eyes swept over him, sizing him up.

"Come on, Priscilla. Get up, it's late, it's time to go."

Priscilla wept behind Matt. He didn't turn. He kept his eye on Richard, willing him to throw the first punch.

"You'll have to come through me to take her." Matt braced for attack.

"No one is taking anyone, anywhere," Cole said from the doorway. He adjusted the door that hung precariously on its broken hinge. Richard, outnumbered, stepped back.

"Richard, is it?" Cole asked, as if they were all sitting down to tea and cake.

"Richard Markus III," he said and he turned his attention from Matt to Cole.

"I am arresting you on the charge of trespassing, assault, and battery of Priscilla."

"You are doing no such thing." Richard made a move toward Priscilla, and Matt blocked access to her with his body.

Cole stood beside Matt. "You are under arrest."

Richard moved away from both of them and went to the door where he ran smack into Jaffrey, who had returned with Lord Harper.

"What is the meaning of this?" Lord Harper boomed in a voice that made Priscilla whimper in fear.

Matt, confident that the situation was under control, turned to crouch down in front of her. Priscilla shook and cowered in the corner of the room.

"Priscilla, you're all right. You're going to be fine," Matt whispered. Matt reached out to touch her, and Richard started screaming.

"Get your hands off my wife!" he screamed at Matt, who ignored him.

Priscilla shook with fear in front of him. She covered her face as she tried to move further into the corner. Matt remembered she had been beaten badly for talking to a man, never mind a man touching her. Out of respect for her, he moved back.

"I'm coming back for you. There is no where you can hide from me, Priscilla. I'm coming back for you..." Richard howled in rage.

Cole pushed Richard face down on the dining room table and handcuffed him with some assistance from Jaffrey.

"When I get my hands on you..." Richard screamed until Cole dragged him up off the table and out the door of the cottage.

"Priscilla!" Richard screamed, as Cole dragged him across the street.

Lord Harper stepped inside the carriage house.

"I'll send you to my lawyer tomorrow morning. Matt can take you in on the stagecoach. This man is an animal. This cannot continue."

Matt watched as Priscilla kept her eyes down, on the floor.

"Thank you," she murmured to Lord Harper.

"I'll have Dr. Davies come check on her tonight. Matt, make sure he gets here and she has some assistance."

"I think we should proceed with moving her into the basement of Hillcrest, if that is still all right with you? He'll be locked up tonight, but Cole can't hold him. She can't stay here without any protection."

"I agree. As soon as Dr. Davies has seen to her, bring her to the basement."

"Priscilla, you are not in this alone," Lord Harper said gruffly. "You will not be returning to that criminal. You are safe here in Oakland, and you can stay at Hillcrest until you are back on your feet. There is lots of room in the basement to do your work."

Lord Harper left the carriage house, and Matt turned to Priscilla, who kept her face buried in her hands. Matt stood by awkwardly. He shuffled his feet a bit and shifted his weight from one foot to the other. He wanted to go to her; he wanted to hold her; he wanted to beat the life out of Richard Markus III. Finally, he couldn't stand by and watch her suffer any longer, so he went to her and crouched down in front of her.

"Priscilla?" Matt very gently placed his hand on her shoulder. She flinched at his touch.

"Leave me," she wept into her hands.

"I can't leave you. You're hurt. Come on, let me see," Matt begged. "Richard is in jail — he can't see us. He can't see this. I want to see how bad it is."

Priscilla finally let her hands drop. Blood had poured out of her nose, and her lip was split. Her eye was starting to swell.

Just then, Dr. Davies knocked gently on the door. Matt looked up at him.

"Matt, maybe you should give us a moment." Dr. Davies suggested softly.

Priscilla tried to hide her face again.

"I'll be right back," Matt whispered. He got up and left her in the capable hands of Dr. Davies. He left the carriage house and went into the barracks right across the street.

"Matt..." Cole exclaimed.

"I want five minutes with him. Just five," Matt demanded.

Cole stood up. "Sure."

Together, they went to the jail cell, and Cole shot a warning look at Matt.

"Five minutes, no cuffs, don't let me kill him because I don't want to go to jail." Matt spoke through a jaw clenched tight.

"Done," Cole agreed.

Cole opened the jail cell and took the cuffs off Richard Markus III. The men squared off in the basement of the barracks.

"Two against one?" Richard paled as he sized up both Matt and Cole.

"No, one on one." Matt stalked around him like a predator.

"What do you want?" Richard's face paled in fear.

"I understand if Priscilla speaks to a man, she gets beaten by you. I just spoke to her, so I'm here to take the beating on her behalf."

Richard's eyes narrowed.

"Come on, Richard," Matt taunted. "You're used to fighting. I'll let you throw the first punch."

"I won't be treated like..."

Matt smashed his fist into his nose hard enough to draw blood.

"I'm not here to talk." Matt bared his teeth at Richard. "Should we get you a horse whip? I hear you are good with them."

"Don't leave me here with him!" Richard screamed at Cole. "I am in your custody! I am under your protection."

"Five minutes," Cole reminded Matt.

Richard screamed insults at Cole, which caused Min, who was in the other jail cell, to start moaning. *What a mess.* Matt watched Richard's eyes widen in fear as he hauled back to hammer him with his fists. When Matt's fist slammed into Richard's jaw with every ounce of his strength, he couldn't wait to hit him again.

The fight was over much sooner than five minutes to Matt's complete disgust. Richard hardly fought back, and when he finally went down, Cole didn't need to drag Matt off. He dragged Richard's bleeding and battered body back into the jail cell. When Matt made a move toward him, Cole stopped him.

"I want to say something." Matt shook Cole's hands off.

"Don't hit him," Cole warned Matt.

Matt scowled at Cole, convinced he was the bossiest person in the province.

Matt crouched down and smiled with satisfaction when he saw that Richard's face was in much worse condition than Priscilla's. He leaned close and held him by the throat while he spoke right into his ear.

"If you come after her again, this is a little taste of what I can and will do to you. If you raise a hand to Priscilla, these fists are coming after you. I will hunt you down like the dog that you are."

Matt stepped away from Richard; he walked away from the jail cells without even a backward glance at Min.

"I understand you are staying here in the barracks with me. I'll make up a bed for you. No sneaking down in the night to finish what you started here." Cole jerked his head toward Richard.

"Thank you."

Matt left the barracks and went to check on Priscilla. Dr. Davies had cleaned her face. She tried to stifle a gasp of pain as he placed a very tiny stitch in her eyebrow. Matt hovered protectively as Dr. Davies cleaned the wound. Matt's heart ached in sympathy when he noticed her knuckles whitened as she gripped the edge of the table from the pain.

Once Priscilla's wounds were treated, Dr. Davies turned his attention to Matt. "Are you all right?"

"I'm fine," Matt said gruffly.

Dr. Davies tidied up and placed a little bottle of laudanum beside Priscilla.

"I want you to put fifteen drops in your tea before bed. I think you should retire now. You are very distraught." Dr. Davies put his instruments away and tidied up the bloody rags he' had used to clean up Priscilla's face.

"Matt, do you have any injuries I need to see to?" Dr. Davies looked pointedly at Matt's bleeding knuckles.

"I'm fine, thanks." Matt reached out to help Priscilla down off the dining room table. She swayed in his arms as he held her up. Dr. Davies discreetly left them alone. He propped the broken door shut against any prying eyes and left them.

"Are you all right?" Matt's arms tightened around Priscilla. She trembled against him.

"No," she whispered, she laid her head against his shoulder. "What did you do?"

"I let him know that if he beats you, I beat him." Matt's jaw clenched in anger.

"He'll be furious." She peeked up at him quickly and then she laid her head back down against his shoulder.

"I don't care. He's a bloody mess in the bottom of a jail cell now."

"There will be hell to pay, and it will be me that pays it," she said sadly. He could feel her heart pounding in fear against him.

"No." Matt stroked his hand gently up and down her back, trying to comfort her. "You will not. I won't have it."

Priscilla straightened up and pulled back, out of his arms. She moved away from him and stood by the sewing machine on loan from Mrs. Bennett. Her eyes filled with tears again.

"He destroyed it. Clearly, someone told him I was working in my trade. Part of the reason he came tonight was to drag me back, and he started with destroying the sewing machine so I wouldn't have any way to support myself."

Matt said nothing. He watched her run her small hand along the top of the machine where Richard had smashed it with a fire poker.

"He destroys everything." Her voice caught. Matt knew about that feeling of defeat; of utter helplessness and the resulting hopelessness in the face of a lunatic.

"We can get another sewing machine." Matt picked up the fire poker and replaced it by the fireplace, so she wouldn't be reminded of the violence it had been used for.

"But he'll keep coming back." Tears welled up in her eyes and spilled down her cheeks. "He'll never stop. He'll never, ever, ever stop."

Matt's heart broke apart in pain as he watched the girl who had interviewed his horse and wanted to worship the sun completely break down. "I'll go with you to talk to the lawyer tomorrow," Matt promised. He couldn't stop himself. He gathered her in his arms and held her until she stopped crying. She felt delicate in his arms; he wanted to go back to the barracks and finished what he started.

Eventually, Priscilla pulled away from his embrace again and wiped her tears on a fresh handkerchief.

"Lord Harper has a lawyer he recommends," Matt reminded her.

"Will it do any good?" Her voice sounded dull.

"Of course, it will. Come on, I'll walk you to Hillcrest." Matt held his hand out, and she tentatively took it. She turned his hand over to examine his knuckles.

"What does it feel like?" She bit her lip as she looked at him.

"What?" Matt tilted his head.

"To hit him." She swallowed hard. "What did it feel like?"

"Priscilla, I'm not proud of it, but I really quite enjoyed it." A smile played on Matt's lips.

"Did you beat him pretty bad?" Her eyes were wide.

A broad smile broke out across Matt's face, his first smile in this very long horrendous day.

"He'll live," Matt said dryly.

To his surprise, Priscilla giggled.

"What is so funny?" Matt gently brushed a piece of hair that was stuck to the tears on her face.

"Did you leave his cuffs on?"

"Priscilla, Cole took the cuffs off so it would be a fair fight, but the thing about men who beat women — they're not so good when they face someone their own size."

"Did he hit you at all?" Her eyes clouded with worry.

"He tried." Matt picked up all her luggage and stepped aside so she could exit the carriage house in front of him.

"Are you hurt?" Priscilla bit her lip and turned to face him.

Matt Hartwell shouldn't have done it. He told himself not to. He put her luggage down and he went to her and took her face in his hands very gently. "Priscilla, on the other side of this door, we have to be very proper. Extremely proper. I know you are married... but... from the first minute I saw you..." Matt couldn't form the words.

"Shhh. We can't talk about that." Priscilla put her hands on his chest as if that could stop him from speaking.

Matt swallowed hard and stopped speaking.

"You are an honourable man. I can tell. Everyone in this community speaks highly of you. We will say nothing." Priscilla spoke the words harshly. "Until I am legally done with him... no words. Promise me."

"Right." Matt's heart plummeted as he honoured her request. "I promise."

He hoped she knew his tone promised much more than just respecting her wish of propriety.

"Don't... don't look at me like that, Matt." Priscilla's voice shook again. He took a step back out of respect for her wishes. She was scared. Not of him, he knew that, but of the emotion they were both feeling. It rose up between them and threatened to draw them closer.

Finally, Priscilla pulled open the broken door, and together they went to the entrance to the basement. Matt stiffly put her luggage in the room where the inhabitants of Hillcrest could ride out any prairie storm.

"Do you need anything else?" Matt asked from a safe distance away. He wanted to drag her into an embrace and tell her his whole world had collapsed today. He wanted to... he wanted a lot of things.

"I am fine." The basement of Hillcrest was rock on rock. She looked around as she shivered. Matt knew it must seem like he was leaving her alone in an ancient prison.

"The coach leaves at 9:00, so I will come for you ten minutes before."

"All right."

"Don't cry, Priscilla," Matt begged her helplessly from the doorway. "He's not worth it."

Priscilla tried to wipe the tears away and more replaced them.

Matt sighed. "Don't forget to take some laudanum tonight. Try to get some rest. I'll be back tomorrow."

She nodded.

He opened the door and closed it behind him. For a brief moment, he pressed his forehead into the wood. "We will find a way," he vowed before he tore himself away.

Chapter Twenty-Six

Sun streaming into Cora's whitewashed cottage bedroom awakened her. She stretched her arms over her head as she blinked. She smiled at the bouquet of lilacs Lucy had placed on her bedside table. Rested and happy, she bounded out of bed, put together a picnic lunch, selected a new book of poetry, and packed everything on her bicycle, intending to search for sandbars.

Manitoba in full bloom made Cora glow inside as she hopped on her bike. Cycling down Crescent Street, she grinned at the raised eyebrows of Mrs. Daindridge and Mrs. Carr as they clutched at each other in front of the post office. Women on bicycles clearly shocked their sensibilities. Cora could almost hear their minds working.

A woman on the run from her husband and another one on a bicycle. The state of women and femininity in this community is under attack!

Ignoring their frowns, she waved and rang her bell at them. As she got to the end of Crescent Street, she noticed the stagecoach pulled up to the back door of Hillcrest. Cora's eyebrows drew together in concern when she noticed the carriage house door hung precariously on its hinges. Skidding to a stop, she gasped as she watched Matt and Priscilla walk toward the stagecoach. Badly beaten, Priscilla's left eye was black, her lip was split. Even from across the street, she could see Priscilla wince as Matt gently took her arm to help her across the lawn.

Cora quickly cycled over to them. Her face creased in concern.

As she drew closer, the early morning light was unforgiving. Priscilla's eyes were flat with hopelessness. She wore a black dress. Very plain.

"Priscilla!" Cora's bike skidded to a stop in front of her new friend. "What happened?"

"He found me." Her voiced sounded dull.

"Oh, Priscilla." Cora's stomach tightened with concern. "Are you all right?"

"No." She turned and went to the stagecoach.

A muscle stood out in Matt's jaw, his movements were jerky with fury as he helped Priscilla into the carriage.

"Where are you going?" Cora refused to be brushed off.

"Lord Harper has arranged for a lawyer to look at my petition." Priscilla's eyes were lowered, she didn't look up as she spoke.

"Oh." Cora put her bicycle down and stood by the coach. "That's good. If Lord Harper uses him, he'll be good, I'm sure."

Priscilla covered her face with her hands.

"I hope the best for you," Cora said quietly.

She moved out of Matt's way; he placed a lap robe across Priscilla's knees.

"He'll win." Priscilla's voice cracked with fear. "He always wins." Priscilla spoke with such sadness Cora's heart broke. All the light that previously shone from Priscilla was snuffed out.

"We should be going." Matt pulled the door of the stagecoach shut.

There was so much suffering in Matt's eyes that Cora's heart splintered even further.

"Of course." Cora stepped back.

"Good day, Miss Rood." Matt tipped his hat and crawled up on the buckboard.

"I hope so," Cora said quietly as the coach rolled out of Oakland. Cora went to her bicycle, crawled onto it, and slowly pedaled home. Seeing Priscilla's face made her sad and scared. The light went out of the day.

***

As Matt drove the stagecoach to Brandon, he tried not to think about where Min was today — in jail awaiting trial. His mind raced as he worried about what Richard would do when he was released. He tried to take comfort in Priscilla's safe relocation to the very thick and secure walls of Hillcrest.

He slapped the reins down, and only one sentence pounded through his brain.

Can the courts really use a divorce petition to order her to return and render conjugal rights?

Bitterness filled Matt's mouth as he thought of delicate, lovely Priscilla being forced back to Richard's bed. Richard, who Matt knew delighted in hurting and humiliating her. Matt dragged the horses to a halt in front of the law office. Once they were tied and settled, he went to the coach and opened the door for Priscilla. She tried to appear composed. He held his hand out to assist her from the coach. Together, they stood shoulder to shoulder in front of the law office. Men hurried to and from offices, their eyes flicked over Priscilla. When the men saw her face, they looked at Matt accusingly. He forced down a sick feeling as all these men who worked as lawyers, accountants, and clerks could see a woman abused so viciously, but not one stopped to inquire if she was safe with him.

Is that why violence against women continues so rampantly? If men with positions of power do not step in and stop this on behalf of defenseless women, where will it stop? Men cannot turn a blind eye to this!

Patiently, Matt waited for her to indicate that she was ready to meet the lawyer. She slowly pulled on a pair of gloves. Black again. She tucked some hair behind her ear.

"I think I'm as ready as I'll ever be," she murmured softly.

He held the door open for her, and together they entered into the lobby.

"Priscilla Markus is here to see Mr. Levinson." Matt spoke for her because she seemed to be on the verge of a complete collapse.

"Right this way." The clerk motioned to an office with chairs in front of it. They sat silently for fifteen minutes until the door opened.

"Mrs. Markus?" Whip thin with piercing blue eyes that missed nothing, Mr. Levinson gestured them into his office. His eyes widened in shock and he frowned at Priscilla's face. Ever the lawyer, he gathered evidence before he spoke.

Matt wondered if any book in this office had a law that could protect her. He hoped the clutter in Mr. Levinson's office was organized in some fashion.

"Please be seated. Who is responsible for her face?" His eyes narrowed as he directed the question to Matt.

"Her husband served her with a petition yesterday. When she didn't return, he did this to her. He only stopped because I showed up." Matt growled the reply; he couldn't stop the angry edge from creeping into his tone.

"Did you run away to be with this man?" Mr. Levinson asked Priscilla so bluntly she gasped.

Matt opened his mouth to speak, and Mr. Levinson stopped him with a look.

"I want to hear it from her. I don't like surprises at trial."

Both men watched as Priscilla twisted a handkerchief between her hands as she gathered her thoughts. Another clock ticked on the mantle, and Matt's nerves were so raw he itched to fling it in the street and then drive his stagecoach over it about thirteen times to be sure it stopped ticking.

"I did not run away to be with anyone." Priscilla's eyes were rooted firmly on the floor. "I left Mr. Markus because he threw me down a flight of stairs in the fifth month of my pregnancy. His abuse caused me to miscarry." Her voice dipped in sadness. It clearly caused her great pain to recount that tragic event. Matt desperately wanted to speak for her.

"I see." Mr. Levinson read over Priscilla's petition swiftly. His mouth hardened as he read the last paragraph. The paragraph Matt and Priscilla had both memorized. The decree demanding restitution of conjugal rights. Just thinking of it made Matt's hands clench into fists.

"Can the courts use a divorce petition to order me back to render conjugal rights?" Priscilla's voice shook with fear.

"Yes." Mr. Levinson didn't even look up at her; he searched for a notepad on his desk. "Do you have any evidence that he has committed adultery?"

"What?" Matt sputtered.

"Here's how it works." Mr. Levinson shot Matt a hard look, indicating that he should stop interrupting. "When a woman gets married, she comes under the law of her husband. The courts do not intervene in how a man runs his household."

"Runs his household!" Matt erupted. He stood up and towered over the lawyer.

"If you can't control yourself, you'll have to leave. Sit down, sir." Mr. Levinson glared at Matt. "Divorce in Canada is a thorny subject. We are a new country, still governed by English law. Here's how divorce works. A man can divorce a woman if he suspects she has been unfaithful. All he does is petition that she has committed adultery, and it is very simple in that case. A wife, on the other hand, has to prove adultery *and* abuse. She has to prove that he has committed adultery and that her life is endangered in order to obtain a divorce in Canada. Adultery, on the part of the husband, is not enough to sever the marriage bond in the eyes of the court. Typically, if a woman has been corrected, as long as her life is not in danger, the courts do not consider that to be their jurisdiction."

"Corrected?" Matt sputtered. "What do you mean?"

"The court would look at this and believe there must have been some misconduct he was correcting. He is fully within his rights to run his home however he sees fit." Mr. Levinson jotted notes down as he spoke.

Matt's jaw dropped in horror. "That's obscene."

"That's the law." Mr. Levinson shrugged.

"How can it be a different standard?" Priscilla's face creased in confusion.

"It appears to be." Mr. Levinson nodded his head.

"No, not appears to be." Priscilla straightened up and glared at the lawyer. "It *is* a different standard for men and women!"

"I'm not done," Mr. Levinson continued. "If, by some miracle, you can prove abuse and adultery, he doesn't have to give you a penny. You leave with the clothes on your back. Nothing more. You need to be certain that you can prove adultery in addition to the abuse, or there is no reason to file an affidavit."

"He killed my son." Priscilla choked on a sob.

"Were there witnesses?" Mr. Levinson didn't blink.

Matt's blood ran cold as it became evident there was no way to protect Priscilla under the law. Worse, Richard had started proceedings to *ensure* the courts would send her back. The way the lawyer spoke, it was as if the miscarriage was so difficult to prove that the courts might just ignore that little incident.

"The butler." Priscilla twisted a handkerchief between her hands.

"Still in his employ?" Mr. Levinson spoke like a man who had heard everything and was convinced there was no way to help women in this situation.

"I'm not sure." Priscilla's voice sounded strangled.

"You need to find out. But again, as I said, no adultery, no cruelty, no divorce."

"How does one prove a husband has committed adultery?" Priscilla asked timidly.

"Typically, a wife notices that she has contracted a venereal disease. The courts cannot refute that evidence. Granted, of course, that she has no immoral activities in her background. Unchaperoned interludes with other men." Mr. Levinson looked pointedly at Matt. Priscilla gasped.

Matt watched helplessly as tears gathered in her eyes.

"Let me get this straight." Matt leaned forward in his chair. "If I had done this to Priscilla's face, I would be charged with assault and battery."

"Of course."

"But her husband can do this, and there is no criminal charge."

"That is correct."

"The courts turn a blind eye to women who are being beaten in their own homes." Matt tried and failed to understand this.

"The courts do not interfere with how a husband runs his household."

"You and I both know that men who beat women never stop, and it typically escalates... he will kill her."

"We can prosecute him if he kills her, for sure."

"That's comforting." Matt threw his hands up in the air; his lips thinned in disapproval.

"So, you can drop all this, go home, render conjugal rights, and try to be a better wife." Mr. Levinson cleared his throat. "That's what I suggest because if we go to court with this, they'll send you home. You don't meet the burden of proof."

Matt gripped the armrests of the chair so hard his knuckles were red, raw, and white at the same time.

Priscilla took a deep breath and let it out slowly.

"If he kills me? Do you face any sort of repercussion for sending me back?" Priscilla lifted her chin in defiance.

"It's not me personally sending you back. The court will send you back. If he kills you, we prosecute him, for sure. Your husband would hang." Mr. Levinson blinked once and returned to his notepad.

"Unless he could prove that I provoked him?" Priscilla spoke so harshly Matt moved closer to her.

"No." Mr. Levinson dragged his eyes away from his notepad. "There is never justification for a man to kill his wife..."

"But he can beat her with impunity."

"He should *not* beat her with impunity."

"But you need to prosecute men who *do* beat women. This isn't right," Priscilla sputtered, losing her patience. "You know that this is completely unfair."

"It doesn't matter what I think or feel." Mr. Levinson spoke like a man who had quit feeling quite some time ago. "The only thing that matters is the law. What the law says, what we can prosecute and defend."

"Laws change though." Matt heard the defeat in Priscilla's voice. He could hear it; the laws would not change fast enough to save her. "What does it take to change a law?"

"The criminal code is legislation, so legislation has to change. This league of suffragettes wanting equal rights... I think they are fighting for the divorce laws to be equal for men and women, but really, the majority of women...the *vast* majority of women, are happy in their homes."

"What if you don't fall into the category of the vast majority?" Priscilla's voice trembled, and Mr. Levinson shifted uncomfortably in his chair. "What if your life is just waiting, terrified for the next fit of rage? What then?"

"It is not my place to offer counsel about marriage. I am here to tell you what the law will intervene in and what it will not. Under the law, you have no legal rights. I am really sorry, but that's all I can say. I can send an affidavit that would buy you some time, but honestly, you can't fight him. You won't win."

Matt wanted to take her hands to stop her from wringing them. This entire altercation was like watching a lamb be led to slaughter.

"I want you to send an affidavit. I want a judge to hear that he caused me to miscarry my..."

"He'll say he didn't know you were pregnant. He'll say you provoked him... it really depends on the judge." Mr. Levinson's voice was a low drone.

"Just write it down," Priscilla cried out with such frustration Matt couldn't help himself; he moved to put his hand on her arm. The look she gave him was tortured. This simple act was not acceptable. He knew it. He immediately dropped his hand. "I don't want to be comforted. I want justice. I came here for justice. I am an innocent victim here, and my unborn son certainly was as well. I want a judge to see him for what he is. There must be a way to prosecute on behalf of my son."

"I'll send the affidavit, but I am urging you to realize, you can't fight him in court. He'll win. You're not the first woman in this state... I am afraid you won't be the last."

"And the men with all the power don't care." Matt marveled that Priscilla didn't cry. She held Mr. Levinson's eye and didn't look away.

"It appears that way." Mr. Levinson spoke cautiously.

"I am going to write a letter to the court that in my professional opinion your return to Mr. Markus would be detrimental to the point that I fear your life would be in danger. Really, that's the best I can do. The good news is he has to pay all your legal bills. The courts do not expect women to pay for their defense. Under the law, a husband has to cover that expense." Mr. Levinson offered that advice as if it were great strides in women's rights.

"Good thing because I can't have a bank account without his permission." Priscilla's voice was iron hard. "So, it would be pretty tricky to pay a lawyer without a bank account, wouldn't you say?"

"I know it seems unfair..." Mr. Levinson held his hands up in defense.

Priscilla stood up, and Matt stood up with her.

"It doesn't *seem* unfair, Mr. Levinson. It is grossly unfair. It is a travesty that the court in this country exists and does nothing for half its citizens, and if I may say, the vulnerable half. I can't defend myself against him. When he beats me, there is nothing I can do but beg..." Priscilla's voice caught.

Fury crawled up Matt's chest and threatened to choke him.

"I thought the courts were supposed to protect everyone, not just men."

"I wish it were different," Mr. Levinson said in a voice that was so resigned Matt knew he was not about to seek justice for her.

Priscilla stood up and took a careful step back, as if she were in danger from him. "As I said, I will add a letter to your affidavit, but please, Mrs. Markus, don't get your hopes up."

"What hope, Mr. Levinson? I have no hope at all."

Matt knew her worst fears were confirmed. Anger tightened Matt's jaw as her hands dropped in defeat. She struggled to put her gloves back on because her eyes were so full of tears she couldn't see. He yearned to reach out to her, but she teetered on the verge of breaking apart. He worried that with one touch from him she would shatter.

"Men like you, who have law degrees, you have a moral responsibility to try to amend the laws... you must add your voice to the women's..." Priscilla's voice broke.

"Mrs. Markus." Mr. Levinson cut her off, and Matt seethed. His body tensed, ready to step in at her slightest indication.

"It's not that simple. All I can do is my best with what is in front of me. I'll go to court for you, I'll fight this, but at the end of the day, we're all going home. That's all that is going to happen here."

Priscilla finally managed to get her gloves on. She straightened up and addressed Mr. Levinson tearfully.

"Mr. Levinson, may God have mercy on you for the lack of care and understanding you have shown here today."

Mr. Levinson's face went white. "I can't change the law."

"But you don't have to defend it as you have. You could say you disagree... you could at least not speak derisively of women who are suffragettes, who are fighting for equality. You should be ashamed of yourself."

Mr. Levinson's mouth thinned with disapproval.

Priscilla turned on her heel and left the office. Matt followed closely behind. She hauled open the door of the coach and slammed it shut behind her. Matt heard sobbing from inside the coach and wisely crawled up onto the buckboard and looked for a store that sold sewing machines.

Matt's mind raced. He had to sit his exams in three days. What on earth was he going to do with his mother? Who would protect Priscilla when he was gone? Cole couldn't keep Richard Markus III in prison any longer. Priscilla was in desperate danger. Matt thought about pointing the horses south and running as far from here as he could get.

Chapter Twenty-Seven

Ada's eyes swept around the drawing room at Hillcrest to see who was already in attendance. She nodded at Priscilla. Lady Harper must have asked her to attend, even though she was beaten and bruised. Ada steeled herself as she watched Mrs. Daindridge and Mrs. Carr's eyes gleam at Priscilla, as if she were a feast of gossip they were eager to tear into.

Lady Harper stood by the jade-coloured fireplace, and everyone drew their attention to her. "We have some sad news. Mrs. Bennett, would you address the ladies with what you know, so we can plan to assist?"

Mrs. Rood picked up a pencil and prepared to take notes.

Ada took her place at the front of the room. "As many of you know, Mr. Hartwell has been dealing with some tremendous family difficulty since his father died."

Sympathy clouded Priscilla's face as Ada spoke of Matt's predicament.

"You may not be aware of this, but Mrs. Hartwell has not been able to cope, to the point that she cannot speak."

The room of women gasped in surprise.

"Also, there has been a terrible accident. It seems Min..."

"Oh, that terrible Min," Mrs. Daindridge hissed to Mrs. Carr. Their hearing wasn't what it once was. What Mrs. Daindridge thought was a whisper was loud enough for everyone to hear.

"Mrs. Daindridge, please, this has been a tragedy for the Hartwell family," Ada tried and failed to take the edge of anger out of her voice. Mrs. Daindridge and Mrs. Carr pushed her to the limit.

"Excuse us, Mrs. Bennett. Please, continue." Mrs. Daindridge snapped her mouth shut and had the good sense not to argue.

"Long story short, Min is not returning to Mr. Hartwell's care. However, Mr. Hartwell is going to Winnipeg in two days to sit his exams. Dr. Davies has requested that our group give some thought as to who would be in a position to assist Mrs. Hartwell while he is gone."

"I am available." Priscilla stood up. Every eye riveted to her as she stood before them, beaten with a black eye and split lip. She didn't flinch at the stares.

"Mrs. Markus, I don't know if you should... you are still in a fragile state." Mrs. Holt's eyes softened in sympathy.

"Most inappropriate! A married woman in the home of a single man." Mrs. Carr sniffed.

"While that man is in Winnipeg, sitting exams, I think we can all agree that it will be very difficult for them to be in an unchaperoned or disapproved state with half the province between them." Ice splintered Ada's voice as she addressed Mrs. Carr. "The fact is we are all up to our eyes in seeding. Our daughters are needed at home to assist. Mrs. Daindridge and Mrs. Carr would you prefer to step in to render assistance?"

Mrs. Daindridge and Mrs. Carr clamped their mouths shut and clutched at each other in support.

"Priscilla, if you would move into Matt's house in two days to care for Mrs. Hartwell, we would all be grateful. We do not want Matt to miss his exams. We will help you in any way that we can."

"Of course, Mrs. Bennett. It is the least I can do."

As the meeting adjourned, Mrs. Bennett noticed Jaffrey hand Priscilla some correspondence. She hoped the envelope contained good news.

***

Matt moved Priscilla's new sewing machine, dress form, piles of fabrics, and her clothes into his house the day before he was due to leave for Winnipeg. He looked around his grim drawing room. Shame ate at him as he saw his gloomy house through her eyes. The rugs needed to be taken out and beaten years ago; the heavy draperies were thick with dust. The cook stove had a layer of grease on it. He had done all the dishes, but had run out of time. They were stacked up precariously in a dish drainer that likely needed a thorough scrubbing. His shoulders slumped in mortification.

Priscilla settled her dress form in the parlour and smiled at him. A smile that did not reach her eyes. She seemed thinner than before.

"I am really sorry I didn't have time to tidy up. I don't know how to thank you, Priscilla." Matt put her box of materials down near the dress form.

"I owe you for stopping Richard." She looked up at him. He winced; the bruises on her face gutted him. Her eye was slowly starting to heal. No longer as black, it yellowed in spots at the edge.

"You don't owe me anything," Matt corrected her.

"Before you go, I should show you this." Priscilla's voice caught. Her eyes met his briefly and then dropped down to the floor. He knew this look — defeated. "So that you know exactly where we stand."

He took the paper from her. He saw both emotional and physical pain in the way she moved. She turned from him and picked up a handkerchief.

Matt opened the paper, his eyes skimmed over it.

"Contempt of court order!" Hot fury washed over Matt. "I can't understand this. Is this actually saying what I think it's saying? If you don't go back and render... render... oh my goodness. If you don't return in two weeks, you are in contempt of court? We are going to fight this."

"Matt." Priscilla moved to him and put her hand on his arm. "There is no *we*. Contempt of court is serious. I have to run. You protected me from Richard, but you can't protect me from the King's Bench. Listen to this wording..."

"I read it," Matt protested. He didn't want to hear the words.

"This court doth pronounce and decree that the petitioner and respondent were and are lawful husband and wife, and that the respondent, within two weeks from the service of this order and decree on her, return home to the petitioner and render her conjugal rights. It is further ordered that the petitioner do pay to the respondent the costs of this action." Priscilla's voice broke on the words *render* and *conjugal rights*.

"They are ordering me home. They call it rendering conjugal rights, but I call it rape. I can't do it. I can't let him... I have to run. I will stay here with your mother for two weeks, and then I'm going to leave. Maybe you could drive me to the train. Once I sell everything that I have and finish Cora's wardrobe, I have enough for train fare and to set up in another community. I see no other alternative."

"Until he catches up to you." Matt's stomach tightened with fear that she would leave. He took a step forward. "Then what, Priscilla? He will never let you go, and you won't have anyone to protect you."

"I'll have to change my name and be very clever. Maybe I can disappear in the United States." Priscilla's voice caught as she blinked back tears.

Matt went to her. She held her hand up. "Please, Matt, don't get involved in this. It's not going to turn out well for anyone."

"I am already involved... I want to keep you safe." Matt held his hands out in supplication.

"You can't." Priscilla's voice sounded flat. "He'll get to me. As soon as you're home, I'll disappear. When you take me to the train, if you would help me trade and pawn everything I took when I left, that would help me a lot."

Matt couldn't process it. There had to be a way for the courts to protect her. Her lawyer didn't care.

We need a different lawyer.

"Priscilla, leave this with me."

"What can you do?"

"Gather evidence," Matt said quietly. "I'm in the city anyway. If I can get evidence of adultery, we can fight this. You can't go into a brothel, but I can."

"Why do you think he would be in a brothel? I can't imagine he would have another woman. He wouldn't have another woman." Priscilla shook her head.

"I'll sit my exams, and then I will gather as much evidence as I can. I have two weeks in Winnipeg, so I can shadow him and see if I can... catch him at something."

"What if you get hurt?" Priscilla twisted the handkerchief between her hands in fear.

"I won't get hurt," Matt said softly.

"What if you hurt him?" Priscilla took a tentative step closer.

"I won't. He won't even know I'm there." Matt wiped a tear that trickled down her cheek. "If I can't find enough evidence, I'll take you to the United States myself."

"I'm not in a position to repay you for this kindness." Priscilla tucked a stray hair behind her ear.

"You're looking after my mother. You can't imagine how much that helps me." Matt smiled at her fondly. "I better go." Matt strode to the kitchen and took the coffee can down from a shelf. "This is the housekeeping money that is set aside for the rest of the month."

Handing her this money to run his household in his absence seemed strangely intimate. "If you need more, I have already let the merchants know that you are to put anything you need on my accounts in town. I am a telegram away if anything happens." Matt dithered around like an old grandmother, worried about her safety and her comfort. "Will you be all right?"

She nodded. "You better go. I wish you the best of luck. I hope you get the best mark. I don't want you to be distracted by this situation. You should focus on getting a good grade." Priscilla held the can of money for a moment and then put the tin back on the shelf.

"I hope you get some rest here." Inwardly, Matt groaned. Leaving her here, in this gloom with his catatonic mother was awful.

"Matt, you are never late. You have to go." Priscilla bit her lip.

"Right." Matt stood awkwardly at his own door.

"Don't hesitate to call for Dr. Davies if you need him. If anyone shows up in town that makes you even the slightest bit nervous, tell Cole. He'll make sure you're safe while I'm gone. Please treat this house as if it were your own."

"I will."

"Take care, Priscilla." Matt's eyes flicked over her, as if committing her to memory.

To both of them it sounded like 'I love you.' They couldn't say it, nor could they acknowledge it. Matt Hartwell slipped out of his house and vowed justice for this woman if it was the last thing he did.

***

Priscilla woke early the next morning and made breakfast for Mrs. Hartwell. She had just started cleaning up when a knock on the door made her clutch at her heart in panic. She peeked out the window before opening the door.

Twenty W. C. T. U. members stood on the verandah.

Priscilla let them in.

Surprised flickered over Mrs. Hartwell's face as they filed into the Hartwell residence.

Ada Bennett and Mrs. Holt were leading the pack.

"We watched him pull out of town with the stagecoach and knew the coast was clear!" Ada smiled at Priscilla with a gleam in her eye. Her wagon was loaded with perennials and all sorts of garden equipment. "I'm going to redo his flower beds."

"Mrs. Bennett, will he mind?" Priscilla peeked around her at the league of women who were there to revamp poor Matt's house. It sorely needed it. The weight of his responsibility had clearly crushed him. The house was so gloomy Priscilla strained to see.

"We love Matt. Always have. We didn't want to embarrass him by coming over here and getting his house in order, but now that he's gone. Well, ladies. Let's get to work."

The ladies handed Priscilla yards of plain muslin.

"Would you be so kind as to make new curtains for every window? Min kept it so dark in here, it was terrible. Let's let some light in." Ada smiled as she added some lace to the top of the pile.

"Will he like lace on his curtains?" Priscilla frowned doubtfully.

"I thought for his mother's room." Ada's eyes twinkled at Priscilla.

"Perfect." Priscilla smiled. The handmade lace was beautiful.

Priscilla laid the fabric out and started cutting. She watched as Ada tore down every speck of heavy curtain. Layers of fabric to keep out the sun were removed. Clouds of dust came down with the curtains. Once they were all torn down and thrown onto the verandah, happy spring sun poured into Matt Hartwell's home for the first time in ten years.

Mrs. Holt let out a faint cheer as the heavy curtains in the kitchen were dispensed of and as the sun poured in, Mrs. Hartwell blinked and squinted from her spot near the cook stove.

Mrs. Holt quit cheering as she added water to the reservoir. Soon she was up to her elbows in grease. As far as kitchens went, it was disgraceful. Mrs. Daindridge and Mrs. Carr rolled up their sleeves and nodded to the younger women to get to work. They started stripping every piece of bedding, washing it and hanging it to dry. The sheets were bleached white in the sun. Every window was scrubbed with hot water and ammonia so they gleamed. By the end of the day, the entire house had been taken apart and scrubbed. Finally, they left a meal to cook in the cook stove. Priscilla had never seen the like of it.

The women were exhausted, but their eyes gleamed with happiness as they surveyed their work.

"Matt will like this," Ada pronounced. She had a smear of dirt under her left eye that she didn't bother to wipe away. "He will be really happy. I wish we had time to change Min's room."

"I can work on that tomorrow. I have two weeks here," Priscilla offered.

Before I run.

"I'll take her bed out of there right now. I think the room needs to be changed into something completely different. He likely has a lot of bad memories."

"I think I have an idea." Priscilla grinned.

The next day, after having breakfast with the still silent Mrs. Hartwell, Priscilla went into Min's room. With the bed gone, there was only a chair and a dresser. Priscilla thought of how cramped Matt's room was with his big architect easel and all his books and papers in a corner of his room. Priscilla decided he needed a place to work.

She slipped down to the mercantile for paint and requested some assistance from Mr. Rood to put up shelves. It took her a week to get the room just as she wanted it. Once the room was repainted, she organised a space for him to read in peace. She placed a little table by the big chair and piled books on it from his bedside. The easel he worked at was positioned between the two windows so he could take advantage of all the natural light. A vase full of lilacs brought the smell of spring into the room.

Recovered pillows from the settee downstairs were placed on his chair, and she rolled up a soft afghan for him to use if it was chilly. Finally, she hung new curtains of heavy grey muslin and swept them back so the sun could shine in. A smiled played on her lips as she stood back to survey her handiwork. Maybe he would find some peace here in this room with all traces of Min removed.

Priscilla heard a movement behind her and turned in surprise. Mrs. Hartwell had come upstairs.

She stood back as Matt's mother shuffled into his new work space. His window overlooked the pasture land behind them. Mrs. Hartwell ran her fingertips along the easel and settled into Matt's chair.

"It's a beautiful room for him, now. I think he will design lovely buildings here." Priscilla smiled at Mrs. Hartwell in expectation.

The older lady gave Priscilla a gentle smile.

Is she making sure Min is gone?

Once Mrs. Hartwell was settled in for the night, Priscilla let herself into Matt's room. She snuggled down into his pillows and breathed in the faint trace of him.

Please, please come home safe.

***

Matt watched a mother assemble her two boys and their father on the steps of the university to photograph the event. The father must have been sitting exams today and she wanted to record the day for their family. The little boys had wide smiles and in between photographs, they jumped around with excitement. Matt fought the ache of being here on the steps of the university all alone as he moved toward them and offered to take a picture so she could be in the photo, too. As he documented this day for this beautiful family in the spring sunshine, he wished his sister wasn't so sick that she had to be put in jail for her actions. He wished his mother wasn't plagued with such sadness.

If only Priscilla were here, she would celebrate this occasion, too. Careful, don't think like that. She's not yours.

Matt struggled to push thoughts of her out of his head. He loved the way she celebrated simple moments that he long ago stopped taking time to notice. He smiled through the pain as he handed the camera back to the woman.

Brownie portable camera, he'd heard of those. All of a sudden, he had a thought. Photographs would be irrefutable evidence... his mind raced. Exams first, and then it was time to search out, document, and destroy Richard Markus III.

Chapter Twenty-Eight

O nce his exams were completed, Matt had a whole week in Winnipeg to try to find evidence against Richard. His first stop was a photography studio where he bought the best Brownie camera on the market. Then he found the Markus residence. He wandered around the park across the street from the house as he waited for Richard to finally leave for the day. Once Richard was gone, Matt took the steps two at a time and tapped on the front door.

The butler promptly opened the door.

"I need to speak to you, sir." Matt stood tall.

The butler regarded him coolly.

"Mr. Markus is gone for the day." The butler tried to close the door on him. "It's you I need to speak to." Matt leaned in.

The butler somewhat reluctantly allowed him into the front foyer.

"I'm the man that's been keeping Priscilla safe after Markus pushed her down the stairs, caused her to miscarry, and now is suing her for divorce. Not the usual kind, a divorce petition that allows her to be held in contempt of court if she doesn't comply with his terms. He wants...well, just read it."

Matt thrust the summons into the butler's hands. He read the contents quickly.

"This has nothing to do with me. I am a butler, nothing more. I don't interfere in Mr. Markus's life." Matt noticed the fear in his eyes.

"She nearly died." Matt's voice hardened. "I had to take her to a doctor who was barely able to save her life. She lost the baby, of course. She lost that on your watch. You didn't stop him from throwing her down a flight of stairs."

"I don't know anything about that, sir." The butler shifted uncomfortably.

"Or stop him from whipping her with a horse whip." Matt's voice sounded ragged with emotion.

"I don't recall that event." The butler's eyes slid to the side, away from Matt.

"You won't testify to the truth," Matt hissed. "Priscilla tells me you got him drunk so you could get her to the hospital."

Silence.

"If you won't testify, could you tell me which brothel or where I can find his mistress?"

The butler gasped. "He has never..."

Losing his patience, Matt's voice deepened to a low growl. "Men like Richard aren't faithful to their wives — you know it, and I know it."

"I am not in a position to help you."

Matt's eyes narrowed. "When I am done with Richard, you will need another job. You should start looking now."

The butler swallowed hard. "You won't win against him. He has money, power, and privilege behind him."

Matt shrugged. "I won't see her back in his bed."

The butler's face was a mask of indifference.

"What if she were your daughter? What would you do?"

The butler moved to the door to open it and escort Matt out. "I didn't have children. I gave my life to the service of the Markus family. I won't speak against him."

"You took her to the hospital." Matt's eyebrows drew together in confusion. "She thought you took her there to save her life."

"I did. If she died in this house, Mr. Markus would be charged with murder. He is a good man. He is misunderstood."

Matt's jaw tightened in anger. "The hospital missed part of the placenta, and she was within days of dying."

"It was a tragic accident."

"Accident." Hot fury roared through Matt. His fists clenched at his sides. "You would testify *for* him? If you lie on the stand, they will send her back. Back to him, to more beatings — you have to speak the truth. Her life is at stake."

The butler didn't reply.

"It's a terrible crime when the intentional miscarriage of an innocent child, a child she wanted, doesn't cause a man to do the honourable thing."

The butler held the door open and inclined his head. "I will testify that I witnessed a terrible *accident*. Mr. Markus was very upset about the miscarriage. He was grief stricken. That is what I will testify to."

I want to take you by the lapels, slam you against the wall, and beat the truth out of you.

Instead, Matt walked out the door.

"You will have to live with this. You have blood on your hands," Matt warned.

The butler looked at the floor, and Matt knew with certainty this man had spent a lifetime hiding the truth. The line between honesty and cover up had been blurred so many years ago, who knew the truth about Richard Markus III, or II... how far back did this treachery go?

Matt left the butler and prepared to follow Richard to the end of the earth, if necessary, to gather evidence.

Chapter Twenty-Nine

L ucy buzzed into Cora's cottage with breakfast and correspondence from Toronto.

"Good morning, Cora." Lucy made tea as Cora picked up a letter from Mrs. King.

"It is a beautiful morning." Cora tried to smile despite the fact that her stomach clenched with worry over the contents of the letter.

"I can't stay — I am off to visit my sister. Do you want to come with me? Or do you have plans for the day?" Lucy poured tea into a china tea cup embellished with crocuses.

"I am going to go bicycling this morning. I am supposed to meet with Priscilla to be sure my new wardrobe fits." Cora settled down in front of her breakfast. "Thank you for the tea."

"Oh! That sounds like a great day — enjoy it! I will see you later." Lucy gave Cora a hug. "I am so glad you are looking refreshed and happy — enjoy your day." Lucy let herself out of the cottage. Cora pulled a shawl around her shoulders and braced herself as she opened the letter.

Dear Cora,
Please accept my sincere apology. Since the day Eli gave you such a terrible ultimatum, he has suspended activities at Hope House. In order to open it again, I have had to prove myself and regain his trust. He has made certain demands of me that are humiliating.
I believe this charity is necessary, so I am gritting my teeth and complying. My life has consisted of house arrest unless he requires my presence at social outings where I smile brightly and pretend my heart is not broken. My life is a sham, but a necessary sham; he has finally allowed me to reopen Hope House. I am not allowed any assistance from

the suffragettes and not permitted to contact them in any capacity. I am trying to ignore my pain and focus on those who need my assistance.

Under no circumstances are you to return to Toronto. Eli is spiraling into depravity, and if you come back here, I fear for your life. I have no idea how far he will go. Stay safe and stay far away from Toronto.

I write this, so you know that you are not the only one who suffered at his hand. I paid a terrible price for not listening to you when you said to drop the petition. I was remiss. My sincere apologies and I hope the best for you in Oakland. May you find peace and happiness there. Has Sol joined you? I hope he has. I will never know because you cannot return any correspondence to me as all my letters are opened. I snuck this letter to Mrs. King at my doctor's appointment. It would infuriate Eli to know I had contacted you. I walk a fine line these days. This letter is sent to you at great risk to my person, but I had to warn you.

Stay safe my friend, be happy in Oakland.

Warm regards,

Adeline Pitman

Worry snaked through Cora as she placed the letter back in the envelope. *Adeline, I'm so sorry I can't help you.*

Tears stung Cora's eyes as she thought about Adeline trying her best to re-open Hope House when her own hopes must be completely dashed.

Cora's heart weighed heavy.

How do I get around this law? How can I protect you when the law considers you property? The law doesn't see you as a person — I don't know how to fight that anymore. Everything I have tried has failed.

After breakfast, she bicycled to Priscilla's and tried to shake off the feeling of doom from Adeline's letter. She took a deep breath of late May, spring air. Her eyes feasted on the new spring green around her. Slowly, the heavy gloom she felt started to ease. She had done her best. She had failed. If in the future a way to assist presented itself, she would seize the opportunity. Depraved Eli or not.

Cycling through Oakland, Cora let the peace of the community settle into her heart. She smiled at mothers who gave children kisses and lunch pails and then sent them off to school. The ladies swept their front steps while they chatted with their neighbors before getting back to housework. These women, Cora knew, shared everything from cups of sugar, to words of encouragement.

Cora wondered if the ladies sweeping their steps were speculating about the news that Min had been arrested and would not return to Oakland. The entire community seemed to breathe a collective sigh of relief that Matt would finally have some well-deserved peace. The women of Oakland were concerned that Matt's mother would have to be placed in a care facility of some sort, but this new 'Priscilla woman' was stepping in while he was away. Single man. Married woman. Unheard of. However, Ada Bennett sanctioned the arrangement, which meant while there were knowing glances and lips pursed in disapproval, no one dared speak against Ada. The gossips held their tongues but kept their eyes peeled for any indiscretion.

Cora ignored the speculations and headed over to Matt's house on her bicycle. She cycled past Mrs. Charbonneau's house and thought she caught a glimpse of the hermit peeking out the window. Such a beautiful spring day; it was sad the woman was shut away inside.

She skidded to a halt in front of the Hartwell's shiny clean house with flowers in a flowerbed. Matt's mother sat on the front porch in a rocking chair holding a kitten.

"Good morning." Cora propped her bicycle against the wrought iron fence and smiled at Mrs. Hartwell. She peeked through the front window to see Priscilla standing in a shaft of sunlight that slanted over her and illuminated her work area. After pinning fabric to a dress form, she stood back and tapped her fingertip against her lip in concentration. Frowning at her work, she took the pins out and started to re-pin the fabric.

Cora smiled at her. Priscilla was a designer at work, and the house could fall down around her — until it was the right line, the right shape, she'd keep working. Cora stopped smiling when the sunshine illuminated the bruises. The thought of Priscilla being beaten by Richard in the carriage house made acid churn in Cora's stomach. She knew Matt stopped the beating and replaced her sewing machine. Cora had always liked Matt Hartwell, but since this incident she had more respect for him than ever.

She knocked on the door and smiled at the kitten Mrs. Hartwell was playing with. Cora recognized the fine hand of Ada Bennett here. Ada, a cat lover, believed many things in life could be cured by spending an hour with a kitten.

"Cora!" Priscilla smiled wide as she opened the door and welcomed her in.

"I hope it's all right that I stopped by today. How are things progressing with my wardrobe?"

"Of course, come in. Can you stay for tea and cake? I was about to take a little break."

"That sounds lovely."

"Do you prefer lazy daisy cake or chocolate?" Priscilla smiled at her, then headed to the pantry.

"One of each, of course." Cora settled down at the dining room table.

Priscilla laughed. "Have you had lunch?"

"I did. It is Lucy's mission in life to feed me every two hours, and so now I'm worried my new dresses won't fit."

"You look much better." Priscilla found tea cups and saucers and set the table.

"I feel much better. Ada Bennett put me on a strict regimen of eating every day, three times a day, riding my bike at least three miles, and reading novels, not law books, in the park. She is most insistent, and I think the bicycling is making me so exhausted I sleep all night. How are you?"

Priscilla gave Cora a quick smile that didn't reach her eyes. "I'll be fine."

Priscilla turned from Cora, went to the cook stove, and poured hot water from the kettle into a tea pot. "I have two shirtwaists finished, three skirts, and your new-fangled corset. So, that'll help with all the bicycling requirements."

"That's pretty fast work!"

"I'm going to leave town next week, so I wanted your wardrobe squared away. I have your swimming costume almost finished, so maybe you could try it on..."

"Leaving town?" Cora frowned.

"I think it's the best option." Priscilla opened the pantry. Cora noticed it was organized, labeled, and well stocked. Either Matt had fierce organizing skills, or Priscilla had taken his house in hand. Cora suspected the latter. Priscilla returned to the table with the tea pot.

"Where are you going?" Cora bit her lip in concern.

"It is probably best that no one knows where." Priscilla returned to the pantry and brought two cakes to the table.

"I see." Cora's spirits fell.

Priscilla served the cake, and as she took a delicate bite, she winced. Cora winced with her.

"I've never made a swim costume before, so I am interested to see what you think of it." Priscilla scooped up more cake for Cora.

Cora knew she wanted to change the subject and cursing her own cowardice, let her.

"I'm sure it's perfect." Cora smiled.

They finished their tea and cake, then got to work.

The swim costume would show her knees. Pale with anxiety, Cora hoped she had the nerve to wear it at Bennett's. No one would see her, but the thought of being caught in public in this costume made her heart pound!

"It's purple." Cora's breath caught.

"Very dark purple." Priscilla laughed at the dismay on Cora's face.

Cora grimaced as she pulled it on. She turned to see herself in the mirror.

"It's scandalous." She smiled slyly at Priscilla.

"It looks like freedom." Priscilla grinned back.

Both of them heard the knock on the door at the same time. Priscilla jumped in alarm.

"Are you expecting a visitor?" Cora clutched at her very exposed throat.

"No." Priscilla's hands trembled.

"Let me get it." Cora placed her hand on Priscilla's to try to stop the tremor.

"You can't in that outfit!" Priscilla's eyes widened with fear.

"Right. Throw me a robe." Cora pulled Matt's robe over her outfit and followed Priscilla down the hall.

Together, they crept down the stairs to the front door where the banging started again.

"Priscilla, I know you're in there." It was a woman's voice. Tension eased from Priscilla's shoulders.

"Who do you think it is?" Cora tightened the robe around her.

"My grandmother." Priscilla visibly stood a little taller and smoothed her hair back, as if getting ready to face an attack.

"She sounds furious."

"I can't leave Mrs. Hartwell out there with her. I have to open this door. This is so embarrassing. Here I am with a client, and my crazy grandmother is on the front step. I'm so sorry."

"Never mind calling me a client. I'm your friend. Let me deal with it." Cora put her hand on Priscilla's arm.

"No. I better answer. This has been brewing for a while." Priscilla took a deep breath and opened the door.

"What are you doing here?" her grandmother hissed as she entered the house. She completely ignored Cora.

"I am caring for Mrs. Hartwell. Would you like some tea?"

"I would like my granddaughter at home with her lawful husband, not living in sin with Matt Hartwell."

"Oh! You're misinformed. Matt is in Winnipeg, Grandmother. He is sitting his exams. I am here with his mother. As soon as he is home, I will be relocating."

"You are a whore like your mother." Mrs. Charbonneau's words bit into Priscilla. Cora took a step forward in order to step in between them and protect Priscilla if necessary.

Mrs. Charbonneau leaned toward Priscilla as she prepared her next verbal attack. Cora yearned to move forward and intervene.

"I am not a whore." Priscilla's voice caught with fury.

"You are gallivanting around the country," Mrs. Charbonneau hissed at her. "It's time you returned to your husband."

"I am not returning, now or ever." Priscilla crossed her arms over her chest.

"You have to. The courts ordered you back."

"How did you know?" Priscilla sounded strangled. "Doesn't matter. The courts can order me back to render conjugal rights until they are blue in the face — I'm not going back."

The cake in Cora's stomach turned to acid at Priscilla's words. *Court ordered rape.* It couldn't be true.

"You made a vow. Do you think you can just walk away from your duty? What makes you so special? This is only going to make things worse for you. If you had returned when I sent you..." Mrs. Charbonneau's eyes narrowed.

"If I had returned when you sent me, I would be dead of fever. I will not return." Priscilla's hand shook as she opened the door, indicating that her grandmother was not welcome to stay.

"You vowed." Mrs. Charbonneau shrieked at her.

"He vowed a few things, too. Hmm. Let's see. Love and honour. There was no love, no honour in what happened between us on the stairs. So, next time you send him some correspondence, you can let him know I intend to disappear. You are welcome to leave." Priscilla responded with such vehemence Cora wanted to cheer.

"You're no better than a prostitute. Do you know what they are saying about you staying here in Matt's house? It's outrageous."

"You are right. This is Matt's house, and as it is not my home, I don't think Matt would appreciate you coming here without an invitation. Unexpected visitors disturb his mother..."

"You're planning to run away with Matt Hartwell." Mrs. Charbonneau spoke over top of Priscilla, determined to have her say.

"No, I am not." Priscilla spoke through teeth that were clenched tight.

All right, that's enough. Cora stepped in between them.

"Mrs. Charbonneau." Cora finally found her voice. "I think it's time you left. It would be best if you didn't return."

"Who are you, then?" Mrs. Charbonneau turned her attention and her rage to Cora.

Cora was thankful for the robe that covered her scandalous bathing costume.

"Cora Rood."

"I heard about you. Some terrible suffragette who thinks men and women can be equal... a lawyer, aren't you?"

"Men and women *are* equal. We're waiting patiently for society to catch up." Ice edged Cora's tone.

Mrs. Charbonneau's eyes flashed with fire.

Why does that terrify you so much? Why does the thought of equality pull anger out of you? What happened to you? Why are we fighting this battle with men and women? Older women, who should be leading this movement... women like Mrs. King.

"If you do not leave..." Cora squared off with Mrs. Charbonneau. She stepped closer, forcing Mrs. Charbonneau to take a step back. "I will have to ask Cole McDougall to escort you out of this house."

"You didn't answer my question. Who do you think you are? Do you really expect me to believe you're a lawyer? It's preposterous," Mrs. Charbonneau hissed at Cora.

Just say no. Just tell her you are not a lawyer. Just say it. Say it. Mercy. . . I can't say it. Deep down, under all the defeat, if I could stand up in court and destroy people like this awful woman in front of me, I would.

"I am not asking you to leave again." Cora's voice hardened.

"Do you know what men think of women like you?" Mrs. Charbonneau took another tack. Her head tilted to the side as she contemplated exactly where Cora might be weakest.

"Priscilla, would you please send for Cole? Mrs. Charbonneau needs to be evicted from this property." Cora didn't take her eyes from Mrs. Charbonneau as she spoke.

"Ah. You speak like a lawyer. It's true, then." Mrs. Charbonneau looked down her nose at Cora. Her harsh tone implied she should crawl away in shame.

"Please, Priscilla, you can take my bike. Get the constable so we can press charges right now."

Priscilla moved to the door; Mrs. Charbonneau took a step back, indicating her intention to retreat.

"No. You don't need the constable involved. I'll go. Know this. You can't outrun your husband forever." Mrs. Charbonneau's face flushed red with fury. "Eventually, he'll find you. You." She pointed at Cora. "You are a disgrace to women everywhere. You're filling this girl's head with nonsense. She can't win. She's making everything worse."

Mrs. Charbonneau went to the door.

Cora stood beside Priscilla. "Get. Out. And if you know what's good for you, you won't come back."

"You're threatening me?" Mrs. Charbonneau's eyebrow arched in challenge.

Cora squared her shoulders. "I can and will bring the law down on you."

Mrs. Charbonneau turned on her heel and marched out of the house, across the lawn, and banged the gate shut behind her. They watched from the verandah as Ada Bennett leaped out of her path.

Ada's eyebrows raised in confusion.

"That was unpleasant." Cora looked at Priscilla to see if she was in tears.

Together they helped Mrs. Hartwell into the house.

"She's awful," Priscilla said as she handed Mrs. Hartwell her kitten.

"Priscilla, what happened?" Ada asked.

"My grandmother is a vicious woman. She accused me of living in sin with Matt."

"Oh, good grief." Ada rolled her eyes. She put lilacs in water and placed them near Mrs. Hartwell's rocking chair. Cora watched Mrs. Hartwell tentatively reach out to touch the blossoms. "Why do people jump to such negative conclusions?"

"Very good question," Cora agreed as she bent her head over the bouquet of lilacs and took a deep breath to calm down. Her heart pounded from the confrontation with Mrs. Charbonneau.

"Any news of Matt?" Mrs. Bennett asked Priscilla.

"No. Have you heard anything?" Priscilla's eyes lit up with joy.

"No. I happened to be in town, so I was hoping to hear if he passed and what day you expect him. We have a graduation gift for him I would leave, if it is all official."

"As soon as I hear, I will let you know," Priscilla promised. "Join us — we were interrupted when Cora was trying on her new wardrobe.

"I want your opinion." Cora grinned at Mrs. Bennett, determined not to allow Mrs. Charbonneau to ruin their day.

"I have ten minutes before Mr. Bennett will be by with the carriage."

"Is everything all right?" Priscilla's face creased in concern as she addressed Ada.

"I'm afraid not. Lady Harper woke up with pains in the night, so John brought me in to check on her. Sadly, she lost the baby. Very unfortunate."

Priscilla's eyes filled with tears. "I'm so sorry. Does she need someone to sit with her?"

"If you could get past that terrible Biddy, I would suggest it. Unfortunately, Biddy is there and keeping everyone at bay. It's peculiar." Ada frowned with concern. "Priscilla, are you all right?"

"I'll be fine. Let's try clothes on." Priscilla tried to smile and failed. She turned to gain composure before leading them back upstairs to see the rest of Cora's wardrobe.

"Priscilla, if you are upset..." Cora went to her and put her hand on her shoulder.

"I keep thinking the whole village might be thinking that I'm here, living in sin with Matt. Do you think the whole village is saying that?" Priscilla's voice broke.

"Absolutely not. The village is saying that they are glad Mrs. Hartwell is in good hands," Ada answered firmly.

Priscilla dashed tears out of her eyes as she turned to Ada.

"You're sure? I would hate to bring any reproach on Matt's good name."

"I am. Even if they were saying such a mean-spirited thing, it's not true. What do you need, Priscilla? What would help this situation?" Ada sat on the bed where Cora's clothes were on display.

"I need a divorce, and I need to be safe. I can't return to a man who deliberately caused me to miscarry. I certainly can't render... uh... well. I can't. To all of it."

Cora's blood ran cold as she listened to Priscilla speak.

Don't get involved. This is not your fight. You gave up law. Stop, Cora, you will only get hurt... you'll get her hopes up, and you can't deliver justice.

"Priscilla." Cora couldn't help herself, she dove head long into how to prosecute this case. "Is your lawyer prosecuting Richard for the miscarriage?"

Priscilla turned away. Cora met Ada's eyes, grateful for her friend. "He said it would be my word against his. He said unless the butler would testify..." Priscilla spoke so softly they strained to hear.

"Hogwash," Cora sputtered.

Priscilla's head snapped up. She turned around to face Cora.

"What do you mean hogwash?" Priscilla dug a handkerchief out of her dress pocket.

"You don't have any rights under Canadian law, but your unborn child does." Cora's eyes lit up. "Richard needs to be arrested for murder. Today. Under Canadian law, everyone is guilty of an indictable offence and liable to imprisonment for life who causes the death of any child, which has not become a human being, in such a manner that he would have been guilty of murder *if such a child had been born.*"

Priscilla gasped in surprise.

Ada stood up. "Is that true?"

"That's the law. That's the battle Priscilla's lawyer has to fight. Not divorce court. Criminal court."

Oh my goodness. I was going about it all wrong! Not divorce court you stupid girl! You have to destroy Richard and Eli in criminal court. Oh! Priscilla and Adeline, there might be some hope yet!

"He says I can't win that way." Priscilla's forehead creased in confusion.

"He, like all of them, doesn't care. Make them care. Insist on this. You can have him arrested and knock him down before you go to divorce court. You need to go back and try again. But, you need evidence. What hospital did you miscarry in?"

"Winnipeg General."

"Then you came home very sick?"

"She had retained placenta from a miscarriage. She had bruising on her hands and wrists consistent with being pulled off a banister. I would testify to that, and I know Dr. Davies would." Mrs. Bennett rattled off a testimony as if she was already on the witness stand.

Cora smiled. She could see the entire court proceeding in front of her.

"You need evidence."

"Matt is looking into the adultery while he is in the city."

"Perfect."

"I thought you weren't practicing law anymore." Priscilla's head tilted to the side as she smiled at Cora.

"I'm not," Cora said grimly. "Just let me look over the documents before you go back to war."

"War?"

"Yes. War. You're going to have to be tough, and your lawyer tougher. I can't do it. I can't go in there and be the lawyer you need, but I can look over the documents." Shame washed over Cora at Ada's look of naked disappointment.

It wasn't enough, and she knew it. Not a lawyer in the land was going to take Priscilla seriously. This was a tricky case to try. One where it would be her word against his. His word held more weight in court. However, with Ada on the stand, Priscilla on the stand, Dr. Davies on the stand, it was possible to win it. What lawyer would fight this for her, on her behalf? Well, one would, but she was sniveling in her brother's cottage trying to hide from the world and all her responsibilities.

Ada Bennett didn't need to say a word. The look she gave Cora was chastisement enough.

"I hope someday you can practice law again. You seem to have a knack." Priscilla held up a skirt.

"I don't." Cora gave her a pained look and turned away. "I'm not sure of much, but I know I will never practice law again."

Cora avoided Ada's eyes.

"Because of what you are running from?" Priscilla asked sympathetically.

Cora let out a sigh. "I'll put your case together. I don't have what it takes to stand up and..."

"Oh, Cora. If you would look at the documents, that would be a big help." Priscilla smiled so broadly her eyes shone with happiness.

"We'll ask Dr. Davies to request your documents from the hospital, and we'll wait for evidence from Matt. Then we reconvene," Cora stated.

Priscilla hugged Cora with excitement.

"Careful. Don't get your hopes up." Cora spoke warily. "You might have to run. The legal system is all men — they don't typically side with women. Please, don't look at me with all that hope."

"It used to be all men," Ada said softly to Cora. "Until one woman pushed all the boundaries and forced them to admit her into law school. That woman didn't stop until they let her train to be a barrister no less."

"Ada." Cora put her hands up in defense.

"That woman is still here, in this room, and she is equal to this task." Ada spoke simply.

"You don't know what I've been through..." Cora's eyes were tortured.

"I want you to come out to my farm tomorrow. The train comes through at 10:30. You and I need to talk. Privately." Ada went to the window and waved at her husband. "John is here. I can't stay. I'll see you tomorrow."

"Of course." Cora's heart dragged to her feet. This would be the longest lecture in the history of mankind.

If it's not Jean King pushing me around, it's Ada-blessed-Bennett, and she's impossible to say no to.

Ada swept out of the room.

"So sorry about that. Please, don't feel any pressure on my account. I'm sure if the documents are in order, my lawyer will do the right thing." Priscilla tried to ease the tension in the room.

Cora sighed. He won't. He won't even look over those documents.

"In case you change your mind about practicing law, I'll whip up a black dress. Extra severe." Priscilla grinned mischievously.

"I won't," Cora said honestly.

"You might." Priscilla smiled.

***

The first night Matt spent in the shrubs across the street from Richard's house there was no movement. Nothing happened.

The second night. Still nothing.

Discouragement ate at Matt until finally, on Friday, Richard hopped into a carriage at around 9:00 p.m. Matt scrambled for his bicycle and followed the carriage to 380 Fort Street. He watched with bated breath as a woman, very scantily clad, opened the door and invited him in.

Matt pulled out his camera and took pictures of Richard entering her home.

Got you.

Just as he placed the camera back in its case, he saw movement out of the corner of his eye. A police officer, two of them.

Matt scrambled to hide the camera at the bottom of his bag and moved to get on his bicycle.

"You there. Stop."

Matt froze in place. "How can I help you, officers?"

His heart pounded hard with fear. Not of what would happen to him, but the camera. If something happened to the camera, there would not be evidence. Without proof, Priscilla would be tied to this adulterer forever.

"What's in the bag?"

They think I'm a burglar.

"A camera."

"Hand it over."

Matt handed the bag to the police, who dumped it on the street.

"That is my camera. I would ask you treat it carefully."

"Are you some sort of peeping Tom?" The bigger cop gave Matt a hard look.

"I'm investigating for an upcoming trial."

The one cop rolled his eyes at the other cop. "That's what they're calling it now? You've likely got photographs of ladies changing in front of windows. So, let's take care of that right now."

Matt watched as the police officer opened the case and pulled the camera out.

"Would you consider letting me get that film developed, and if it *is* women in their altogether, you could charge me with... uh... what is the charge for that? A stiffer penalty than just loitering, right?" Matt looked wildly from one to the other.

"Sounds like a lot of work." The cop shrugged as he flipped the case open and pulled the film out to be exposed to the street light.

Matt lunged for the camera, but the other officer tackled him to the ground and handcuffed him.

"Let's get you processed and off the streets for the night," the bigger cop said as he hauled him up.

The officer tossed the camera behind a shrub and left it there, then both dragged Matt to the police station.

Once processed, Matt slumped down in the prison cell and thought about how he could prove Richard was having an affair with the woman who lived at 380 Fort Street in Winnipeg, Manitoba.

By the next morning, stiff, sore, and furious, he had a plan.

Chapter Thirty

Cora hopped on the train and was on her way to Ada's by 10:00. She watched the Manitoba fields as they passed by. Newly planted, the whole world seemed like it had just woken up. At the Switzer train stop, Cora was let off on the vast prairie. Only a sign, a bird, and prairie grass to greet her. She walked down the path to the Bennett's farm. As she got closer to the bridge, she saw Emily Wheaton hanging wash out to dry. Cora waved, and Emily quickly dashed back inside the cabin. Cabin was a grand term for the squalor Emily Wheaton lived in. Cora's heart ached in sympathy at the scene.

Poor Emily.

Cora walked across the bridge, up the hill, and down the lane to the Bennett's home. Ada's clotheslines were already full, and her sheets, filled with spring air, billowed out and settled back down.

Ada waved from her verandah. Cora's eyes lit up as she soaked in the beauty of the river as it flowed by. Apple orchard in bloom, grass freshly clipped, and a garden peeking through with new green made her happy. She turned her attention to Ada and wondered how bad the scolding would be.

"You made it!" Ada smiled at her friend. "I'm so glad you could come out. With all the travel into town with Lady Harper, I'm behind on my house. Come in. I have a treat for you."

"Ada, I'm going to have to cut out some treats or these clothes aren't going to fit for long," Cora groaned. The entire community of Oakland seemed bent on stuffing her to the gills at every opportunity.

"Please, stop griping about your weight. You came here a skeleton. You finally look like you aren't going to blow away with a gust of wind. Get in this kitchen," Ada demanded.

The kitchen was overflowing with baking, from one end to the other.

"Put me to work, Ada, it looks like you're swamped." Cora rolled up her sleeves and hoped she could head off the lecture if she was working.

"Absolutely not. You are my guest. I'm going to fill these bread pans, and we're going to talk. How are you feeling now? You are keeping food down? Riding your bicycle?"

"I'm much better." Cora sat down at the table.

"How are your nerves?" Ada's eyes swept over her friend.

"Pretty good. I'm feeling well."

"Good." Ada put a steaming cup of tea and a hot cinnamon bun with extra butter in front of her.

Cora weakened in regard to saying no to treats as she breathed in the scent of fresh cinnamon bun. "My favourite."

"I know. I did that on purpose." Ada smiled at Cora and poured herself a cup of tea. She sat down across from Cora.

"What is your next step?" Ada asked simply. "You fought for five years to be a lawyer, and now you are not going to practice. What are you going to do?"

"I don't really know how to answer that." Cora cut patterns in the butter with her knife.

"Why don't you start from the beginning?" Ada's voice was gentle.

"Since I got out of jail, I can't seem to find the will to keep going. To keep fighting." Cora's heart wrenched as she spoke.

"So, have you decided to give up the law altogether?" Ada cut straight to the point.

"Yes." Cora's gaze dropped to the table.

"Why?"

"I'm terrified to go back to jail."

Ada looked as if she were formulating her next line of reasoning. "How often do lawyers get thrown in jail for practicing law? I'm curious."

"Rarely." Cora put her head in her hands. "I know when I say it out loud, it seems ridiculous. They get sent to jail for participating in rallies and leading a group of women into battle, only to be tortured while imprisoned."

"You lost a battle at a women's rights rally. That must have been devastating." Ada reached across the table and held Cora's hand.

"It was." Cora took a deep breath as the memories tortured her.

"What happened to the women in jail?" Ada tilted her head to the side as she waited for Cora's answer.

"They were all beaten very badly, and the guards made me watch." Cora's eyes glistened. "We were at their mercy, and there was no mercy."

"Why you?"

"I led the rally, and I am connected to Lady Bronwyn. They wanted me to see what I was up against." Cora dashed tears from her eyes. "Then it was my turn."

"I'm very sorry." Ada's eyes were soft with sympathy. "What happened then?"

"When the morning guard showed up, most of us were released. Eventually, everyone got out. They got on with their lives. We pressed charges, and it went to court, but it doesn't fix what it did to me. I can't seem to get past it." Cora bit her lip.

"Do they hold you responsible for the events of that night?"

"No." Shame flooded through Cora.

"But you do?" Ada probed to get to the root of the problem.

"Ada." Cora scrubbed her hands over her face.

"You're taking responsibility for everything that happens in the women's rights movement." Ada presented the facts like a lawyer. No emotion, only logic. "These are grown women — they can make their own decisions. They chose to rally. They can again, with or without you."

Cora took a deep breath and let out a long sigh.

"What is your goal for your life, Cora? What do you want now, more than anything?"

"I'd like to eat this cinnamon bun in peace," Cora growled.

Ada threw back her head and laughed. "Come on. Answer me. I want to know. What do you want?"

Cora abandoned the cinnamon bun and got up from the table. She stood at the window, her back to her friend; her shoulders slumped as she clenched her teeth.

"Everything I want, I can't have."

"Let's assume it's within your grasp. What is the first thing that comes to mind?" Ada refreshed the tea in their tea cups.

"I want equal rights for women." Cora kept her eyes on the river. "I want the law to stop men from being able to beat their wives, with little to no recourse under the law. I know the temperance movement wants to ban alcohol, Ada. I respect that. However, what I want goes further. Instead of banning alcohol, let's prosecute *all* violence in the home. In addition to that, I want the law to apply equally to men and women. There should be no double standard in court."

"Why? Why has *that* been your life's goal? You were raised in a good family — you had everything. What do you know of violence in a home?" Ada's voice was so gentle, Cora turned back to Ada with fresh tears in her eyes.

"Oh, Ada. I have never spoken of it," Cora whispered. "I came here prepared for a lecture, not this... not this kindness."

"What happened, Cora?" Ada sat still and waited for Cora to speak. Taking a shaky breath, Cora returned to the table.

"I was nine. My mother had gotten really sick, and my father was so busy with harvest, they sent us to live with my aunt for a month while mother recovered in hospital."

"You and Wil?"

"Yes. Thank goodness Wil was with me. At first, everything was fine, but we noticed our aunt seemed nervous all the time. Her hands shook, just like Priscilla's. One day, a man came by the house — he was lost, actually. My uncle saw it. Once the man left, he started screaming and beating my aunt. He accused her being immoral with that man. Not in those words. Harsher words, terrible words." Cora put her hands over her ears as if she could still hear him. "The beating kept going. He hit her over and over, and he didn't stop. We were all screaming and crying, and the beating got worse. Oh, Ada, when I close my eyes, I still see it.

"I buried my face in Wil's chest, I was so traumatized. My uncle stopped and dragged me away from Wil. Turned out, he enjoyed an audience. Wil went wild and tried to intervene. He got beaten, too. I couldn't stop screaming. When the belt came down on Wil, Aunty Lucinda tried to protect him with her own body. She kept herself between the belt and Wil." Cora covered her face in her hands. "Finally, she stopped moving, and I thought she was dead. He warned us, if we said anything, he'd kill her."

"Oh, Cora." Ada's eyes were soft with sympathy.

Cora took a very deep breath. "That wasn't the worst."

Ada bit her lip as Cora continued. "When he was finally done, and she was a bloody mess on the floor, he pulled her up and cut all her hair off. In front of all of us." Cora's eyes filled with tears at the memory. "He was so calm. He kept jeering at her, baiting her. He said, 'no one will look at you now.' We all cried. Her sons and her daughters, Wil and me. We cried with her, and the more we cried, the happier he seemed. Oh, Ada, the humiliation on her face — I can still see it all these years later." Cora wiped tears away at the memory.

Ada sat quietly, waiting for her to continue.

"Wil and I changed that summer. We banded together with their children, and I remember it was hard to sleep because we lived in constant fear of setting him off. Finally, mother was well enough for us to go back home. So, we told our father. We went into his study and told him everything, even though we were terrified that Aunt Lucinda would be killed. Being dead would be better. I remember Wil wept as he spoke of it — we were so upset. Of course, no one in the family knew. My father's face went grey as he listened to the whole thing. He was absolutely horrified that we were there and subjected to that.

"You remember our father — he was determined to do the right thing. He immediately looked into legally intervening, and guess what he found out? If she left, she would not have any rights over her children. The courts immediately grant custody to the father. She couldn't leave the children, so she stayed to protect them. I remember at nine years old I said to my father, why can't you do anything? He used the terms 'no recourse under the law.' That was the first time I heard that term." Cora stopped crying and her eyes hardened. "Not the last."

"Your father always was a progressive thinker." Ada's tone indicated approval.

"He raised us to believe men and women were equal. You can imagine my surprise when I was dropped into the real world. When I went to school and training, it was a rude awakening. Life changed again when I had my bachelors in mathematics at the age of sixteen. I'm not bragging about that. My parents believed if you can do something, you should. My father would not take no for an answer. He said my mind could not be wasted, I needed to be in the best schools. To him, it was simple. So, when I was educated to that degree, I was stunned at how men treat educated women — it was awful. Then the D. W. E. A. got ahold of me. They asked if I would go into medicine."

"Why did you choose law?"

"There were already women in medicine. Amazing women fighting that battle. There are no women in law. I, as you know, am the first one. Someone had to be first." Cora shrugged. "I chose law to seek recourse for my aunt and women like her. It seemed unconscionable that women were second class citizens until they are married. Then, after marriage they have no rights at all. I thought women like my aunt should be safe and raise children in safety. It's like my eyes were opened, and once I saw the inequality in the law, I had to demand change. For her. For all women, everywhere."

"I didn't know about your aunt." Ada's eyes were soft with sympathy.

"Not just her, now." Cora shook her head. "I've been in the tenements in Toronto. When we rally, that's where the women come from. It breaks my heart. Every time. I can't seem to be callous about it."

"Nor should you be." Ada shook her head and sipped her tea. "Have you changed your mind then?"

"I grew up, Ada. I see what we are up against." Cora sat down at the table.

"You knew what you were up against at the age of nine," Ada reminded her gently.

"There is a big difference between witnessing violence and being the victim of it. I vowed, while I lay on the bottom of a jail cell with a fractured jaw, that if I ever got out, I would never rally again. I would never lead women into battle like that, to be subjected to anything that terrible again. I thought I would get over it, but coming up against Eli Pitman and failing so miserably, that was the last straw. I'm done." Cora couldn't take the anger out of her voice.

"I see it differently." Ada spoke softly.

Cora's head snapped up and her eyes narrowed.

"Hear me out." Ada buttered a cinnamon bun that neither of them would eat. "You know what it feels like to be hurt and know that no one is coming to the rescue. You have experienced the pain and the humiliation. It puts you in a better position. All this anger that comes from witnessing injustice, you can use that to keep you down or you can tap into it to spur you forward. If I needed someone to fight on my behalf, I don't want the girl who has no idea what it feels like. I want a warrior on my side who has been there and says, that's enough. No more. You are letting injustice *defeat* you. I say, let the injustice spur you on."

Cora's lips thinned. "You don't seem to realize what I'm up against."

"You don't seem to grasp how much ground you will *lose* for the women's rights movement if you stop," Ada said sharply.

Ada and Cora locked eyes. Cora didn't look away.

"Easy for you to say in your happy, clean kitchen with a man that loves you and three lovely children," Cora hissed.

"You could have that, too." Ada shot back. "I know you, Cora. That's not your purpose. You didn't start all of this to stop now when you are two weeks from being sworn in! First woman barrister. They tried to tell you solicitor was enough, and you laughed at that and demanded they let you be a barrister. First woman lawyer in Upper Canada and Great Britain, and you are thinking about getting married and making cinnamon buns? No. You're not going to be happy here long term. Marriage and children and making a home is enough for most women, but *not* for you. You need a challenge or you will slowly become stagnant and die of boredom."

"You don't know what the men in power are capable of," Cora roared back at Ada. "All I feel is fear. I still feel so much fear."

"Ah. That's it." Ada leaned back in her chair. "The little nine-year-old girl who saw inequality was taught to fix it, the law had to be changed. Law doesn't change unless it is challenged. That little girl was *thinking*. The woman in front of me is *feeling*."

"She's thinking, too." Cora spoke through clenched teeth.

"No. Since you got here, you've been talking about how you *feel*. Not once have I heard what you think. You're feeling pressure from the D. W. E. A. It is a high profile case, challenge it and fail to defeat Eli in a court of law. They wanted to use that case to throw the double standard in the face of the court. Hard to ignore a double standard like that, isn't it? We're not talking about some uneducated shop girl. Adeline Pitman sounds like a force to be reckoned with. Powerful amount of money behind her. You were supposed to champion women's rights through her." Ada's reasoning hit deeper.

"They wanted an epic *fail* so the courts would have to re-evaluate divorce law. They didn't mind sacrificing me or Adeline on that alter," Cora shrieked at her. "I'm sick to death of failing, Ada! You know my background. I never fail. Until now. Now, I am *expected* to fail at every turn."

"Sometimes, Cora, we choose to lose a battle in the fight for women's rights while we prepare to win the war." Ada's eyes locked with Cora's. Cora didn't look away. "You know very well that a loss that huge could cause legislators to look at the law again. Your voice will be a leading force in demanding equal rights. You can't stop now."

"Do you really think so?" Cora choked on the words. "You think I have what it takes, after all I've been through?"

"I don't think." Ada stood up and placed her hands on the table. "I know."

Cora stood up to face Ada head on.

"I'm afraid to watch the law let another woman down." Cora's jaw clenched in anger. "The terror we felt at being in the kitchen of my aunt's home, watching her be beaten and humiliated, has never left me. How do I represent Priscilla, watch the courts fail her, and know that Priscilla will be forced home to more abuse? How do I live with that?"

"Not trying is a form of failure," Ada said simply.

Cora closed her eyes and hung her head.

"Stop focusing on fear. It's emotion. Start thinking. Priscilla has already been let down in every way a woman can be. At least, if the law lets her down and she runs, she knows she tried. The court lets her tell her story — it gives her a voice. Even if they fail her, she will be able to stand up to him and expose him for what he is. What is holding you back?" Ada words dug into a part of Cora's soul that she had carefully built walls around. Fresh pain and shame cut into her as Ada spoke. Cora's neck cramped with tension.

"You're brilliant, Cora, so stop listening to your heart. What does your head say? If Priscilla was your client, what would you do, what would be your first step?" Ada demanded.

Cora rubbed the back of her neck.

"Richard needs to be taken by surprise." Cora dropped her hands and lifted her eyes to Ada. "He's used to calling all the shots. He needs to be unsettled. Have him arrested for murder. That's what I would do. I would strike hard and fast and see how far we can provoke him. He would be stunned to face me in divorce court, and I would use that. He'd be careless, coming up against a woman."

Ada's face broke into a smile. "You would use your gender to manipulate him."

"Yes, I would absolutely use my gender to manipulate him. He won't know to be terrified at how far I will go to seek justice." Cora's eyes hardened as she spoke.

"You can't stop." Ada breathed. "You are an inspiration."

"Oh? Really. Well, not such an inspiration, Ada. My conscience bothers me every day that I left Adeline to face who knows what. If I do this, I'm back in the fight. I'll have to go back and destroy Eli Pitman. I've thought of nothing else. Adeline would lose in divorce court, but I know, deep down, past all the fear, that I could set things in motion, with the right evidence, to annihilate him in criminal court. Like you say, Ada, lose a battle to win the war. Men like Eli are criminals at best, but animals really. If I dig hard enough, if I'm patient, I can catch him, and I can destroy him. He won't see it coming — he doesn't know what lengths I'll go to."

"So why aren't you doing that?" Ada sat back down and took a delicate sip of tea. As if she hadn't pushed her friend to accept the greatest challenge facing women in this new century. She sat at the table as cool as a cucumber. As if there were no threat to Cora's life or sanity. "You got into this for a worthy cause. You need to finish it. Not for the D. W. E. A. Forget the politics, Cora. Finish this for the nine-year-old *you* who knew, deep down, the laws needed to change.'"

"What if I fail?" Cora crossed her arms in front of her chest.

"What if you win?" Ada spoke with such force Cora's eyes met hers again. "What if you win for Priscilla? Come on, Cora. This is court-ordered rape, and you know it," Ada roared. "Her choice is to return or run. So, not trying means we've all failed. She's vulnerable in either scenario. Will your conscience allow you to let her return or run?"

"You shame me, Ada." Cora swallowed hard.

"That was not my intent. My intent was to lovingly encourage you."

"This has been a lot of screeching and hollering for loving encouragement!" Cora reprimanded her friend.

"We're passionate about women's rights." Ada shrugged, making no apology for her arguments. "We both love Priscilla."

"I've thought of nothing else since her grandmother went after her. That kindled a fire in me I thought was long burned out," Cora admitted quietly.

"What do you need?" Ada, ever practical, sat up straighter.

Cora rubbed her forehead as she conceded. "I'll need a black dress. I'll have to have a firm to work under, and I need to see the paperwork up to this point."

"I spoke to Mr. Birch in Oakland, and he said you could work under him for the duration of the trial." Ada's eyes gleamed at Cora. "I told him you needed two weeks to finish your term so you could be sworn in. He said he would sign off on that. I asked Priscilla to make you a black dress for court. She already had it half sewn when I suggested it. Priscilla has all the paperwork. She will bring it to your cottage today. I understand Matt will be home shortly, so whatever evidence he gathered in Winnipeg will be on the top of the pile."

"You were pretty sure of yourself," Cora growled.

"No, Cora, I'm sure of you," Ada said simply. "You stubborn girl, I'm sure of *you*. I know you. I know your heart. You can't turn your back on a girl facing rape or running to the States. I knew you wouldn't let that happen, Cora. We have nothing to lose here. The only way this can go is up. Priscilla deserves happiness, and you are her only chance, so stop sniveling, and let's get a strategy."

"You are the worst friend anyone ever had in the whole world." Cora shook her head as her mind began racing through how to win. "I'll look at the documents. I can't promise anything."

"You better hurry. She's in contempt of court if she doesn't return by Friday."

"Friday? You mean next week?" Cora clutched at her throat in concern.

"Did you see that?" Ada grinned triumphantly. "You're already in this fight. I knew it. You just needed a nudge. Friday, next week. But this is already Thursday, so you have a lot of work ahead of you."

"I better get back to town."

"You can take Mae's horse. We'll bring her home from the livery stable tomorrow." Ada went to the front verandah to ask the hired man to saddle Brownie and bring her to the house. Cora finally ate her cinnamon bun while she waited for her horse to be saddled.

Ada returned to the kitchen. "When we are done with this, I promise to spend a day on a sandbar with you."

"I will hold you to that." Cora stood up, and Ada hugged her hard.

Brownie neighed at the front door.

"How fast is this horse?" Cora hadn't been on a horse in years and felt nervous at the thought.

"Nearly dead," Ada reassured her.

"Perfect." Cora climbed on the horse and felt Brownie take a deep breath, like a sigh.

"Cora." Ada leaned against the verandah pillar. "You can do this. I am so proud of you."

"We'll see." Cora adjusted the reins in her hands.

"You are an inspiration for women everywhere. I will be cheering for you every step of the way."

"Thank you, Ada, you are a good friend."

Ada nodded and went back to her kitchen.

Cora spurred Brownie forward; she put the thought of the battle she lost in a jail cell out of her mind as she prepared for war.

Chapter Thirty-One

The police released Matt the next morning. He washed away the smell of jail, dressed in his best suit, and made his way to a florist. He purchased the biggest bouquet of flowers he could find. As soon as he had the flowers, he made his way to 380 Fort Street. He checked his watch, 11:00 a.m.

Is it too early? He scrambled around behind the shrub where the police officer had tossed his camera and found it. The film was gone, but the camera was all right. He dusted it off and found the case that had been left on the ground beside it. Finally, after watching the house, he noticed a movement in the front window.

He took a deep breath, went to the front door, and rang the doorbell.

No answer.

Please come to the door. Please.

He rang the bell again.

Nothing.

He sat down on the front step and was contemplating his next step when he finally heard footsteps behind the door.

The door opened a crack. The woman peeked around. She looked at him, and her eyes narrowed. He stayed back a few steps.

Is she nervous of a man on her doorstep or suspicious?

"I'm not sure if I have the right house?" Matt smiled broadly at the woman. "I work for Mr. Markus. He asked me to have these flowers delivered to this address."

He watched her eyes shift from angry to delighted.

"Oh! They are beautiful!" she exclaimed as she held her hands out to take them.

Matt tried to look away; Richard's mistress was barely dressed.

"I am meeting with Richard later." Matt kept his eyes level with hers. "Would you like me to take a note to him? Just so he will know you received the flowers?"

"Good idea!"

"I have a pen, paper, and an envelope." Matt offered and she handed the flowers back and took the pen.

She smiled and wrote a note. She tucked it in the envelope and sealed it.

"I will get that to him right away. Thank you so much." Matt took the note, handed her the flowers, and as he turned away he heard a voice.

"Who is it, mama?" A little boy with brown curly hair and bright blue eyes came to the door and peeked around his mother.

"A nice visitor." She tousled his hair. "Daddy sent flowers."

Matt's blood ran cold.

Daddy.

"I'll get this note to Mr. Markus straight away." Matt sounded strangled even to his own ears. "Oh! I almost forgot. Mr. Markus sent something to you, too, young sir."

The little boy looked up at Matt in expectation. "He asked me to make sure you were a very good boy first."

"I have been!" The little boy jumped up and down with excitement as Matt pulled the camera out of its case.

"I think I better double check that with your mother. Madam, has he been a good boy?"

"He is the best boy." She smiled so much love at her son; Matt's heart broke for both of them.

Do you know Richard is married? How long has this been going on?

He crouched down to eye level with the little boy.

"This is a new kind of camera." Matt smiled at him as he loaded a new film and then closed the case. He handed it to the little boy. "I hope you enjoy it."

"This is so generous. I better add to that note. Can I quickly get another piece of paper?"

"Of course." Matt tried to sound casual. Evidence of a mistress and a son was going to liberate Priscilla.

She returned in record time, a robe belted over her scandalous night dress. She handed him a folded note and smiled broadly as she handed it over.

"You can let Richard know we are very grateful."

"I will indeed. Have a nice day ma'am, and you, young sir."

Matt's stomach churned in worry as he waved at the little boy. He tucked the evidence of Richard's adultery in his breast pocket, picked up his bike, and rode away from 380 Fort Street.

When Richard sees the flowers and the camera, will he know? He would be furious with her. What would he do to her?

You can't protect everyone.

Matt tried to shake that thought off and failed. When he was a block away, he opened her note. She wanted Richard to come by at 8:30. The note she added said Edward loves his new Brownie camera, thank you for being such a loving daddy.

Matt folded the note very carefully. Here it was — irrefutable evidence. He placed it in his pocket and wished with every fibre of his being a child was not involved. He couldn't bear the thought that his actions would cause this woman and her son any harm.

At least her child is alive.

That thought did not sooth his conscience. He rode to the nearest police station and asked to speak to the inspector.

"How can I help you?" The inspector frowned at Matt.

"There is a woman who lives at 380 Fort Street. I happen to know that her... uh... man is beating her."

"Are they married?"

"No. But, if you could send someone around tonight just to be sure..."

"Sir, we don't have enough police officers to be patrolling where someone might get hit. Come on. What are you thinking?"

Matt wanted desperately to get home to Priscilla. Friday, she would be held in contempt if she did not return. It was Monday. Dr. Davies had paved the way for him to pick up her hospital records; he now had evidence of not only adultery, but a whole family.

I can't leave Edward and this woman, Valentine of all names, to Richard's fists. He'll learn about this, and he'll hurt her. I can't let that happen.

Matt left the police station and went to the telegram office.

'All evidence collected, home before Friday.'

Matt bought another camera and found a better hiding spot to wait for Richard to show up. He didn't. Matt sighed and prepared to stay there every night until he did.

Finally, Tuesday at 8:30, Richard's carriage rolled down Fort Street, and Matt, camera ready again this time, held his breath as Richard got out of the carriage and went to the front door. He snapped pictures as the door opened and Valentine came out. She hugged him, right there on the front step. Matt held his breath as he watched them talking. He couldn't see Richard's face. He waited until they went into the house. Within a few minutes, he heard something smash.

Matt put his camera down, scrambled to his feet, and raced to her defense. He pounded his fist on the door.

The smashing inside the house stopped and a furious Richard Markus opened the door. His face registered surprise for the split second it took Matt to pound his fist into his jaw. He dropped like a rock at the front entrance.

Matt's heart broke when he saw the flowers proudly displayed on the little table, presumably their dining room table. Edward and Valentine were holding onto each other and crying. The camera lay on the floor, smashed to pieces.

"Who are you?" Valentine wept as she held onto Edward, who sobbed inconsolably.

"I'm here to help you." Matt went to them and handed Valentine a handkerchief.

"You ruined everything." She pressed the handkerchief against her bleeding lip.

"I am so sorry this happened to you." Matt crouched down and helped her up off the floor. "He's married. I know his wife. He nearly killed her. She needs to divorce him, and I needed evidence. Why don't we go together to the police station, and you can press charges against him so he doesn't do this again."

"Press charges? Are you crazy?" Valentine's eyes widened in fear. "Who do you think pays for this place? Where do you think my next meal is coming from if I kick him out? I have a little boy to think about."

"But he beats you." Matt's eyebrows drew together in confusion.

"What alternative do I have?" She wiped her eyes and kissed Edward on the top of the head. "I can work at back-breaking work for half the wages a man makes, but who looks after my son?"

Matt stood awkwardly by her as she started weeping again. She held Edward close to her.

Matt scrubbed his hands over his face.

"Look. I wanted you to know that Richard is married. His wife had to run from him. She is filing for divorce. I don't know what that will mean for you, but if there is any way to get away from him..."

"There is no way to get away from him." Valentine held her hands out in surrender. "This is how it is. Would you please leave now? I think you've done enough."

"Of course, I'll leave. Are you safe if he regains consciousness?"

"I'll go to the neighbor's." She swallowed hard.

"I'll walk you there." Matt couldn't reconcile the thought of leaving a woman and child in the home of a man who would beat them all over again.

Her eyes flicked from Richard to Matt. "Why are you being so nice?"

"You deserve better than this," Matt said simply.

"Lots of people would say you made your bed, now you have to lie in it."

"I'm not most people, and it's not my place to say anything of the sort."

She wiped her tears on her skirt.

"This isn't right," Matt said gently. "You should never have a man lay a hand on you, and your son shouldn't watch it. So, let's go to the neighbor's and think of what your next step is. Is there a place for women who have to run away from bad husbands? I'm sorry. I have no idea."

"Come on, Edward, let's go to the neighbor's." Valentine sighed as she put clothes together and then stood at the entrance of the shabby house she had endured many beatings to stay in.

Matt watched as Richard started to stir. Fear flashed across Valentine's face; Matt stood between them.

"You go. I'll make sure he doesn't follow tonight." Matt held the door open for her. "I wish I could do more."

She nodded.

"Valentine?" he called after her.

She turned on the front step.

"This is my name and address." Matt jotted down his information on a piece of paper. "Please, let me know where you end up so I can send young Edward a camera to replace the one he lost here today." Matt watched helplessly as her eyes filled with tears again. "I'm sorry. I didn't say that to make you cry."

"Why aren't you calling me a whore and telling me I'm a terrible person?"

"Miss, I am here to see justice for Priscilla and had no idea I would stumble into this. I don't use that word. I want to do the right thing for everyone. If I can help, please let me know. He's getting up so you should run, and I'll look after this. Please be in touch. Let me know that you and Edward are safe wherever you decide to go."

"Whoever she is, this Priscilla, she's a lucky girl," Valentine said sadly.

She disappeared down the street while Matt waited for Richard to regain consciousness, so he could beat him again.

Richard stirred and finally got up on all fours. Matt crouched down to face him.

"I am going to kill you." Richard collapsed back down on the floor.

"Maybe." Matt shrugged. "So far, this is our second fight, and I've won both times, so I'm not so sure you're capable, actually."

"I will hunt you down, and I will kill you." Richard spat out a tooth.

"Listen, if you're done threatening me, know this: Priscilla is not returning on Friday."

Richard glared up at him.

"I am not a violent man, but I will protect Priscilla, Valentine, and Edward to the best of my ability." Matt leaned close and said very calmly in his ear, "You come after Priscilla, you'll deal with me. Valentine is to let me know if you lay a hand on her or Edward again. I'll be back. Got it?"

Richard dragged himself to his feet. Matt stood back and let him get his bearings. Blood poured from his mouth. He swayed, and Matt shook his head in disgust. He could not in good conscience beat him any further. "See you in court."

Richard lunged at Matt's back as he went to the door. He tried to tackle Matt to the ground. Furious, Matt flung him off. When they stood face to face, fear flashed in Richard's eyes. Matt's lips thinned, his fists clenched, and he laid into Richard. He wanted to ignore the voice in the back of his head saying, 'don't kill him.'

When Richard went down, far too soon, Matt's conscience forced him to step back. He saw Edward's smashed camera in the corner of the room. Matt's eyes narrowed at the rags soaked with blood from Valentine's bloody nose and lip. He wanted to drag Richard off the floor so he could beat him down again and finish him off, right there in the shabby little house that he kept his mistress and son in. All while he lived in opulence. Matt forced himself to take another step back.

"Priscilla is not coming back to you. It's over," Matt said to Richard's still form.

His hands shook with rage as he picked up his camera, got his bike out of the shrub, and caught the last train to Brandon.

***

Cora left Brownie at the livery stable and made her way back to her cottage. Sure enough, a few papers were on her table by the front window. Lucy had left a big bouquet of lilacs, and there was a letter standing up against the vase.

Cora regarded it warily.

What now?

She looked it over. The stamp said Gimli. Gimli — Icelandic settlement — Sol. Cora's heart hardened. She marched to the cook stove and tossed the second letter from Sol inside. Tears filled her eyes as she watched it burn.

Immediately, she wished she could snatch it from the flames. She wondered about the contents of the letter. Her heart yearned to read it.

He sold me out for a farm. It's over. I handed him my heart, and he handed it back. Done.

Cora's eyes flicked over the documents. Citation to appear in court for Friday, June 8. Contempt of court order if Priscilla didn't return to Richard Markus III by Friday, June 8.

He has a good lawyer. Good thing I'm better.

"Cora?" Wilbur stood at her front step and knocked gently.

Cora went to the door and opened it. "Come in."

"I got a letter from a man from Gimli?"

"I don't want to know." She returned to her documents.

Wilbur frowned at his sister. "What happened?"

"My client hired him as a bodyguard."

"And..."

"And he traded me for a farm in Gimli." Cora spoke in a clipped tone.

"Hmm. He's worried sick about you. He sent me a letter telling me you would likely burn his. He wants to be sure you are safe. He wants to explain that Eli..."

"I don't want to hear it." Cora turned her back to Wilbur and placed the documents in order of dates.

Wilbur ignored her refusal to listen. "Eli told him if he didn't leave, Eli would have you arrested on charges of fraud."

Cora straightened up.

"Also, something about thirty families..."

"I don't want to hear it," Cora snapped. Her eyes stung with unshed tears.

"The police were there to drag you away if he so much as made eye contact with you." Wilbur refused to be put off. "I don't know what that means, but he's asking if you are safe. He knows you won't have a thing to do with him. He doesn't blame you, but he wants to be able to sleep at night, and the thought of you in danger... I can read it to you. Word for word so I don't get it wrong."

"How can I trust that?" Tears stung Cora's eyes.

"He seems like a good man." Wilbur shrugged.

"He left me, though."

"Looks to me like he left you to keep you safe. Anyway, I'll send a telegram letting him know you are safe here with me and that you aren't returning to Toronto until you are called to the bar. That will put his mind at ease. There is no reason to be cruel. He cares about your safety. Supper is ready in a half an hour. Are you joining us this evening?"

"Of course, thanks, Wil." Cora wanted to read Sol's letter to Wilbur. She itched to pluck it from his fingertips and devour it. He would hand it over without protest, but she sat on her hands and willed herself not to ask for it.

Better this way. Clean break. He's on a farm in Gimli — that was his dream. My dream is dead, so there is no future for us. Better it ends right now without any further hurt.

"All right. See you at supper." Wil smiled. "Are you representing Priscilla?"

"Apparently."

Wilbur smiled broadly. "I am really glad to hear that. I am not a sensitive man, Cora. I'm not really very good with words, but sometimes I look at you and what you have accomplished, and I think our father would collapse with pride. Our mother, too of course, but you were special to father. He thought your mind was a gift. It is, Cora. You are brilliant, and I know that if the women's rights movement lost you, well I think it would be a tragedy. I wanted you to stay here in Oakland with us. I intended to help you find a house and a place to practice law until Lucy rolled her eyes and told me that it would hold you back. We'll cheer for you from Oakland and keep a light on for you."

"Wil." Cora's eyes filled with tears at his words. "I don't know what to say. I'm not so sure I can go back. I haven't finished my articling. I don't know…"

Wil hugged her hard, and suddenly uncomfortable, he shrugged. "You'll go back. You've only ever been on loan to us. I knew it when you demanded to be a mathematician at sixteen. I'll leave you to it."

Wilbur closed the door on the cottage, and Cora took a deep breath.

"Oh, by the way, *if* I return to be sworn in, Eli and his men will likely kill me," Cora said to the empty room.

The very thought of going up against Eli and his men made her heart pound with fear.

Chapter Thirty-Two

ole picked up Matt at the train station, and they raced back to Oakland.

"You go and take her the good news. I'll deal with the team."

"Are you sure?"

"Of course."

Matt couldn't stop himself from sprinting home. His pocket contained two papers; one that changed his life, and one that would change Priscilla's.

What will it be like to come home to Priscilla when she is actually mine? Will that day ever happen?

He stood outside the gate, and his jaw dropped in surprise. His mother sat on the porch in a shaft of sunlight. She played with a small orange kitten on her lap. As the kitten batted a ribbon on her new dress, she smiled. Her hair had been carefully curled and brushed back off her face.

Priscilla.

His mother gave him a tentative smile, and he smiled back.

The flowerbeds were different. Not a weed in sight. Pink and white striped petunias nodded among other flowers he didn't know the names of.

"Hello, Mother." Matt leaned down to give his mother a kiss on the forehead. The kitten yawned at him as he patted it on the head.

He hesitated at the door. Matt's eyebrows raised; Priscilla had painted his front door. He hadn't realized how shabby it looked until a fresh coat of paint and a pot of flowers on each side of the doorframe cleaned it up and made the house instantly inviting. Happiness bloomed inside him just looking at it.

He knocked on his own door out of respect for Priscilla, who wasn't expecting him. He didn't want to scare her.

"Come in!" Priscilla called out.

He opened the door and stood in his front room. The state of the room stunned him. Gone were the heavy curtains, and with them the gloomy darkness Min demanded. Not a speck of dust was permitted to land anywhere in this house. If his mother hadn't been on the front porch, he would have wondered whose house this belonged to.

"Mrs. Bennett, I'm in the kitchen," Priscilla called out.

Priscilla had taken over his drawing room. Her work space was neat and tidy. She had swept the sheer curtains back, and sun streamed in over her work area. The sun illuminated lace and ribbons and all sorts of finery. She was clearly in the middle of a big order. He blushed as he looked at a lacey undergarment she had pinned to the dress form. She had a bouquet of lilacs on her work table beside a curly tape measure. She had tied a pretty ribbon around a vase he didn't recognize.

Because Min smashed every vase.

Matt moved from her work space to the entrance of the kitchen. She'd made new curtains for the kitchen windows, too. The curtains were edged with lace and tied with a pretty bow. With her back to him, she swiftly stacked wood in the fire box and then placed her bread pans in the cook stove.

"Sorry, Mrs. Bennett, I'll be right with you," she called out. She snapped the door to the cook stove closed and filled the kettle, then set it down.

Finally, he cleared his throat. A deep, gravelly sound Mrs. Bennett couldn't make.

She jumped a foot in the air and whirled around. "Oh, Matt! You scared me to death!"

"Sorry. I didn't mean to scare you."

"You're home early. I didn't expect you for two days." Priscilla smiled at him and pressed a hand to her chest.

"We're running out of time. I got everything done and came straight home."

"Did you pass?"

Matt handed her a piece of paper with good news. She opened it and smiled at his mark.

"Matt! Ninety-three percent!" Her eyes gleamed with happiness.

"I am now officially an architect."

Priscilla smiled at him. "Of course, you are! I never doubted that for a minute. Matt, I have something to show you — I hope you aren't mad. I took a liberty here, and I think you'll like it."

"Mad at you?" Matt moved closer and ached to take her in his arms. He yearned to feel her against him, but he didn't dare. "I can't imagine being mad at you."

"Oh, well. I don't know." Priscilla smiled shyly. "Come on. I'll show you."

She led the way up the stairs.

She stood in front of the door to Min's room. His chest tightened at the thought of stepping into her old room, so many terrible memories of her there.

"Close your eyes," Priscilla demanded.

Matt complied; he would have jumped out a window if she requested it.

He heard the door squeak on the hinge; he'd have to oil it.

"Open them."

He opened his eyes to view a light grey room with his architect easel in between two windows. Min's old room was directly over the living room, so the same sun that slanted down over Priscilla's work area downstairs illuminated his. She had made draperies that were heavy but tied back. Sheer curtains allowed the light in. She had taken Min's bed away and on the table by the chair, she had stacked his favourite books and a big bouquet of lilacs.

He didn't know what to say. The only words he could think of were Cole's.

These women, Matt, they hold all the hope in Oakland.

Priscilla wrung her hands. "Matt, are you upset? Maybe this is too soon after... after what happened."

Matt heard the worry and fear in her voice. Choked with emotion, he went to the window to get himself under control. She placed a tentative hand on his arm.

"You loved her. I am so sorry, Matt." Priscilla's voice trembled on the verge of tears. "This was too soon, and I took such a liberty with this. I apologize..."

Matt turned to face Priscilla. He put his arms out, and she went right into them. He pulled her hard against him and picked her up so her face was level with his.

"I love it."

"Really?" She sighed with relief as she hugged him. "You scared me."

"I don't know how to thank you. I don't even know what to say." Matt tightened his arms around her.

"Well, when you're driving the getaway stagecoach, that will be thanks enough," she said dryly.

She pressed on his shoulders, indicating he should let her down. He didn't want to, but he did.

"No, you're not running." Matt dug around in his breast pocket and pulled out two notes.

"Matt, we've been over this. I have to run. They will make me go back."

"Priscilla, I stayed in Winnipeg until I found enough evidence to give you concrete proof of adultery. You will win your divorce case now."

"How?"

"Just read these letters, and then I'll explain the whole thing."

"Your knuckles are bruised." Priscilla's face creased with worry.

He yearned to reach out to comfort her. He didn't.

"Never mind my knuckles," Matt said gruffly.

"Did you fight him?" Her eyes filled with tears.

"It doesn't matter."

"Did you?" she demanded.

"Yes."

"I hate that you have to fight on my behalf. It's awful. It's so coarse, such a crude affair..." Her voice caught with emotion.

"I am happy to fight on your behalf, Priscilla, but this time it wasn't for you. Richard has a woman and a son that he keeps at 380 Fort Street in Winnipeg. I basically tricked her into giving me information that would entrap him, so when I left, all I could think was that her and her son were going to pay the price. I couldn't leave them undefended. Sure enough, a couple nights later, he came back and I stopped him from hurting them."

"What?" Priscilla gasped as if someone had punched her in the stomach. "He has another woman and *son*?"

"Yes." Matt helped her to the chair.

She sat down and put her face in her hands.

"How old is his son?"

"I'm not sure, maybe three or four."

"He had this woman before he met me."

"I'm so sorry, Priscilla," Matt said simply.

"Is there anything else?"

He didn't tell her about being arrested. She would worry, and he didn't want her to worry.

"I went to the house the next day with a bouquet of flowers from Richard. I told her that he couldn't meet her at the agreed upon time, would she send a note letting him know when he could return. This is the note she gave me."

Priscilla took the note and read it.

Hello Richard,

Come tonight at eight thirty.

I can't wait to thank you in person.

Yours, Valentine

Priscilla ran her fingertips over the note.

"She did. I'll take you in tomorrow first thing, and we'll see what the lawyer can do before Friday." Matt's pulse quickened at the thought that she would soon be free.

"What if it isn't enough? What if there is some sort of loop hole and they force me to go back to him? I can't do it." Priscilla's lips trembled in fear.

"If you lose, and I don't think you will, not with this evidence, I will help you run as far and as fast as you want. No one is making you go back."

Priscilla took a deep breath. "Matt, Ada got involved, and I am firing the lawyer we spoke to before."

"What does that mean?" Concern flooded through him.

"Ada spoke to Miss Rood, and she agreed to look at my paperwork. Ada also spoke to Mr. Birch so..."

"Do you think Miss Rood can handle this? Are you sure?" Matt's eyebrows drew together in a frown. "Do you really think a woman lawyer is going to be up to this challenge?"

"Ada seems to think she's up for the task, and when my grandmother stopped by Miss Rood ordered her from the property." Priscilla crossed her arms over her chest. "I really think she cares, and I don't think Mr. Levinson does at all. I want someone who will care about me to defend me."

"It's your decision, Priscilla. If you and Ada think she can do it then I guess that's who you should hire. I just worry that a judge might not take her seriously. I don't know. It seems risky."

"It's the day after tomorrow, and I think it's too late now to change things. Did I make the wrong decision?" Priscilla's eyes filled with tears; she bit her lip in fear.

"No matter what happens, it will be all right. If you think she can do it then I know she can. I promise you, Priscilla, he's not going to hurt you in any way, ever again."

Priscilla nodded and brushed tears away with her fingertips.

He wanted to reach for her, cradle her face in his hands, and kiss the worry away. Instead, he put his hands in his pocket.

"You should know, my grandmother came by and upset your mother." Priscilla's face clouded with sadness.

"Did she upset you?" Matt tried to keep his voice gentle. The thought of Mrs. Charbonneau attacking Priscilla in his house didn't sit well.

"No." Priscilla took a shaky breath, which told him she was lying so he wouldn't be upset. "I'm fine. I just wanted to be sure you knew because you entrusted your mother to my care, and I... don't want you hearing about that from someone else and being... uh... angry with me."

Priscilla's hands shook with fear as she looked at him, trying to gauge his reaction.

"Priscilla." Matt held her trembling hands firmly in his. "I want you to listen to me very carefully."

Priscilla's eyes dropped to the floor.

She's afraid.

"Priscilla." Matt let go of her left hand so he could stroke her cheek gently to get her attention. She flinched. Immediately, he dropped his hand. "Priscilla, if you get a divorce from Richard, you *might* allow me to court you. I don't expect it. It's an option. I would like that very much, but you have been through a lot, so I'll wait for you to decide. If you *do* choose to allow me to court you, that is not the way things are *ever* going to be between us."

Priscilla's eyes flicked up from the floor to him and then back to the floor.

"If a neighbor said someone came to the house and threatened you, I would be concerned for you, and I would find out who threatened you, and I would go to that person and make sure they knew that was not acceptable. Or I would help you handle it, if that's what you wanted. There is never, ever going to be a day that I am angry with you to the point that I would hurt you or let anyone else hurt you."

Priscilla put her hands over her face. Matt's heart splintered at the pain she was trying to hide.

"I don't expect you to believe me. I expect to spend a lot of time winning your trust. I promise you, right now, you are safe with me, and I will keep you safe from everything that scares you or hurts you. That promise comes with no strings attached. I'm waiting for you to let me know." Matt reached for a clean handkerchief, and when she finally let her hands drop, he wiped the tears from her cheeks carefully.

Priscilla dragged her eyes back to him. "What if I can't... ever..."

"Then you can't ever." Matt shrugged as he put the handkerchief in his pocket.

"But then you will have wasted all this time..." Her voice broke.

"You make me happy, Priscilla." Matt took her hands in his.

"Why? Why do I make you happy?"

"When you said, you wanted to be a pagan so you could worship the sun. You had your head tilted back, you wanted to celebrate that day, even after all the horrible things you'd been through. I want a girl who knows how to talk to horses and celebrate every happy thing around her. Since I met you, I feel like better things are ahead. You made me hope again, after years of thinking nothing would ever improve. When I got to know you, I was drawn to your respectful, hard-working, and resourceful personality. I shouldn't say this, but I will — you are very, very beautiful."

"Matt, you shouldn't say such a thing." Priscilla blushed five shades of red.

Matt shrugged unrepentantly. "It's true."

"What now?" Priscilla took a deep breath and let it out slowly.

"When do you meet with Miss Rood?"

"I have given her all the paperwork. We were waiting for the hospital documents and whatever you found."

"I have all of it. Should we go now?" Matt stood up and held his hand out to her.

"The sooner she can build this case, the better." Priscilla placed her hand in his.

"Priscilla?" Matt held the door open for her.

"Yes?"

"Thank you for this." Matt smiled warmly, he inclined his head to his new work area. "This is the nicest thing anyone has ever done for me."

"The entire W. C. T. U. did this. I just helped." Priscilla smiled brightly.

"This room, though? Did you do this room, or did they?"

"I did." Priscilla brushed a piece of hair out of her eyes. "It was my pleasure."

"It's very nice. I really like it. Uh, the pink flowers in the flower beds — I'm not sure that's appropriate for a bachelor, though."

"They are called bachelor buttons," Priscilla said slyly.

"They are not." A deep chuckle bubbled out of Matt. "You're kidding. Really?"

A bright smile played on Priscilla's lips. "Really."

Matt stood back so she could leave the room in front of him. "I wonder if I will always have *bachelor* buttons in my front flower bed."

Priscilla turned around in the hallway and grinned at him. "We'll see. Thank you for this." Priscilla lifted up Valentine's note.

"Of course. I told you, you're not going back." Matt followed her down the stairs.

Priscilla went to the kitchen, took the bread out of the cook stove, and set it on a wire rack to cool. She re-read the note, hardly daring to hope in the release it promised. Her heart soared with the belief that this note was enough for a judge; she would be free of Richard's fists, forever.

Matt told his mother they were just stepping out for a few moments and they would return right away. Priscilla, satisfied his kitchen was in order, joined him at the front door.

"Ready?" Matt asked her as he held the door open for her.

"Yes." Priscilla carefully folded the note in two and left the house in front of him.

Chapter Thirty-Three

Cora looked up from her documents as Matt and Priscilla walked across the lawn to the front door of her cottage. Matt knocked on the door, and they smiled at each other with so much love and hope Cora worried there wouldn't be enough evidence and the hope glowing from them would be dashed.

She opened the door and gestured them in.

"Thank you so much for agreeing to look at the documents." Priscilla smiled shyly.

"Before we get started, are you sure you are up for this?" Matt asked Cora.

Cora bristled visibly. "What do you mean?"

"I just wonder if... well... I don't mean to be rude, but are you sure you are up for this? Richard is terrible. He has money, power, and prestige in his favour."

"I'm up for it or I wouldn't have taken it on." Cora gritted her teeth.

Up for this indeed!

"Ada had paperwork sent over. I'm wondering what else you have?" Cora directed this statement to Priscilla, intending to ignore Matt completely.

Priscilla handed the love note and photographs over. Cora examined the evidence and read the letter swiftly.

"How did you get evidence of adultery and a *son*?" Cora's eyebrows shot up in surprise.

"Long story." Matt held a chair out for Priscilla to sit at Cora's table before he sat down.

"There is no reason to worry about the divorce trial. This photography. It's brilliant. How did you think of this?" Cora's eyes were wide; she couldn't ignore him.

"I was standing on the steps of the university and a mother was there with her sons taking pictures. It hit me that this would be irrefutable evidence, right? There was a lot on the line. All I could think was if I didn't get this evidence, Priscilla would run, and I couldn't tolerate the thought of it."

Matt put his arm around Priscilla. His eyes were soft with concern as he looked at her. Cora couldn't suppress her eye roll. They were like love's young dream, and they needed to be cunning. Between the two of them, they didn't have a ruthless bone in their bodies.

I'll have to be ruthless for all of us.

Cora sighed. "Priscilla, are you ready to go into Brandon tomorrow?"

She watched Priscilla straighten up and square her narrow shoulders. "You guarantee they can't make me go back to him if this whole thing fails?"

"This will not fail." Cora spoke with such conviction that Priscilla visibly relaxed.

"All right. Then let's do it. What's first?" Priscilla leaned forward to hear the process.

"Tomorrow, we fire your lawyer. We take your medical evidence to the constabulary and advise them that Richard will be ready for arrest after your contempt of court hearing. I will, of course, contest that, and I will win. As soon as you are no longer in contempt, the divorce trial is set, and Richard will be arrested. You can start to relax a bit knowing he's behind bars and can't hurt you, once he is in custody." Cora straightened the papers and photographs so they were neat, tidy, and ready for trial.

Priscilla took a deep breath and let it out slowly. "If we go to court and they don't believe the evidence, is there any chance they can force me to go back? I just want to be sure."

"I know you are scared." Cora placed her hand on Priscilla's forearm. Priscilla trembled with fear.

"No, I passed scared months ago. I am absolutely terrified that I will walk into that courtroom and they will drag me back to Richard." Her voice broke on a sob. Matt leaned forward and put his arm along the back of her chair. He put his hand on her shoulder.

"We have photographic and written evidence of adultery, and we have confirmation of abuse from a doctor. We also have Dr. Davies and Mrs. Bennett ready to testify on your behalf. You have all the grounds the court requires for divorce. You have nothing to worry about from the court proceedings tomorrow." Cora and Matt waited patiently while Priscilla wiped her tears away.

"Do you think we will ever see a time that the courts can't order a woman to return and render conjugal rights?" Priscilla asked Cora softly. "That is the paper I am the most afraid of."

"I am not sure." Cora rubbed her forehead. "Unless there are more women ready to challenge the law, things won't change."

"I see," Priscilla said sadly.

"We can only do our best." Cora's fingertips fiddled with the file. "It is very difficult Priscilla, to come up against this double standard. I completely understand how terrifying it is. You should be very proud of your strength. Very few women challenge the law, and when they do, they are alone in that challenge. It's hard when the judge, jury, and barristers are *all* men. So, women seeking justice are up against a wall of men, who have never experienced the sort of vulnerability that you have experienced. The men making laws likely have never required the protection you require, so they don't mandate that protection through law."

"I wouldn't dream of going in there tomorrow without you. Mr. Levinson would have handed me over and not thought twice." Priscilla took a deep breath and let it out slowly.

"You are very kind to say that. When I got here, I had no intentions of ever setting foot in a courtroom again." Cora smiled at Priscilla.

"What changed your mind? If you don't mind me asking."

"Ada Bennett reminded me why I started. All the years of school and finishing my term of articling and the abuse that came along with that process, well, it made me lose sight of my original purpose and the bigger picture, so to speak."

"What was your purpose?" Priscilla leaned against the back of her chair.

"To give a voice to the innocent and oppressed." Cora's eyes met Priscilla's. "That was my original purpose. If laws change and equal rights come out of it, that's a happy benefit. I needed an arena to use my voice and to give other women a voice. Court is the perfect place to expose the inequality in the law. That's why I chose law — this is my true path. Sometimes we just need to be reminded."

Priscilla reached for the photograph of Valentine's son.

"Even if we lose the trial regarding your son in criminal court, it's a win due to the fact that you have challenged something that is wrong and forced the men in that room to acknowledge that it is wrong. The divorce trial is already won with this evidence. You have nothing to worry about, Priscilla."

Priscilla's eyes filled with tears again.

"Without the butler's testimony, we don't know how this criminal trial will go. I will warn you, I believe you *will* lose that trial, so please prepare yourself for that. Get a good rest tonight. We battle tomorrow." Cora reached out to her and squeezed her hand hard.

"Your extra severe black dress is done." Priscilla placed the photograph back down on the file.

"Perfect." Cora tucked the photograph away.

***

The next day, Matt, his four horses, and the stagecoach were all polished to a high shine. Matt showed up half an hour early, and the three of them made their way to Brandon. When the coach ground to a halt in front of the law office, Priscilla was shaking with fear beside Cora.

"I've never fired a lawyer before. I'm not sure how to do that."

"Would you let me do it?" Cora grinned. "I would really enjoy it."

"Sure." Priscilla breathed a sigh of relief as Cora led the way into Mr. Levinson's office.

"Have you decided then?" Mr. Levinson directed the question to Priscilla. "You are supposed to be in court this afternoon."

"I have decided not to return."

"I see. It is my duty to advise you, they will find you in contempt of court."

"If that's the best you can do, Mr. Levinson, your services are no longer needed in this case." Cora wrote down Richard Markus's address on a piece of paper. "You may send your bill to Mr. Markus to pay for the costs incurred up to today. Good day, sir."

"Who do you think you are?" Mr. Levinson stood, in an attempt to tower over and intimidate Cora.

Cora took a step toward him as her eyes locked on his. "I am Cora Rood. First woman lawyer for Upper Canada and Great Britain."

Mr. Levinson's eyes narrowed at her across the desk. "You can't be. I don't believe it."

"Believe it." Cora's eyes narrowed; she ignored the sneer on his face. "You have a good day, and when I win this, I'll let you know how I did it."

Cora swept out of his office with Priscilla and Matt close on her heels. A spark of confidence began to blaze inside her. The documents and photos would exonerate this woman.

What a privilege to be part of it!

"Where to now?" Priscilla's eyes were wide.

"Police station, then we face Richard in court." Cora smiled at Priscilla with encouragement.

The constabulary buzzed with officers.

Cora spoke to the clerk at the front entrance. "We need to speak to the inspector. We are here to report a crime."

Within minutes, they were escorted into a room to be interviewed. Matt settled Priscilla into a chair.

"I'm Inspector Cook. How can I help?" He picked up a pencil and waited to take down the information.

"Mrs. Markus would like to report a crime." Cora nodded at Priscilla to speak.

Priscilla's voice trembled. Inspector Cook became increasingly protective of her as her story tumbled out. His eyes hardened at the brutality of the abuse. As it became clear he was taking her seriously, she sounded stronger.

The inspector took detailed notes. Cora could practically see his mind work as he listened to Priscilla. Pushed down flight of stairs, intent, butler will testify it was an accident, Dr. Davies will testify there was intent to do bodily harm. Bruising on wrists corroborates testimony that she was forcibly pushed. Documentation from hospital supports the testimony regarding miscarriage. He stopped Priscilla to look at the documents from the hospital. He squinted in disapproval as he read over the proof of ongoing abuse.

"Unfortunately, the hospital in Winnipeg missed some of the placenta, so we have further documentation of a surgery Dr. Davies had to perform to save her life. He will testify in court about the extent of damage inflicted on Mrs. Markus's person."

"We'll arrest him today. When are you done with him in court?" The inspector directed his question to Cora.

"He will be in court this afternoon at 2:00. We have a citation to appear to fight this contempt of court order."

"May I take a look?" He held his hand out for the documents.

Cora handed the inspector the court order to return to render conjugal rights.

"Dear lord." Inspector Cook gasped. "This is... this is disgusting."

"We need him in court this afternoon," Cora reminded him, "but he's all yours after that."

"If you lose, he'll be in our custody. Is that what you're thinking?" Inspector Cook put the documents down.

"I won't lose." Cora stood up and pulled her file together. "Richard off the street is good for my client *and* his mistress."

"Who did you say you are?" The inspector's eyebrows rose as Cora tucked the file into the crook of her arm.

"I'm a lawyer, sir. I am here to represent Mrs. Markus. Will I see you later then, or one of your men, perhaps?"

"I'll bring him in myself." Mr. Cook tidied up his notes. "Are you prepared to go to trial very soon? Cases like this are not on the books for long."

"We are ready." Cora held her hand out; the inspector shook it. "Thank you so much for taking this case seriously. I mean it, sir, I really appreciate it."

"I'd horsewhip him myself if I could get away with it. We'll pick him up after court. You have nothing to fear from him now. Unless you lose in court. If the butler lies, it could go either way."

Cora shrugged. "At least we know we have done all we could for her child."

"Of course. My condolences, Mrs. Markus. I wish you all the best."

Hope grew in Cora's heart as she watched the inspector shake Priscilla's delicate hand. His hand engulfed hers. He intended to use the law to protect her, as he should. Inspector Cook nodded to Matt, and in some sort of unspoken way, he seemed to indicate he was turning Priscilla over to him to protect her. "Keep an eye on her. This is a terrible business."

Cora fought so hard against men and had been hurt so deeply, she had forgotten there were some good ones among the awful. Here were two, right in front of her. As they exited the police station, Cora smiled at the thought of striking at Richard with irrefutable evidence.

Once they were settled in the courtroom, fifteen minutes early, Priscilla twisted her handkerchief between her hands in fear. Cora placed her hand on hers. "You're all right," she whispered as they waited for Richard and his lawyers to show up.

"I wish Matt could be here." Priscilla dashed at a tear that escaped down her cheek.

"No. They would run with that and accuse you of adultery. Stand up. The judge is entering the room." Cora and Priscilla stood as the judge went to the bench. Cora checked her watch. Five minutes early.

Drat. Old judges are notoriously non-progressive.

Divorce was so unheard of that it caused raised eyebrows all on its own, never mind with a woman lawyer presiding. This would be tricky, but the evidence spoke for itself.

Finally, Richard entered with three lawyers. He leered at Priscilla like a predator about to pounce. The grin on his face made Cora bristle with anger. Priscilla trembled beside her.

"Where is your legal counsel?" the judge asked Priscilla.

"I am legal counsel for Mrs. Markus, your honour." Cora's voice rang out like a bell.

"Approach."

Cora went to the judge; she straightened her spine and refused to wilt under his hard look.

"Is this some sort of practical joke?"

"No, your honour, I have nothing but respect for your courtroom. I am Miss Rood, I am just finishing my term of articling with Mr. Birch from Oakland. He asked me to come and stand in for him, as this is a simple citation regarding a contempt of court order. He believed I could handle this on my own."

"I'll allow it today because, as you say, it is a simple citation. However, if you want to step foot in this courtroom again, I want Mr. Birch with you to supervise. You will bring evidence of your qualifications if you intend to represent Mrs. Markus in divorce court."

"Of course. I would be happy to bring that documentation." Cora's teeth clenched in anger. "Thank you for allowing me to represent her today."

"Not much choice is there?" The judge's eyes narrowed at Cora.

"Thank you." Cora's clenched jaw ached with the pressure of remaining respectful.

"Proceed."

Once Cora had returned to the desk, the judge spoke to both legal counsels.

"According to the affidavit, this court finds the marriage legal. The contempt of court document orders Mrs. Markus to return to Mr. Markus and render conjugal rights. Has Mrs. Markus returned to render her conjugal rights as directed?"

"She has not, your honour." Richard's counsel spoke for him.

"What say you?" The judge gave Cora a hard look.

"We have new evidence to present, your honour. This evidence has only recently been presented, and we wish to enter it as evidence to adultery and cruelty."

"Approach."

The judge swiftly read the notes and the documentation from the hospital.

"Mr. Markus has a son with this woman, this Valentine Champalone?"

"There is no proof of this." Richard's counsel was quick to reply.

"This is a note calling him daddy. Proof enough for me. The contempt of court order is nullified. I set the divorce trial date for Monday next week. You lay a hand on this woman in the meantime, I will have you arrested for assault. We reconvene on Monday at 11:00 a.m. Miss Rood, bring your supervisor."

The gavel banged down.

"What is he saying? He believes this insanity about Valentine? What's going on?" Richard protested.

The judge left the bench, and Cora feared Richard would grab Priscilla. The bailiff moved closer to ensure he wouldn't touch her.

Richard shook off the hands of the lawyers when they tried to subdue him.

"You think a piece of paper is going to keep you from me? Some order in a court can make our marriage null? You're mine, Priscilla, and I guarantee you are coming home with me. Maybe not today, but on Monday for sure." He lunged at her, and two of his lawyers held him back.

Come on, try it...

"Mr. Markus," boomed Inspector Cook from the back of the courtroom. "You are under arrest for assault and murder."

Richard panicked and tried to run.

Cook pounced on him, put him in handcuffs, and dragged him from the court. Richard's lawyers were hot on their heels. Priscilla and Cora collapsed into their chairs.

"So, it begins," Cora said to Priscilla quietly.

Priscilla grabbed Cora's hand. "If you hadn't been here, I can't even think about..."

"This is our first win." Cora squeezed her hand hard. "It won't be our last."

Priscilla and Cora got to their feet and held onto each other as they left court.

"It's all right now?" Matt held the door to the coach open and helped Priscilla inside. He held onto her hand longer than necessary, as if verifying for himself that she was all right.

"Contempt of court is removed." Cora let out a breath she didn't realize she had been holding.

Matt let out a long sigh of relief.

"We are going to divorce court on Monday." Priscilla's lips were white with fear. "Only two days of worry, I guess."

"It's won," Cora said to Matt. "Nothing to worry about here. It's as good as done."

"Thank goodness." Matt opened the stagecoach door.

"Let's go home." Cora crawled in beside Priscilla and held onto her while she cried. Relief replaced the fear. "You're all right. Everything is going to be all right now."

Unless Richard wins in criminal court. If he does, he'll come back for you, and you won't be safe in Oakland.

Chapter Thirty-Four

Matt dropped Cora off at her cottage before taking Priscilla back to the carriage house at Hillcrest. He pulled the horses to a stop and went to help her out of the carriage, relieved that she appeared to be calmer.

He walked her to the door.

"Do you want some tea before you go home?" Priscilla asked shyly.

"I would. I wanted to let you know, I am away tomorrow. Dr. Davies has not seen enough improvement to leave my mother in my care. He gave me some options. I decided on a care facility in Brandon, so I can check on her often."

Priscilla tilted her head; her eyes softened in sympathy.

"Oh, Matt, really?"

"Dr. Davies said he needed to see more improvement for her to stay in my care, and she hasn't improved. There is some municipal assistance that they are using to pay for her care. I am supplementing that, of course, but my father left us a trust, so she will have the best care."

"Will they let her keep her kitten?" Priscilla asked softly.

"I'll make sure of it." Matt smiled at her gentle concern.

Priscilla made tea and placed oatmeal cookies on a plate. The carriage house was gleaming and freshly stocked. Matt made a mental note to thank Jaffrey for moving Priscilla's things on his behalf.

"Are you all right with this decision?" Priscilla bit into a cookie. Her question drew his mind back to the matter at hand. "First your sister, now your mother?"

"I would be lying if I said I wasn't relieved. When I think back over the last ten years, I am not sure now how I ever coped at all. It's nice that the decision is out of my hands."

"I don't want to sound like I don't trust your judgment, but can you tell me why you waited so long?" Priscilla bit her lip.

Matt shrugged. "It was a slow progression. Once father died, we were all devastated, of course. I sort of assumed that they took longer to deal with it because..."

"Because why?" Priscilla tilted her head.

"I'm not sure how to say it." Matt watched Priscilla to gauge her reaction. "I just sort of thought that they are women, and women sometimes are more emotional, and um... have a harder time with things such as this, or that is what I was told anyway."

"You were told that women are weepy and crazy, and you just had to put up with it?" Priscilla shook her head at Matt.

"Something to that effect." Matt held his hands out in surrender. "I was fifteen! What did I know of women? I still don't know much about them."

"Most of us are not weepy and crazy." Priscilla laughed at him.

"I can see now, I was misinformed." Matt chuckled. "Anyway, I thought it was my job to be the man of the house and deal with everything. I was wrong. It was a terrible mistake to leave Min with mother that long unsupervised. I should have asked for help years ago. Some part of me was very embarrassed, and the other part of me didn't see a solution. I'm sick about it, actually."

"Matt, it is so tragic, isn't it?" Priscilla's eyes softened in sympathy. "All that pain and suffering. Poor Min and your poor mother."

"Poor Min!" Matt gasped in outrage.

Priscilla held up her hands. "Hear me out, Matt. Min must have very serious problems for her to act in such a way. She must have suffered greatly to be that miserable for that long."

Matt frowned at Priscilla across the table.

"She's lucky I have the strength of will that I have. I wanted to strangle her to death, and I still do," Matt said mutinously.

"She is very sick. She is incurable, Matt. Your mother is very sick, too. You did your best." Priscilla softened her tone. "I'm so sorry about your mother."

"Me, too." Matt sipped his tea.

"Do you want me to come with you to help get her settled?"

"I would really like that, but I think it's dangerous. I am hearing gossip in town about you leading me astray." Matt grinned at the outrage on her face. "Married woman from the city and all. I think, in order to protect your reputation, we should be very cautious."

"I'm leading *you* astray!" Priscilla's mouth dropped open with disdain.

"That's what I've heard." Matt smirked at her.

Priscilla's eyes flashed. "What if you are leading me astray?"

"Impossible. I am known far and wide as a gentleman." Matt bit into a cookie.

"Matt Hartwell." Priscilla gathered steam to blast him.

He held up his hands in surrender. "I'm kidding. It's wrong. I disagree. But, if someone is going to lead me astray, I am glad it's you." Matt smiled.

"Looks like you better get used to bachelor buttons in your flower bed, sir. I think they will be appropriate for a long time." Priscilla tossed her hair back.

Matt's eyes darkened with the challenge. "I'll win you over."

Priscilla arched her eyebrow and glanced at him out of the corner of her eye. "We'll see."

She got up and went to the cook stove to put more water in the kettle. Matt went to her; he took the kettle from her hand and replaced it on the stove. He bracketed her with his arms against the countertop, and she gasped in surprise. His eyes searched hers, looking for fear, but her dark eyes snapped with excitement as she leaned back. He gently caressed the side of her face with his fingertips, and her eyes slid shut and then very slowly opened again. Desire radiated between them as he tenderly pressed his lips against hers. He pulled back to be sure she wasn't scared. She smiled up at him in encouragement, so he kissed her again. His heart pounded as her hands slid up his arms and twisted in his hair, pulling him down, allowing him to deepen the kiss.

"Careful." He pulled back. "Your lip is still healing. I don't want to hurt you." His fingertips brushed against the split in her lip.

"Matt?"

He dragged his eyes from her mouth to meet her gaze.

"Yes, Priscilla."

"I think next spring, different flowers are in order for your front flower beds. Bachelor buttons will be misleading." She smiled tentatively up at him.

"You put whatever flowers you want in those flowerbeds, miss. Can we get back to you leading me astray?" Matt's arms tightened around her. "I was rather enjoying that."

"You kissed me!" Priscilla protested.

"Priscilla," Matt disagreed. "Women are far too powerful in matters of the heart. Men don't stand a chance. You have been leading me astray since you renamed my horse and tried to turn me into a pagan to worship the sun with you. One thing I will agree with." Priscilla squeaked when Matt lifted her onto the countertop so their faces were closer to the same level. "Next year, no bachelor buttons."

Priscilla grinned at him, at what he was implying, and then she laughed. Hope welled up in his heart as he laughed with her before he kissed her again.

***

First thing Saturday morning, Cora hopped on her bike and went to Priscilla's.

"You owe me." Cora smiled at Priscilla, who had a mouth full of pins. "One day of peace and happy before I step back in the ring."

Cora's eyes swept over all the garments in Priscilla's dining room.

Priscilla pressed the pins into a pincushion before she spoke. "I was going to work today. That river doesn't look very clean at all."

"The train leaves for Bennett farm at 9:30. I have a lunch here from Lucy, and I want a day of happy and fun. Let's go."

"I don't have a swimming costume." Priscilla grasped at that straw and clung to it.

"That's why we're going to the Bennett's sandbar. There isn't a soul in sight, plus it's easy to walk to. Come on."

"I really should..."

"Me, too." Cora interrupted. "This might be the only day."

"Why?" Priscilla squinted warily.

"Before we face Richard in divorce court, I need this one day of peace. Once I am called to the bar to be sworn in, I will have to return to Toronto. I finish my term of articling next week. Mr. Birch files the papers next Friday. Then I wait for the call. It shouldn't be long, as the rest of the class was finished articling at the end of May. I took a few weeks longer. Come on." Cora checked her watch impatiently.

"I hate the thought of you in Toronto." Priscilla bit her lip.

"Me, too, but I've come too far. I have to go back. Let's go. I don't want to think about Toronto today."

"You *did* get the contempt of court document nullified." Priscilla wavered.

"And rewrote all your petitions and affidavits, too, so you owe me. Let's go."

"I do love the Bennett farm," Priscilla said in surrender.

"Great." Cora smiled at Priscilla as she put her pincushion aside. "Let's go to the train."

Once they got to the Bennett's, they carried the picnic blankets down the hill to the sandbar where Ada planned to join them after she fed her men lunch.

They walked through mud that made them sink to their knees. Cora laughed so hard she fell over.

"Cora, that is not just mud — that is also cow patties..." Priscilla grimaced.

Cora laughed harder.

"You have to help me up," Cora begged, holding the blankets over her head so they wouldn't be covered in mud. Priscilla tiptoed through the muck and took the blankets.

"I'm not going anywhere near you. You're a mess," Priscilla said primly, as she stood back from the pit Cora had slid into.

Cora took another step, lost her shoe, and sunk deeper.

"You realize this is something children do. Play on sandbars, get mud up to their necks. This is inappropriate for grown women!" Priscilla protested as Cora hooted with laughter.

"Oh, Priscilla!" Cora gasped from the depth of the mud, head-to-toe covered. "I need to be a child for a day. So do you, and so does Ada. I've been much too serious for too long."

"It is beautiful here," Priscilla conceded then took a deep breath and let it out slowly.

"Yes, it is. It's so beautiful, it is time to let go of all the stress I had to endure in Toronto." Cora struggled out of the mud pit. "I'm leaving it right here, on this sandbar. If I could just get out of this mud and get to it!"

When Cora had finally freed herself, they settled on the sand and put their feet in the water. The June sun beat down hot on their heads. Mud dried on Cora's bathing costume. She grabbed the rope that the Bennetts kept tied to a stump and dove into the river. Cora let the current pull her. She tugged on the rope to drag herself back and let the river take her again. Happy memories flooded back to her, worrying about nothing but playing in the water. Once she was sufficiently washed off, she dragged herself back up the slope of the sandbar and sat down beside Priscilla.

"Priscilla, I am letting the peace of this river soak right into me. Don't you love this?"

The breeze and the river melted her worries away. Exactly like she knew it would.

Politely, Priscilla declined to answer as she brushed mud off her cheekbone and grimaced.

"Why don't you stay here?" Priscilla asked. "You love it here."

"Things are tough there, but I hate unfinished business. I think a part of me always knew I would have to go back. Being part of family law reminded me of that."

Priscilla twisted open the top of the thermos of lemonade and poured them each a glass.

"Oh, this mud!" Ada interrupted them as she called out. Cora laughed when Ada sank to her knees. "I need to get John to build me a dock," Ada grumbled. Cora went to her and dragged her out of the mud.

"I brought you some lunch in case you run out of food."

"Is it lunch time? I lost track of time." Cora opened the picnic baskets.

"Well past." Ada settled down beside them.

Priscilla opened a tin of sandwiches.

"Egg?" Cora asked Ada.

"Of course." Ada grinned as Cora took a sandwich and handed the tin back to Priscilla. "With dry mustard. People always forget the dry mustard — it's the most important part. You might need a little extra salt."

"I always need a little extra salt." Cora sprinkled some on her sandwich.

The three of them sighed as they watched the long grass sway in the breeze.

"You were saying?" Priscilla took a sip of lemonade and stretched out on her blanket.

"I left Toronto absolutely terrified and heartbroken. My new fear, since court the other day, is this: I am more afraid to live without hope and without purpose than to go back and deal with Eli. Coming here and seeing how a community can pull together to help Matt and you, Priscilla; it has healed me. It wasn't something I saw in Toronto. Ada, you reminded me of my purpose. The opportunity to represent you was a gift, really. I got to see firsthand how the law could protect you. The entire process worked for you — the courts, police officers, the inspectors, everyone. I feel like my hope in humanity was restored yesterday."

"I know you have to return." Ada handed Cora some cake wrapped in wax paper. "But I worry about you in Toronto on your own."

Cora took a bite and wanted to swoon in delight. "I can't let Adeline down. I had a letter from her, and Eli has taken bullying to a whole new level. I have to go back and find out if she is all right. The only place to be sworn in is at Osgoode Hall. So when I get the call, I must go."

Ada sighed, and they turned their attention to Priscilla.

"Priscilla, are you having fun yet?" Cora teased, as she brushed sand off her bathing costume.

"No. I've never been this muddy in my life. I am enduring this day for you."

"Come on. Into the river. You have to try it."

"I. Will. Not!" Priscilla protested.

"Just try it," Cora insisted.

Priscilla rolled her eyes, sighed as she picked up the rope, and waded in.

Cora smiled as she watched her new friend float in the current.

"Do you think you'll win on Monday?" Ada asked quietly, so Priscilla wouldn't overhear.

"Yes. Monday I am not at all worried about. The criminal trial though, I have no idea. If he gets out, I am worried about what sort of vengeance he'll seek. She lives alone, works alone. She's vulnerable, and he's really terrifying."

"We'll have to figure something out." Ada watched Priscilla float in the current.

"That grandmother would tell him every step. If he doesn't get convicted, she'll have to leave Oakland." Cora's shivered with worry for her friend.

"Maybe." Ada tidied up her dishes and turned to face Cora. "I'm proud of you."

"Never mind that." Cora turned over so the sun could dry her back.

"I mean it. She's had proper representation, and it matters. What you do matters a lot."

"I'm worried about Matt. He finally has a taste of happiness, and she's going to have to run anyway." Cora settled her head on her crossed arms.

"He'll go with her." Ada smiled. "That boy is smitten. He's not letting her out of his sight."

"People will talk," Cora warned.

"Who cares? They'll talk anyway. She's made for him, and he's made for her. It's obvious when you spend a minute with them. He loves her. He will treat her with tenderness and will be happy to take care of her no matter what comes their way. Matt Hartwell is lovely."

They both turned their attention to Priscilla, watching her pull herself against the current and then let the current pull her again. "Priscilla is special. Matt said it best. She sailed in and brought light back into his very dark life. I wish them all the best. It is my sincere wish that they'll let John and I host the wedding. We need a wedding here."

"Lucky, Priscilla." An emptiness ached inside Cora; she tried to ignore the pain. "You have them married already."

"It's just a matter of time," Ada said confidently. "Maybe you'll run into your bodyguard in Toronto."

"He's long gone," Cora said bitterly.

"If you have feelings for him. You should let him know."

"I like my heart intact. I don't want him to step all over it." Cora bristled.

Ada smiled at Cora.

"How did you make out?" Cora flipped onto her back as Priscilla dragged herself up the bank.

"It is wonderful!" Priscilla said as she wrung river water out of her hair. "I think I'll be doing this again soon!"

Ada got up off her blanket. "I better get back. I have to get supper ready. Come up when you're ready."

"How are we getting home?" Priscilla dropped down beside Cora.

"I left a note on Matt's door to come out and pick us up." Cora smiled mischievously at Priscilla.

"He can't see me like this!" Priscilla panicked. "I look like a drowned rat!"

"You look lovely, Priscilla!" Ada said, as she tried and failed to get around the mud. "I'll make up an extra plate for Matt. He took his mother to Brandon today, didn't he?"

"Yes, he did. Thanks, Ada."

"Come up soon. Supper is in an hour."

Cora went back to the rope and dove into the river.

As the current dragged her, she put the thoughts of Sol, Eli, and Adeline firmly out of her mind. She smiled at Priscilla, who laughed as

Ada struggled through the mud to get back to her precious kitchen. Monday, Priscilla would stand up to Richard, then at his criminal trial, too. If Priscilla could stand up to bullying of that sort, she could, too. New courage had surfaced during the standoff with Mrs. Charbonneau. The courage intensified as she stood down Mr. Levinson. Cora knew, deep down inside, there was no turning back now.

Cora dove down and swam as hard as she could against the current. Finally, exhausted, she let the flow of water pull her down the river. Somehow, the current forced her mind to calm and left only peace in her heart. Peace and a newfound strength.

Cora shook her head and took a deep breath.

It's time to prosecute some really bad people so, get ready, Richard. I'm coming for you, and when I've defeated you in every court, I'm coming back for you, Eli... count on it.

Chapter Thirty-Five

O n Monday morning, June 11, at 10:45 a.m, the day they had been hoping for and dreading all at once, Priscilla sat beside Cora on a hard chair in the courtroom. Mr. Birch, Cora's supervising lawyer and an elderly gentleman, patted Priscilla's shoulder as the bailiffs hauled Richard in. Priscilla stiffened beside her.

Richard vibrated with fury. "You're taking these cuffs off, I presume."

Cora put her hand on Priscilla's arm. Priscilla stared at the table, refusing to look at Richard.

Cora heard a movement behind her. A young woman and little boy took their seats in the courtroom. Cora's neck slicked with anxious sweat. Valentine Champalone, large as life, looking exactly like her photo.

Is she here to testify that she had lied in the note? Has she been threatened? Have they paid her to lie on the stand?

The judge entered the room.

"All rise. The honourable Judge Madden presiding."

Cora wondered what the judge thought of Richard in handcuffs with three lawyers flanking him, contrasted with two women and an elderly lawyer.

He took a seat and asked Mr. Birch to approach his bench. Mr. Birch slowly, and with great care, picked up his cane and tottered over to the judge.

"You are allowing this woman lawyer to article in your firm?" The judge's eyebrows rose in skepticism.

"I am, sir."

"Do you have her transcripts and credentials?"

"I believe she brought them, your honour."

"Approach." Judge Madden sighed.

Cora leaped up with her documentation and presented it to the judge.

"Woman lawyer, I ask you, what next?" the judge grumbled to Mr. Birch.

Cora, with great difficulty, kept her mouth shut.

Mr. Birch shrugged as he leaned on his cane.

Judge Madden's eyes narrowed as he handed the documents back to Cora. "This looks in order. Let's proceed."

"In the matter of Markus v. Markus, we are here to rule if this marriage is legal and binding. What say you?" The judge directed the comment to Cora.

Priscilla, very cautiously, put her hand up. The judge's eyebrows shot up in surprise. No one expected her to speak.

"Yes?" Judge Madden asked.

Priscilla stood up.

"Your honour, I have an unusual request. Possibly, this is out of line." Priscilla kept her eyes down. "Would it be possible to speak to Mr. Markus for a few minutes before this court decides on our marriage? Maybe his cuffs could be taken off?"

"Do you think you could reconcile?" Judge Madden's eyes gleamed with hope.

Not a chance! Not on your life.

"I think we should try." Priscilla dragged her eyes up to the judge.

Cora shook her head no. Her heart pounded in her throat at the thought of Priscilla alone in a room with Richard.

"I don't see any harm in that. If a marriage can be saved, we should do all we can. I call a ten-minute recess." The judge banged his gavel down.

Cora's eyes widened in fear.

"Have you lost your mind?" Cora hissed at Priscilla.

"I just want a conversation with my husband." Priscilla turned her back on Cora.

Fear pooled in Cora's stomach as the bailiff removed Richard's cuffs before he followed Priscilla out of the courtroom.

Cora and Richard's lawyer, Mr. Collier, scrambled after them. By the time they got to the little room, the door had snapped shut. Cora knocked politely.

Richard opened the door.

"No need for you to attend." Richard sneered with contempt.

"She is entitled to legal counsel at every minute of this proceeding." Cora stood her ground and moved to accompany Priscilla.

"Absolutely not."

"It's all right, Cora." Priscilla's voice sounded quiet in the room. "I'm all right. I just have something to say to Richard."

Richard's lawyer jostled Cora out of the way. He whispered in his ear, and Richard's mouth hardened.

"Richard, if I don't have a lawyer here, you don't need one either," Priscilla suggested meekly.

Cora stood at the threshold of the door and gave Priscilla a pleading look.

Richard closed the door on Cora and his lawyer. They stood there, completely dumfounded.

At a loss, Cora turned to Mr. Collier. "I'm Cora Rood."

The lawyer sneered at her outstretched hand and ignored it. Cora crossed her arms in front of her chest.

"A woman lawyer?" He sniffed. "This is going to be very, very easy."

Cora gritted her teeth and sat down on the bench by the closed door. She sat on her hands so she would not wring them in fear.

***

"Are you ready to return?" Richard's eyes swept over her. Priscilla shivered in revulsion. "This has gone on long enough. I'll speak to the judge on your behalf and tell him this has all been a complete misunderstanding."

Priscilla took a deep breath to try to control the fear churning in her stomach.

"This is the last time we'll talk." Priscilla straightened her shoulders. "I wanted to give you an opportunity to apologize to me. For killing our son."

Richard stood up so quickly his chair flipped over. Priscilla stood up, too. Her eyes locked with his; she knew he would be furious at a show of strength from her.

"I did not kill our son," he hissed furiously. "They are trying me on Thursday. I'm looking at life in prison. You will drop the charges, and you will come home. This has gone on long enough."

"You peeled my hands off the banister." Priscilla moved around the table so she could face Richard with nothing between them. "You held me for a moment before you pushed me down the stairs. I am going to testify to that in court, Richard. I can't make you pay for the injury to me, I have no rights here, but my unborn child does. You will pay for the loss of his life."

His fist hit her so fast and so hard, blood spurted from Priscilla's nose. Knocked to the floor, she tried to crawl away from him.

"You will drop the charges!" he roared at her as he dragged her back up off the floor. Priscilla tried to brace herself for another attack. "I am facing a murder trial with life in prison!"

He shook her hard. Blood from her nose spattered across his chest.

"I'll watch them throw you in prison for life," Priscilla baited him with her words. "I will laugh when they toss the key away so you never see the light of day again. Once I walk out of that courtroom, I will never, ever think about you again."

Her words stoked the fire of rage in his eyes. She held her breath as he plowed his fist into her jaw with such force, she hit the wall before she fell to the floor. She heard Mr. Collier and Cora trying desperately to get in the room, but they sounded very far away.

Richard pounced on her just as his lawyer finally, with the assistance of the bailiffs, broke the door open with his shoulder.

"Richard!" Mr. Collier and two bailiffs dragged Richard off Priscilla so he couldn't hit her again.

Cora dropped to her side immediately. "What is the meaning of this?"

"Get him out of here!" Mr. Collier pointed to the open door as he stood between Richard and Priscilla. "You just lost this case. This is on you."

Richard grabbed his hair with his fists. "She provoked me! It's not my fault... Priscilla, you did this on purpose! Tell the judge my wife provoked me!" Richard's eyes were wide and wild with fear as the full weight of what he had done crashed down on him.

"Get this animal away from my client." Cora roared at Mr. Collier. "He better be in handcuffs, or we won't be returning to court." She pointed at the bailiffs then handed Priscilla a handkerchief to clean her face.

Mr. Collier's face purpled with anger as he dragged Richard back into the courtroom. Cora heard him cursing under his breath.

"Aren't you going to clean your face?" Cora helped Priscilla struggle to her feet.

"I'm ready for trial." Priscilla swayed and held onto Cora.

"You're bleeding on everything," Cora whispered.

"Didn't you say sometimes we lose a battle while we prepare to win the war?" Priscilla smiled at Cora, her teeth red with blood. "Let's go to war."

Cora saw Priscilla in a new light and with a whole new respect.

I thought you were a timid little dress designer, but you are a warrior. If your jaw had been broken in a jail cell, I daresay you would have found a different way to fight. I need to take a page from your book.

Cora shook those thoughts off, and her arm tightened around Priscilla's waist.

"I'm a little dizzy." Priscilla leaned on Cora.

"Can you do this?" Cora bit her lip with concern.

"Of course. I'm going to be divorced at the end of this. This was the last beating. Can *you* do this?" Priscilla's eyes searched Cora's.

"I was born for this." Cora held Priscilla up, and together they walked into court.

Both of them ignored the gasps from the judge and courtroom attendants. The judge's eyes widened in disbelief.

"What is the meaning of this?" he asked Richard and his counsel.

"She provoked him," Mr. Collier had the nerve to say. "She planned this all along, your honour."

Cora's eyes narrowed to slits. She took a deep breath.

Stay cool and calm.

Judge Madden shot Richard a hard look.

"We'll reconvene tomorrow. She needs a doctor." Judge Madden banged his gavel down.

"I would like to see this to the end today. I'm all right," Priscilla begged the judge.

"Your face... you should take some time to clean up your face."

"This is nothing. If you send me home with him, it will only get worse. I would like to finish this trial today, please." Priscilla's tone suggested she would not take no for an answer.

Priscilla's face would pull sympathy out of anyone; Judge Madden was no exception.

"All right, we proceed." His eyes narrowed as he addressed Richard's counsel.

"We request his handcuffs be replaced," Cora said coolly.

"Agreed, bailiff, return his handcuffs. I will not have violence in this court."

Tension eased from Cora as the handcuffs were returned. Richard tried to make eye contact with Priscilla, but she ignored him and kept her eyes fixed on the judge. "Is there any contest to what is here in this affidavit?" The judge directed that to Richard's lawyers.

"We would like to ask Valentine Champalone to testify." Mr. Collier's voice seemed high with anxiety. "The note and the photograph have an easy explanation."

If Valentine lies, it will be her word against Matt's. Matt will tell the truth, and the photograph does not lie. This could come down to the judge.

"Proceed."

Cora and Priscilla held their breath as Valentine made her way to the front of the court.

After she was sworn in, she took her seat in the witness box. Cora took a deep breath as Mr. Collier stood.

"Can you tell us, how do you know this man?"

Priscilla cleared her throat. Valentine couldn't tear her eyes from Priscilla as blood dripped from Priscilla's nose onto her dress. Her eyes softened in sympathy, then darted from Priscilla to Richard and back to her. Priscilla's eyes locked on Valentine's, and she didn't look away. A door opened at the back of the courtroom. When Matt walked in, Valentine looked at him, and her face crumpled.

Valentine opened her mouth to speak and then closed it. Mr. Collier tried to block her view of Priscilla.

Is she remembering all the times her face looked like that? Is she worried that he will turn his rage to their son next? What is she thinking? Please tell the truth.

"Excuse me, Mr. Collier, I can't see the witness with you standing in front of us." Cora watched Valentine's resolve crumble as she looked at Priscilla's face.

He scowled at Cora but moved so Valentine could see Priscilla.

"He..." Valentine tried to look away from Priscilla but couldn't drag her eyes from her.

"You rent from him. He is your landlord," Mr. Collier prompted.

"Objection, your honour, testifying." Cora got to her feet.

"Sustained. Mr. Collier, this has to be her testimony, not yours."

Valentine started to shake. "He is my son's father." Valentine pressed her handkerchief to her mouth. She stifled a sob.

Mr. Collier sighed, walked back to his table, and dropped into his chair, defeated.

"She's lying." Richard stood up.

"What say you?" The judge pointed at Cora.

"Miss Champalone, can you tell the court how long you have been the mistress of Mr. Markus here?" Cora asked her simply.

"Four years."

"And you have a son with him?" Cora presented the photo of Richard Markus III, embracing Valentine Champalone.

"Yes. Edward."

"Your honour, we believe Miss Champalone's testimony corroborates the photographic evidence of adultery. No further questions for this witness."

"The witness is dismissed." Judge Madden banged down the gavel.

Valentine went to her son and put her arms around him.

"According to this most current affidavit and this testimony, the petitioner, Mrs. Markus, has grounds to divorce. She has provided the burden of proof regarding adultery, and the hospital reports speak to cruelty." Cora's voice rang out in the courtroom. Mr. Birch placed his hand on Priscilla's shoulder.

"Any evidence to the contrary?" Judge Madden directed the question to the lawyers at Richard's table.

"Tell them she's lying! This is a set up!" Richard hissed at his legal counsel.

"It's over," Mr. Collier murmured back to Richard. "No. No evidence to the contrary." Mr. Collier jotted something down. His face flushed red with embarrassment.

"I rule this marriage dissolved, as it meets the burden of proof both of adultery and abuse on the part of Mr. Markus. Decree nisi is to be issued. Mr. Markus, in accordance with Canadian law, will pay the fees incurred by Mrs. Markus. Court is adjourned." Judge Madden banged down the gavel.

One decision and one bang of the gavel ended the potential for a lifetime of suffering. Elation soared through Cora. Justice had been served for the weak and oppressed, and she rejoiced at her part in it.

Judge Madden left the room, and Priscilla stood up beside Cora.

"This isn't over." Richard tried to lunge at Priscilla. Cora marveled that Priscilla was able to hold her ground. The bailiffs held Richard between them.

Cora held her breath in fear as Priscilla walked right up to Richard and stood in front of him with the bailiffs holding him securely between them. Matt scrambled through the attendants to get to Priscilla.

"I will see you Thursday, in court, where you will answer for what you did to your son." Priscilla moved close to him and whispered into his ear. "I'm not done defeating you."

Richard attempted to lunge at her for the last time, but the bailiffs dragged him out.

"Come on, fighter." Cora hauled Priscilla in the opposite direction, out of court. Once the courthouse door closed, Matt turned to Priscilla, his face white with worry.

"Priscilla, are you all right?" He reached for her to assist her to the carriage.

"I need to get cleaned up, for sure. Is there anywhere we can go?"

"I'll take you to the hospital." Matt opened the door to the carriage and helped her in.

"No need. It's a split lip and a bloody nose. It's all right."

"We're going to the hospital." Matt's tone indicated that he had no intentions of changing his mind. Cora helped Mr. Birch crawl into the coach.

"What is decree nisi?" Priscilla held a handkerchief to her nose to try to wipe away any blood that hadn't dried.

"You are as good as divorced." Cora smiled broadly. "It's over. Next step, criminal court on Thursday."

***

Once Priscilla, Cora, and Mr. Birch were tucked into the stagecoach, Matt noticed Valentine and Edward come out of the courtroom and stand on the street corner. She blinked back tears as she fumbled in her bag looking for a handkerchief. Matt went to her side.

"How are you?" Matt handed her a clean handkerchief that she accepted gratefully.

"He paid me to lie about our relationship. I asked for half up front." Valentine wiped her tears away.

"Is it enough to live on?" Matt asked.

"I found a job at a laundry in the hospital here in Brandon. Turns out my sister is in a bad situation, so we're going to live together and raise our kids together. We will work opposite shifts. We'll be all right." Valentine took a deep breath and tried to stop crying.

Matt crouched down and ruffled Edward's hair. "I have something for you, young sir. If you would give me a moment."

Matt went to the stagecoach and found the camera he had used to incriminate Richard. He brought it back to Edward.

"If you are a very good boy, you can have this." Matt looked from his mother's shining eyes to Edward's.

"I am a very good boy." Edward jumped up and down. Matt smiled at his enthusiasm.

Valentine's eyes filled with tears, again.

"I hear you get to move into a new house." Matt handed him the camera. "Now you can take some pictures of your new friends."

Happiness glowed on Edward's face as he hugged the camera to his chest.

Matt straightened up to speak to Valentine in a low tone. "On Thursday, they try him for murder. If he gets off, you will be in danger from him. If he threatens you or comes after you, please let me know. Send a telegram to Matt Hartwell in Oakland, and I will be here to deal with him in a heartbeat."

"Thank you." Valentine's shoulders slumped. "You are very kind. Priscilla is lucky. I'm sure you will be very happy together."

"If you hadn't told the truth, she would still be married to him. I owe you a great debt, and I won't forget it. If you need me, don't hesitate to contact me. I wish you all the best." Matt held out his hand; Valentine shook it. "I mean that."

Valentine nodded; she took Edward's hand, and together they made their way home.

Matt crawled up on the buckboard and slapped the reins down to take Priscilla to the hospital. He worried if Richard won in criminal court, what would their next step be? His hands clenched into fists on the reins at the thought.

Chapter Thirty-Six

The next day, sun streamed in the window of Cora's bedroom. She stretched out in bed as the events of the day before flooded back to her. She winced as she thought of Priscilla's face, but then her heart glowed with happiness as she remembered they'd won. Priscilla took a gamble. Letting Richard attack her one last time was not the loss of a battle, it was a necessary defeat to win the bigger war. Cora curled to her side and bunched a pillow under her head as she thought about that.

Is this where I got it wrong? I kept looking at the little battles I lost, without remembering the big picture. Each little battle lost contributed to winning the war on women's rights because even though we lost some, we were still fighting. Ada is right. The injustice of those losses can defeat you or they can spur you on. The only way things can change is if the double standard women are up against is in the forefront of the court.

What if Aunty Lucinda had a lawyer like me? I might have lost, but it would have brought the horror of domestic abuse and the lack of law to regulate it to the forefront much sooner. How many women would have been assisted and rescued had we demanded protection under the law long ago?

The time is now. You were right, father. If you can do something to better the lives of your fellowman, or in this case woman, we absolutely should.

Despite the win they had, Cora shivered with fear. If Richard won in criminal court, how long would Priscilla be safe?

Cora's thoughts drifted from Priscilla to Adeline.

What about Adeline? She says Eli is spiraling into depravity...what does that mean? Is he doing something criminal we can prosecute him for? Lose her battle in divorce court but annihilate him in criminal court?

Filled with renewed energy and determination, Cora sprung out of bed. She hummed while she got dressed and, after breakfast, took her bike to Priscilla's.

"Come in!" Priscilla smiled broadly from the doorway.

"Good morning! I'm here to celebrate your win yesterday and make sure you are all right."

"Never better. Are you all right?" Priscilla poured tea into two tea cups. "Your first time back in court went rather well, right?"

"Yes, very well. I don't want to put you on the spot, but I do need a favour."

"Sure. If I can help, I will." Priscilla placed oatmeal cookies on a plate and offered them to Cora.

"Once I am called to the bar, I will need to go back looking like a man. I need you to cut off my hair and make me a suit. If I go back as a woman, I'm a target."

"Dear heavens. What sort of threat are you up against?" Priscilla's eyes widened in fear.

"The worst sort," Cora said grimly. "Can you make me look like a man?"

"Of course. But your hair..."

"It'll grow back." Cora straightened up and faced Priscilla.

"Will you tell Mr. Rood?"

"I can't keep the call to the bar from him. He doesn't need to know I plan to find out what sort of criminal activity Eli Pitman is engaged in."

"When will you leave?" Priscilla's face fell.

"I don't know. Mr. Birch filed my papers, and I assume I will be called to the bar with the rest of my class. They were anticipating July 25."

"I better get started today then." Priscilla pushed her plate of cookies out of the way and reached for a box of patterns.

"Thank you." Cora sipped her tea. "Do you need my measurements?"

"No, I still have them from your dresses."

"Priscilla, I don't want a protest on my hands. I ask you to tell no one that I am returning to find dirt on Eli."

Priscilla's eyes were troubled. "Are you sure you shouldn't have some protection?"

"Make me look like an ugly man, and I should be all right." Cora bit into a cookie.

"I don't think I can make you look ugly, Cora. You are beautiful." Priscilla bit her lip in fear.

Cora waved the compliment away.

"Maybe we should give you a little more disguise? Like some padding?"

"Whatever you think." Cora finished her cookie, drained her tea, and stood up. "I'll leave that up to you."

"Do you think we'll win?" Priscilla cleared the table of dishes so she could start on Cora's suit immediately.

"Priscilla, I'm not so sure."

"If he is not convicted, I have to run." Priscilla kept her back to Cora.

"How will Matt react to that?" Cora asked quietly.

Priscilla turned around. "I don't have a choice."

Cora went to Priscilla and wrapped her arms around her friend.

"Don't panic yet. You have a lovely business here. You are safe here. Try to stay calm until you have a reason not to be. Richard is in jail. Take a deep breath."

"I wish you weren't leaving." Priscilla dropped her forehead onto Cora's shoulder.

"Me, too." Cora gave her one last hard squeeze before she let her go. "You'll be all right. You are just shaken up. When I'm gone, talk to Ada. She can get a soul through any sort of tribulation, and she loves you."

"You think so?" Priscilla blinked tears back.

"Ada Bennett has enough love in her heart for everyone. She told me once that hope and love reside together, so when your hope starts to fade, she has an endless supply. Go see her after I go. Talk to her about this." Cora smiled at her friend.

"I'll have that suit ready." Priscilla smiled sadly.

"Thanks. I will leave you to it."

***

On Wednesday evening, Cora strolled down Crescent Street to meet with Mr. Birch. Her shoes clicked on the hardwood floor as she settled into one of his chairs by the front window of his office. The window looked out onto the street where horses and carriages went by. Couples were out for a stroll in the beautiful summer evening. Wilbur and Lucy were in front of their mercantile; Cora smiled at them as Wilbur locked the door, held out his hand to Lucy, and together, they went home. As she waited for Mr. Birch, she looked at the portraits of the men in his family who had worked as lawyers.

What a legacy! Will I ever have a child to follow in my footsteps?

Thoughts of children made her think of Sol, which caused Cora's heart to seize in pain.

After a few minutes, Mr. Birch called her in. She followed him down the narrow hallway to his office that looked out over Victoria Park.

Mr. Birch handed Cora her papers, which he had signed, verifying she had finished her period of articling. He passed her a brandy and filled his pipe with tobacco.

Cora held onto the file and could barely believe what she was looking at. Five years of fighting. Done. Now she waited for a call to the bar.

"First woman lawyer in Canada and Great Britain, and I got to be part of that." Mr. Birch's eyes were warm with approval.

"I'll post these papers tomorrow from Brandon." She took a tentative sip of brandy.

"I took the liberty of sending a telegram to one of the benchers today. Malachi Marks, maybe you've heard of him. I informed him of your work with me. I mentioned that your papers are on the way and that I would expect you to be called to the bar with the rest of your class." Mr. Birch took a long drag of smoke into his lungs, held it, and released it slowly.

"Really?" Cora gasped. "How do you know Mr. Marks?"

Mr. Birch's bushy eyebrows shot up. "I was called to the bar with him. Got into some slight altercations when we articled at the same firm. Let's just say he owes me a favour if he intends to enjoy my continued silence. I may be old, Miss Rood, but I still have a bit of a standing with the benchers. I went to school with more than half of them."

"If only I had known a few years ago, I could have used some of those connections," Cora said ruefully.

"Looks like you did well enough on your own." Mr. Birch took a long sip of brandy, then a long drag of his pipe.

Cora shrugged. "They say they anticipate some resistance at the swearing in."

Mr. Birch took another long drag. "Ridiculous. Don't let it intimidate you. Walk in there like you own the place. It's the only way."

"What do you think will happen tomorrow for Priscilla?"

"I wish I knew." Mr. Birch sipped his brandy again. "The verdict could go either way. Terrible business that was. You did well."

"I'm not so sure how to thank you for this." Cora ran her fingertips across the file.

"Be a good lawyer and stand your ground. No need to thank me. This is a professional courtesy. Any lawyer would have done the same."

"I'm not sure of much, Mr. Birch, but I guarantee most lawyers would not extend me professional courtesy if there was a gun to their head," Cora said bitterly.

"You threaten them." Mr. Birch looked out his window at the tops of the trees in the park. Cora could almost see his mind work as he formulated his next thought. "You don't mean to, but you challenge how they view women. You are very clever, Miss Rood." Mr. Birch turned and held Cora's gaze. She listened intently. "Your father isn't here to say this to you. So, I'll do it on his behalf."

Cora's throat burned with unshed tears as dear Mr. Birch spoke of her father.

"He was a good man and a great friend to me. So, I want you to listen carefully. The men trying to stop you were raised to believe women are inferior. They truly believe women are not as intelligent as men. Cora, five minutes in your company forces them to re-evaluate that opinion. Their treatment of you has nothing to do with you and everything to do with an archaic way of looking at women that absolutely needs to change. You will be on the forefront of that change. You will have some failures, for sure. But you will succeed. Ultimately when history looks back at you, they will see only the success. You are the woman who dared to be Upper Canada and Great Britain's first female lawyer. A barrister no less."

Mr. Birch shook his head. "I will be adding a picture of you to my front wall. To be part, even this tiny part, of your success makes me proud. Know this; not everyone is ready for change, but that can't stop you. When you walk into Osgood Hall, you hold your head high. Very high, because you will bring the women's rights movement to light in a court that disgusts me with its double standard. Women having to prove adultery *and* abuse, having no legal right to their children or property once they are married. It's despicable. You will change it. I guarantee it. The women of this society are desperate for your voice to be heard in the courts on their behalf."

"Thank you, Mr. Birch. I appreciate it." Cora swallowed down hot salty tears at his words.

Together, they sipped their brandy and watched the sun bleed orange and pink across the prairie sky. Thursday was fast approaching, and the criminal trial loomed in Cora's mind. Priscilla would know for certain if she could stay in Oakland or have to run for her life. Cora let herself out of Birch's Law Office. Once Priscilla had her answer, it would be time to return to Toronto — Eli's territory. A shiver of fear raced down her back.

Chapter Thirty-Seven

Thursday, June 18, 1904 arrived — the day of the trial. Dr. Davies, Cora, Priscilla, and Matt made the journey to Brandon. Priscilla and Cora dressed head-to-toe in black. As the stagecoach ground to a halt, Cora's stomach flipped in nervous anticipation.

Cora sat beside Priscilla in the courtroom and reached for Priscilla's ice cold hand. She watched as the twelve-man jury entered. She scanned their faces, mostly middle age. Cora bit her lip as the lawyers entered with Richard. A new legal team today. The lawyers that lost his divorce case had apparently been fired and replaced. Priscilla trembled in fear beside her. Her handbag fell off her lap and crashed to the floor.

Cora retrieved the handbag and passed it to Priscilla with a sympathetic look.

"Cora, I can't stand this. If he isn't convicted, I'll be looking over my shoulder forever." Priscilla's eyes widen with fear. "The prosecutor needs to win this."

Finally, the time for Priscilla to testify came; Cora gave her hand a hard squeeze.

"The prosecution would like to call Mrs. Priscilla Markus to the stand."

"Stay strong," Cora whispered in her ear. "Remember, you have no rights in this courtroom, but your unborn child does. Make sure your statements bring your *unborn son* into this trial."

Priscilla nodded; she listened to Cora but kept her eyes on the judge. She straightened up like a fighter about to go into the ring. Nervous, terrified, but courageous nonetheless.

Priscilla took the stand, and Cora held her breath.

"Please tell the court what took place on April 30, 1904," Mr. Harris, the lawyer for the prosecution stated.

"We had been for supper at a fundraising event, and my husband had quite a bit to drink that night. When we returned home, he was furious at me for speaking to a gentleman who was in attendance." Priscilla twisted a handkerchief between her hands.

"So, he was upset with you *before* you left the fundraiser?" Mr. Harris scratched a note down on the notebook in front of him.

"Yes."

"What sort of conversation were you having with the gentleman?"

"He was asking me if I was available to design a gown for his fiancée. They were to be married in three months, and he knew I was trained by Emmaline Prue. I said I would have to ask my husband if I was permitted to work on a project that was so big."

Perfect. Good girl. Permitted. Great word.

"You tried to explain this to your husband?"

"I have learned to try to stay as silent as possible when he is upset with me."

"What happened when he asked you about your relationship with the gentlemen from the fundraiser?"

"I told him he asked me to design a dress. Richard didn't believe me. He accused me of being intimate with the gentleman."

"What reason did he give?"

"Sir, when my husband gets drunk, there is no reasoning left."

"Did your husband know you were pregnant on April 30, 1904?"

"Yes. He knew I was pregnant, and he knew it was his child. Until he was drunk, and then he lost his reason." Priscilla lifted her chin.

"So, describe for the court what happened that night."

"He slapped me so hard I ran from him. I knew if I could just get to the spare room and lock the door, I would be safe. I have hidden there before. I raced up the stairs, and at the top of the stairs I lost my balance. I held onto the banister so I wouldn't fall, but he was behind me." Priscilla stopped, took a deep breath, and then continued. "He reached around me and grabbed my wrists. He yanked my hands off the banister. Just for a moment, he held me upright. I thought he would help me onto the landing. I was mistaken. Instead of helping me to the safety of the landing, he pushed me down the stairs. I was falling so fast, I couldn't stop myself. He screamed that he would never raise another man's child. He purposely threw me down the stairs to end this pregnancy in a jealous fit of rage. In his intoxicated state, he believed I had been unfaithful to him, which is not true."

The jury gasped then fell silent. Cora watched their faces carefully. They were horrified. Priscilla seemed particularity vulnerable as she tried valiantly not to cry. She carefully pressed her handkerchief to the eye that was still black from his fist.

"I did *not!*" Richard screamed. He jumped to his feet; it took both lawyers to subdue him. Priscilla shook with fear, and Mr. Harris moved so she couldn't see Richard.

"Order!" the judge bellowed. "You will have your turn, Mr. Markus, but not just yet."

Richard settled down reluctantly.

"What happened then?"

"The butler came to help me up, but Richard said to leave me there. I couldn't get up."

"Then what happened?"

Priscilla took a sip of water before responding. "The butler poured him a brandy. He got him drunk enough that he passed out, and then the butler helped me to the hospital."

"Winnipeg General?"

"Yes, the miscarriage caused terrible cramping pain. The staff there told me the baby had been a boy."

"I would like to present Mrs. Markus's chart at this time." The prosecutor handed the report to the judge, who skimmed over it.

"Let the record show that the doctor on staff verifies that the miscarriage was a result from a fall down stairs.

"Mrs. Markus, was the doctor concerned about any other injuries you had sustained?"

Cora watched the defense team tense in anticipation.

Clever.

"The doctor was concerned about the whip marks on my back."

"Objection!" Mr. Collins had the biggest mouth on the defense team; he shouted the loudest. "Mr. Markus is not on trial for anything but the miscarriage. The way a man exercises authority in his house is of no business to the Canadian court!"

Mr. Harris addressed the judge, but spoke directly to the jury. "Your honour, I would like to remind this court that under Canadian law, whipping is never to be inflicted on any female, no matter what the offence. To take a whip to a pregnant woman is most heinous. This man has put himself *above* the law of Canada. In addition to murdering what would have been Mrs. Markus's first-born child."

Perfect. You presented that perfectly. The jury is horrified, and you just won this case. Wonderful.

"Objection! Prejudicial!" Mr. Collins's face turned purple, and Cora wondered if he would drop to the floor from a stroke.

"Goes to motive, your honour. This indicates a history of disregarding Canadian law. Men of honour live according to the laws of this land. As Canadian citizens, we don't flout the law. We know, in this court, a man is the ultimate authority in his home, and as such is within his rights to correct his wife as he sees fit. That is not disputed."

Cora burned with fury at the statement.

"However, he must recognize the law of the land as he does so. No man is above the law. If he would disregard this law, what else is he disregarding in his home? Every home and every man is subject to Canadian law, is he not?"

Careful, don't grandstand... but you are brilliant, and I will be using this line of reasoning when I'm back in family court.

Cora watched the defense drag Richard back into his chair.

"Objection overruled."

You've won it. You did it!

Cora couldn't take her eyes off the lawyer for the prosecution. He was an elderly gentleman, but his mind was sharp as a tack. She wanted to stand and applaud, but she didn't dare.

"She fell! It was an accident," Richard screamed.

Richard shook his attorney's hands off. Cora held her breath. The bailiffs hovered.

"Your honour, this man clearly has no respect for your courtroom, in addition to the law of Canada. He's intimidating my witness."

"One more outburst and you will be removed from this court and held in contempt."

Richard. You. Are. Done.

"Mr. Collins, your witness."

Cora's neck tensed in terror as Mr. Collins checked his notes and then stood to cross examine Priscilla.

"I'm sorry to hear of your miscarriage, Mrs. Markus." Mr. Collins spoke softly.

"Thank you. It was a tragic event."

"I'm curious. How did you end up in the care of Dr. Davies in Oakland, Manitoba? That's a long way from Winnipeg General Hospital." He had the audacity to chuckle softly.

"I went to see my grandmother." Priscilla sipped her water.

Good girl. Give him only the facts, nothing more.

"Did your husband know you were going to Oakland to visit your grandmother? Did you have permission for that trip?"

Cora bristled at the word permission.

"I ran from home because I was afraid to go back after the miscarriage. I was terrified of him after he pushed me down the stairs."

"Would he have *allowed* you to go if you had asked permission, as you should have?"

Cora vibrated with fury at his line of questioning.

If there was even one woman on the jury, they would be horrified at this line of questioning!

"Wouldn't most loving husbands want their wife to find comfort from a grandmother after losing their first child?" Priscilla's hand shook as she set the water down. She couldn't take the edge out of her voice. Mr. Collins heard it and pounced.

"Permission to treat the witness as hostile?"

"Proceed." Judge Lawrence said.

Mr. Harris sat up straighter, ready to intervene.

"How did you finance this little trip to Oakland, Mrs. Markus?"

Priscilla's face flushed red.

"Wives are not permitted to have bank accounts without their husband's permission, are they? Did your husband sign for you to have a bank account?"

A hot fist of anger clenched around Cora's heart, making it hard to breathe as she kept her eye on Mr. Collins.

"No." Priscilla whispered.

The jury murmured.

"I can't hear you." Mr. Collins taunted Priscilla.

"No," she said firmly. "I was not permitted money or to work."

"That's right. You are a dress designer. A professional dress designer, right?"

"Objection. Relevance? What is this?" Mr. Harris roared from his table.

"I'm just trying to understand how this woman financed a trip to Oakland and how she has lived in Oakland since she ran away from her lawful husband even when the court *ordered her back.*" Mr. Collins held his hands up indicating his confusion.

"Overruled. Answer the question."

"I was given many gifts at my wedding. I took them with me when I left and sold them to pay for the train ticket."

"A married woman cannot own property, and everything that is hers is property of her husband when they are married. Any gift given to you belongs to him. Ergo, you stole from him."

The jury gasped.

"Those were gifts from my friends to me." Priscilla's voice shook.

Cora's stomach cramped in fear watching him bait and attack her.

"Everything, including *you*, became his property when you signed the marriage document. You have no access to anything without his permission. I believe you to be headstrong and independent! Isn't that right? No respect for your husband, obviously, stealing and then running from your husband. Shameful! Then, when you got *caught* you claim he pushed you down the stairs! Where were these grandiose claims before?"

"Objection! Testifying!" Mr. Harris called out.

"Overruled."

"He did push me down the stairs. That is not a claim, Sir, that is a fact." Priscilla's voice shook.

"A fact? Do you have a witness to that? Because we're going to hear eyewitness testimony that you fell. An accident. Really, Mrs. Markus." Mr. Collins shook his head. "Mr. Harris has said a bit about ignoring the laws of the land. Let's talk about the law that you refused to comply to. You were ordered back to your husband by the King's Bench, and you refused!"

"Objection! The contempt of court order was thrown out of court. Is there a question here?" Mr. Harris called out to the judge.

"Sustained. Move along, Mr. Collins."

Cora stood up. She kept her eyes locked on Priscilla. She shook her head no.

No emotion. Once you show emotion, you are done. Come on, Collins, ask about the divorce. Come on. Open that door. Take the risk that this group of men will be furious about a woman filing for divorce. Let's talk about his affair with Valentine. Come on, do it.

"I was afraid for my life. I ran to my grandmother. I could not live with a man who deliberately terminated my pregnancy. I will never go back to him. I am afraid of him." Priscilla looked at the jury. "I am terrified of him."

"No wonder you provoked him. You are a headstrong girl — you have no regard for the sanctity of marriage."

"Objection, badgering!" Mr. Harris stood up.

Priscilla stood up. The jury murmured as they watched her.

"I think that a man beating his wife with a horse whip crushed the sanctity of marriage, Mr. Collins. A man that can take a whip to his wife can certainly, in a fit of rage, throw her down a flight of stairs. If all you have to accuse me of is taking some funds necessary for my survival, if that's all you have on me, I beg you to stop wasting the court's time. I am an innocent woman, but whatever you think of me doesn't matter because we are not here to discuss me or my husband. We are here to discuss my son. *My son!*" Priscilla gripped the railing of the witness box as she leaned over it. "My son — he killed my son!"

"Objection!" Mr. Collier called out, but Priscilla spoke over him.

"I had to bear the physical effects of a miscarriage. Do you know what it feels like to miscarry a child after being pushed down a flight of stairs with partially healed whip marks on your back? Do you? Or to have a fever rage through you and have the rest of the placenta scraped out of your womb so you don't die. Whatever you think about me, whatever you think about Richard and his eyewitness doesn't alter the fact that a child died at his hand, and I had to bear the pain of it. I don't care about me. I am here to ask for justice." Priscilla broke eye contact with Mr. Collins to address the jury. "Justice for my son."

Holy cats, Priscilla! You should be a lawyer! That was brilliant!

Priscilla sat back down; her hand shook as she picked up her water glass.

"Move to strike." Mr. Collins put his hands on his hips.

"The jury will disregard that statement."

The jury would never disregard that statement! Cora broke out in goose bumps from the truth of it.

"You admit you stole from your husband, ran away, and refused to return."

"I needed to recover. I was in a great deal of pain — Look at my chart. I nearly died of sepsis. I did what I had to do to protect my own life."

"No further questions for this witness."

Priscilla returned to her seat beside Cora. Cora reached for her; her hands were ice cold and shaking.

"You did that perfectly," Cora whispered in her ear.

"He's going to lie... he's going to destroy what I just said," Priscilla said against Cora's neck. Her voice shook; Priscilla sounded like she was on the verge of a breakdown.

"I don't think so. That was powerful. I didn't know you could speak like that."

"Just like you said, I saw it in their eyes. I had no worth to them. Thank goodness, my son has rights in this room. I clearly have none." Priscilla pulled a handkerchief out of her pocket and wiped her eyes.

The prosecution would like to call Dr. Davies."

Oh, thank goodness for Dr. Davies.

"Can you describe the state of Mrs. Markus for the court?"

"On May 1, Mrs. Markus was carried into my clinic. She was so weak and fevered she couldn't walk. Upon our initial examination, we found she had a very high fever. Mrs. Markus had suffered a miscarriage as a result of a fall. I immediately performed dilation and curettage to remove the remaining placenta that had become septic. Twenty-four hours without surgery, she would have died."

"In addition to the injury consistent with a fall down the stairs, what other injury did you find?"

"Objection! Prejudicial."

"Your honour, Mr. Markus says she fell. Mrs. Markus said she had her hands pulled off the banister and was then pushed. I want the doctor to tell us if there was any evidence, physical evidence, that Mrs. Markus's hands were forcibly pulled off the banister."

"Overruled."

"The injuries to Mrs. Markus were extensive. She had bruising on the top of both her wrists. The markings under her wrist were made by four fingers. Can I show you, Mr. Harris, if I could see your wrist?" Dr. Davies placed his hand on top of Mr. Harris's wrist and showed the jury. You'll notice where the finger mark bruising is. It is consistent with someone pulling up on a wrist like so. She had four marks along here and one mark that would be a thumb right here. It's a perfect handprint. There is no question that she had her hands pulled off something."

"So, this bruising would be from someone holding her wrists facing her or behind her?"

"Behind her."

"How can you be sure of that?"

"I'll show you on your wrist again. You'll notice where my thumb is on your wrist, the bruising pattern would be completely different if I was facing you."

"In your professional opinion, the fall down the stairs terminated the pregnancy?"

"Oh yes, the damage sustained from that fall caused her to miscarry."

"Was this the last time you treated Mrs. Markus?"

"Objection. Relevance."

"Withdrawn." Mr. Harris walked back to his table and checked his notes.

"May I mention one more thing?" Dr. Davies suggested so politely; Cora held her breath in anticipation.

"My conscience will not allow me to be silent on this matter. I've never, in my entire professional career, seen a lash taken to a woman."

"Objection!"

"Please, your honour." Dr. Davies held his hands out in supplication. "I am a doctor, and as a doctor, I cannot say that the whipping she sustained wouldn't have *also* weakened her. The fall, for sure, would terminate a pregnancy. But in addition to lashing, well, sir, it is obvious to me he was acting with reckless disregard for the life of his unborn child. No man would treat his pregnant wife in this way..."

"Objection! Opinion!" The defense team leaped to their feet.

"Sustained."

"Your witness," Mr. Harris said to the prosecution. He sat down and wrote on his legal pad.

Cora shook with worry that the defense would destroy Dr. Davies.

"The bruising that you mention, do you have any evidence that the bruising happened at the same time as the fall? Can you say for sure that the bruising was before the fall or even on the same day?"

"The marks were deep purple, and in my professional opinion, they were very recent. I believe that she was bruised the same day as the fall. I believe them to be part of the same event."

"Is it possible that the bruising could have been sustained the day before?"

"It's possible." Dr. Davies's mouth thinned in disapproval. "Clearly, there is a pattern of disturbing domestic violence in Mr. Markus's home."

"Move to strike." Mr. Collins roared at the judge.

"The jury will disregard that last comment."

They opened the door on previous abuse. They opened that door! They are desperate. Are you going to walk through it? You have this. You won it. Please, please redirect.

"Redirect." Mr. Harris stood up.

Cora stopped herself from cheering out loud.

"Do you think the bruising happened the same day as the whipping?"

"Your honour! Objection!"

"They brought up previous abuse. I'm just following their lead."

"Overruled. Proceed."

"If we're speculating that the abuse was the day before, well, what if it was at the same time as he took a horse whip to her back?"

Cora's eyes swept over the jury, their eyes were narrowed as they watched Richard Markus III slink down in his seat.

"No. Not the same day as the whipping." Dr. Davies corrected Mr. Harris.

"Oh?" Mr. Harris's eyebrows raised. He leaned against the table and crossed his arms. "How do you know that?"

You are good. Letting your witness correct you. Perfect.

"Mr. Harris, the lash marks were partially healed. The bruising on her wrists was, as I mentioned, very fresh."

"As fresh as the fall down the stairs?"

"Objection! Testifying."

"In your professional opinion, can you say with certainty that Mrs. Markus sustained the bruising consistent with her hands being pulled off a banister the same day as the fall down the stairs?"

"In my professional opinion, the bruising pattern corroborates her account of the events. There is no question in my mind."

"Just so we are clear, as a doctor, you are testifying that Mrs. Markus's testimony of events is true and correct."

"The physical evidence clearly supports her account of the events. I swear it."

"No further questions." Mr. Harris sat down and wrote on his note pad again. Cora itched to go and read his thoughts.

The prosecution rested their case and Cora held onto Priscilla's hand as the defense called their first witness.

"The defense would like to call Mr. Moore, the butler, to the stand."

Once Mr. Moore was sworn in, the defense started questioning. Cora held her breath and Priscilla's hand.

"Mr. Moore, would you tell the court what you saw on April 30, 1904?"

"I saw Mr. Markus get into an altercation with his wife. It was a terrible accident. She fell down a flight of stairs. As soon as I could, I took her to the hospital and had her examined."

"You're certain Mr. Markus didn't intend to harm Mrs. Markus?"

"I swear it."

"Your witness."

"So, Mrs. Markus was at the top of the stairs, and Mr. Markus was at the top of the stairs. Where were you standing?" Mr. Harris, the lawyer for the prosecution asked.

The butler shifted in his seat.

"I was down the hall."

"Describe the scene."

"Well, it all happened so fast." Mr. Moore refused to meet Mr. Harris's gaze. He scratched his eyebrow.

"So, Mrs. Markus was holding onto Mr. Markus or he was holding onto her? Please describe what you saw."

The butler shifted in his seat and started to sweat. "All I saw was her foot slip, and she fell down the stairs. It happened so fast, I couldn't be sure of anything else."

"So, he could have peeled her hands off the banister, but you just didn't see it."

"Objection! Speculation."

"Overruled. Careful, Mr. Harris."

"You can't be sure of anything else, but you are saying with certainty she *wasn't* thrown down the stairs. Well, that is speculation if I've ever heard it."

"I saw an accident. That is all I saw." Mr. Moore's face paled with worry.

"How long have you worked for Mr. Markus?"

"I worked for his father. I've known him his whole life."

"Were you aware that Mr. Markus beat his wife with a horse whip? Or was that an accident, too?"

"Objection, badgering. We are not here to discuss the whipping, only the fall down the stairs."

"Overruled. Answer the question, Mr. Moore."

"I was aware of no such thing."

Well done, sir, you just re-introduced the whipping and let the jury know this man would cover it up because there is no way something like that could happen in the house and the servants wouldn't know about it! Servants know everything!

"You've known Mr. Markus his whole life. Are you surprised to learn of this?"

"Of course. I had no idea such an altercation had occurred."

"An altercation. There's that term again. You used it in regard to the fall down the stairs. I wonder if you mean to say assault. They both start with an A, maybe you got them confused. At any rate, a very different term. Most people would consider this a heinous *assault* on a woman. Yet, you call it an altercation."

"Objection, is there a question here?"

"No further questions for this witness." Mr. Harris sat down.

"The defense calls Richard Markus III to testify."

After Richard was sworn in, Mr. Collins asked, "Can you describe the night of April 30, 1904 for us?

"We were at a fundraiser, and I saw my wife flirting with another man. I was upset so I suggested we go home."

"How upset?"

"It bothered me to see my wife acting inappropriately in public. I got home, we resolved things, and as we went upstairs to bed, we were both on the top step and her foot slipped. I tried to catch her, but she fell down the stairs."

"Did you push your wife down a flight of stairs?"

"Of course not. She tripped, and she fell. I would never do anything to hurt my unborn son. It was an accident." Richard smiled at the defense team.

His son, not his wife... did you catch that?

"You were happy about having a child?"

"Of course. Who wouldn't be?"

"Your witness." Richard's lawyers handed him over to be slaughtered by the prosecution. Cora wished fervently that she could prosecute the case so she could annihilate him with questions.

"You would never do anything to hurt your unborn son. How do you feel about hurting your wife?"

Perfect.

"Listen, I have a right to run my house the way I see fit." Richard's chin jutted out, and he sneered at Mr. Harris.

"No. You don't." Mr. Harris ignored the jury as they murmured to each other. "I will explain why. As citizens of Canada, we have to live in accordance with Canadian law. The law, as it stands, allows you to correct your wife but only within the boundaries of law."

"Objection. Is there a question here?"

"Oh, I have a question. Absolutely. Would you like to tell the court why you took a horse whip to your wife? What conduct were you correcting?"

"Objection! He is not on trial for the whipping!" The defense jumped to their feet.

"Sustained. Mr. Harris, be careful." The judge shot him a hard look over his glasses.

"You are here to tell me, sir, that your wife tripped and fell down the stairs?"

"It was an accident." Richard's face reddened with fury.

The voice of two men against one woman.

"You look upset, sir, are you upset? Are you angry with me?" Mr. Harris tilted his head.

"Objection! He's badgering this witness." All three lawyers roared from the table where the defense team sat.

"Withdrawn." Mr. Harris turned around to take his seat; he shot a grin at Priscilla, who held Cora's hand so hard it felt like it might break. "No further questions.

"If there are no further witnesses, we will hear closing arguments."

"I need a minute. I think I should go," Priscilla whispered into Cora's ear.

"No, you need to stay. They need your face in front of them when they hear the closing arguments."

"He's going to win." Priscilla put her face in her hands. "There's not one woman on that jury. This is all men deciding about justice for a woman — there is no justice here." Priscilla's voice broke.

"Just a few more minutes, and we'll leave while the jury deliberates." Cora put her arms around Priscilla. "It's almost over."

The prosecution began their closing arguments.

"His word against hers." Mr. Harris's voice was low and smooth. "Who do we believe then? Do we listen to the eyewitness testimony of a butler in Mr. Markus's *employ*?" He paused and let the jury connect the dots that if Mr. Markus paid him for services, why not pay him to testify? "The butler is clearly a man who has a history of covering up, what was the word he called horrendous abuse?" Mr. Harris went to his note pad and checked his notes. "Yes. He used the term *altercation*. I don't know about you, but if a man took a horse whip to me, I would not call that an altercation. If he pushed me down a flight of stairs, I'd be calling that what it really is. Assault.

"Let me lay the facts out for you. Mr. Markus was upset with his wife. The physical and medical evidence verifies that Mr. Markus does not use restraint when correcting Mrs. Markus. She presented at the Winnipeg General Hospital with partially healed wounds from a horse whip.

"The bruising on her wrists proves that someone stood behind her and peeled her hands off of something. She says the banister she was clinging to in order to save the life of her unborn son.

"Why should we believe her?

"Gentlemen, we have no choice. The physical evidence and the testimony of a doctor corroborates her account of the events. We have to act on this because a child is dead.

"A child is dead," Mr. Harris repeated, and then so they would all let that sink in, he continued. "Forget the abuse to Mrs. Markus for a moment. We are here to rule on whether or not this man caused his wife to miscarry. We are here to give a voice to a child whose life was terminated by the hand of his very own father. The criminal code is very clear, gentlemen. Mr. Markus is liable to imprisonment for life because he caused the death of a child which has not become a human being, in such a manner that he would have been guilty of murder if that child had been born. If he had pushed his two-year-old son down the stairs, we wouldn't be discussing this. There is nothing more vulnerable than an unborn child. If we, as the gentlemen of this society, do not protect the vulnerable of our society, then shame on us." Mr. Harris paused and looked at each jury member. The entire court watched him in rapt attention.

"Do you really have any doubt that Mr. Markus, in a fit of rage, threw his pregnant wife down a flight of stairs causing her to miscarry? Dr. Davies, a well-respected doctor in his community, swears she was pushed. A man who has no history with either of them. Mr. Markus is guilty of causing the death of his unborn son. Jury members, we are men. Men protect women and children first, before our own safety and our own convenience. Your duty is to find Mr. Markus guilty of murder." Mr. Harris's eyes pierced each of the jurors before he sat down at his table.

Circumstantial evidence against eyewitness testimony. Dicey. This could go either way.

The prosecution stood up to deliver their closing arguments.

"We wish to remind you all, Mr. Markus is well respected among his peers. Now that Mr. Markus realizes that Canadian law forbids punishments involving a whip, we can assume that would never happen again. The truth is he had an altercation with his wife. Haven't we all? Gentlemen, I think we can all remember a time that a woman pushed us a *little* too far. Who can sit in judgment of that? If we're going to call guilt on the odd incident here and there, well lock me up." Mr. Collins had the audacity to chuckle and shake his head.

Some on the jury nodded in agreement. Cora took a deep breath to try to calm the rage that roared through her.

How dare he?

"They resolved it, and as they were retiring to bed, his wife slipped. The butler, Mr. Moore, is an eyewitness to this event. He confirmed that an accident occurred. You've heard a lot of speculation about bruising that appeared to be fresh that might corroborate the evidence that he pulled her hands off the banister. It is very possible that the bruising on her wrists was *days* old.

Gentlemen, this is his word against hers, but remember, he has an eyewitness. Women tend to be hysterical at the best of times. Certainly, the loss of a child would make any member of the fairer sex lose their reason. Isn't it possible that Mrs. Markus is emotionally distraught from miscarrying a child and her emotions ran away from her? Speaking of running away, how can we trust the word of a woman who ran from her husband after she stole from him? Let's consider this a very difficult situation that arose from a tragic *accident*. You must find him not guilty. Thank you."

Cora's mind flashed back to the face of her aunt while her hair was crudely cut off and fell around her. The same look of shame and humiliation showed on Priscilla's face. Cora wrapped her arms around her.

"Jury members," the judge stated. "You are here to decide if Mr. Markus is guilty of causing the death of his unborn son. The butler says it was an accident. The doctor is convinced, due to the physical evidence, that Mr. Markus is responsible for the miscarriage. The penalty for intentionally causing a miscarriage is life in prison. That is what you are to decide today. The jury is dismissed to deliberate." The judge brought the gavel down.

Priscilla bolted to her feet and ran halfway out of the courtroom while Cora tried to keep up.

Chapter Thirty-Eight

"Come with me." Cora opened the door to a room off the hallway, and Priscilla entered the room before her. Matt stayed close behind.

"What do you think?" Priscilla collapsed into a chair.

Cora pulled a chair up beside her.

"Priscilla." Cora put her hand on Priscilla's shoulder. "Priscilla, you were brilliant in there. You spoke very well, and you presented your case perfectly. You could not have done better."

"My safety, my life, comes down to twelve men on a jury and a judge, also a man." Priscilla covered her face with her hands. Matt knelt down in front of her and handed her a fresh handkerchief. "What do they know of the violence women experience? How will they rule on something as foreign to a man as miscarriage? They don't know what that feels like. I don't think there is any sympathy at all on that jury."

"I don't know," Cora answered honestly.

Priscilla wiped her eyes with the handkerchief.

"Miss Rood, could we have a moment?" Matt asked Cora.

"Of course. I'll come for you when the jury makes a decision."

Cora left the room; she leaned back against the closed door and heard Priscilla start to cry.

***

"Priscilla." Matt pulled Priscilla up into his arms. "You're all right."

"I am going to have to run now. He'll find me." Her voice was muffled against his shirt. "My business is just getting started, and I'm happy in Oakland."

"Shhh." Matt tightened his hold on her while she trembled in fear.

"Matt, I am not safe. I'm not safe anywhere." Priscilla wept.

"Priscilla." Matt pulled back a little and cradled her face in his hands. "I promise, you can stay in Oakland, and I guarantee you will be safe. He will never hurt you again."

"You can't be everywhere." Priscilla took a deep breath and let it out slowly. "I can't stay, and you know it."

"We don't even know if he is going to be released. Let's talk about this when we have all the facts," Matt reasoned.

Priscilla pressed her face back into his shoulder. His shirt absorbed her tears.

"I can't bear this, Matt." Priscilla's voice broke on a sob.

"It's almost over." Matt rubbed his hands up and down her back in an effort to calm her down. It worked. Priscilla relaxed a bit against him. "You have been through a lot, Priscilla. Too much for anyone. If you need to run, I'll help you do that because I really care about you, and I want you to be happy."

"Please be patient with me." Priscilla laid her head against his shoulder and sighed.

"Of course." Matt's heart ached for her. "Priscilla, you were the first person to bring sunshine back into my life, and with that sunshine came a hope that things could be better for me. I want to do the same thing for you. If he gets away with this, we'll come up with a plan. I'll help you run."

"Really?" Priscilla dried her eyes and tilted her head. "You would do that?"

"Of course." Matt's smile did not meet his eyes when he promised to help the one person whom he loved more than anything walk away if the court did not put Richard away for life. "While we have a minute, I wanted to tell you about a recent agreement I signed."

"Oh?" Priscilla pulled back a little so she could dry her eyes and clean up her face.

"I need a place to meet and discuss plans with clients. There is a building on Crescent Street that is available for rent. The trouble is, it's quite large, so I was going to ask if you wanted to put your business in there, too. The second floor is an apartment. Lord Harper has a midwife coming from England, I understand, to assist Lady Harper. So, in case you don't want to share the carriage house with her, this building seems perfectly suited for both our needs."

Priscilla sat down. "I'm not sure what to say."

"There are absolutely no strings attached. It's the only building available, and you would have the front section of the main floor. I would work in the room behind you. In the city, I noticed dress designers make displays for the front window. I thought you could maybe do the same thing, so your work area could face the street. You could live on the second floor. Your spaces would be completely private."

"Matt, this is a dream come true! This is so very generous. What would I be expected to pay?" Priscilla bit her lip, waiting for his answer.

"I think we could renegotiate the payment schedule after you are settled," Matt offered cautiously.

There is never going to be a day that I take a penny from you.

Priscilla took a deep breath. "I think that sounds wonderful. If I can stay, I would love a storefront." Priscilla smiled at him tentatively. "This is most generous of you, Matt. If I can afford it, if I can stay. I have always dreamed of my own place to work, design, and display. How much is the rent right now, so I can figure out what it might be in the future? I would hate to get all settled and then not be able to afford it." Her eyes clouded with worry.

Cora tapped on the door.

Matt smiled and gave her a figure that was a quarter of what he was paying for rent as he went to the door.

"That's so inexpensive! What a tremendous deal!" Priscilla's eyes shined with excitement. Matt could tell she was already thinking about how to set up her displays. "All right, we'll share a store!" Priscilla smoothed her hair back. "I'm ready to go back in." She faced Matt before he opened the door. "Do I look all right?"

Priscilla's eyes and nose were red and raw from weeping. Matt saw the split in her lip she hadn't covered. Defending herself and her unborn child in court had exhausted her and left her with dark circles under her eyes.

"You are beautiful," Matt said sincerely.

Priscilla's eyes filled with tears.

"Don't cry, Priscilla. Please. Don't cry. Everything is going to be all right. I promise." Matt handed her another handkerchief — all of hers were soiled and in a crumpled mess in the bottom of her handbag.

She took a deep breath and let it out slowly. Her hands shook as Matt turned the doorknob.

"I don't think I can... I don't think I can face this." Priscilla wiped her tears away.

"He's not your husband now. You are divorced. If he tries to hurt you, he has to fight through me. I guarantee I will stop him, and we'll all go home."

"The divorce isn't final for six months," she reminded Matt quietly.

"I know, but legally, you are free now. You are just waiting on paperwork. He can't hurt you now. I promise."

Priscilla nodded.

Cora's face was white with worry when Priscilla emerged from the little room.

"Ready?"

"I think so. That was fast. Is that good or bad?"

"I'm sorry, I don't know." Cora reached for her and helped her into the courtroom. Matt, as promised, stayed at the back of the courtroom and waited.

"All rise."

Cora held Priscilla's hand as the judge entered the room. Once he took his seat, the rest of the court took their seats. The faces on the jurors looked grim.

Is that good or bad?

"In the matter of the province versus Richard Markus III what say you?"

"We find the defendant guilty."

Priscilla slumped against Cora with relief. Cora struggled to hold her up in case she fainted.

It's over. The whole thing is over. Priscilla can stay. She can stay safe in Oakland. It's only here, in court, where she could be ultimately free, and she's free!

Priscilla put her hands over her face, and Cora put her arm around her shoulders. Priscilla didn't look up as the judge declared the sentence. Richard was going to prison for the rest of his life. The divorce papers would take six months; she had to wait for the decree absolute, but for all intents and purposes, she was free. Free to be with Matt if she chose. Free to work and heal.

The people in the courtroom dispersed shortly after the verdict was issued. Cora held onto Priscilla as the full scope of what that verdict meant settled on them. The noise around them seemed far off. Cora watched as a weight lifted off Priscilla.

"I feel like I pushed against a gate and it finally let go, and now I am off balance," Priscilla murmured. She watched as Richard was dragged out of the courtroom, away from Priscilla for the last time.

I had a hand in this. The system can work if we work the system. Not in all cases, but in a few, and I want to be part of the few that succeed.

Once the door closed behind him, Priscilla turned to face Cora. "You did it. If you hadn't fired Mr. Levinson and stepped in, I don't even want to think about what would have happened."

"Priscilla, it's you who won this. I just presented it. You determined what you would tolerate and didn't take no for an answer. You demanded your rights, and you had the courage to follow through, no matter the consequences. I learned a lot from you in this ordeal. You taught me to be true to justice and follow through. No matter the cost. I lost sight of my purpose and my voice in Toronto. Standing up for you reminded me why I started this in the first place."

"If it wasn't for you, I would have had to run. I can't even imagine it." Priscilla shuddered with the thought of having Richard following her for the rest of her life.

"It's time for me to go back and fight. Not just Eli, the whole thing. My place is in a courtroom defending women like you. Not moping around my brother's cottage and hiding from the world. Not practicing real estate law. I need to get back to the front line of this battle." Cora stood up.

"Well, my friend, your suit is ready." Priscilla stood up beside her. "I will forever be in your debt. I don't know how I can repay you for this." Priscilla stopped her before they opened the door to the courtroom.

"Priscilla, we're friends. Friends don't care about payment." Cora shrugged.

"I couldn't have survived today without you," Priscilla said simply.

"You would have. I saw you on the stand, young lady. There's nothing you can't do." Cora linked her arm with Priscilla's.

"I knew that about you when you fired Mr. Levinson." Priscilla grinned at Cora as they opened the courtroom door.

"That was particularly gratifying." Cora chuckled.

Together, Cora and Priscilla held onto each other as they left the courtroom and walked out into the bright June sunshine.

Chapter Thirty-Nine

"It's hideous," Priscilla moaned. Cora stood in front of the mirror in a man's suit. Padded shoulders and a padded stomach were added to try to disguise her figure; it worked. The clothes and padding transformed Cora into a short, portly man.

"I love to design beautiful things. I feel like my talent has been used for evil instead of good." Priscilla frowned.

Cora threw back her head and laughed. "It's perfect. I can slip back into Toronto, and no one will be the wiser."

"I hope you are right." Priscilla hugged Cora very hard. "In case that Icelandic boxer shows up, I made a few nightgowns that will take his eyes out. Never before has an ancient spinster worn something like this."

Priscilla held up lacy, filmy, beautiful nightgowns that looked impossibly delicate.

"Priscilla! I couldn't wear something like that in front of anyone I would die of mortification! Most inappropriate!"

"I made you a few robes." Priscilla held up robes that were as sheer and beautiful as the nightgowns.

"I asked you to make me plain nightgowns. These are..."

"Beautiful. Wear them. If you have to look like a man all day, at least you will look like a woman at night."

"You're as bad as Adeline, making me look like a tart."

"You could never look like a tart!" Priscilla howled at the thought.

Cora frowned. "I need to be taken seriously."

"Not in the bedroom, you don't." Priscilla smiled wickedly.

"Especially in the bedroom," Cora said grimly.

"Oh. I hope this Sol is up to the challenge."

"Sol is farming in Gimli. I have no need for frilly nightgowns. They are beautiful but extravagant." Cora put them aside and got changed back into her dress. She didn't dare wear a suit in Oakland, Mrs. Daindridge and Mrs. Carr would collapse.

Priscilla waved at her friend as she got on her bike and rode off.

A week later, Cora was summoned back to Mr. Birch's office. His eyes sparkled with happiness.

"I got a telegram from Malachi Marks you might be interested in."

"Oh?"

"Young lady, you are being called to the bar on the 25 of July with your class. They have requested an address. Where would you like your paperwork sent? I wasn't sure what to tell them, as you will be travelling back to Toronto. I was to pass on Malachi's warm wishes."

Malachi Marks has warm wishes for me! Is that even possible?

"Really!" Cora gasped. Eyebrows raised, she thought of the best possible scenario. "Could you send the paper work to Mrs. King? I have her address here."

"Certainly." Mr. Birch jotted the name and address down.

"That's that," Cora said quietly. "It's happening."

"Yes. In a month. What will you do now?"

"I would like some time in Toronto before being sworn in."

"If those plans fall through, if you get bored, I have some real estate law you could have a go at." He smiled to let her know he was speaking in jest.

"I appreciate the offer. A whole summer in Oakland, Mr. Birch, would be wonderful. However, I believe real estate law should be banned when the sun shines like this." Cora stood up and held her hand out to Mr. Birch.

He shook it heartily.

"I should give Mrs. King a telegram to let her know to expect my paperwork. Shall we go to the telegraph office together?"

"Certainly."

Walking with elderly Mr. Birch was an exercise in patience. Cora longed for the speed of her bike as they strolled along Crescent Street.

Once at the office, Mr. Birch carefully hung his cane on the railing, got out his notes, adjusted his spectacles, dropped his cane, picked it up, readjusted his spectacles, picked up a pencil, and tapped his pencil against his lips as he thought about the message he was going to send. Finally, and with great care, he wrote a note to Malachi Marks.

Cora stifled a sigh as she waited politely and thought about how to word her telegram to Mrs. King.

June 25, 1904.

Mrs. King,

Called to the bar on July 25.

Paperwork will be sent to you.

May I stay with you before being called to the bar? A telegram to follow once I arrive in Toronto.

Cora

Fear knotted her stomach as she thought about trying to find out what criminal activity Eli was up to.

She gave feeble Mr. Birch a gentle hug and returned to her cottage to tell Lucy the good news. This was something that would require a celebration.

***

That night, at supper with Lucy and Wilbur, Cora handed Malachi's telegram to Wil. His face broke into a wide smile.

"It's happening. I can't even believe it, Wil!" Cora said.

"I'm so proud of you. Are you worried though, about facing that terrible Eli Pitman again?"

"I am scared stiff."

"Maybe you should go with her." Lucy directed the comment to Wil.

"Of course, I can go with you." Wilbur's eyes lit up at the suggestion.

"But you can't live in Toronto with me forever. I have to do this. I'll be all right. I'll be with Mrs. King. It will be fine."

Wilbur frowned. "I don't like this."

"Wil, I have no choice. I can't stay here terrified. The fight is in Toronto. I have to go."

Wilbur sighed deeply with worry.

Pain shot through her heart at the memory of how Sol used to sigh exactly like that.

"We'll talk about it again tomorrow," Wilbur warned.

It was Cora's turn to sigh.

Bright and early the next morning, Wilbur watched Cora hop on her bike with lunch and a book. Satisfied she was off for the day; he slipped to the telegraph office and sent a telegram to Sol Stein in Gimli, Manitoba.

Mr. Stein,

Cora is called to the bar July 25, 1904.

According to her schedule, she will arrive in Toronto July 15.

She plans to stay with Mrs. King but has not given her an exact date. This is very concerning. It will be up to you to find her. She says she has a job to finish, and I fear for her safety.

If you are not able to be in Toronto with her, I will make other arrangements. Please advise at your earliest convenience.

Wilbur Rood.

By the end of the day, tension eased from Wilbur's shoulders as he read the reply.

Mr. Rood,

I will be in Toronto no later than July 10, 1904. D. W. E. A. has already contacted me to retain my services.

She'll be safe. I guarantee it. Best if she doesn't know. Let me handle her.

Sol Stein

Wilbur took a deep breath to release the terror that had settled on him at the thought of Cora in Toronto without protection.

Sol Stein, if you can 'handle her,' I tip my hat to you.

***

After endless days of sandbars, tea parties, and long walks with Priscilla, Cora tried to prepare her mind and her heart to return to Toronto. Her sense of accomplishment for being called to the bar warred with the certainty that Adeline was suffering. If there was a way to alleviate the suffering of her friend, she had to find it.

"Where are you staying in the city? You haven't given Mrs. King a definite date." Wilbur pestered her again as he double checked the locks on her luggage. "This is dangerous enough as it is. I hate the idea of you at no fixed address."

"Depends on where Eli is. I need to dig up dirt on him. I have a disguise. I have a plan. Trust me." She adjusted the strap on her handbag.

"Cora," Wilbur pleaded. "I trust you! I don't trust him or his men. They followed you here. I hate this. I forbid this."

"Wilbur, you can't forbid this." Cora crossed her arms in front of her chest.

"What if you get hurt?"

"I got hurt before, and I survived."

Oops! Cora turned her back and sat on her trunk to close it.

"What do you mean, young lady?" Wilbur's voice croaked in fear.

"They threw me in jail and hurt me badly." Cora squared her shoulders and turned to face him. "I'm going to wage this war in a courtroom, Wil, not on the streets. I will be very careful."

"Threw you in jail!" Wilbur disregarded her last comment. His jaw clenched tight with fury and fear. "Send me a telegram every day. I mean it. Every. Single. Day."

"I will," Cora promised.

"I love you." Wil pulled her into his arms and hugged her so hard she couldn't breathe.

"I love you, too." Cora finally pulled away; she had a train to catch.

Wilbur and Matt loaded her luggage into the stagecoach, and Cora saw the concern in Wilbur's eyes as she stepped into the coach.

"Stop worrying. You are like an old grandmother!"

Wilbur shut the door on the stagecoach and spoke through the window to Cora. "I will never stop worrying about you until the day I die."

"I'm going to be very careful," Cora promised.

"A telegram. Every. Single. Day," Wilbur repeated.

"I promise."

Matt slapped down the reins, and Cora was off. She watched Wilbur from the back window until Matt turned a corner and she couldn't see him anymore. The green beauty of Manitoba in summer greeted her as the stagecoach moved across the prairie to Brandon. Eventually, they ground to a halt in front of the train station. Matt hopped down from the buckboard to assist Cora at the platform.

"I don't even know how to thank you for what you did for Priscilla." Matt carried her luggage off the coach.

"Believe me, Matt, she did a lot for me, too."

"Are you sure you should be returning?" Matt frowned in concern.

"I have to. Oh!" Cora handed Matt a large envelope. "Can you mail these? They are Priscilla's name change documents. She refuses to be called Mrs. Markus anymore. I wonder how long she will be Charbonneau though; Priscilla Hartwell has a lovely ring to it."

Matt blushed.

"Take good care of her, Matt, she's precious."

"I will." Matt shot her a happy smile. "Thanks again, for everything." Matt shook her hand.

"Be very happy." Cora grinned at Matt. "You deserve it."

Matt made his way back to his stagecoach. Cora watched him leave then dashed into the train station.

She changed into her suit with lightning speed. The suit that made her look like a short portly man. No handbag to put her ticket in, instead a breast pocket. The ticket wouldn't fit, so she rummaged around in the pocket.

What is this? Notes... two notes?

Cora pulled out the notes as she settled into a seat on the train. She read them swiftly.

She smiled at Ada's phrase.

You are equal to this task — A

Priscilla had just folded a note in half and wrote Cora on the top. She opened the note.

Thank you. P

Her eyes misted with tears as she read those two words. Cora closed her eyes as love and hope bubbled up out of her heart for these two amazing women. She wiped at the tears and tucked the precious notes back into her breast pocket. Cora rested her head on the back of her chair and watched the flat fields of Manitoba race by as the train whisked her back to Toronto. She tried not to think about the fear that crowded in on her.

She closed her eyes as she heard Ada's voice in her head. *'Let the injustice spur you on.'*

Determination stiffened Cora's back.

Hang on, Adeline. I'm scared, but I'm coming for you.

Chapter Forty

The train ground to a halt in Toronto five days before Mrs. King expected Cora to arrive. Five days with no fixed address made her nervous and determined to find criminal activity the courts could use to prosecute Eli. Cora hoped to bring an end to Adeline's suffering.

Cora pulled the brim of her hat down then slid her fingertips over the camera to reassure herself that it was there. She hoped to find an opportunity to use it. One last look in the mirror revealed narrow eyes, thin lips, and a face pale with anticipation and fear. Toronto — Eli's territory — she squared her shoulders.

Cora purchased a bicycle before she checked into a hotel as close to Bleaker Street as possible. From her hotel room, she could see his penthouse. The Bleaker House, a place where lumberjacks typically resided, was rough and sparse. She frowned at the bed with thin sheets. Not the luxury she was used to at Wilbur and Lucy's. Settling her binoculars at the window, Cora sat by the window and waited.

A crash from the hallway interrupted her thoughts. Heart in her throat, she peeked out the door and watched a man throw another man into the wall. As quickly as she opened the door to see what was going on, she snapped it shut. Her hands trembled as she double checked the lock. Even dressed as a man, she realized she wasn't going to survive long here.

Finally, darkness settled over the city. Squinting through her binoculars, she focused on Eli's apartment. Fear pooled in her stomach as she watched the man, who had completely obliterated her, hop into a carriage and take off into the night. She raced down the stairs to her bicycle and followed him.

Brothel.

Gritting her teeth, she made her way into the brothel through a back door. She ordered a drink from the opposite end of the bar then hid behind an enormous lumberjack. Eli held his hands out to a young prostitute. Cora's eyes narrowed as she watched them — fourteen, if the girl was a day. Her heart ached for this young girl. Royce stood guard at the bottom of the steps. She noticed two other men at the entrance; their eyes scanned the room. Royce's eyes never stopped moving. Cora's neck tensed with anxiety as his eyes slid over her.

He doesn't recognize me. But he will soon enough. I can't be this close.

Finally, Eli was done in the brothel, and she followed his entourage home. Three bodyguards.

What is he up to other than brothels?

Cora hung back. The carriage turned down Bleaker Street; he was going home. She waited a long time in the shadows to be sure he was in his apartment and his hired men went home for the night. Finally, she made her way up to her room and watched from the window until his lights were off.

Disappointed that the first night following Eli didn't produce any sort of results, Cora lay on the hard, narrow bed that smelled like body odor and tried to sleep.

The next morning, Cora went to a men's store to purchase more clothes. Royce had seen her in the one suit she owned. This time, she bought pants and shirts and three different hats, all black to fade into the background. She dressed for another night of surveillance and spotted herself in the cracked mirror over her wash basin. She would be mistaken easily for a fourteen-year-old boy.

Perfect.

Eli went to a different brothel this time, and Cora didn't dare enter. Eli's men were everywhere. Something was up. They were edgy and on high alert. She expected his carriage to return to Bleaker, but it didn't tonight. Heart hammering with anticipation, she followed Eli and his bodyguards as they neared the docks and entered another bar. The crowd standing around the entrance was rough; lumberjacks, sailors, and the like. Her stomach knotted with fear at the thought of entering.

After a few moments, she entered from the back alley. At the back of the bar, she spied aprons hanging in the passage way between the bar and the door. Quickly, she slipped one on. She grabbed a tray and started clearing tables. The majority of men were drunk, except the bodyguards, and they didn't care about a young man clearing tables.

Royce's eyes swept over her and narrowed. He moved to the bartender and murmured to him. Terrified, Cora scurried to the kitchen with her tray. Heart in her throat, she peeked out at them speaking and saw the bartender shrug. After putting water on to heat, she watched Eli as a man sat down at his table. Her eyes widened as she watched, through a crack in the wall behind the bar, Eli and Judge Bram order drinks. Cora stood still; she didn't dare breathe in case the treachery she witnessed disappeared before she could obtain evidence.

How many legal proceedings had been unjustly ruled on because of these two men sitting here?

Drinking together and having a cigar at 1:00 in the morning.

What are they discussing? How long has Judge Bram been turning a blind eye to Eli Pitman?

Cora's eyes darted around the kitchen. Seeing she was alone, she brought the camera out of her bag and put the lens between a crack in the wall and the door. She had Judge Bram and Eli together in a frame when a large man stepped in front of the crack; all she could see was black. Clenching her jaw in frustration, she waited until he moved. She held her breath.

When Eli took an envelope out of his pocket, Cora's eyes widened. She photographed Eli as he handed Judge Bram an envelope. She kept taking photos until they wrapped up their business. As if on cue, a prostitute joined them at the table. Cora snapped pictures of the prostitute as she flirted with Eli.

Judge Bram got up to leave, and Eli turned his attention to the young woman on his lap. He followed her upstairs. Cora sighed, put her camera away, and returned to doing dishes. Every few minutes, she looked through the crack in the wall to make sure Royce was still in the bar and not coming back to inspect her in the kitchen.

Finally, Eli returned to the bar, and he and his men left. She straightened up and got ready to follow. She hung her apron on the hook by the back door, but Royce remained and motioned that he wanted a drink. The bartender complied.

Defeated, she had a sinking feeling that Royce was going to stay here and follow her. Cora's stomach knotted with fear as she washed a glass.

How long will Royce stay here? What will he do if he recognizes me?

Cora gave up the pretense of doing dishes and kept her eyes glued to the crack in the wall; she watched the bartender pour Royce another drink. She took off her apron, picked up her bag with the camera, and snuck out the back door. Moments later, she heard footsteps behind her.

Royce.

Her heart hammered in her ears as she made her way down a dark street, hoping to lose him. He got closer, and her palms slicked with sweat. Unfamiliar with this part of town; all she could be certain of was the danger these streets held. She slipped down a back alley and spied an open door into a tenement. As she tiptoed into the room, she froze in her tracks at the sound of snoring.

Heart in her throat, she saw a very old man passed out drunk on the floor in a pool of urine. She shuddered in revulsion and locked the door as quietly as possible. Her entire body trembled in fear that the man would regain consciousness or Royce would start breaking doors down to inspect the tenements. Royce left no stone unturned. He looked behind trash cans. Frustrated, he kicked them over and prowled up and down the alley. He seemed to grow bigger as he stalked back and forth.

Finally, after more than an hour, he cursed as he gave up and walked away. Slowly, her heartbeat returned to normal. She checked her watch. Three a.m.

As silently as possible, Cora got up, unlocked the door, and left the apartment. She stayed in the shadows as she slipped down the back alleys, hoping to get back to her hotel without any interference. Her heart pounded in fear when she heard steps behind her. She didn't turn to look; she ran.

Finally, back in the safety of her hotel, her hands shook with adrenaline as she placed the key in the lock. Gasping for breath, she opened the door to her hotel room.

She sighed with relief as she stepped across the threshold.

A very large hand clamped over her mouth and silenced her scream while an arm of iron circled her waist.

Chapter Forty-One

Screaming in terror, Cora clawed against the hand clamped over her mouth. In this terrible hotel, not one man would raise an eyebrow over a woman screaming. The man dragged her back against the solid wall of his chest.

Royce!

She fought against the arms holding her in place.

"Don't scream," he hissed into her ear. "What are you doing following Eli Pitman to a brothel?"

Icelandic accent.

Sol.

Fury roared through Cora as she thrashed against him as hard as she could. She felt like a butterfly trying to break through brick. Battering and pounding on any inch of exposed flesh.

"Stop." He flipped her around to face him and pushed her against the wall. "You're only going to hurt yourself. Every time you hit me, it hurts your hands, and I don't feel it."

Her eyes narrowed to slits, and she fought harder.

"If I let you go, will you scream?"

She clawed at him in answer. His hand hardened on her mouth.

He pinned her to the wall with such force she could barely breathe and couldn't move. He leaned forward so he was speaking into her ear.

"Stop it," he growled. "I am not leaving until I've said what I have to say. You didn't have the decency to send me a letter to let me know you were safe. I can't believe you would be so callous. Stop. You're not going anywhere until you hear all of it. I don't want you to hurt yourself."

Cora tried hard to bite the inside of his hand but couldn't. She squirmed against him, even though she could hardly move.

"Did you read my letter?" Sol demanded.

Eyes flashing with fury, Cora tried to and failed to twist out of his grasp.

"I'll take that as a no." He shifted; Cora struggled to breathe. "The day I left you in the law office, Eli Pitman told me if I didn't walk away right then, those thirty Icelandic families would be on the street that night. I couldn't be responsible for that. He left me no choice. You would have left, too, if only to protect the children. You cared about those people like I did."

Her glare softened; Eli had threatened her with the same thing.

"He also said that if I didn't leave, he would have you thrown in jail for fraud. I know, and you know, that he is capable of falsifying records. I couldn't risk it. I knew jail is your biggest fear. He told me that Adeline would be disgraced and Hope House would be sold. He said he would make her watch him sign the papers before having her arrested for fraud."

Tears stung Cora's eyes at his simple sincerity. He lifted his hand away.

"The worst thing to admit to you is this—" His eyes met hers, and he held her gaze. "Thirty Icelandic families with little children facing spring storms on the streets. Adeline, the woman I worked for, facing unjustified incarceration for who knows how long. So help me that was not my reason for going." His voice dipped low. "I couldn't be responsible for Eli sending you to jail, and I know he holds all the power in Toronto. I couldn't bear it, Cora. I knew I could protect you physically from Royce and his men, but I couldn't stop him from destroying you with falsified documents in court."

Tears glittered in her eyes.

"I had thirty seconds to make a decision." He ran his fingertips over her previously fractured jaw. "I panicked. I was so afraid of you getting hurt. Can you ever forgive me, do you think? Or is this all over?"

He didn't run because he doesn't like intelligent women. He didn't sell me out for a farm. He left to protect me. Cora struggled to process that thought.

His eyes were tortured. She could see the pain in them by the light of the moon spilling in through the window.

"The minute I ran, I knew it was wrong. But I honestly didn't see any other alternative. It was the hardest thing I've ever had to do. Tell me you weren't hurt." His fingertips stroked her jaw again. She slid her eyes shut; the caress woke a desire inside her, weakened her.

Sol put his arms around her and held her hard. Her body melted into his.

"Please say something. I am so sorry," Sol said into her neck as she burrowed deeper against him.

"I didn't read your letter because I thought you wanted a farm instead of me." Cora's voice cracked with emotion. "I thought you sold me out, and my heart was so broken, I couldn't bear to read any excuse you might give. I burned your letters."

"What about your brother's letter?"

"He tried to read it to me, but I hardened my heart," Cora whispered. "Now I know, you ran to protect me, and I ran to protect Adeline. I can't hold it against you when I did the very same thing. I completely overreacted. I don't trust men to do the right thing, and I am going to need to change that."

Sol pulled away slightly. Cora looked up at him and bit her lip.

"When we were in the kitchen and I was carrying the soup for you, you asked me a question I didn't answer, remember? You asked if I'd gone soft for you." Sol traced her cheekbone with his fingertips.

"Have you?" Cora swallowed hard.

"I couldn't stop thinking of you for one minute over the last two months. All I wanted to do is ask if you can forgive me?"

"Of course." Cora's voice caught on the words as she created a little distance between them. He looked at her with such intensity, she felt a shiver of apprehension as his eyes flicked over her pants and shirt

Of all the days to be dressed as a fourteen-year-old boy!

Cora reached up and ran her hands across the top of his shoulders.

"He promised you would be safe from his men if I left." Sol brushed hair back from her face. "Were you? I want the truth."

"I was. Royce followed me all the way to Oakland. He dragged me onto the train." Cora took a shaky breath.

Sol's jaw tightened. "Royce hurt you?"

"I hesitated when I was on the platform because I thought he was in the train car behind mine. I panicked and stepped back off the train. Royce took me by the arm and forced me to get on the train."

Sol's eyes flashed from blue to black with such intensity, she wondered what he might do.

"When I was on the train, he took me to my seat and let me go. He made sure I left Toronto. When my brother picked me up at the train station in Brandon, he left me. I didn't see him again until tonight."

Sol took Cora by the upper arms and looked into her eyes. "This is no time for a brave face. If Royce hurt you in any way, I want to know."

"He didn't." Cora shook her head as she reached for him. His arms tightened around her. "I was terrified that you were Royce. How did you find me?"

"You wouldn't return my correspondence, but everyone else in our lives did." Sol rolled his eyes. "The D. W. E. A. are in a froth because you are to be sworn in and it's a triumph for women's rights and no one can find you. I'm surprised they didn't send a convoy to Oakland and bring you back by force. Anyway, the minute they heard that you had completed your time of articling, they were concerned you would run into trouble if you try to enter Osgoode Hall to be sworn in. So, they wanted to hire me to ensure you were sworn in unscathed.

"Your brother let me know you were all right and he sent me a telegram when you left Oakland. When he said, you were on your way, I jumped on the next train back to Toronto. I was terrified you would get here before me. So, here I am. The D. W. E. A hired me to be in Toronto by July 5. Apparently, I have lost my ability to say no to women. I've been here scouring the city, waiting for you."

"How did you know this was me?" Cora pulled back and gestured to the outfit she was wearing.

Sol smiled at her and cradled her face in his hands. "I would know you anywhere, no matter what you are wearing." He hesitated for just a brief moment, searching her eyes for acceptance before he pressed his lips to hers with heart-stopping tenderness. Desire radiated between them as he smiled against her mouth and kissed her again.

A fire lit inside her, and she reached up and pulled him closer.

"Or not wearing," he said so suggestively she weakened and held onto him to stay upright.

"Are we talking or kissing?" She teased as his lips moved down her neck; he pulled her closer so her body fit against his.

"Kissing." He smiled as his lips met hers again and silenced them.

Until this moment, in Toronto's seediest hotel, she had no idea women could have any sort of power over men; her whole life experience had been a lie. The minute she could get out of the pants and shirt and into proper feminine clothing and wield even more power, she would. She pulled back, so he did, too.

"I know, we have to stop." Sol groaned. "There can't be any shady business between us." He pulled his hands through his hair.

"Is that what it's called?" She grinned despite the disappointment that winged through her.

"When you have been sworn in and my term of employment is over, watch out." He kissed her one last time as if sealing the promise. "On the way up to Gimli, where we'll farm and have scads of children, we can get our family started on the train."

"I'm not having scads of children on a farm in Gimli. Horrors!" Cora gasped. "I'm *not* going to Gimli."

Sol grinned. "I'll win you over."

"You won't." Cora moved closer to him, back into the circle of his arms, to test out her new-found feminine power. To see just how much influence she could wield over him. "I'll seduce you back to my side."

She watched his eyes flash at the word seduce.

"I suggest," she purred. "If you stay in Toronto, we can have a small yard, and one tomato plant."

Sol's eyes smoldered with heat as she ran her hands along his shoulders.

"I will need at least two tomato plants to be considered a farmer." He pulled her against him harder than before. She gasped in anticipation.

"I'll warn you Sol, I am very used to getting my way." Cora smiled as he kissed her again.

"I noticed that about you," Sol said dryly. "You might be spoiled, but I'm a stubborn Icelander, so maybe you've met your match." He sat down on the settee and tugged her to sit down on his lap so they could be eye to eye. "Not a decision we are going to make today." He pulled her forward for one last kiss. "What is your next step?"

"I'd rather forget the next step and kiss you again," Cora answered honestly.

"Me too. However, I have to answer to Toronto's biggest union of old prudish women, and if your virtue is compromised, I have no idea what they will do to me." Sol tugged her closer, kissed her gently, and then let her go.

"I can't believe Sol Stein is afraid of the D. W. E. A?" Cora tilted her head to the side.

"Terrified," Sol confirmed. "What is your next step?"

"We need to verify criminal activity on Eli's part." Cora traced her fingertips across the very hard muscle of his shoulders. His shoulders slumped as the tension eased out of him at her caress.

"You have to stop that, or you're going to lose your virtue in the world's worst hotel room."

She dropped her hands and shot him a flirtatious smile. "All right. No more caresses for you. Back to Eli. If we lose in divorce court, I have to find and be able to prove enough criminal activity so the prosecution can annihilate him in criminal court. I saw him pay off a judge. I photographed it, but it was so dark in the bar, likely the photos won't be good enough. They'll say it was a business deal. There has to be something we can hang him for." Cora's jaw clenched.

Sol laughed. "Such a lady!"

"Never mind lady. I have a job to do. He's terrible. You know it, and I know it. We just need to find it and parade it in a court of law." She straightened up; her eyes gleamed with the challenge.

"New rules." Sol's fingertips stroked underneath her jaw; Cora's muscles loosened.

"I will find dirt on Eli — that's my job. There will be no more detective work for you." His voice purred in her ear; a kick of desire pulsed through her. "What is *your* next step?"

Cora's eyes snapped open; she pulled his hand away. "You were trying to distract me!"

"Did it work?" Sol grinned slyly.

"That is very underhanded, sir." Her eyes flashed with outrage.

Sol shrugged unrepentantly.

"I have to find criminal activity." Cora dragged herself away from him. She went to the window to show him her binoculars and notebook.

"This is all very cute." Sol got up to join her. "I think it's adorable that you are trying to find enough criminal activity to get Adeline a divorce."

Cute! Adorable! Cora bristled. All the passion and desire she had felt on the settee fizzled, and her body quivered with rage now instead of passion.

"I'd like to hear all about it when you are safely tucked into Jean King's happy home. I am to deliver you there as soon as I find you." Sol wasn't taking no for an answer.

"You are not taking me seriously." Cora gritted her teeth. "You have no right to drag me to Jean King's or anywhere."

"Your identity is compromised, Cora." Sol's jaw clenched as he prepared to override her objections with brute force if necessary. His stance told her he would drag her out of here kicking and screaming, deposit her at Mrs. King's, and not think twice. "There is not going to be any competition between us, miss. We both have strengths, and gathering evidence is mine. I will take the risks from his men, not you.

That is not up for discussion. I will keep you alive as you destroy him in a court of law. In the meantime, your days on the docks are over."

"Hey, I..."

"I just said it's not up for discussion." Sol put his hands on his hips.

Cora's eyes flashed with fury, her shoulders tensed, she straightened. "Everything will always be up for discussion, or it won't happen. I'm your equal, Sol."

"You are *not* my equal, Cora," Sol roared.

Cora's head snapped up at that pronouncement. Her eyes narrowed, and her lips thinned. "If you don't realize that I'm your equal, we are done here. You can pack up and hightail it back to Gimli or whatever iceberg you floated in on. You will see me as your equal and treat me as such, or we're done here." Cora's voice dripped with fury.

"I knew," he countered, "the first second I met you that you are, hands down, the most intelligent person I have ever known. To consider myself your equal in intelligence would be an *insult* to you."

Cora wavered; his response caught her off guard. "There are different sorts of intelligence."

"No. *You* are brilliant. I am not. You are far superior to me in that way." Sol's eyes burned into hers with intensity. She took a step back as she tried to assimilate this new thought, as if he might be trying to trick her somehow.

"Oh." Cora's voice sounded flat. The fight went out of her. Her head tilted back so she could hold his gaze.

"When it comes to legal battles, that will be your job. When it comes to physical battles, that will be my job." Sol towered over her.

"I do not appreciate having decisions made for me," Cora warned.

"I'm not going to fight about this with you. I gave my word to your brother that I would keep you out of harm's way. So, I will. If you get hurt before you are sworn in, I will be henpecked into an early grave by the entire D. W. E. A. and Mrs. King and every women's rights group screaming for you to champion their rights in court. Pack up. You are not staying in this seedy hotel. Time to get you settled so I can do surveillance."

"Where are you going to stay?"

"I'm at Mrs. King's, too. She wants me on site to be sure you are safe until you are sworn in."

"So, you work for the entire D. W. E. A. or just Jean King?"

"All of the above." Sol sighed. "There is no greater proof of how terrified I was for your safety. When Isold was killed, I had sworn off

Rebekah Lee Jenkins

women. Too vulnerable, I couldn't go through that sort of loss again. My vow to never work for women or with them was obliterated when I heard you were on a train back here. The D. W. E. A. sent me a summons — yes, a summons — to be back in Toronto to protect you. They weren't sure if you would be called too, but they weren't taking any chances. That means, Cora my darling, I have approximately eight women hassling me morning, noon, and night as to your whereabouts. Dramatic, hysterical, rich, irritating women. It's a nightmare I can't wake up from."

Cora couldn't help it; she howled with laughter. The thought of Sol up against the entire D. W. E. A. and Mrs. King as his bosses was too much. Cora tried to stop laughing, but the tension of the last two days melded into hilarity. Finally, a grin tugged at Sol's mouth. Cora wiped the tears from her eyes.

"Sol, you are very funny."

"I'm not trying to be," he assured her as he looked out the window and kept a steady eye on Eli's residence.

Chapter Forty-Two

Smiling with pleasure, Adeline slipped into her office. She opened the heavy drapes to let the sunshine in before she tore into her work. She took a sip of tea as she flipped through her correspondence quickly. Deliveries started at 10:00 a.m., she had a typing teacher to interview and scads of correspondence to open and respond to. She smiled as she saw cheques from charities start to roll in.

Adeline despised bookwork and put off checking bank reconciles as long as possible; finally, she slid open the envelopes. June 1 to June 30. Zero balances in her personal account. Her stomach cramped in fear; her heart hammered hard in her chest.

They can't be at zero! This is my private account! How could Eli do this? I thought I was the only one with signing authority?

Her neck slicked with cold, anxious sweat. She put down her letter opener then got up and paced by the window. Royce standing on the sidewalk caught her eye. She stood out of his view and wondered why he was there.

If Royce is here, Eli won't be far behind. What am I going to do? How could he do this?

She turned at the sound of a man clearing his throat at the doorway. Eli leaned against the doorframe to her office. The sun streamed in on him. He crossed his arms over his chest; his lips thinned with anger.

"This is unexpected!" Adeline's shoulders tightened.

"Change in our arrangement." Eli's eyes swept over her like a predator about to pounce.

She moved so her back was to the wall beside the window.

"Oh?" Adeline tried to speak confidently through the tight fist of fear in her throat.

Eli kicked the door shut, locked it behind him, and sat down behind her desk. He read through her open mail.

Her nails bit into her palms as she watched him violate her privacy.

"When I invite you to attend a dinner with the Scotts, I expect you to dress up, show up, smile, and make my guests feel welcome in our family." Eli pulled reading glasses out of his breast pocket and adjusted them on his nose. His eyes skimmed over the bank reconcile, and he smiled at the zeros. "If Randall misses the opportunity to marry Laura Scott because of your foolishness, I will have you committed to the first lunatic asylum I can find."

He means it. He hates me that much.

"You wouldn't dare." Adeline's knees weakened in fear.

"It's an easy thing." Eli stopped pawing through her mail. He got up from the desk and moved over to her. Towering over her, he took her by the upper arms. "A doctor says you are unstable, I sign a paper, they toss away the key. When I require your presence, Adeline, there is no option of declining."

Her mind raced to think of a solution to protect herself. He could do it. He would do it.

"You won't throw me in an asylum, Eli, because it would look bad. You think the Scotts would let their daughter marry a man whose mother is in a lunatic asylum? Think again. Lunatic asylum would be a black mark on your character. You will render our sons unmarriageable. No parents in the land would turn a blind eye to that."

Eli blinked; the argument made sense. His eyes narrowed as he immediately came up with another way to punish her.

"I am selling this house. You have two days to relocate the prostitutes here."

"How will that look, Eli?" Adeline tried and failed to pull out of his grasp. "What will the press do with that, do you think?" Her heart pounded in her ears. "I can see the headlines. Rich get richer. Initiative to alleviate suffering canceled by business tycoon Eli Pitman..."

"I am losing patience with you." He hissed at her; little flecks of spit landed on her face. A vein stood out on his forehead; his hands tightened on her upper arms.

"Don't take this house away from me. I'm begging you, Eli. I will do anything." Adeline swallowed hard. Tears glittered in her eyes.

Eli smiled.

"Yes. You will do anything." Eli pressed her hard against the wall. "You have nothing to give me, Adeline. Everything you possess belongs to me. Bank accounts, Hope House, the bed you sleep in, the clothes on your back. All mine." His right hand held her jaw in place as his lips crushed and bruised hers. She tried to fight him off, but his fingers dug into her jaw, holding her in place. When he pulled away, he smiled. The smile didn't reach his eyes. "I own everything. Even you."

Horror flooded through Adeline when she realized what he was about to do.

The anger and his need to dominate her was unmistakable in his flat grey eyes. She trembled in fear before his predatory gaze, her fear intoxicating him.

"Please don't do this." Panic churned acid in Adeline's stomach.

"I can do whatever I want to you, Adeline." He growled into her ear.

"Eli, I am begging you." Adeline's voice sounded shrill. "Please. I will do anything... not... don't do this."

"We had an arrangement — you broke it." Eli dragged her to the desk. Adeline fought against him; his grip hardened to iron as he relentlessly detailed her loss of personal freedom. "You will host a supper for the Scotts, and we will be the happy married couple they believe us to be." Eli cleared the desk with one swoop of his arm. "Hope House will be deeded to Jean King tomorrow. You will never set foot here again. You are not permitted to take part in any suffragette activity. A letter stating that will be sent to Mrs. King and the D. W. E. A. Your bank account will remain zero. I will close it tomorrow. Royce will now accompany you at all times when you leave the house. I can't trust you, Adeline. Anyone I can't trust is supervised." Eli's fingers bit harder as he pushed her down onto the desk. "I think it's time I reminded you of what your duty is to me."

Adeline opened her mouth to scream.

***

"Friday." Eli buckled his belt and pulled his suit jacket back on. "I'll instruct the servants to have supper ready for the Scotts."

Adeline's hands shook as she pulled her clothes together.

"Buy yourself something nice." Eli tossed a roll of bills on the desk beside her.

Adeline looked at the money. With one hand, she slowly slid it off her desk so it fell to the floor. "You raped me." To her own ears, her voice sounded very far away. As if somehow her mind and her body had separated. Her throat closed on the salty sob that tried to escape. She looked at the floor, unable to meet his eyes.

Eli frowned at her. "I can't rape you — you're my wife."

"I said, no. I screamed..." Adeline tried to stand and move away from him. Her legs buckled, and she sunk to her knees. She put her back against the side of the desk and pulled her knees up to her chest. Her hair hung down around her and covered her face.

Not my desk anymore.

Tears coursed down her face; she didn't bother to wipe them away.

"Adeline, we're husband and wife. You're being melodramatic. Buy a new dress for Friday. You'll feel better. We'll have supper with the Scotts, and maybe after we can..."

"Get out!" Her voice was hoarse from screaming.

"Adeline, stop this. You're embarrassing yourself," Eli reprimanded her.

She shook with shock; it seemed as if she heard him through a very long tunnel.

"Friday at 6:00 p.m., we will have supper with the Scotts. Don't disappoint me again," Eli growled. "You'll regret it."

Desperate to get him out at any cost, she forced the words out. "I'll be there." She lied so he would leave. She picked up the money from beside her on the floor, indicating her acceptance.

"Perfect." Eli smiled and crouched down in front of her. He reached out to stroke her cheek. She flinched and turned away. "It'll be good to entertain together again. Like old times. You are still so beautiful to me."

Acid churned Adeline's stomach into knots. She wondered if he could hear her mind screaming. Devastated, defeated, she couldn't drag her eyes from the floor. She focused on a strip of black thread in the carpet.

"You'll get used to this new arrangement, and all will be well again between us." Eli leaned forward and kissed her forehead. Adeline didn't fight him. The fighting spirit she had relied on to this point was broken, by him, on top of her desk.

She remained silent as he stood up, went to the door of her former office, and with one last look, he frowned at her then left.

As the door shut behind him, she crawled under her desk, curled into a ball on the carpet, and wept.

Chapter Forty-Three

M rs. King handed her correspondence to the butler just as there
was a timid knock at the door.

The butler opened it to reveal the trembling and terrified
form of Mirabel Salter. She shook on the step. Mrs. King's eyebrows shot
straight up.

"Mrs. King." Mirabel Salter swayed against the doorframe.

"Goodness!" Mrs. King held her hands out to her.

Mirabel was disheveled and weeping. "I didn't know where to go."

"Would you please assist Miss Salter to my drawing room and then
send breakfast and tea in to us? That correspondence needs to go at
once to the post."

Mirabel collapsed on the settee, beaten and bruised. Mrs. King
closed the door just as she heard another knock on her front door.

She heard the butler and then an Icelandic accent.

"Miss Salter, I will return shortly. Please, excuse me." Mrs. King
pulled the drawing room door closed behind her, and when her eyes
landed on Cora Rood she gasped.

"You're here!" Mrs. King was not a demonstrative person, but relief
caused her to drag Cora into a tight embrace. Tears filled her eyes as
she looked Cora over.

"What happened to your hair, and why are you dressed like a
man?" Mrs. King frowned in disapproval.

"Long story." Cora smiled at her.

Sol hovered over Cora protectively.

"I want to hear all of it," Mrs. King insisted.

"I have been following Eli, and we ran into each other last night."
Cora blushed, her eyes darted to Sol, and he took a step closer to her.

Sol's ears were bright red and about to burst into flame.

"I see." Mrs. King gave Sol a hard look. "I trust you were safe with Sol, on the *streets*."

Sol held his hands up. "Mrs. King, while I am in your employ, her virtue is safe with me."

"And after you are *not* in my employ?" Mrs. King's eyebrows shot up to her hairline.

"All bets are off." Sol grinned. He loved to tease Mrs. King. She drew herself up to her full height in indignation. "I would like to leave her here in your capable hands to do whatever you ladies do. I have training this morning and surveillance this afternoon and evening."

"Before anyone goes anywhere, I think you should see who is in my drawing room." Mrs. King's lips thinned.

"Who?" Cora's eyebrows arched in question

"Mirabel Salter." Mrs. King closed her eyes briefly as if gathering her strength.

"Mirabel!"

"We have a situation," Mrs. King said quietly.

"Lead the way, Mrs. King. That's what we are here for." Cora prepared mentally for the *situation*.

"Young lady, you are here to be sworn in, exactly seven days from now, or have you forgotten? The entire women's rights movement is holding their breath, and you stroll in here in men's attire and almost no hair." Mrs. King shook her head. "You have no time to be all caught up in a drama involving Mirabel Salter."

"I have hair — it's braided. Mrs. King, I assure you, I am ready for Osgoode Hall. Once I am sworn in, I can practice law on my own. I will do all that is in my power to assist Adeline. So, let's interview Mirabel and see what sort of dirt I can find on Eli."

Mrs. King pursed her lips and turned on her heel.

Sol sighed, and Cora shot him a look.

"Hysterics and drama. I can't do this," he grumbled against her ear. His breath against her neck woke butterflies in her stomach.

"One step closer to destroying Eli. You'll survive." She grinned at him and followed Mrs. King into her lavish drawing room.

Sunlight streamed in on potted palms and fresh cut flowers. A decorative tea service gleamed in the sunshine.

Mirabel Salter held a handkerchief to her lip. Cora gasped at the state of the girl. Sol's eyes narrowed.

"What happened, dear?" Mrs. King asked softly.

"I don't even know where to start." Mirabel sobbed into her hands.

"Mirabel, we're all aware you are Eli Pitman's mistress. No need to pretend anything, just the straight facts, my dear." Mrs. King settled down on the chair and faced Mirabel.

Cora pulled a chair up, and Sol took the tea and food from a servant and closed the door so there would be no eavesdropping on this sensitive situation. He carried the food to the ladies and poured tea for them all. Cora smiled as he retreated to the doorway with a cup of tea and a piece of toast. She knew weeping mistresses were far too much emotion for him.

"I'm pregnant," Mirabel sobbed.

"Oh, my dear." Mrs. King shook her head.

Across the room, Sol sighed.

"Eli made an appointment with a doctor, to force me to have an abortion. I refused to go, then Eli lost his patience. He told Royce to force me to go."

Cora swallowed hard. "Mirabel, that is terrible. When did that happen?"

"Two days ago." Mirabel took a fresh handkerchief from Cora.

Mrs. King put two sugar cubes into the tea and handed it to Mirabel.

"Drink this, dear, you need to keep up your strength."

Mirabel wiped her eyes and took a sip. "Thank you. I have nowhere to go. I was hoping I could be in Hope House, and I know that I was a terrible spoiled child at that meeting. You can't imagine what it feels like to have to beg to be given shelter, Mrs. King. I am ashamed of myself and my situation. If you turn me away, I don't know what I will do."

"Of course, you can go there." Mrs. King patted her hand gently.

"Would you smooth things over with Mrs. Pitman?" Mirabel looked from Mrs. King to Cora.

"No one is going to the streets. We'll figure this out." Cora leaned forward and sipped her tea. "Is there anything about Eli and his activity that you can tell me?"

Mirabel tucked her feet up under her skirt. "Why?"

"Mrs. Pitman is suing Mr. Pitman for divorce. Any information you can give us would help her case. Since you need her to provide a place to live and recover, it would be best if you cooperated." Cora's voice hardened.

Mrs. King frowned but didn't intervene.

"I don't know much about his business except he wanted me taken care of before Thursday. I heard him say to Royce, 'Bluebell will be at the docks on Thursday. Get her fixed up before that.' As if I were some sort of to-do list." Mirabel's eyes saddened as she picked at a loose thread on her skirt.

"Would you be willing to testify in court that you have lived with Eli Pitman for the last year and a half?" Cora stepped into her natural role as lawyer.

"What will he do to me if I testify?" Mirabel's hands shook with fear.

"If you want to avail yourself of a house Adeline built with her own two hands, after Eli forbade any of the suffragettes to work with her, I suggest you start telling the truth." Cora's clipped tone caused Mirabel to look up in alarm.

"Are you saying that if I don't testify, I can't stay at Hope House?" Mirabel's eyes widened in fear.

Cora opened her mouth to speak then closed it. She thought of the proper phrasing for a moment. "Can you give me your word that you will testify in a court of law that you have been Eli Pitman's mistress for the last year and that you are carrying his child?"

Mirabel looked from Cora to Mrs. King. Both women leaned forward to hear her answer.

"Yes." Her head dropped in defeat.

"Do you need a doctor, dear?" Mrs. King, a humanitarian first, wanted to see to Mirabel's physical and emotional state before building a case.

"I can't afford a doctor." Mirabel wept piteously. "I have nothing."

"We'll take you to a doctor before settling you at Hope House."

"What if Royce comes for me there?" Mirabel wiped her eyes on her handkerchief.

"There is a security guard there," Mrs. King said soothingly.

"What did Royce do to you, Mirabel?" Cora asked softly.

"Does he have to be in the room?" Mirabel pointed to Sol.

"Sol, could you give us some privacy?" Cora asked.

"Don't go far — I need to speak to you and Cora privately before I take Miss Salter to a doctor." Mrs. King spoke to Sol as if she were a principal and he an unruly student.

"I'll be right outside." Sol leaped at the chance to exit from the drama unfolding in the drawing room.

"We can press charges if we know what he forced you to do." Cora brought their attention back to the matter at hand.

"When I said no to the abortion, he went crazy and wanted the doctor to perform the abortion anyway."

Mrs. King closed her eyes, absolutely horrified.

"And then what happened?" Cora probed gently, mentally taking notes. Her fingers itched for a legal pad to write on.

"The doctor said he wouldn't touch me. He reminded Royce that abortion is illegal and performing one was risky enough for his professional career, that if I testified against him, he would go to jail for life. So, when Royce couldn't bully the doctor, we left, and Royce said there was no going back to Eli. If I kept the baby, I no longer had Eli's protection. I started screaming at him to take me back to Eli, and Royce hit me and he said since I was no longer under Eli's protection, he could do what he wanted to me." Mirabel swallowed hard. "I tried to run from him, we were in the alley, and a man who looked homeless stepped in. Gray-something. Ash-something, I think? Odd name, I thought. Anyway, he stepped in and he looked as scary as Royce. Turns out he is a police officer. As soon as he stepped in, I didn't stay around, I ran. I went home, and my mother wouldn't open the door." Mirabel covered her face with her hands.

A knock at the door interrupted them. Cora frowned.

Now what?

"Excuse me. I must have another guest." Mrs. King's eyebrows drew together in confusion before she left the drawing room.

Cora rubbed at the tension in the back of her neck. "Mrs. King will take you to the doctor and then to Hope House. Why don't you have something to eat?"

The door to the drawing room opened. "Cora, would you join us?" Mrs. King's voice sounded shrill.

Cora swiftly went to the door and gasped. Adeline took one look at Cora and fainted on the floor of the entryway.

Chapter Forty-Four

"**D**o you have smelling salts, Mrs. King?" Cora went to Adeline and knelt beside her.

Mrs. King returned quickly, and Cora uncapped the salts; she waved them under Adeline's nose. Her body jerked as she regained consciousness.

"You're all right. Just stay still. No need to rush. Just take your time." Cora stroked her friend's hair back from her face very gently. Adeline's eyes filled with tears. "Whenever you're ready, Sol will carry you to a spare room. Shhh. Not just yet."

Adeline buried her face in her hands and wept. Cora's eyes widened in alarm as she looked at Sol and then bent her head over her friend.

Once Adeline calmed down, Cora placed her hand on her arm. "Is it all right if Sol picks you up and takes you to the spare room to lie down?"

Adeline struggled to sit up. "I can walk."

Sol helped Adeline up off the floor; she stood on shaky legs. Sol hovered in case she collapsed again while Cora scrambled to assist her.

"Which room should we take her to?" Cora asked Mrs. King.

"Follow me."

Adeline took three steps and clutched at Sol to remain upright.

"Let me carry you. You can barely stand," he requested gently.

Adeline nodded her agreement.

Mrs. King led the way into a spare room that hadn't been prepared for guests. The air hung heavy around them. She opened a window as Sol placed Adeline on the bed. She curled in a ball away from him. He straightened up and stepped away from her; Sol shot Cora a look of helplessness.

"If Royce comes here, you have to get rid of him — he can't know I'm here." Adeline's voice shook. "Sol, you have to give me your word."

"Of course. Adeline, did Royce hurt you?" Sol asked. His eyes met Cora's, she recognized this look; he was begging her silently to step in.

"No. Not Royce — Eli." She pulled a pillow against her body and curled around it.

"Can we have a moment, please?" Cora asked Mrs. King and Sol. She sat down on the bed and stroked Adeline's shoulder.

The door closed behind them. She waited for Adeline to gain control over her emotions.

"Adeline, what happened?" Cora dreaded the answer but asked anyway.

She shuddered and turned to face Cora. "This morning, very early, I went to work at the house, and Eli came by. He..."

Cora took her hand in her own.

"Take your time. No need to rush. We have all day."

"Could you ask the maid to draw a bath?" Adeline's voice sounded small.

"Certainly." Cora's stomach clenched. She went to the doorway and gestured to a maid. "Have a bath drawn for Mrs. Pitman, immediately." When she returned to the bed, she picked up Adeline's hand again.

"I opened my bank reconciles, the balance in my personal account is at zero. Every penny. Gone. Eli stood at my door." Adeline's voice trembled. "After he forced you out of Toronto, he demanded things of me. If I kept up my end of the bargain, I could keep the house for the girls. Anyway, he says I violated the terms of our agreement. Hope House will be gifted to Jean King. I am no longer permitted to set foot in Hope House. My accounts are closed. I am to entertain our future in-laws on Friday. I said no. He raped me." Adeline's tone was flat and dead.

"Adeline!" Cora gasped.

"Call a doctor, and he can verify I was raped. We can use that as cruelty and abuse, and if there is any good that can come of it, at least I have the terms I need for divorce."

Cora closed her eyes briefly. She covered her eyes with one hand and rubbed her eyebrows.

"What?" Adeline's eyes glazed with fear. "What is it?"

Cora stood up and paced to the window. She looked out, looking for Royce.

"Can you please give me a moment?" Cora's voice shook with emotion.

"Of course." Adeline sounded puzzled.

Cora left the room, leaned back against the closed door, and pulled her hands over her face. She paced up and down the hallway shaking her hands to try to relieve the tension.

"Are you all right?" Sol sat between the drawing room containing the mistress and the spare room containing the wife. In the midst of this chaos, he tried to distract himself by reading the paper.

"I..." Cora's voice broke with emotion. She put her hand over her mouth to stop a scream from erupting. "I have to go back in there..." She gestured wildly at the door.

Sol leapt to his feet and took her by the arm. "Come on. Into the study. Tell me. What is going on?"

He closed the door. Cora paced to the window keeping her back to him.

"If you need to scream or cry or whatever, it's fine. Just tell me. What are we up against? Let me help you."

"Eli is signing Hope House over to Jean King."

"Not so bad." Sol was quick to point out the positives.

"Please, just let me say it all." Cora's voice was dull, her face white with anxiety as she turned to face him. "He raped her."

"I don't understand." Sol's eyebrows drew together.

"If you don't understand that a husband can rape his wife, you need to walk out of this house and take the first train to Gimli," Cora roared at him. "Your services are no longer required."

Sol held his hands up in surrender. "I didn't mean that, Cora. I didn't mean that at all."

Cora pressed the heels of her hands into her eyes. Sol stood in front of her and rubbed his hands up and down her arms. "I didn't mean that." Sol's voice shook.

Cora took her hands away and blinked back tears.

"I'm sorry your friend got hurt," Sol whispered.

"That's not why I'm upset. It's part of it, but it's not the worst part." Cora dashed tears away.

"Cora, there is nothing worse than rape," Sol said gently.

"Yes, Sol. Yes, there is." Cora's voice caught on a sob.

Sol's eyes were wary as he reached for her and she sidestepped him, as if his hands on her caused her to lose her train of thought. She needed clarity.

"Rape that is not illegal. It's worse than regular rape. She thinks that I can use this to establish cruelty and abuse, and I... I can't...." Cora pressed her hand to her heart as if trying to stop it from shattering.

"What are you saying?" Sol frowned. "I don't understand. Rape is a criminal offense."

"There is no law regarding rape between husband and wife," she whispered. "The courts do not recognize it. No way to prosecute it. She doesn't have grounds to divorce." Cora could barely form the words. "She is lying on the bed thinking, this is it, she's finally free, and I have to go in there and tell her she doesn't have grounds." Cora's voice escalated with anxiety. Sol dragged her against him as she broke apart.

"We have a pregnant mistress in the drawing room," he reminded her gently.

Cora cried harder.

"I didn't say that to upset you," Sol said helplessly.

"Sol." Cora pulled back. He pulled a clean handkerchief out of her breast pocket to dry her eyes. She wiped her face clean and then met his gaze. "I have to prove adultery *and* abuse. Adultery alone is not enough. Rape between husband and wife is not considered illegal since she is technically owned by him. Legally, he can do what he wants. I cannot get a divorce for her. What he has done isn't enough."

"Cora." Sol shook his head. "This is insanity. There must be a way, the law can't allow this, it is outrageous."

"It continues to go uncontested. I can't help her. There is no recourse for this in court." Cora shook her head and dashed tears out of her eyes.

Sol took a deep breath and let it out slowly.

"What do you need to destroy him?" Sol stood taller.

"The only thing we can possibly use is abandonment, and even that is a long shot."

"How do we prove that?"

"Mirabel said she would testify that she had lived with Eli for over a year. I need proof."

"Her testimony isn't enough?" Sol's eyebrows arched.

"She could panic and say she doesn't feel like testifying. She's a spoiled child. I want to present definitive proof. If we could get records that he's been living there for a year, that would be proof. We need to know who owns the building and get receipts, or break in and see if there is evidence on his desk."

"I'll do that today." Sol offered.

"I'll come with you."

"No. Cora, it's too dangerous." Sol shook his head.

"I need to go and do this. Please." She placed her hands on his chest.

"I don't like this." Sol's voice hardened.

"Neither do I, but I know the law, I know what I'm looking for. Royce is looking for Adeline. He won't be at the apartment. Eli will be at work. We'll be fine."

Sol's mouth thinned with worry as he checked his watch. Cora noticed the heavy silver wedding ring was gone. In the midst of this horror, her heart skipped a beat.

"It's 1:00. We should hurry." Sol relented. "But this is it. After this, you leave all this to me."

"First, I have to speak to Adeline, and then I'll change." Cora ignored his protest and put her hand on the doorknob. "Could you tell Mrs. King to keep Mirabel here for now? Maybe she could bring in a doctor to see them both?"

"I will speak to her now." Sol joined her at the threshold of the room. "Listen, Cora, we're going to do the right thing by Adeline. He won't get away with this. We'll figure it out."

A firm rap at the door made her leap away from him.

"You're very jumpy." He looked at her with sympathy.

"Adeline is requesting your presence." The maid blushed as her eyes flicked over Sol. Cora rolled her eyes.

"Do you have that effect on all women?" she asked as the maid skittered and giggled down the hall.

"What effect?" Sol asked innocently.

"Do you know what you look like?" Cora's voice caught with desire as she asked this question, knowing full well they had no time for this.

Sol looked down at himself and shrugged. He clearly didn't see himself as he was — an icy blond, blue-eyed Icelandic boxer in his prime. Strong, broad shoulders, hard abdomen, long powerful legs. One look at him had men fearing his fists, but women swooning, like the silly maid at the sight of his muscles, even under a shirt. Sol innocently had no idea that the maid and Cora's pulse raced at the sight of him. Cora tried to ignore the heat that pulsed through her whenever he touched her.

"Never mind." Cora said more to herself than to him. She shook off thoughts of Sol and redirected her focus to Adeline. "Let's get back to work. I'll talk to Adeline, get changed, and get my camera. After you bring Mrs. King up to speed, would you be a dear and bring the carriage around?"

"You're bossy." Sol grinned at her.

"Get used to it." Cora smiled sweetly. "Let's go."

Cora walked past the room with a huge tub of hot steaming water and knocked on Adeline's door.

"Come in."

"Your bath is ready. It's just down the hall. I'll have a maid assist you. Adeline, before you go, I need to clarify something with you."

Adeline sat up on the bed.

"Adeline, what happened is terrible. I am so sorry." Cora took Adeline's hands in hers. "It is hard to say this, but rape is not recognized as illegal in court between husband and wife."

Adeline's face went white.

"I am not saying that you can't petition for divorce," Cora said quickly. "Here's what we have. There is testimony from Mirabel Salter that she has lived with Eli for over a year and she is pregnant with his child. I am going to cite abandonment. Right now, Sol and I are going to his apartment, and I am going to try to find evidence that he has been there a year, a rental agreement or something. We are going to fight this, and somehow we are going to win it."

Adeline didn't look up.

"Please, have a bath and have something to eat. I have to go. We have only a few hours before Eli gets home, and we need some evidence before that. I will be back later. I hate to leave you like this."

Adeline finally looked up.

"He'll win." The light had gone out of her eyes.

"Don't give up, Adeline. If there is a way to win this, I'm going to find it. I promise." Cora squeezed her hands hard.

As Adeline crawled off the bed, Cora called a maid to assist her and then flew to her room and grabbed her camera.

Sol waited at the entrance. He opened his mouth to make one last attempt to stop her from accompanying him, so she interrupted him before he could protest. "Let's go."

Chapter Forty-Five

Together, they raced up the fire escape to reach the penthouse balcony. They carefully tested each window. Cora found a window into the kitchen that slid open.

"You won't fit through that window, miss." Sol's shoulders were too broad to even consider it.

Cora hoped her hips would fit. She started unbuttoning her top.

"What are you doing?" Sol's ears turned red.

"I have to remove some layers to fit through this window. If you would turn the other way, please?" Cora hesitated until he complied.

"Are you dressing like a man from now on? Or are you going to return to female attire in the future?" Sol whispered.

"I like pants." Cora pulled off her shoulder padding and stomach. She quickly pulled her shirt back on and buttoned it swiftly. Buttons in the front. So much easier than women's blouses that buttoned in the back. "Makes life easier. I didn't realize how restrictive women's clothes were until I got rid of them. However, I have to live in society, so I will have to go back to feminine attire. You can turn around now."

Sol turned, and his eyes swept up and down the empty hallway.

"I think I can fit through now."

"What was under that shirt?"

"Padding to make me look like a man." Cora shrugged.

"You certainly don't look like a man now." Sol's eyes gleamed in appreciation.

"Let's get back to the task at hand. This window is open if you would just lift me up and slide me through?"

"Sure."

She stood in front of him, and he put his hands on her waist to pick her up. Immediately, he dropped his hands. "You aren't wearing a... this is just you under this shirt."

"Who else would it be?" She grabbed his hands and placed them back on her waist. "Can you concentrate, please?"

"I'm trying," Sol admitted as he lifted her and she put her feet through the window. Her head rested on his shoulder while he carefully fed her body through the very narrow window.

"I hope my hips fit," she whispered.

"You forgot to remove the padding there?" he asked innocently.

"I didn't need any padding there. Thanks for pointing that out," she growled as her hips caught on the window frame. She squirmed, twisted, gasped a bit in pain but finally slithered through. Her feet landed on the countertop in the kitchen, and Sol held his hand against her head so she didn't bump it on the windowsill. "That was quite a lot of touching, sir."

"I think in some cultures we would be married," Sol responded dryly. "Quick. Open the door. There is no time for chit chat."

Cora went to the door and let him in. He immediately closed the window in the kitchen and tidied up the countertop where her feet had landed.

"Are you planning to clean the entire apartment?" she teased him.

"No. I just want you to be able to take him by surprise. No trace that we've been here." After handing her the camera, he hurried to the front of the penthouse and opened the door, so no one would take them by surprise.

Cora pounced on Eli's desk. Her fingers raced over files until she finally found a file folder entitled 'Penthouse.' Quickly, she took pictures of every receipt back to when he had actually moved in with Mirabel. She photographed the lease agreement and subsequent receipts. Mirabel's name was on nothing. This was a long shot to begin with; it seemed longer now.

She continued to scan through the files, and one was titled 'Bluebell.'

The ship Mirabel mentioned.

Her curiosity got the better of her. Confused, her eyes read over the ledgers swiftly.

April 1904. One line had 14, $75, the next line 16, $40. The line after said 17, $35. Cora's eyes swept through pages of these lines of numbers and prices. Confused, she photographed every paper. A new page for every shipment, and every shipment went to warehouse 699. Clipped to the front of the file was an empty page. Dock 318 and warehouse number 699, July 25, 1904. She itched to take the file.

Eli owns warehouse number 699 and July 25, 1904 is the next shipment. This corroborates Mirabel's story about the dock on Thursday. What is 14, $75?

Cora's heart pounded in her ears as she looked over the documents and photographed every single paper that corresponded to every shipment. She had no idea what it meant, but her stomach clenched. Instinctively, on some level, she knew whatever this was, it was bad...very bad.

"Cora. You have to hurry. We have to go," Sol hissed from the doorway.

Regretfully, she pulled herself away from the desk. There was no time to investigate further.

Swiftly, she took a picture of the closet where his clothes hung beside Mirabel's. It was the best she could do. She took one last sweeping look around the penthouse and noticed jewelry on the dresser. She tiptoed over and took a picture of all the jewels Eli had bought Mirabel.

Sol gestured at her to move faster, and she left the apartment. He carefully locked the door behind her and handed her the padding, which she crammed into her bag.

Together, they ran down the servant's stairs and exited the building. They walked swiftly to Mrs. King's carriage that was waiting six blocks away. Cora jumped in first, and Sol followed her in; he slammed the door shut behind them.

"Sol. He has a paper on his desk indicating he will get a shipment on Thursday. I don't know what it is, but Mirabel said he is always on site for that shipment, and there are lots of papers documenting what comes in that day. The boat is called "Bluebell." It is the same day I get sworn in. We have to be in that warehouse to see what it is." Cora's eyes widened in anticipation.

Sol braced himself for a fight. "Absolutely not."

"Dock 318, warehouse number 699, July 25th. That's what it said. I don't understand what this means, but it's bad. I can feel it," Cora said ominously.

"You are never going to be in that warehouse." Sol held his hands up in protest.

"If it is criminal activity, we will need two witnesses," Cora said over top of him. "There is no one else in this city we can trust. I have to be there."

"I don't like this." Sol's jaw clenched hard.

"I don't either." Cora's eyes flashed at him. "This might be crates of tea from England and I'll have to design another plan." Cora tapped a finger over her lips as she thought. "If it is something I can prosecute him for, I take full responsibility if anything happens."

"If anything happens," Sol warned. "I'll never forgive myself."

"If there was another way, I would say let's do it the other way. There is no other way. Please. You have to take me with you."

Sol sighed. "You are really difficult."

"I've been called much worse." Cora grinned.

July 25, 1904 loomed in both their minds. First, a swearing in at Osgoode Hall and then a stakeout. Cora's stomach knotted with anxiety as she contemplated both events.

Sol's eyes softened with sympathy. He leaned forward and took her hands in his. "We'll catch him. I guarantee it."

Cora swallowed hard. "We have to."

Chapter Forty-Six

A t 5:00 a.m., Cora's hands trembled with anticipation, her nerves stretched to the brink. She thought about the itinerary of her day.

Her call to the bar to be sworn in was enough for anyone, and that would take until at least 3:00 p.m. However, under the cover of darkness, a big shipment would arrive at warehouse number 699 on dock number 318. Her mind went over those numbers obsessively.

Cora took a minute to sit at her window and look over the back yard of Mrs. King's home. Perfectly tended, the early morning sun woke the day lilies and roses. Trying to let the beauty of the day soothe her, she rolled her head back and forth to relieve the tension in her neck.

Who will try to stop me from swearing in? Will Royce be there? Will Eli be there?

A gentle tap at the door startled her out of her thoughts.

"Breakfast." The maid entered her room and left a big breakfast on her desk. "Anything else?"

"Would you draw me a very hot bath?"

"Certainly." The maid nodded and curtsied before she left the room.

Cora ate her breakfast in near silence; the clock ticking was the only sound as she sipped her tea. Apprehension gnawed at her stomach, making it difficult to eat. As she stepped into the hot scented bath, she hoped the water would ease the fears that made keeping her breakfast down difficult.

Finally, she could put it off no longer. Cora dressed very carefully in her most severe, plain black dress as the benchers dictated. After plaiting her hair, she took a look at herself in the mirror to tie the regulation white tie. Deciding to carry her robe, she gave herself one last look — stern, severe, and completely void of emotion. Satisfied she looked the part; she leaned forward and examined her eyes in the mirror. She could see, underneath that façade of hardness, beat the heart of a woman. A passionate woman who was outraged at the lack of rights for women under the law, horrified enough to make exposing it her life's work. Now, with the status of barrister, she could finally do something about it. Those feelings could not show today, but she looked forward to letting them loose on Eli if she found what she needed tonight.

Cora smoothed her hands over her hair to be sure there were no loose ends. Seven-thirty. Time to go.

Sol waited at the entrance as she walked down the stairs toward him.

"You look... uh..." His eyes swept over her as he scrambled for words.

"Like a ninety-year-old librarian in a bad mood?" she suggested with a smile. "Or as we know me to be an... hmmm what do they call me? Oh yes, ancient spinster."

"I was going to say you look very serious," Sol said cautiously.

"Like a *serious* ninety-year-old librarian and ancient spinster! Perfect." Cora rolled her eyes.

"Nervous?" He pulled her into a tight hug.

"I am worried about what I'll face on the steps. What kind of protest do you think?"

"Nothing to worry about on those steps, miss. You leave that to me." Sol pulled back and then held his arm out to her.

Cora's face paled as she nodded. "What if there are a lot of protestors?"

"Then a lot of them will get hurt." Sol shrugged. He opened the carriage door, and they climbed in together.

"Did you pick this attire?" His eyes swept over her dress.

"No. It took them two months to decide what they would allow a woman to wear in court. They insisted on a black dress under the black robe and no hat. I have to appear with my head uncovered."

"Did they say why?" Sol frowned.

"They stalled me every possible way they could. They don't give explanations. I didn't ask. I just got the most severe black dress I could and carried on." Cora took a deep breath to calm her nerves. "This might get very ugly, Sol. There has been five years of opposition. What if you are outnumbered?"

Sol leaned forward so his forearms were on his thighs. He took her cold hands in his. "Whatever happens on those steps, I will fight through it. Just stay behind me. You are safe. I guarantee it."

The carriage pulled her inexorably forward.

She nodded.

"You all right?"

"I think so." Cora gasped as the carriage rounded onto the street in front of Osgoode Hall. The crowd on the front steps astounded her.

Sol's entire body tensed. She could feel it right across the carriage; he went from sympathetic and kind to battle ready. His lips thinned as he counted men blocking the front door.

Every single woman who was affiliated with the Dominion Women's Enfranchisement Association and the Women's Christian Temperance Union filled the steps and the front lawn.

Cora held her hand to her throat.

"Sol," Cora breathed. "There are... how many women are here?"

"I'd say around two hundred?"

"Oh my goodness," she said breathlessly.

"You're not going to faint, are you?" His eyes flicked over the crowd and then back to her. "If you faint in that mess, Cora, it won't be good."

"I won't faint. I'm wearing my bicycling corset. I can breathe easily." Cora couldn't tear her eyes from the people on the steps.

Men had gathered in protest. They had posters protesting suffragettes and their activity.

"Sol, there's thirty men there. You can't get me past thirty men." Cora's voice sounded shrill in her ears.

He held his hard, broad hand out, and she clasped it. He squeezed her hand, assuring her of his strength. "Nothing to worry about. Come on. Let's go. Stay behind me when we get to the men."

"Oh, there are more men showing up." Cora trembled in fear as three carriages showed up, and men piled out of them.

"Look closer, they're police." Sol let out a long breath of relief. "I was hoping he would join me."

A mammoth, shaggy-looking police officer came to the door of the carriage. He looked like he'd spent the night on the streets. Sol opened the door with a wide smile and they shook hands.

"I heard you might run into some resistance. We are here to lend a hand." The police officer's voice sounded like an axe being dragged through gravel. He was almost as tall as Sol and as broad. Face stern, he held his hand out to Cora.

"Cora, this is Asher Grayson. He's a detective with the Toronto Constabulary," Sol said.

Cora held her hand out and shook hands with the man who looked like a cross between a homeless man and a detective, with black hair and grey eyes. He hadn't shaved in days; his face was dark with rough black stubble on his jaw. Mr. Grayson looked terrifying. He gave her a curt smile, no nonsense.

"I counted thirty resisters, and what would you say, two hundred women in white promoting suffragette activity?"

"Fair assessment," Sol agreed.

"You want to take the men, and I'll take the women?" Mr. Grayson asked Sol slyly.

Sol chuckled. Cora glanced over at him; she had never seen him with men, only sighing about the drama that women were engaged in all around him. He relaxed in Mr. Grayson's company, stopped sighing, and was eager to take on the men in front of them.

"I want to be in the front, with Cora behind me. I can't sit back and watch anyone else get her in there. No disrespect intended. I'm sure your men could get her past these men, but if someone comes after her, I want to be the one to crush him."

"I expected nothing less. I saw you up against the Romanian. I pity any of the men on the steps that get in your way, Stein." Grayson straightened his shoulders and stepped aside so they could exit the carriage.

"What Romanian?" Cora asked.

"You've never seen him in the ring?" Grayson's eyebrows arched in question.

Cora frowned. "No. Never."

"I don't think ladies need to be present at boxing rings." Sol's ears burned red.

"No one wants to come up against your man here. He's fierce. You can lead the charge in any operation for me, sir. Let's go. Clock's ticking. I've got ten men here. We'll put Miss Rood behind you, and I'll be right behind her. My men will flank us, five on each side. Anyone tries to fight you, Stein, let my men deal with it. You just get her past the door. There are press inside, and you are on your own with them, Miss. Rood. Stein, when you get her safely inside, you are welcome to check and see who was at the protest. You can help us subdue anyone who looks like a threat to this lady. By subdue, of course, I mean use any force necessary to bring the scene under control. Let's get her in the building." Mr. Grayson nodded at Cora.

Sol got out of the carriage first and held his hands out to Cora. She took a deep breath and placed her hands on the tops of his shoulders. Once he helped her out of the carriage, she straightened.

"There's twelve of you and thirty of them." Cora clenched her teeth together to stop them from chattering.

"No problem." Sol shrugged. "You have nothing to worry about. I would've got you in there if it was just me against thirty."

"You're pretty sure of yourself!" Cora frowned.

"Cora, I fight for a living." Sol shrugged. "Whenever you are ready."

Two hundred suffragettes turned to look at her. They parted on the steps to let her through. When her foot touched the bottom step, they broke out in applause. The sheer force of their excitement and cheering hit her right in her heart. Her eyes locked with Lady Bronwyn, Mrs. King, Mrs. Colton... the faces were familiar and they showed their support the best way they could. Their presence. They couldn't physically fight the men who were trying to stop her, but they could give her confidence before she faced the protesters.

Lady Bronwyn held her hand up to stop the applause.

"Cora Rood, first woman lawyer for Great Britain and Canada."

The women roared their support. Once the crowd calmed down, Lady Bronwyn continued. "You have shown us your determination and your true grit. We know you will be successful in this, as you have been in all your endeavors. Please, feel our support for you." She held her hands up, and the women burst into applause. She then held her palm out to her assistant, who brought a necklace to Cora. "On behalf of the Dominion Women's Enfranchisement Association and the Women's Christian Temperance Union, I want to present you with this suffragette badge of honour. A woman lawyer is a huge stride in the battle for equal rights. God bless you, Cora Rood."

Lady Bronwyn put the necklace around Cora's neck, kissed her on both cheeks, and held her in a hard hug.

"Glad you showed up," she whispered in her ear.

Cora took a very deep breath. "Wouldn't miss it."

"Are you ready?" She held Cora in front of her, gauging her strength.

"I am," Cora said simply.

Lady Bronwyn let her go. Cora held her hands up to indicate she was going to speak to the crowd.

"Ladies," Cora called out.

The women hushed.

"I will remember this moment always. I can't thank you enough. It is my sincere hope that a woman lawyer will be able to expose the double standards we face in court. Thank you for your hard work in promoting me and your continued support. From this day forward, whatever we as women face in a court of law, you will have the opportunity to have your sister represent you." Cora bowed to her audience as they cheered their approval.

Cora straightened and watched more police gather on the sidewalk inside the fence. She lifted her chin and went to Sol's side. As she neared the last row of women, Sol stepped in front of her, and Mr. Grayson stepped behind her; five police officers stood at each side. The men howled at her and waved anti-suffragette propaganda. When she continued forward, they threw rotten fruit and tomatoes; Sol quickly pulled his coat off and put it around her to protect her clothes.

"Just get her safely inside, and we'll arrest these... uh... I'll say it later. I can't swear in front of a lady. Men, steady on. Keep in formation." Grayson's body tensed as they moved into the center of the protest. Cora pulled Sol's coat over her head so she wouldn't be covered in rotten tomatoes.

Sol and the police officers were pelted but walked forward without flinching. Cora molded herself against Sol's back. As he struck men down who came at him, she could feel the power and vibration of each punch he threw. Tears formed in her eyes at the thought that he had to physically fight her through the crowd. The men hated her that much. Finally, they stopped. Sol dragged the door to Osgoode Hall open. He pulled her inside, and just as the door shut, a tomato splattered on the glass.

"You all right?" Sol was completely covered in rotten tomatoes. Fists clenched, he was desperate to get back out into the fight.

"You're covered." She dashed tears out of her eyes as she took his coat off. "In stinky rotten tomatoes. I'm so sorry. Please tell Mr. Grayson's men, I am so sorry."

"It'll wash off. You're crying, Cora. Are you hurt?" His eyes darkened in worry. He ran his hands over her to see if she had been hit.

"No. I'm just... that was really scary. Were you scared?" Cora tried to control herself and stop crying from fear.

"I rather enjoyed it, I am ashamed to admit." Sol grinned. "You didn't get anything on you?" His eyes swept over her again to assure himself that she was unhurt.

"I wish I had. The press is right over there, ready to document this." She took a deep breath and let it out slowly. "This is appalling! The way they are acting."

Sol took her by the upper arms. "You wiped the floor with them — you took the top mark at the bar exam. You didn't tell me that, by the way. No wonder they are protesting. You're the most brilliant lawyer in the whole group."

Cora shrugged.

"As soon as the crowd is under control, I'll be in to watch." Sol's face broke into a wide smile. "I'm proud of you, but I can't hug or kiss you. I'd get you covered in tomatoes. But, later..."

"Later we'll be trying to catch Eli at whatever happens at his warehouse in the middle of the night."

"One thing at a time. Go in there and keep your head held high." Sol smiled and picked his filthy coat up off the floor. He hesitated before he opened the door to the chaos of the police arresting the protesters.

"Break some jaws out there." Cora smiled tremulously.

"Count on it. I'll be back for you," Sol promised.

Cora shivered with anticipation at what his statement implied. She took a deep breath and turned to see the press. The press yelled questions at her; she declined to answer. It took her a long time to get past them. Finally, she pulled her black robe on, and walked swiftly toward the judges at Osgoode Hall.

Her breath caught in wonder as she entered the convocation room. Hands shaking, breath caught in her throat, she closed her eyes for a moment and took a very deep breath. This was it. She moved forward and turned to see the women enter the hall to watch Cora Rood be sworn in as a barrister.

When she was called to the bar, Cora got to her feet and smoothed her skirt. She placed her trembling hand on the Bible and took a deep breath to ensure her voice would be strong.

"I accept the honour and privilege, duty and responsibility..." Cora spoke clearly. Once she was done, silence hushed over the convocation hall. She left her hand on the Bible for one brief moment as she thought of her mother and father.

I wish you were here. This was such a hard fight, father. The challenge you presented when I was nine took a big toll. I add to the oath I just took — I will fight to promote equal rights in court. I will fight to remove the words 'no recourse in a court of law,' and I will do it for you.

A slice of pain shot through her heart at the thought of her parents. Cora tried to shake off the sadness that came with the knowledge that she would turn around and there would be no family to cheer her on. One of the judges cleared his throat, indicating that she was done and it was time to move on.

Cora slowly slid her hand off the Bible; she turned to look out over the entire convocation hall. She ignored the impatience of the judge as her eyes swept over the crowd. She saw men with hard looks for her, men who had stalled her, treated her with utmost contempt. The open hatred on some of the men's faces caused her breath to catch. Her jaw and her dignity had paid the price for standing up to that level of hatred. Fear pooled in her stomach as she caught the eye of benchers who despised her. Men she would have to continue to stand up to for as long as she practiced law. She straightened; her eyes narrowed at them as she held their gaze.

A double standard doesn't change unless it is exposed. You can't stop me now, and I will pave the way for more women to follow me. That's a promise.

Cora's eyes locked with Malachi Marks. His face was as impassive as granite; she nodded ever so slightly at him, and his nod back was barely perceptible. Her eyes swept over women glowing radiantly because she would fight on their behalf. The gleam in the women's eyes overwhelmed her. Most didn't know what she was up against. Many of them, she knew, would be let down because of the bias in the law. A law she could only expose, not change.

Finally, feeling overwhelmed with sadness, her eyes swept the crowd looking for a friendly face that just wanted her to be happy, to be her best.

Her eyes settled on a big, blond Icelandic man, knuckles raw, covered in rotten tomatoes, whose smile went from ear to ear. Cora Rood's ancient spinster heart soared with happiness.

Chapter Forty-Seven

Sol's eyes scanned the convocation room. The freshly minted lawyers shook each other's hands in congratulations but pointedly ignored Cora. A slow burn of anger simmered in him as he watched the men turn their backs to her and finally exclude her completely. He had read about their mock trial in the newspaper. The lawyers had all dressed as women, according to the papers, and the trial that year had ridiculed women viciously. Furious at having to share their graduating class with a woman, they had lashed back at her the only way they could — treating her with utmost contempt behind her back. Sol was glad Cora hadn't attended.

He yearned to go to her as she stood to the side, alone. Finally, the crowd broke so she could leave the convocation room. Sol couldn't get near her as the ladies swamped her. He watched Lady Bronwyn hold her arms out for an embrace. She held Cora in such a way that the press who were photographing the event had a clear look at Lady Bronwyn's face and Cora was in profile.

The men hated her, treated her with contempt, and the women wanted her to further their agenda at whatever cost. Frustrated, Sol's eyes swept the crowd, looking for any danger. Satisfied that Eli's men weren't in attendance, he moved closer to Cora.

"I am so proud of you! We have festivities planned. I am hosting lunch in your honour. You'll need time to change." Lady Bronwyn's eyes were bright with excitement. "Please, make sure Mrs. Pitman knows she is invited. Sol, you are welcome, too."

A luncheon with the D. W. E. A. Sol suppressed a groan.

"Mrs. Pitman is indisposed," Cora explained as she pulled out of Lady Bronwyn's embrace.

"Oh. That is unfortunate." Lady Bronwyn's face fell. "Either way, we're excited to host you. We'll see you as soon as you can manage!"

With that, she turned to her husband. Lord Bronwyn gave Sol a nod. He had been the man's bodyguard on three separate occasions and had been treated by him as serving class each time.

Lord and Lady Bronwyn excused themselves, and Sol took Cora's hand.

"I so badly want to hug and kiss you, but I am covered in tomatoes." Sol shook off the discomfort he felt from being snubbed by Lord Bronwyn and instead smiled at Cora. He wanted her to be happy.

Together, they walked out of Osgoode Hall to their waiting carriage. Once Cora settled in, he crawled into the carriage after her.

"Back to Mrs. King's and then to the Bronwyn's?" Sol asked.

Cora looked out the window; she didn't meet his eye. "You don't have to go to the Bronwyn's. You can just come for me after, if you would rather. I know you would hate it." Her voice sounded flat.

"No, I can go. Whatever you want."

"I saw that snub." Her eyes flicked to him and then back out the window of the carriage. "It's all right. Leave me there for lunch and come back for me. You can go and train or whatever you like to do."

Sol's brows knit together.

The sadness in her eyes bothered him.

***

She tried to stop the tears from spilling down her face. She focused on the huge iron and rock fence surrounding Osgoode Hall. When the carriage pulled away, she tried to ignore the pain in her heart as she focused on trees and the couples walking on the street. She took a deep breath and let it out very slowly. Sol reached for her hand and gave it a squeeze. His knuckles were raw, and his sleeve was covered in tomato. Cora turned her attention to him. Sadly, she traced her fingertips over the bleeding skin.

"Everything all right?" He leaned forward, careful not to let his clothes brush against hers.

"I'm sorry. I am happy, really I am. I just keep thinking that if my parents were alive, they would have been so thrilled to be here today." Tears spilled down her cheeks, and she tried to dash them away. "Once I finished my oath, it struck me that they weren't here, and they are not going to be here for any important days." She bowed her head. "This day, the day I'm sworn in, is one of the most important days in my life and for women, and here I am trying not to feel so sad. What an idiot."

"I saw how they treated you, Cora. It's really wrong."

She nodded and looked back out the window of the carriage.

"I have something for you. Your brother wanted to be here today. He sent this so you would have something from your family to mark this special day." Sol pulled a little box out of his pocket.

She turned her attention back to him as he handed her the box. She opened it and smiled. A locket — inside were photographs of her parents. A diamond, emerald, and garnet sparkled on the front. Suffragette colours.

"Your brother asked me to pick this out for you and to put those photographs in it. He wanted me to tell you that he is giving this to you on behalf of your father and mother, who would be so proud of you. There is a letter for you to read."

Cora's eyes filled with tears as she held the locket and the faces of her parents looked back at her.

"It's so perfect." Her eyes filled with tears again.

"Let me." Sol took the locket, put his arms around her, and fastened it at the back of her neck.

"Do you and my brother send telegrams every day?" She tried to lighten the mood.

"You may be a progressive woman, miss, but I am still old fashioned. I telegrammed him to let him know I am currently keeping you alive."

"You did?"

"Of course, I did. He is worried sick about you. I telegram him often. He's very nice and cares about you a lot. I think we will be great friends."

"I'm sure you will." Cora looked at the locket again. "Suffragette colours. That was really kind of him to think of that."

"He wants you to succeed. Something we both have in common."

"I have a lot of good men in my corner." Cora's eyes filled with tears all over again.

Sol pulled his shirt off so he could hold her without getting tomato all over her convocation robe. His undershirt was soaked through in some spots but not too bad.

"Come here." Sol pulled Cora into his arms and held her as she wept into his shoulder. "I'm so sorry."

"Me, too."

When the carriage halted in front of Mrs. King's, Sol kissed the top of Cora's head. She had been quiet in his arms for two blocks.

"We're here," he said gently.

Cora sat up and wiped her tears away.

"Are you up for this lunch?"

"I have to be." She wiped her eyes again.

"This is the problem with being a public figure, right? The public owns you now?"

"Very true. I didn't know what I was getting into." Cora sighed. "Oh no. I'm turning into you, sighing constantly."

Sol laughed as he crawled out of the carriage ahead of her.

Together they went into Mrs. King's house. The butler raised an eyebrow and immediately sent water to Sol's room. Cora requested a maid to help her change. The dress for the luncheon was particularly charming. Purples and mauves, Priscilla's insistence, with beaded trim that moved with her. The maid adjusted her hat, and she finally pulled on gloves. Cora packed her bag with her pants, a black shirt, and her camera.

Sol waited for her at the entrance, and his eyes lit up when he saw her walk swiftly toward him.

"What is in the bag?" he asked warily.

"My clothes for later."

"Cora. You are not going to the warehouse with me." His tone warned her as he opened the door, and together they got back into the carriage.

"Sol. Re-evaluate that comment and never make it again." Cora leaned forward. "I won't move, I won't say a thing. I have to be there, I have to see for myself what happens in that warehouse tonight."

Sol took a deep breath and let it out slowly. "We'll talk about it later."

"Sol, I'm coming with you. We're a team."

The Bronwyn mansion loomed in front of them.

Sol's jaw clenched hard; he sighed a sigh that started at his knees.

"I'm coming," Cora insisted.

"You're not."

Chapter Forty-Eight

A
fter enjoying a lavish lunch and best wishes, Cora joined Sol in the carriage. She secretly revelled in his red-eared embarrassment as she changed into her man's suit.

"First," Sol relented when he realized it would come to brute force to stop her from participating in the stakeout. "We survey the area from up there." Sol led the way to a four-storey building.

They climbed the stairs onto the roof, and Cora rubbed her arms as the temperature dropped and drizzly rain started to fall. From their vantage point, they had a perfect view of the warehouse. Sol held binoculars to his eyes.

"I have something that might help." Cora pulled a roll of paper from her bag.

"What is it?"

Cora unrolled the large paper. "I got this from the tax assessment office. I asked if there was a building permit for this property."

"Cora, that's brilliant."

Cora shrugged that away. "I have been studying it. There are three coal chutes on the north side of this building. According to the plans, your shoulders and my hips should fit." She grinned at him. "If you notice, there is a door here that leads to the stairs, up to a mezzanine where we can watch whatever he drags in there tonight."

"Let me get Grayson involved," Sol requested. "We'll put you somewhere safe."

"Eli's men know I'm back in the city. The only place I'm safe is with you." Cora moved closer and put her hands on his arm. "We can do this. If Grayson is there, he'll arrest Eli."

Sol's face creased in confusion. "I thought you wanted to destroy him in criminal court."

"Yes, but I have to face him in divorce court first. He has to believe he has won in that court."

Sol sat down on the low wall. "That is very confusing."

"Please, trust me. I have a plan."

"He might be importing fabric or tea or something that isn't criminal."

"I have a plan B for that. If he is engaged in criminal activity, tonight is the night."

***

Together, after dark, they tested the doors and coal chutes that faced the wharf. Everything was locked up. Defeat settled over them as they hid in the inky darkness. Cora scratched her eyebrow as she thought about the plans. There was no other way into the building.

"Stay here. I'm going to take out that guard the next time he walks by. It's the only way in." Sol got up and crept to the corner of the building. Cora's eyes widened.

The guard came back after fifteen agonizing minutes. Cora cringed when Sol dropped the guard with one punch. He found keys to the warehouse in the unconscious man's pocket. After they tried what seemed like thirty keys, one finally opened the door. Cora's heart pounded in her throat with fear that another guard would find them. Sol opened the door and placed the keys in his pocket. He dragged the guard behind some piled up building material so that he wouldn't be found. Together, they slipped into the warehouse and went up the steps to the mezzanine so they could watch the shipment come in from a height where they would not be seen.

Cora curled her body against Sol as they settled in to wait.

"What happens if they find us?" The full gravity of how dangerous this was made her weak with fear.

"I'll have to fight us out of here," Sol said grimly. "Your brother will never forgive me. If something happens and the guards come for us, you crawl under this tarp."

"The fish tarp?" Cora's nose wrinkled from the smell.

"Yes, the fish tarp." Sol's voice hardened. Cora could tell he was afraid that she was here with him. "You crawl under there and leave me to the guards."

"Let's hope it doesn't come to that." Cora shuddered.

"If it does... promise me you'll stay under that tarp until a police officer comes for you." Sol shot her a hard look.

"I promise." Cora swallowed around the knot of fear in her throat.

Silence. There was no movement anywhere.

"What if it is tea? What if I dragged us to this and we have nothing at the end of it?" Cora hissed at Sol.

"Then we do your plan B." Sol moved ropes out of the way so if there was an attack, he would have solid footing to fight back.

Another hour dragged by, and Cora rubbed her eyes.

Sol looked at her sympathetically. "You're exhausted."

"I'm all right."

Suddenly, he moved closer, pulled her tight against him, and put his hand over her mouth. "Don't scream." Her eyes widened in surprise. "I don't know how you feel about rats."

Her body clenched.

"That's what I thought. There are some rats to your left. If I let my hand off your mouth, you can't scream," he whispered into her ear. "Shhh."

He took his hand away from her mouth carefully, testing her resolve to be silent.

"I'm not tired anymore. I feel like I'm going to have a heart attack!" Cora whispered into his ear.

He moved her so his body was between her and the rats and then held her against him tightly. "Do you realize that the only time I get to hold you is in jail cells and rat-infested warehouses? Where you are either soaked from being in a spring storm or wearing men's clothing? I am starting to feel cheated. This is not the sort of courtship I envisioned with an ancient spinster."

"You're trying to distract me." She wiggled in closer to him.

"Is it working?" Sol asked against her neck.

In a man's shirt, her neck was exposed to him, not buttoned to her jaw like a woman's blouse. "Yes." She shivered with delight.

"Shhh, look, there's a light from a ship."

Cora took a deep breath and let it out slowly. They took their positions by the edge of the mezzanine and watched as the ship docked.

"This is no good. Eli isn't here." Cora wanted to weep in disappointment. Rats to her left, armed guards in the warehouse below, and no Eli.

***

"He'll be here." Sol moved both of them to gain a better vantage point. "Eli doesn't think the law applies to him. He'll waltz in here large as life."

A very long half hour later, Eli strolled in, flanked by four bodyguards. Cora shook with fear beside Sol at the sight of him. Sol dragged her in front of him so that her back was against his chest. Sick with revulsion, she kept her eyes glued to the scene in front of them as the warehouse door opened. Her jaw dropped in horror as she watched the scene unfold.

Girls. Oh mercy, he's selling girls.

Eli Pitman was procuring girls as prostitutes; and by the look of it, some no more than children. Cora shook in Sol's arms. She wanted to document the entire scene with a camera, but there was no use. It was far too dark in the warehouse. So, she forced her eyes to stay on the horror in front of her. She committed each terrible, depraved movement to memory.

"Shhhh," he whispered.

Together, they watched in horror as Eli examined the girls. One had enough spirit left to slap his hand away. He backhanded her, and Cora flinched. Sol's arms tightened around her while he kept his hand hard on her mouth in case she screamed.

As Eli groped them, the girls cried; Sol cursed near Cora's ear. She reached up and put her hand over his mouth. He could do nothing for these girls, and she could feel him tense and ready to protect them from Eli. Too many armed guards — he'd be shot and killed on the spot. They dared not even blink as they watched the depravity unravel in front of them. When Eli was finally at the end of the line, a man approached from the entrance that opened to the street.

"Looks like a very lucrative crop of girls." The short and heavyset man with an Irish accent approached Eli. Sol tensed again; his hand hardened on Cora's mouth. "These English girls are the best, aren't they? I'll need fifteen percent this time, Pitman."

Eli raised his gun and point-blank shot the man instead of answering his question. His expression didn't change. The man dropped; the girls screamed.

Sol's arms tightened so hard around Cora she could barely breathe. Shaking, with acid burning in her stomach, the only thing keeping Cora's eyes forward on the revolting and deviant mess in front of her was the day she would sit in court and give her testimony. Her word and Sol's would have Eli swinging from a rope.

"Paying off cops is getting too expensive." Eli put his gun back into its holster. "Dispose of him, Royce. Cartwright and Baker, get these girls distributed. Payment to be brought to me tomorrow morning, 8:00 a.m. sharp. Dismissed."

With tears in her eyes, Cora pulled Sol's hand away and watched helplessly as thirteen girls, who tried to hold their clothes together and hang onto a shred of dignity, were dragged, weeping, out of the warehouse.

Royce pulled the dead cop away by his heels.

Now that the criminal activity was over, she could cover her eyes with her hands. It didn't help. The horrendous events were burned into her memory. She watched it over and over again behind her eyelids. "Sol, I've made a terrible mistake." She wept into his ear.

"Never mind that, there is no time for tears. We need to get out of here alive. Shhh." He covered her mouth with his hand again. "Stop, you have to stop crying. When all the men disperse, we have only a few hours before sun up. We have to get out of here undetected. Cora, please. Stop."

Guilt washed through her, and made her feel hot and cold at the same time; her throat choked on a salty sob.

We should have involved Grayson. Eli should have been arrested tonight. Thirteen girls will disappear into the streets and brothels. We'll never find them, and it's my fault.

Finally, the warehouse was silent. All the men had dispersed to complete their nefarious duties and assignments. As dawn broke, they could wait no longer; they crept down the stairs of the mezzanine. Sol opened a door to the side of the warehouse and braced himself to be attacked. No one saw them as they slipped out of the warehouse and made their way down a back alley as fast as they could. Satisfied they weren't followed, they moved swiftly, staying in shadows, until they reached their carriage eight blocks away.

They jumped in, and Sol slammed the door shut behind them. The carriage driver slapped the reins down, and as distance started to increase between the warehouse and their carriage, they let out a very long breath of relief.

Cora covered her face with her hands.

"You're all right. You're safe. Come here." Sol pulled her onto his lap and into his arms.

Cora buried her face in his chest and couldn't stop the sobs that tore out of her. "I'll never forgive myself."

"What are you talking about?" Sol pulled her away from his shoulder to look at her.

"You wanted to involve Grayson, and I said no. This is my fault. I should have involved the police. Grayson could have involved the entire constabulary..."

"You don't know who Eli shot?" Sol's eyebrows were high on his forehead.

"No." Tears coursed down her cheeks. Very gently, Sol wiped her tears with his sleeve.

"Police Inspector Logan." Sol's eyes hardened.

"What?" Cora gasped.

"Who knows how deep this corruption goes. Grayson couldn't have gone in there on his own. He might have been set up, too. No, Cora, there was no other way."

"Can we trust Grayson?" Cora's eyes were wide.

"Grayson is the only cop I know that is clean. He's the best chance we have."

Cora swallowed hard. "I feel sick."

"This is the first man you've seen killed?" Sol's eyes softened with sympathy.

She nodded slowly.

"It's a hard thing to see." He pressed her head against his shoulder.

"Who will those girls be sold to?" She moaned as she wiped her eyes with his shirt.

"There is nothing we can do for those girls, Cora. Put that out of your mind. We can only take Eli down and hope to stop white slavery where we can." Sol's arms were tight around her.

The carriage ground to halt in front of the King house.

"To bed with you, miss." Sol pulled her out of the carriage.

"No. Not yet. I have to serve Eli with a divorce petition." Cora's stomach churned with fear at the thought of facing Eli. "Once I serve him, he'll know I'm at the King's and he'll send men to come for me." Her voice escalated with fear.

"I'm looking forward to that." Sol grinned in the early morning light. "No to all of that. No serving him with papers yet. You need to sleep — you are exhausted. You can't think straight, and when you go up against Eli, you have to be sharp."

"All right." Cora shoulders slumped. She picked up her bag, and Sol held out his hand to carry it for her. Her eyes looked stamped in purple; her arms dragged with exhaustion.

"Bath first — you are covered in rat... uh... leavings."

Cora shuddered.

The butler gasped at the sight of them as they made their way into the entrance of the King mansion.

"Cora," Sol said as he helped her to her room. "Please, don't cry."

She wiped at tears as they fell down her face.

"But... Sol, those girls. Those little girls." Cora broke down. Exhaustion and grief took her to her knees in front of him. "I can't bear to think of it."

Maids hovered around them. "Draw a bath, please, and bring Miss Rood some breakfast," Sol instructed as he dropped to his knees in front of Cora, gathered her against him and held her as she splintered.

Chapter Forty-Nine

Eventually, she calmed down in his arms as the storm of emotions passed.

"I want you to stay here, with me." Cora's hands shook as she wiped her face on her sleeve.

Sol swallowed hard. "Mrs. King will not approve of that."

"I don't care." Cora's chin trembled. "I close my eyes and I still see it. I will never sleep again."

"The bath is ready. I left breakfast on the desk," the maid said to Sol.

"Thank you." He nodded.

"Eat or bath first?" Sol asked Cora as he detangled himself from her.

"I'll never eat again," she moaned.

"That's enough. Come on. Toast, tea, bath. That's the order."

He dragged her up off the floor and made her eat two pieces of toast covered in poached egg. As Cora picked up the tea cup, her hands shook so hard tea splashed over the rim.

"Don't say, I told you so." Cora's shoulders slumped in defeat, her eyes glittered with tears. "Don't say, I'm too delicate to gather evidence," she wept.

Sol reached forward and gently took the cup from her hand. He held it to her lips so she could drink the hot sugary tea without spilling it everywhere.

"I wasn't going to say anything of the sort." Sol put the empty tea cup down and then took her shaking hands in his. "You watched a man sell thirteen girls into slavery and then shoot a police inspector. I'm horrified, too. If you weren't upset, I would be worried." He pulled her onto his lap and stroked her back as she wrapped her arms around his neck and pressed her face into his shoulder.

373

"Really?" she cried against him.

"Really." Sol picked up a napkin and wiped her tears away. "Here's what I think, Cora. Up to this point, you've tried very hard to be as much like a man as you can be in order to do your job. You said emotion is a weakness and you can't show any weakness. I say stop that thinking, Cora." He turned her to face him; he cradled her face in his hands. "You are a woman, and being a woman lawyer is powerful. The devastation you feel today will drive you to demand change." Very gently, he wiped tears from her cheekbones as he continued to talk. "Don't apologize for feeling this deeply about the women who are looking to you to protect them in a courtroom." Sol cradled Cora's face in his hands. "They need someone to be outraged."

"*You're* not crying," Cora wept.

"I'm crying on the inside," Sol admitted.

"Really?"

"Sobbing my heart out." Sol sighed as he hugged her tight against him.

Despite her tears, a smile tugged at her lip. She didn't want to leave his warm embrace.

"Get cleaned up, and I'll check on you before you go to sleep," Sol promised. Cora got to her feet and dragged her weary body to the threshold of the room.

The maid helped her bathe and get into her nightgown; her eyebrows arched as she looked at Cora in a dainty, lacy nightgown cut to flatter her figure. A nightgown no ancient spinster had *ever* owned, past or present. The maid departed, and Cora stood by the bed as Sol pulled the heavy drapes shut to ensure no sunlight came into the room. Once the room was dark, he turned to her. His eyes met hers; she trembled as his gaze traveled over her.

"I don't typically dress like this." Cora fidgeted with the lace on her nightgown. "Priscilla, my friend, was trying out new designs, and she doesn't listen to what her clients want. This is far too extravagant... just so you know, I am not some sort of... well, you know. A woman who... uh... wears things like to... uh... seduce men. You know. That sort." She dropped her eyes to the floor.

"That's a disappointment," Sol said so gravely, she knew he was teasing her.

Her face fell anyway; she reached for a robe and tried to cover up as best she could.

"Sorry, I shouldn't make a joke with you today when you are so upset. I'm sorry. Don't, please, don't be embarrassed. You are beautiful, Cora." Sol closed the distance between them.

She looked up from the floor. "Thank you." Cora bit her lip. "They call me a spinster lawyer for a reason, Sol. No one has ever looked at me this way, in this sort of attire." Her voice caught with raw anxiety, she bit her lip. "The way you are looking at me now."

"I see." Sol's voice was soft.

Cora nodded as she pulled the tie on the robe very tight. "So, I'm not sure how you feel about me being some sort of ancient spinster. That's what Mr. Crest called me, and Priscilla was thinking it but was too polite to say it." Her voice caught in her throat. "I'm not sure what you're thinking just now." She finished rambling and fidgeted with a silk ribbon on her robe. A robe that looked like you would have to battle through yards of flounces and frills to get to the woman underneath. Her eyes met his. As she recognized the desire that smoldered there, nervous tension caused her to drop her gaze to the floor again.

"I love ancient spinsters," Sol said simply; his eyes crinkled at the corners as he smiled at her.

"Really?" She bit her lip as she dragged her eyes from the floor to him.

"Really. Cora, ancient spinsters are my favourite," Sol confirmed. "I am the luckiest man in the entire world. That is the only thing I am thinking right now."

Sol took another step toward her. "I'm also thinking that I would really, really like to kiss you, with your permission, of course."

Her pulse leaped in her throat.

"That would be nice." Cora croaked the words out.

"You know that maid is going straight to Mrs. King, and she's going to be banging on this door in three minutes," Sol warned her.

"Then we should make them a very good three minutes," Cora suggested, sounding nothing like an ancient spinster, as Sol pounced on her.

Just as their lips met, Mrs. King knocked firmly on the door.

"Cora, if Sol is in there, it's time to send him straight out." Her voice sounded shrill.

Cora's breath caught as Sol's lips slid down the side of her neck. She shivered in his arms as the banging increased.

"Sol Stein, come out of Cora's room at once!"

Cora gasped as Sol scooped her up and carried her to the bed.

"I heard that, Cora! You have a reputation to uphold," Mrs. King roared against the door.

"She's going to have a stroke," Cora whispered.

Sol's lips moved back up her neck to her jaw and then her lips.

"She'll stop banging on the door then," he said then deepened the kiss.

"Sol, come out of there at once!" Mrs. King demanded.

Sol sighed and tore himself away. He straightened up to comply, but Cora dragged him back.

"I am getting a key!" Mrs. King sputtered in fury.

"I have to go." He tore his lips from hers. "I *really* have to go. We'll have lots of time for this when we're settled on my farm in Gimli."

Farm!

"I am not going to be a farmer in Gimli!" Cora sat up in protest, going from passionate to horrified in a single moment.

"Cora, have a good rest. We can talk about that later." Sol grinned. He straightened up; his ears were red as he went to placate Mrs. King.

***

Cora fidgeted with the divorce petition as they stood at the entrance of Eli's empire the following Monday. Gulping down her fear, she entered the lobby after Sol opened the door for her. Cora spoke to the clerk at the front desk while Sol watched the door and Cora simultaneously.

"I have a petition for divorce for Mr. Pitman," Cora said to the man behind a massive oak desk.

The man's eyes narrowed as he looked at the petition.

"Who shall I say dropped it off?" The man looked from Sol to Cora and then back to Sol. Sol inclined his head at Cora.

Cora leaned across the desk. "Cora Rood, a lady lawyer, dropped this off for him. You can tell him I can't wait to see him in court."

This is it. An open window straight into chaos.

Eli would fight back. Hard.

I will not give up on this... you will go down. I will destroy you. I can't fix everything, but I can help this one woman.

"His lawyers can reach me at this address to set up a meeting."

She gave him the address of Mrs. King's home. His eyes narrowed further.

"Is this some sort of trick?"

"No. I suggest you give this to him right away."

Cora and Sol went back to the King residence and waited for the storm.

Early the next morning, a summons to meet with Eli's counsel was delivered with Cora's breakfast. Adeline immediately burst into tears when she saw the summons. When her legs buckled in fear, Sol helped her into a chair.

Cora read the counter petition; her spine hardened with steel as she took a deep breath. Straightening her shoulders, she stood up.

"Let's go." She folded the petition, and Adeline trembled beside her. "Can you walk?"

"I can't be in the same room with him." Adeline's voice shook.

Cora knelt down in front of her. Taking Adeline's hands in her own, she met her eyes and held her gaze. "This is your chance to stand up to him."

"Everyone who stands up to him loses." Adeline's eyes filled with tears.

"Please, Adeline," Cora pleaded. "I need you in that room. I know it is very hard, but we need to negotiate, and if you aren't there, it will drag things out. I am asking you to trust me."

Adeline blinked back tears and pressed her handkerchief to the side of her eye. "The only thing I trust is you. I don't trust Eli or the court, only you."

"I'll be in the room. He can't physically harm you." Sol took a step forward, jaw clenched and body tensed, ready for battle as he spoke.

"Thank you." Adeline's voice was flat.

"We are out of time." Desperate to get the proceedings started, Cora stood up.

Adeline lifted her head. "You think I can win the divorce case?"

Not a chance in this life or the next. I'm losing this battle so I can win the war.

"We're going to give it our best." Cora pulled on her gloves and led the way. "We have to go. Adeline, I guarantee that I will fight with every last breath to get you justice. Just come with me and let me do my job."

Adeline took a deep breath and let it out slowly. She stood up; Cora slid her arm around her waist, and together they went to face Eli, with an angry Icelander making sure no one got too close.

Chapter Fifty

Cora's stomach flipped hard with fear and nervous tension. They would meet in a room to hash out a decision without a judge. This was standard. This would fail. Cora would ensure it.

She took a deep breath, and reaching for Adeline's hand, she squeezed it as they walked down the hall. She heard Sol behind her. Knowing he was there gave her confidence. Physically, she was safe; her client was safe. Emotionally, she had to keep the big picture in place. Fail to win. Take advantage of the fact that the men in the room would believe in their own superiority so completely, they would not notice being manipulated. Show them a card by accident while the ace up her sleeve is waiting to drop.

Be strong enough to appear weak.

She hesitated at the door and took a deep breath. She smiled at Adeline's look of terror.

"This is going to be just fine."

The three entered the room. Eli's legal counsel was extensive. Three lawyers to Adeline's one.

One that is a woman.

Eli nodded and rolled his eyes at his counsel, as if to say, I told you. A woman lawyer was no threat to them. Everyone took their seats after the women sat.

How they pretend to be chivalrous with actions, while their hearts are black with hatred for a woman in this position. Equal education, equal opportunity — unacceptable to these men.

Cora was certain Eli and his counsel thought his battle was won before it even started. He grinned like a wolf when his eyes flicked over his wife and then Cora. Adeline hung her head as he looked at her. Sol stepped in between them to give Adeline time to compose herself.

Cora calmly peeled her gloves off her fingers and waited for Eli and his counsel to start.

"We had a deal, you and I," Eli said smoothly to Cora.

"I don't make deals with filth like you." Cora let her eyes clash with Eli Pitman. He didn't look away. Neither did she. Cora straightened up

Go in strong, leave in hysterics. I hate this. I hate that I have to pretend to be so weak. I want to rip you to shreds in court, and I can't.

"This is about the law. You have no power here, Eli. We are all subject to the same code. No deals. Let's begin." Cora opened a file.

"First, we clear the room. Just you and me," Eli said to Cora.

"You want to meet with a lawyer without your legal counsel?" She smiled. She had him.

"You are no threat to me." Eli lifted his chin and looked down his nose at her.

"You need your counsel. Don't be foolish. Eli, *you* need to be protected. *From me.*"

Eli threw back his head and laughed. "You have a funny view of yourself, miss."

"Gentlemen, he wants the room cleared." Cora shrugged.

His counsel pounced on him and whispered intently in his ear. Cora sat and waited.

"She's just a woman. I am not worried about meeting with a woman!" Eli barked at them and sneered at her.

"We're here to discuss a divorce proceeding, so let's do that, shall we?" The lawyer nearest to Eli looked at him sternly. "Respectfully, Mr. Pitman, the counsel wishes to stay."

"Fine. Let's proceed." Eli looked bored and furious at the same time.

Cora looked at each member of his counsel.

"Mr. Pitman, I would like to direct your attention to the following photographs."

His eyes narrowed as evidence of his affair was laid out in front of him.

"This doesn't..."

"Silence," Cora reprimanded Eli. "I'm not done speaking."

As she knew it would, a vein stood out on Eli's forehead. If she didn't have him arrested and tried for murder, he would find her, and he would kill her. Of that she was certain. Sol or not. He would have her dead by the end of the week if she didn't do this right.

"Under Canadian law, adultery isn't enough." The oldest lawyer protested. "You have no proof of abuse. I have no idea what we are doing here. The law is clear on this point."

"I would like to draw your attention to these photographs here. You'll notice the dates on these penthouse receipts."

"He purchased this property a year and a half ago."

"When did he move out of your home?" Cora directed the question to Adeline. Adeline looked as if she would break into a million pieces. Evidence of his affair with Mirabel, the affair that had gutted her, was spread out between all these men. Her head hung in shame.

"Over a year ago. He moved out in the spring of 1903." Adeline's voice was barely above a whisper.

"No evidence of abuse. I can do what I please," Eli growled at Cora.

Eli's legal counsel shifted in their chairs uncomfortably.

Cora looked at them, each of them, and smiled very sweetly.

"Maybe you should speak to your lawyers about the term 'abandonment'."

As she predicted, Eli's face paled; she saw rage spark behind his eyes. He stood up swiftly and towered over her. She leaped up to meet him eye to eye. They squared off over the table, over all the evidence she had against him. Sol stood just slightly behind her. She knew he was ready to step in at her slightest indication.

Eli glared his hatred at her.

"Mirabel will testify that she has been living with you, in this penthouse, for over a year. You really want to gamble on how a judge will call this? Sounds like abandonment to me." Cora's heart pounded with fear as she met Eli's icy eyes across the table. She straightened her shoulders; she'd learned courage from the best in Oakland. If Priscilla could take a fist in the face to ensure justice was served, Cora could certainly stand up to this bully. She refused to be stifled by the fear of jail and the hopelessness that had crushed her since then. This was it. *This* was why she was a lawyer. To expose the double standard, to destroy the likes of Eli Pitman, and to crush an unfair law.

You're up against the wrong woman. You underestimated me.

"I have not abandoned my wife." Eli spoke through teeth that were clenched together in fury. "I have given her everything she desires. I have paid every bill. I will not pay your bill."

"I already explained this to you. Check with your counsel about that, Mr. Pitman." Cora moved closer to him. She spoke a few inches from his face. "As she is your lawful wife, you have to pay her counsel.

Smith v. Smith. You are *uninformed.*" She threw out that bait, watched to see if he took it.

Swallow it down. Let it fester in you. Come on. Hit me. Try to hurt me. Let's see what you are capable of because I know you can't defeat me... I will destroy you. I guarantee it.

Eli seethed. He moved back, just a little bit.

"I bet I can show your utter disregard for your wife in a court of law. I bet I can show that you abandoned her very easily. Your will, for instance. I am certain I can prove that you have not provided for her in the event that something happens to you."

"Of course, I have provided for her and my sons." Eli bared his teeth in anger.

"Prove it," she echoed back to him softly. "In a court of law."

In family court — a court of law that gives you all the rights and Adeline none.

"When can we do this?" Eli moved away from her.

I have you.

"Make my will available. I have never, for a second, abandoned my wife. This is ridiculous," he barked at his counsel without taking his eyes off Cora.

"I can call for a judge to hear this right away," one of the lawyers offered.

Cora watched a lawyer out of the corner of her eye shift in his chair.

"We'll need two days," he corrected his colleague.

To change his will...

"One," Cora countered. "Two days might give you time to change the will. To make it look like you are *providing* for your wife. A will that provides for Adeline takes abandonment off the table. I want this in front of a judge tomorrow."

"Two days," the lawyers restated.

Adeline stood up. She looked so fragile, Cora secretly rejoiced.

"You won't win against me," Eli hissed at her.

"I've already lost, Eli," Adeline said in such defeat Cora wanted to shout for joy. Adeline had no idea what Cora was going to do with Eli in two days... she couldn't. If Adeline had a speck of confidence, she would ruin the entire thing.

"You'll pay for this." Eli directed that statement to Cora.

Cora checked her watch and smiled at his counsel.

"Threat uttered at 11:18 a.m. on August 1." Cora nodded to the clerk. "Make sure you put that in the notes of these proceedings. If anything happens to me, you can be certain Eli Pitman is behind it, or one of his men."

She turned her attention back to his legal counsel. "Please, get your client under control. I would really appreciate it if we could conduct these proceedings without threats."

"We'll see you in court, two days, Miss Rood."

"I said one," she growled at the lawyer.

"Impossible. We need two." The lawyer stood up, effectively dismissing her. Sol moved closer.

She looked at them coolly and then deliberately let her lip tremble. Easy to do; she thought about the fate of the thirteen girls he sold into slavery.

"If you change that will to make it look like he is providing for Adeline... my whole case... will fall apart." Tears filled Cora's eyes. She noticed one lawyer roll his eyes at the other lawyer.

They expected female hysterics and weeping.

I know you. I know exactly how you feel about me. I've heard it for the last ten years. You can't be a mathematician, you can't be a lawyer, you can't be a solicitor, and you can't be a barrister.

Watch me.

The lawyer closest to the wall cleared his throat, embarrassed at the tears that gathered in her eyes. When Adeline saw that Cora was weeping, she started weeping as well, and all the men in the room frowned and then rolled their eyes as they murmured to each other.

Women, what do you expect?

"I'm begging you to play this fair." She let her voice tremble. "You and I both know the law is not fair... *please be honest.*" Cora wiped tears from her cheeks and gathered her evidence from the table.

Please, don't be honest. Run — don't walk — back to your law offices and change that last will and testament...

"Two days." The oldest lawyer put his foot down. "You don't call the shots here."

"All right." Cora dropped her eyes to the table in a show of submission. A submission he expected simply because as a male lawyer, he believed himself to be superior to her. She picked up the evidence of adultery and put it in her folder. She let her tears drop on the table.

Once her photographs were packed away, she reached for Adeline's hand and they slunk out of the room. When Sol closed the door behind them, they heard the entire room full of men erupt into laughter.

Cora squeezed Adeline's hand hard as they left the court house.

***

Once they returned to Mrs. King's residence, Cora tucked Adeline into bed with a book. Satisfied her friend was settled, Cora and Sol went to the constabulary. The brick building dominated the street. They were escorted to Detective Grayson's office, where they were told to wait for him. Any surface not in use had an inch of dust on it. He had stacked files on the floor when he ran out of room on his desk. There was a pile of dirty clothes in the corner as well.

Cora and Sol sat down and waited.

"How does he find anything in this swamp of files and papers?" Sol itched to clean off the desk and line up the pencils.

"I don't know. My desk, at times, looks pretty similar." Cora grinned at him.

"That's going to have to change." Sol shook his head in dismay.

"Oh?"

"I can't live in chaos, Cora. You'll have to make that concession when we're together."

"Together?" She tilted her head toward him.

"Yes." Sol's face was stern. "Unless you intend to stay an ancient spinster. If that is your intention, you are going to need different nightgowns. Immediately."

Cora blushed. "When you say together, you mean in Toronto?"

Just as their eyes met to hash out their future, Grayson opened the door to his office. He settled in behind his desk, rummaged through a desk drawer, and found a pencil. He didn't bother to close the drawer. Cora smiled at the open disdain on Sol's face.

"Sorry to keep you waiting. How can I help you?" Grayson looked from Sol to Cora and then back to Sol, clearly expecting him to take the lead in the conversation.

"We have some information regarding a murder and a white slavery ring." Cora opened her file to show him the pictures of the documents from Eli Pitman's desk. "We both witnessed him shoot police inspector Logan. It appears that Logan has been turning a blind eye to this white slavery ring for a hefty price."

Grayson's head snapped up at that announcement.

"We also saw him inspect thirteen girls he had purchased to be used as prostitutes." Cora's lip trembled as she spoke.

"You both saw this? You are telling me, you will both testify to this in court?"

"Yes."

"I'll go and pick him up today." Grayson stood up.

"I need to request that you do not." Cora opened another file. "His wife has hired me to petition him for divorce, first."

"She won't need a divorce if we have him swinging from a rope for murder," Grayson growled.

Sol shot Grayson a hard look.

"Sorry," Grayson said sheepishly as he looked at Cora. "I'm not used to working with women."

"Never mind that. I'd hang him myself, if I could." Cora waved her hand to dismiss his concern. "Murder is only one aspect of his crimes, sir." Cora laid out the photographs on his desk. "I need to tackle him in divorce court, first."

Grayson's jaw clenched. "I really don't want to wait."

"I have to insist. I know it's unusual, but I am begging you to trust me. The entire women's rights movement will be very grateful, not to mention his wife. Adeline's future depends on the..."

"Women's rights movement, who has time for that?" Grayson interrupted. "He murdered a man!"

Cora lowered her voice. "I am asking you to please wait until you hear from me. When I go in to argue for Mrs. Pitman, if you are in the courtroom, as soon as the proceedings are finished, you can take Mr. Pitman into custody. We need to have him in court the day after tomorrow. I need you to arrest him right after court is adjourned."

Grayson's lips thinned.

"Thirteen girls, we could start to find them right now, if I picked him up today."

Cora's face paled. Sol put his arm across the back of her chair.

"If we do this right, it might protect many, many more girls." Cora's fingertips slid over all the ages and prices on the photographs. "This ring, it's a big one. It has to be taken down, but not at the expense of my client."

"While we're waiting on this court case, what do you suggest we do to keep the citizens of Toronto safe?" Grayson growled at her.

"Mr. Grayson," Cora said sharply. "If this wasn't a matter of grave importance I would not ask it. I know you think this is foolish, but I am begging. Please."

Grayson pulled his hands through his hair.

384

"This is exactly why men don't work with women. They are very hard to say no to." He frowned at her.

Sol nodded his silent agreement.

"When do you expect to be done in court? The day after tomorrow?"

"We should be wrapped up by 3:00 p.m."

"You better hurry." Grayson's eyes narrowed. "If he kills someone else, there will be hell to pay."

She smiled at him radiantly. "I will. Thank you so much."

***

Two days later, Adeline paced outside the courtroom door. A judge would hear their divorce petitions today. Lawyers clumped in the hall arguing with each other, some laughing together. They all looked at Cora in her robes, and their eyes arched in surprise, then hardened in scorn. Wearing their official robes, daring to be their equal. She watched them seethe as they looked at her. Inside her chest, her heart beat hard with anticipation. She noticed a man in the corner of the lobby. He had a tin cup out begging for money. No other lawyer gave him a second look. Shaggy hair, heavy black stubble, and a ripped coat, even gloves with the fingertips removed. Cora shot him a hard look, and he met her eyes briefly before looking away.

Asher Grayson. Oh, thank heavens. Grayson is here, and he is ready for Eli.

She looked away quickly so no one else would pay him any attention. He was dressed this way on purpose. He would take Eli in today, and no one would expect it. She entered the courtroom, took off her hat, and stood tall while the judge called for Pitman v. Pitman. Adeline shook with fear beside her. Cora ignored all of that. She took her stand at the bar, squared her shoulders, and prepared to lose a battle so she could win the war.

Chapter Fifty-One

Cora and Adeline stood as Judge C. Brett Martin entered his courtroom. His eyes flicked over both counsels. Cora saw his eyes widen at a woman lawyer in his court. She couldn't tell what he thought of that.

"The King's bench calls Miss Rood, counsel for Mrs. Adeline Pitman."

"As per the instruction, we are petitioning for divorce on the grounds of adultery and abandonment." Cora spoke clearly and concisely. She ignored the fear that slid around her heart just looking at Eli Pitman.

"What say you?" The judge directed this statement to Eli's legal counsel.

"There are grounds for adultery, but no grounds for abuse. We can prove there has been no abandonment."

"What say you?" The judge looked back at Cora with impatience. His eyes told her she was wasting the court's time.

"I would like to enter into evidence the purchase of a penthouse where Mirabel Salter, Eli's mistress has been living. We have photographic evidence and her testimony, that he lives there with her and has done so for over a year."

"Approach."

Cora presented the documents to the judge and stepped back.

"Your Honour, Mr. Pitman owns property everywhere. He rents to Miss Salter."

That lie hung there, and the judge cleared his throat as he flicked through the evidence in front of him. He looked at Adeline Pitman, and Cora thought she saw his eyes soften. She looked closer at the judge. Early fifties.

Aren't judges usually older?

He was handsome with cool blue eyes and salt and pepper hair at his temples.

"It is disgusting that the law doesn't allow me to dissolve this marriage on grounds of adultery alone," the judge said with such vehemence that Cora's head snapped up.

What! No! I have to lose!

"Unfortunately, a penthouse with a mistress in residence isn't enough."

"I would like to enter into evidence a will that Mrs. Pitman was privy to. She has not been cohabiting with her husband for more than a year, and he has made no attempt to provide for her legally in the event that he passes." Cora held up the document. "This, coupled with the living arrangement, I would like to present as abandonment."

"That will in her hand is outdated." Eli's legal counsel all stood up as she approached the judge.

Her eyes met the judge and she saw that she was defeated.

Perfect.

"Can you present the current will and testament?" the judge asked.

There it was. Cora itched to snatch the will away from the judge.

"This gives half of Eli Pitman's fortune to Adeline Pitman. This divides the remaining assets to his two sons, the issue of said marriage to Adeline."

The judge's eyebrows shot up in amazement. Men were not required to provide anything to wives in the event of their death; this was beyond generous.

Unheard of!

Cora carefully drew a mask of defeat down over her face to hide the sheer joy that washed through her. Half of Eli's fortune!

"How do I know we don't walk out of this courtroom and the will cuts her out and puts Mirabel in... his mistress is pregnant, Your Honour. How do I protect my client when the law is so blatantly biased? How do we protect the lawful wife?" She let her voice raise.

The judge looked at Eli's legal counsel.

"The mistress is pregnant?" the judge asked.

"What does Canadian law think of that? Will Adeline be expected to co-raise this child? How far do you wish the law to further *humiliate* Canadian women?" Cora roared at the judge.

The older lawyer, Mr. Morris, stood up. "They are no longer together, Your Honour. He has already deposited a quarter of his fortune into a bank account for Mrs. Pitman." His voice was as smooth as his hair.

"Unacceptable. As he is the husband, he will retain rights to that bank account. That money needs to be placed in a bank account he has no rights to." Cora demanded.

Eli's face paled. His fists clenched.

Got you.

Judge Martin looked at Eli and then back at Cora.

"May I see that paper?" Cora asked.

Eli's counsel handed her a copy, and she nearly collapsed at the numbers in front of her. She showed them to Adeline, who gasped.

"You're my wife. You are my lawful wife, and you will remain my lawful wife, Adeline. I have never abused you, and I never will. This proves that I will provide for you even after I am dead." Eli stood up as he shouted at Adeline. His lawyers dragged him back down into his seat. They hissed at him to be silent as the judge banged his gavel down hard.

"Order in this court!"

"How can I be sure that the trust will be there for her?" Cora spoke past a throat tense and tight with anxiety. "He could live for thirty or forty years and take that money and redirect it, or drain the bank account. I want that money in a secure bank account. Today. This has been enough humiliation. I will not return to this court and beg and scrimp on my client's behalf at a later date when he has stolen the money from her," Cora roared at the judge. She was grandstanding and loving every single minute of it. The moral outrage was easy to manipulate. The judge ate it up.

"I agree," the judge said firmly. "Let's have that money deposited today. I will issue an order. The bank will send documentation with the reconcile that the sole authority on the account is Mrs. Adeline Pitman. At any later date, if a penny is unaccounted for, we will assume it was stolen by Mr. Pitman. If the money is not deposited today by noon, I will hold Eli Pitman in contempt of court, and I will rule on the side of abandonment."

Eli's face went from white to purple. A quarter of his fortune today and another quarter at his death. He grabbed the lapel of a lawyer on his team and whispered furiously into his ear.

"We will reconvene at 1:00 p.m. You can bring me the bank reconcile, and I will rule on this marriage then."

Cora took a very deep breath. She noticed Sol slip out of court.

He'll tell Grayson to wait. He'll know to do that.

Eli's counsel was visibly nervous as Eli shook with fury. A quarter of his fortune out of his reach and the other quarter tied up legally, in Adeline's account for her to do with as she wished. It was unthinkable. They left the court and retired into separate rooms.

Sol and Cora dragged Adeline into a room and she sat down in shock.

Cora dropped into a chair because now that the trial was paused, the full weight of what she could have lost hit her hard. Her legs buckled and gave out. She put her head between her knees and breathed deep. She gulped air into her lungs past a throat tight with fear at staring down Eli. She trembled in fear. If they didn't come back with that money, Cora rocked slightly at the thought; she didn't have another plan to protect Adeline financially.

What a gamble. Cora's stomach knotted with anxiety.

Sol put his hand on her shoulder. "Are you all right?"

His touch awakened a desire strong enough to burn through the fear. She sat up. His eyes clouded in worry, and his concern brought her to her feet. Sol's eyes were wide when she threw her arms around his neck. She dragged his head down and kissed him. She kissed him so hard, he immediately reciprocated. Joy danced through her heart as he deepened the kiss.

Adeline cleared her throat delicately.

Sol and Cora ignored her.

Cora sunk her fingers into his hair as his hands cradled her jaw; he deepened the kiss further.

Adeline cleared her throat louder. "Excuse me, should I leave? We are in the middle of a trial here... if you would be so kind as to remember I am in the room."

"You are not leaving me to farm in Gimli. I won't have it." Cora tore her lips from his. Sol pulled back. The kiss should have broken the tension between them; it escalated it. They continued to ignore Adeline, who finally left the room in a huff. The door banged shut behind her.

"What farm in Gimli?" He kissed her until she was breathless, and then tried to pull down the tight collar of her dress to gain better access to the inch of skin between her jaw and her collar. He groaned in frustration.

"You know, the farm you left me for!" she shouted in outrage.

He pulled back and smiled. His fingertips tried to erase the whisker burn along her upper lip.

"Oh, that farm! I was under the impression all this time you were just wasting your time as a lawyer waiting for the opportunity to move to northern Manitoba, have twelve children on a farm in Gimli... with me."

"Are we doing this, or aren't we?" Cora shook her head. "I can't handle the suspense. What are you doing? Staying here and keeping me alive to fight for women's rights or going back to your crops?"

"You want me to stay here with you?" Sol's voice washed over her. His eyes locked with hers; excitement raced through her. The prospect of winning this case for Adeline awakened hope inside her in a professional sense, but his voice woke a hope for something better for her future. A future that involved him. All of him.

"I might be persuaded to stay and keep you alive." His voice deepened. "But, I don't like dramatics or hysterics. I like my house tidy. From this day forward, what I say goes."

Cora rolled her eyes and laughed. "No. Absolutely no. To all of that."

Sol grinned and then dropped to his knees. Cora stopped laughing. "If I promise not to drag you to a farm in northern Manitoba..."

"I like where this is going." Cora's breath caught with anticipation.

"If I promise to stay with you in this terrible city and vow with all my heart to love and protect you, ancient spinster that you are, will you do me the great honour of being my wife? To have and to hold for as long as we live?"

Cora dropped to her knees and kissed him again. Gently this time. Reverently.

"It would be my great honour, Sol. I can't go for any length of time without you again. I love you. I love you with everything that I am."

Tears stung her eyes as he pulled a box out of his pocket.

"I was going to wait until after the trial. I was going to wait for tonight, when Eli is safe in custody and Adeline is sleeping with extra laudanum in her tea, but I have a feeling once we get this mess squared away, we're just going to drop right into another one."

Cora gasped as he opened the box to show a ring that was staggering.

"What? How did you get this?" She bit her lip as she looked up at him.

"Well. That farm in Gimli that Eli tried to buy me off with, turns out it was worth a fair bit."

"You sold it!" she shrieked. "All this time, you let me think..."

"While you were defending the rights of Priscilla, I was busy farming," Sol interrupted her. "I am really good at farming, by the way. So, I sold the farm to Silas's parents. Here we are. You'll be happy to know that little Silas you were so fond of already has a pet pig, and he's thrilled to bits to be growing up in beautiful Gimli, Manitoba."

"You put all that money into a ring?" She breathed as he slid it onto the fourth finger of her left hand.

"Of course not, that would be irresponsible. I bought a house, too," Sol said offhandedly.

"A house!" Cora's gasped. This was serious; this was happening.

"Yes. One that is close to Hope House because I think you'll be spending a lot of time there."

Cora's eyes widened.

"It looks like at the end of this trial you and I have new jobs." Sol's eyes burned into hers with intensity.

"What new jobs?" She was breathless, waiting for him to continue.

"After this trial, Jean King will be hiring you to be legal counsel for Hope House, at Adeline's insistence. I was certain you would say yes. I am going to be security for Hope House, and Detective Grayson wants me to join the police department. Once you're settled and the threat is over, I'll be in training to be part of the Toronto Constabulary. I already said yes to that. Our house is close enough for you to ride your bicycle to work and back. So, you can check on..."

"Check on what?" she whispered. She didn't dare move in case this was a dream and everything was going to evaporate. She hung onto his lapels.

"I thought you might want to be close enough so you can check on the nanny." Sol's eyes smoldered as he said it. Confirming that children would be in the future but also her career as a lawyer. "I saw you with that baby in the kitchen of Hope House, and I know with certainty that you might be an ancient spinster lawyer on the outside, but deep down, you want a baby. I just hope you want one with me."

"Sol!" Happiness bloomed inside her. "Not twelve, mind you," she cautioned. "But I would like two."

He grinned and then kissed her.

Tears gathered in her eyes as the emotional storm of being this man's wife hit her hard with every implication of what that would mean. His wife. His children. Him... every day. Every night...him.

Tentatively, she pressed against his chest to make him stop. He complied.

"Before we enter this contract of engagement." She took a deep breath before she presented a few bare facts for his consideration.

"Oh, Cora, I love when you talk like a lawyer. It is so romantic, makes my heart beat hard in anticipation," Sol teased her.

"I'm serious. I have to say this. You might change your mind." Her face paled with anxiety at the thought. She gathered her breath to speak. "My desk will never be clean, and I'm pretty certain the children will take after me. I can't stop the dramatics." Her eyes burned into his. "Very likely, your knuckles will be raw for the rest of your life. I will be going up against terrible predators, angry husbands, bosses who take advantage of female employees."

Cora paused because Sol's eyes hardened at that. She knew down to the ground he wanted in on that fight, to absolve Isold's death in some way. Encouraged, she continued. "I'll be fighting in the center of all of that, until I can't fight anymore. Also, if we have a daughter, I will train her to follow in my footsteps." She paused to gauge his reaction. A very slow smile broke across his face. "Can you handle that? I think it will be quite a bit of discomfort for you. My desk alone will make you crazy." She bit her lip as she waited for his reply.

Sol threw back his head and laughed. White with apprehension, she waited for him to answer.

"Miss Rood, since I met you, I had no idea how much *discomfort* a man could put up with. You haven't said yes."

Cora Rood, confirmed ancient spinster and rider of bicycles, threw herself at Sol Stein, world's tidiest Viking boxer, and kissed him in a way that didn't require a yes.

A tap at the door, to let them know court was going back into session, interrupted them. Sol dragged Cora up off the floor and straightened her clothing.

"Are you ready to go and do this?" Sol tucked a piece of hair behind her ear.

"I am so ready." Cora took a deep breath, "for everything."

"Before we leave, I want you to know how proud of you I am. Watching you in action in court, you are an inspiration, Cora Rood."

"It's called grandstanding. The judge really shouldn't have allowed it."

"I think he was like me. He couldn't take his eyes off you."

Cora turned to look at Sol. "I love you."

"I love you, too." Sol smiled.

"I mean it Sol — you are one of the best men I know."

"You are a very lucky woman," Sol agreed solemnly.

Cora laughed so hard, she wiped tears from her eyes. "I know it. Follow me — I have to lose this trial." Cora smiled as he opened the door.

Together they left the room to find Adeline. Hand in hand. There was no doubt in either mind. They would be married. Immediately. Their life in a spotless, tidy new house on Cherry Street was waiting for them.

But first, Cora Rood had to lose to Eli Pitman in a court of law.

*****

Adeline looked at them and knew immediately, they were engaged. She, despite being a nervous wreck at what they were about to face in trial, hugged Cora hard.

"He told you about the job offer?" she whispered.

"Adeline, I don't know what to say. Of course, I want to be legal counsel for Hope House."

"Cora, you came back to help me. I can't thank you enough."

Cora looked at Sol and then moved closer to Adeline.

"Whatever happens in there," Cora nodded at the courtroom, "I will never forget that you are my friend. I would represent you for nothing. I love you, Adeline. Hope House is going to do amazing things for women in our society. It's a gift to be part of it. You are a woman of sincerity and warmth of spirit, a true humanitarian. I am proud to call you my friend."

"I can't thank you enough." Adeline blinked back tears.

They hugged each other hard. Cora squared her shoulders and wished she could tell Adeline about Eli's upcoming arrest. Instead, she linked her arm with hers. Together as two friends who loved each other, they walked into court.

*****

"All stand."

The court stood as the judge took his seat.

"You may present the bank reconcile," Judge Martin stated.

Mr. Morris presented the bank reconcile to the judge and sneered as he handed a copy to Cora.

She ignored his face and his contempt. Cora swiftly read over the numbers and verified the bank account was only in Adeline's name. Her mind raced at the thought of what this sum could do with interest. The amount made her swoon. Adeline was now, very likely, the richest woman in Canada. Or close to it. She could absolutely change Toronto with money like this. A paper from the bank verified that she was the only one with access to the money. The bank manager signed a note saying that anyone who wished to withdraw funds from this account other than Adeline Pitman would be arrested on site, in accordance with the court's instruction.

"As much as I would like to decree a divorce in this instance, especially as the mistress is pregnant, Canadian law is clear. As this amount of money is guaranteed to Mrs. Pitman and in her name, and as she currently resides in a home provided by Mr. Pitman, it is with great heaviness of heart, I cannot grant a divorce, Mrs. Pitman. The double standard placed on women in divorce court outrages me. However, until legislators remove this double standard, I am subject to it as well. I am not unfeeling as to what this means for you. The ruling is that the marriage between Eli and Adeline Pitman is legal and binding."

The gavel banged down.

"Court dismissed with my apologies to Mrs. Pitman."

The gavel came down again and Cora remained standing.

Eli walked over and stood near Adeline.

"Mirabel's gone. I'll come home." He reached for her.

"Get your hands off me!" Adeline screamed. The entire court jumped to attention; the judge paused and gave Eli a hard look. Sol bolted through the courtroom to wedge his body between them. Eli took a step back and sized up Sol.

Adeline moved so Sol was still between them but she could speak to Eli straight on. "I don't want you back. I will never look at you again. You raped me. If adultery on my part is what it is going to take, I could easily find someone... I just wanted to be sure I could afford the lifestyle I prefer before I go out to find my next man."

Cora's eyes widened at that turn of events. She had an ace up her sleeve, but so did clever Adeline!

"You wouldn't," he hissed, and his lips went completely white as the realization that he had been played crashed down on him.

"Eli, you have no idea what I am capable of. If I walked away from you before all this, I would have been penniless."

"I forbid it." A vein stood out on Eli's forehead.

"Eli, you lost that right with Lucretia Lopez. If that wasn't humiliating enough, Mirabel Salter, a girl the age of your son! You are disgusting. You don't have the authority to forbid me anything. Ever again."

"Adeline." Eli vibrated with rage.

"It's over and it's done. I will never look at your face again." Adeline walked away from Eli without a backwards glance. Sol's hard, strong body was in position to block Eli from following her or harming her in any way.

Cora caught a glimpse of Sol's stern face; he wanted Eli to try to get past him so he could pounce, right here in court.

Eli stood by the table, his hands clenched in fury. The bailiffs hovered. The people in the courtroom hushed at his humiliation.

Cora's eyes widened; she took a step back as she watched Eli's rage get the better of him. Foolishly, Eli tried to push past Sol to follow Adeline out of the room. Sol blocked his path, and Grayson stood at Sol's side.

"Eli Pitman?" Grayson demanded.

"Yes." Eli looked from Sol to Grayson.

"You are under arrest for murder."

Eli blinked in confusion. Slowly, the blood drained from his face as it dawned on him that he was being arrested.

Eli tried to bolt, but Grayson tackled him to the ground and put him in handcuffs. True to Adeline's word, she didn't even turn around to see what the commotion was about. She left the courtroom with her head held high. Eli left in irons, and Cora left with her hand in Sol's.

"Where to now?" Sol asked Cora.

"We have one more legal document to file before we are done for the day." Cora grinned.

"What is that?"

"A marriage license. Shall we?"

Sol's face broke out into a very wide smile.

"After you."

Chapter Fifty-Two

Adeline put the paper with its screaming headlines about Eli Pitman's murder trial, conviction, and hanging aside as she sipped her tea. She shuddered as she thought about the two days it took for them to convict him. He'd paid for his crimes the same week. The house went up for sale the day of his execution. Adeline liked the look of a mansion at the end of Cherry Street near Hope House. She was excited to live near Cora and Sol and was eager to cut down her commute. Jean King handed Hope House back to her at a luncheon where they sipped sherry in the sunshine. Together, they drafted big plans for Hope House.

When the news reached Adeline that she was now a widow, she sipped tea and watched the sun dance on the rose blooms in her garden. Such beauty to be accompanied by such terrible memories. A man she had loved, married, had children with, shared a bed and a home with was no longer in the world. He had spiraled into evil and destroyed countless lives. She shook her head, trying to feel at ease with the loss of Eli. He was gone.

She put half of his estate toward repairing what damage she could. Hope House would flourish; she would guarantee it. With Cora and Sol at her side, there was no battle she couldn't take on. No enemy too great. Cora Rood defeated Eli Pitman. Adeline still shook her head in wonderment at how Cora had outmaneuvered him. She had used her gender, along with the bias men treated her with, to annihilate him. He hadn't seen it coming. Adeline knew she and Cora would fight hard, together. There was so much work to do. The predators among them would never know what hit them.

I could have used this wealth to assist these girls and these women so much earlier. No more wasted time.

Adeline continued to sip her tea as the butler entered the garden with a huge bouquet of flowers. Her eyebrows arched in surprise.

She took the card and read it swiftly. Judge C. Brett Martin.

Hmmm. The handsome judge requests the honour of my presence at a fire and ice ball? Maybe I'll think about that. What's this? Oh. A cheque for Hope House.

Adeline choked at the number — the postscript said this amount would be made available every year, so to budget with this number in mind. Tears stung her eyes at the generosity. She put the cheque down and looked over the grounds of her home. She pressed her hand to her chest at the thought of what that money could do for her charity.

With money like that, we could afford a doctor on site. Maybe a doctor who would specialize in women's health?

Adeline placed the cheque and the card back in the envelope. She stood up, picked up her roses, and went to her desk to return correspondence to Judge C. Brett Martin. She wrote that she was available and would love to attend the fire and ice ball. Perhaps he would like to attend a wedding on September 8 at Hope House, so he could see firsthand where his funds would be directed? She sealed the envelope and smiled as she smelled the roses.

***

It was fitting, according to Adeline, that Cora and Sol be married at Hope House. Something happy to counteract the amount of not so happy they had dealt with since it had opened.

The girls who had been relocated off the streets and into Hope House were thrilled with the assignment to decorate the hall. Adeline happily spared no expense. Anything that could hold a bouquet of flowers held two. The early autumn sun slanted in through all the windows as Cora stopped by to double check that everything was in order. She stood in the dining hall and took a deep breath. She remembered thirty Icelandic families and a heavy pot of soup; she remembered comforting Adeline when Eli threatened to take it all away. She straightened and smiled at the hall. Hope House had survived Eli just as Adeline had. Not just survived, flourished and blossomed.

Who knew what lives would be saved and fixed in this house? Adeline, Mrs. King, the Toronto chapter of the W. C. T. U., the D. W. E. A., and Cora would band together and create *more* of these houses. Cora grinned to herself as she thought about poor Sol Stein. His days of drama were just beginning. Soon though, he would be able to retreat to the all-male world of the Toronto Constabulary. Satisfied the hall was ready; Cora hopped on her bike and rode home to Cherry Street to get dressed.

She unlocked her front door.

Their front door.

Nervous anticipation shivered through her. Soon, in a few short hours, she would be entering this door as Mrs. Sol Stein.

There was a long box on the dining room table. She tilted her head in confusion as she opened it up.

"I think it's your size."

Cora turned and saw Priscilla at the entrance to the dining room.

"Priscilla!" Cora gasped.

Cora's heart soared as they hugged each other hard.

"And a few other people here to cheer you on. This is a very special day. Adeline shipped us all here from Oakland." Wilbur Rood swept Cora up into a bear hug.

Matt slid his arm around Priscilla, his eyes sparkling with happiness.

"Oh, my goodness! I hadn't even dared to dream you would all be here today!" Cora's eyes filled with tears as Lucy Rood hugged her hard.

"Where else would we be?" Wilbur's voice was gruff with emotion.

"I'm so thrilled you are here!" Cora smiled at him.

"Let's get you dressed. The wedding is in an hour, is it not?" Priscilla tapped her foot and checked her watch.

"It is."

Priscilla and Lucy took Cora into the master bedroom with the long box and got to work.

"Open the box. I want to see your face when you see the gown I created with you in mind." Priscilla's eyes gleamed with anticipation.

Cora looked up at Priscilla and bit her lip. Priscilla had a brownie camera ready to document her expression.

When she opened the box and saw the gown, she gasped out loud, again.

Stunning. Yards of tulle and lace. Soft ivory cream. Perfect for a complexion like Cora's.

She pulled the gown out very carefully and wanted to weep with happiness. It made what she had picked out look like a gown you would wear to clean a cookstove. Nothing like this ethereal creation in her hands.

"Priscilla, it is just... I don't even know what to say." Cora couldn't take her eyes off the gown.

"Check the tag. I created a line of bridal wear with you in mind." Priscilla smiled tentatively.

Cora looked at the tag in the gown, and her eyes filled with tears.

"Hope in Oakland," she whispered as she ran her finger across the very discreet tag that only she and Priscilla knew the meaning of. "Oh, Priscilla, I don't even know what to say to you. Thank you is not enough. You didn't have to do this for me." Cora's throat tightened with unshed tears.

"Oh, yes, I did. Without you coming to Oakland when you did, fighting as you did... I would have nothing. You gave me my life and my hope for a bright future back. I have a business where I get to create beautiful gowns and bridal wear all day. I get to share my happiness with clients! Matt and I will get engaged, I'm sure... as soon as the divorce decree comes through, and I am so happy with him. When we get home, we are opening a store together. He let me have the whole front so I can show off my work. If you hadn't come to fight that contempt of court document for me..." Priscilla's eyes darkened as she spoke. "I can't even think about it. Matt says not to ever bring it up again. So, this is the last time. I thank you from the bottom of my heart. Today we are here to rejoice with you and put all this behind us."

"Priscilla, please, I can't hear this. It's too much. I can't..."

"You have to — I'm not done." Priscilla's eyes filled with tears as she spoke from her heart. "There was hope in Oakland, Cora. Hope for me, and I think for you, too. We just had to grab onto it and trust it. I got my life back there and a new love, and you got your confidence back, I think." Priscilla tilted her head to the side. "We both got our *lives* back there. In that courtroom. When you... well, when you did what you do. I can't thank you enough."

Cora dashed tears away as she held onto Priscilla like a life raft.

"All right. No more crying. That's enough. Your eyes will be red! Come on. Let's get you dressed." Lucy Rood, ever practical, handed them each a handkerchief.

Together, they dressed her, and when Priscilla was done, Cora didn't recognize herself. Cora looked at her reflection in the full-length mirror; she tried to blink back the tears shimmering in her eyes. Gone was the ancient spinster lawyer. Gone was the corset that allowed a woman to ride a bicycle. A delighted, gorgeous woman blinked back at her. She peered into the mirror hardly daring to believe the transformation achieved by this gown.

I wonder if Sol will be crying inside when he sees this?

"I want to wear this every day," Cora said breathlessly, "But eventually, it will be time to take it off." Priscilla smiled as a blush bloomed on Cora's face. "Will Sol be able to figure out how to get me out of this thing?" Cora asked timidly.

"He'll have to work for it," Priscilla said dryly.

"He'll figure it out. No fear of that." Mrs. Rood smiled at Cora.

Cora took a very deep breath and checked the time.

"It's time."

They all got into the carriage. After they arrived, Wilbur Rood stood beside Cora in the lobby of Hope House and squeezed her hand.

Cora heard the waltz come belting out of the front of the hall. She walked toward Sol and felt her worries fall away. His eyes widened as she walked toward him, past girls in the process of leaving a life of prostitution behind, past the W. C. T. U. and D. W. E. A. of Toronto that were going to make it happen. Past Adeline Pitman, who stood near a certain judge that had awarded her half of Eli's estate.

The sun slanted down on Cora Rood and Sol Stein as they vowed to love each other.

Sol claimed her mouth in a kiss that made Cora's friends cry with happiness. When they finally broke apart to smile at the audience, Sol slid his arm around her. Cora's heart swelled with love, joy, and hope as she took in the familiar faces in the crowd. For just a moment, everything was still as Cora focused on Priscilla and Matt. Her brother and his wife. Cora spied Asher Grayson, who was not dressed as a homeless man for the occasion, as he sat beside a beautiful blond woman, his wife Melinda. Cora's eyes slid over them all. It was unheard of for a bride to speak at a wedding other than vows, but Cora was not a usual bride.

She could feel Sol, strong and silent beside her. Her eyes met Priscilla's.

"I have something to say." Cora turned her attention fully to the audience. "I would like to address my friends, who brought us here. There would not be a wedding without two women in this audience. First, Adeline when you swept into my office I wanted to hide under my desk."

The crowd laughed.

"You presented the impossible and wouldn't take no for an answer. I thank you for your tenacity and your vision. Without you, I would be stuck in real estate law and talking to a plant. You remained true to yourself and you reminded me that I lost my voice and my purpose. Not only did you push me to be the lawyer I needed to be, you hired this Viking to be my bodyguard, to keep me alive while I did it. You, my friend, are why we are here today. I love you for your strength, your purpose, and the work you do here at Hope House."

Adeline's eyes filled with tears; the handsome Judge Martin sitting beside her handed her a handkerchief and put his arm around her as she composed herself.

"Thank you," Adeline said softly.

"Priscilla." Cora dragged her eyes and attention from Adeline to Priscilla. Priscilla sat up straighter.

"I want to introduce the designer of this dress. When we won against Richard, I saw how the law can protect some women. Your case emboldened me to keep going. To keep righting wrongs. Your case made me face fears and rekindle my courage to conquer them. I wish you and Matt every happiness. You have given me my hope back. Watching you triumph, watching *us* triumph, emboldened me to just keep going, keep righting the wrongs, no matter what the sacrifice. You fought hard. You reminded me that my place was on the front line of this battle. I watched you in awe as you gathered your courage. You reminded me that I had courage, too. The suffragettes will continue to expose double standards, and they will force Canada to change a biased law. But I will know, in my heart, that you gave me the strength to get back up and keep going. I love you for that."

The crowd held their breath as Adeline and Priscilla made their way to Cora for a big hug. Sol was nudged aside as the three women held onto each other. This was more than a wedding; this was a celebration of their victories and their love for each other and a fresh hope for the future. When they finally broke apart, the crowd broke into applause.

The ladies took their seats, and Sol took Cora's arm.

Cora smiled up at him.

"Since my wife has addressed the crowd, it's my turn." Sol looked over the audience. "Thank you, Adeline, for forcing me to be a bodyguard to Cora. You were right. I was glad I took on this job. This tremendous burden turned out to be the love of my life. Priscilla, your case restored Cora's faith in humanity, in the law itself. I can't thank you enough. Without you, without that victory, she might have ended up on a farm in Gimli."

"I assure you that never would have happened!" Cora protested.

The crowd laughed again.

"Now." Sol looked over the crowd. "Because I am married to the most beautiful, most intelligent woman in Toronto, I'm going to kiss my bride. Again."

The crowd held their breath as Sol kissed Cora. They watched as he bent her over his arm, deepening the kiss, claiming her as his own. They murmured in astonishment as she grabbed him by his lapels and claimed him right back.

When they finally straightened up and faced the crowd, Cora hoped they could hear the cheering. All the way to Oakland.

Epilogue

Mrs. Daindridge and Mrs. Carr took a stroll after supper on most nights. Their nightly walks gave them an opportunity to catch up on the events of the day and offset the consumption of butter tarts. They were just rounding the corner onto Crescent Street to watch the sun set when they spied a sewing machine and boxes outside the door of the only vacant building.

"I heard Priscilla is setting up her shop today. It's official. We have a dress designer in Oakland." Mrs. Daindridge had ordered a new slip and various other undergarments from her. She kept it a carefully guarded secret from Mrs. Carr, who was convinced that the fripperies pouring out of Priscilla's temporary shop in the carriage house of Hillcrest were the beginning of the end. Husbands were tiresome enough as it was — who needed to encourage them with lace undergarments? No. Absolutely not! It was outrageous.

Mrs. Daindridge knew Mrs. Carr's thoughts on lace undergarments and resolved she would take her lace undergarments *and* her butter tart recipe to her grave. What Mrs. Carr didn't know wouldn't hurt her.

"You heard that bold Miss Rood married some sort of Viking?"

"I did." Mrs. Carr had sent a handmade quilt. She knew Mrs. Daindridge held a grudge against Miss Rood due to some *perceived* slight which involved her son Darren. Mrs. Daindridge did not need to know about the quilt. She would not approve of quilts being sent across the land for women who didn't recognize a good suitor like Darren. What Mrs. Daindridge didn't know wouldn't hurt her.

"Priscilla insisted she *had* to go to the wedding and Matt already can't say no to her. He's wrapped around her little finger." Mrs. Carr shook her head at the willfulness of this next generation. "In *our day,* you wouldn't expect trips to Toronto with your intended." Mrs. Carr's lips pursed with disapproval.

"They *were* chaperoned," Mrs. Daindridge grudgingly admitted. "Mr. and Mrs. Rood went, too."

"It just seems *flashy*." Mrs. Carr pronounced the word as if it were the worst sort of crime.

Suddenly, she clutched at Mrs. Daindridge as they watched Matt and Priscilla come around the corner of Crescent Street with their arms full of boxes. As quick as their old hips could move, they leaped behind a lilac bush to spy on the couple. Matt put his boxes down and turned to Priscilla. He took the boxes out of her arms.

The old ladies strained their ears but couldn't hear a thing. They watched as Priscilla looked up at Matt, a little confused. He looked up and down the street before dropping down on one knee. Mrs. Daindridge and Mrs. Carr gasped as Priscilla placed her hand on her heart.

They didn't need to hear what she said as Matt took a box out of his breast pocket and slid a ring on her finger. They watched Priscilla wipe tears from her eyes as Matt stood up. They saw her look up at him with so much love; it caused their hearts to melt just a little. Mrs. Daindridge and Mrs. Carr plastered their spectacles against their faces and watched with great anticipation as he took her into his arms.

Matt Hartwell kissed Priscilla deeply as her arms went around his neck. The ladies sighed as Priscilla's hands traced along the hard line of Matt's shoulders.

Their hearts were in their throats watching the obvious love between Matt and Priscilla.

Mrs. Carr held onto Mrs. Daindridge as Matt scooped Priscilla into his arms. They sighed as her hair tumbled free of its pins and cascaded down his arm. They held their breath as he carried her across the threshold of *their* new premises. Matt Hartwell kicked the door shut behind them.

Both ladies strained to look in the window. To their dismay, it was utter darkness.

"Hope in Oakland." Mrs. Carr squinted as she read the sign hanging on the front of the building. "Strange sort of name for a dress shop."

Mrs. Daindridge felt the caress of her new lace unmentionables and thought it was just about perfect.

The End

Acknowledgements

Big thanks to the editors behind the scenes:

Alex McGilvery of Celtic Frog Publishing for his hard work in content, line by line editing, and formatting. I am grateful to you for your hard work and patience.

Julie Sherwood for her work in copy editing.

Ev Marshall and Wendy Holmstrom for their work in proof reading.

Josephine Blake of Covers and Cupcakes, for the book cover, chapter header, book mark and business card design.

Thank you Wendy Mae Andrews and Becky-Jo Fluker for beta reading.

Dana Stam Photography, Photo of Hillcrest for book cover.

Thank you book launch team:

Mom and Dad, Trent, Jody, Sophia and Olivia, Trevor and Melanie, Baily, Azelin, Carson, Wes, Mason and Meika, Betty Levandosky, Tammy, Ava and Mia, Julie and Ashley, Lezlie and Marlee, Becca Green, Ev Marshall and Wendy Holmstrom. Thank you for your hard work on the launch.

A big thank you to Connie Bradshaw at the Souris Library for fulfilling all my research requests and inviting me to come in and speak to the community.

Thank you to the Hillcrest Museum board for allowing me to launch at Hillcrest.

Last but certainly not least, thank you Peter, you are a super huge support. Without you there would be no books and I would be a homeless person. Thanks for paying the bills between book sales and giving me all the time and space I need to write.

Author's note

The first divorce on record in Manitoba was from 1917. Please note, the trials used to create Adeline and Priscilla's divorces are from 1920. That means that less than 100 years ago, women faced this tremendous double standard. Men could divorce due to adultery alone, women had to prove adultery and abuse.

In the interest of privacy, I will not disclose who Priscilla's character was based on, but I will continue to think of her as her trial transcript absolutely haunts me.

Priscilla's story is true. Every heartbreaking sentence. The forced abortions and whipping were so repellent to me I was stunned at what I read.

When I finally got to the end of the transcript and found "Priscilla's" contempt of court document, I didn't believe it. (A copy of this document is on my website. I won't post it until October so there won't be any spoilers!) It seemed too terrible to be true. The courts ordered her back to render conjugal rights by a certain day and when she didn't return she was sent notice that she was in contempt of court. Stunned that the courts wielded that kind of power, I actually didn't believe the paper in front of me.

In real life, this woman had a son, Edward. I am not sure what happened to her or her son. The librarian at the Legislative assembly was fantastic and threw herself into this research, she did find an Edward, same last name as her, that died at the age of one but I hope that was not her child. I can't imagine the level of suffering she endured; to lose a son as well is too much.

After the contempt of court document, there was a letter from her lawyer pleading to revoke that document as he feared for her life. I believe she ran to the United States because the trial ended with a demand from the court that the costs she had incurred to make a defense were to be paid by him. He contested it and that was all there was in the file. I think she ran.

My question as I read the transcript was this— why wasn't "Priscilla's" husband prosecuted for the forced chemical abortions? I knew from researching Til's incarceration, anyone who caused an abortion was subject to life in prison. So, this lady's battle should have happened in criminal court, not divorce court. Thus, the story was born.

A different divorce trial involving a woman being whipped caused me to dig deeper into the criminal code. Women enduring whipping was so prevalent, that there is a picture of it in a medical book. I found it when I wrote The Night They Came For Til, I sort of ignored it thinking it wouldn't be something I would ever run into again. Then I saw it come up again in divorce trials (more than one) and realized it was more prevalent than I thought. I had read in the criminal code of Canada that whipping was never permitted as a punishment for women. (In 1906, whipping was still part of the code and was a sentence that was handed down in addition to hard labour). Thus, I had the prosecution attack Richard for taking a lash to Priscilla because it put him *above the law*. Richard would have been considered the ultimate authority in his home. As such, he could impose restrictions and *corrections* to his wife as he saw fit. This was particularly chilling to me as I thought, who regulates these corrections? (See the research page and read the law paper sited there by Constance Blackhouse.) Her paper and the criminal code is the resource material that I used to write the criminal trial for Richard.

I could tell from the statements and letters from the lawyers to the court that many lawyers were furious at the lack of protection for women in court.

I was shocked at how oppressive the courts of Canada were to women. The law allowing the double standard was not removed until 1925.

If you are interested in the documents, I will put them in my October 2018 newsletter. To receive the newsletter please find me at Rebekah Lee Jenkins.wordpress.com. You are welcome to sign up there. I will also put a record of them on my website.

Ada Bennett is inspired by Elizabeth Buckley. She was the second owner of our family farm. If you love Ada, she has a starring role in The Night They Came For Til.

Cora Rood was inspired by Clara Brett Martin. She was the first female lawyer for Upper Canada and Great Britain. There is very little known about her, other than the fact that she rode a bicycle and fought hard to open the way for women in law.

She obtained her bachelors of mathematics at the age of 16 which speaks to her brilliance. When the benchers of the Upper Canada Law Society offered to relent and let her practice law as a solicitor, she refused. She demanded to practice as a barrister. It took years of fighting to have them agree. Eventually, she got in with one vote.

The night of terror she describes to Ada Bennett happened to a group of women in Washington in 1917. There is no evidence that Clara Brett Martin experienced any violence in her pursuit of practicing law. If she left a record as to why she insisted on being a barrister, she left no diaries or letters to explain it. Her motivation for practicing law was never documented; my writing of her motivation is pure fiction. I do know this; she was so successful that she ended up with her own law firm on Bay Street in Toronto where she specialized in family law. The discrimination in court was so great. By the end she started hiring barristers to represent clients because her presence caused judges to make prejudicial decisions. I concluded that something motivated her to work in family law so I created a scenario that made sense to me. Clara Brett Martin died very early, at age 49. She lived with her sister and was *often* referred to as a spinster. I had a lot of fun with that word!

You might have noticed, the judge who was so progressive in Adeline's case — C. Brett Martin, was a nod to her.

As previously mentioned, other than her education and difficulty with articling, the events of this book are pure fiction.

Author Bio

Rebekah Lee Jenkins has always enjoyed writing as a hobby, but didn't get serious about publishing until 2016. She published her first book *The Night They Came For Til* in June of 2017. Both *Hope in Oakland* and The *Night They Came For Til* are set in her home town, Souris Manitoba.

She was thrilled to be the first writer in resident at the Margaret Laurence House in Neepawa, Manitoba in 2017.

Today, she and her husband live and work in Souris, Manitoba.

You are welcome to read more of her work on her website: rebekahleejenkins.wordpress.com

Rebekah Lee Jenkins

Research:

Petticoats and Prejudice: Woman and Law in Nineteenth- Century Canada by Constance Blackhouse, published by Women's Press, 1991.

Divorce Trial Transcripts from 1917-1925 courtesy of Manitoba Archives.

Criminal Code of Canada, Revised statutes 1906, printed by Samuel Edward Dawson, Law Printer to the Kings. Legislative Assembly, Winnipeg, Manitoba

Pure Patriarchy- nineteenth century Canadian Marriage, Constance Blackhouse, McGill University Law Paper.

Night of Terror leads to Women's vote in 1917. Newspaper article, Washington Post. I found this on the website of Daily Republic.

First Chapter of The Night They Came For Til

I woke up on a ship sailing west with a note from Malcolm, money, clothes, and my doctor's bag. That was it. The list of what I didn't have was longer. My eyes slid shut as I tried to block out the thought.

A week and a half at sea and I still couldn't bring myself to open the note. I was afraid of what it said. My hands shook with terror thinking that Til may be dead. There was no way to manage that thought. The fragile grip holding my sanity would slip; I would be lost. Wincing with pain, I went to my doctor's bag and pulled out the laudanum and the note. A slow, long sip of laudanum, much more than the suggested fifteen drops, swirled through my veins and unlocked the pain, taking the sharp edges away from my thoughts.

I ran my fingers over Malcolm's handwriting, anything to be close to him. I picked up the note to see if I could smell his aftershave.

A knock on the door interrupted my thoughts.

"Your supper, Miss Stone," the steward shouted through the door.

I put the laudanum bottle on top of the note and went to the door to retrieve my tray. I wondered how much Malcolm had paid this little man to serve me my meals so I could stay alone in my berth.

"Thank you." I gave him a tip. I tipped him every day because he was the only thing preventing me from starving to death. Most days I couldn't stand the thought of facing anyone.

I alternated between worrying about where the ship was taking me and not caring. Some were speaking about Canada— I shut their voices out. I was so sick I wanted to die, then I wanted to fight something, and in the end, I lay there day after day, as my body slowly healed. The bruises were fading; the cuts were healing. Before long, I could sit without wincing in pain. My body was young and resilient; inexorably it healed and left my mind far behind, still broken.

Fragments of the past came back to me, often when I was sleeping. The memories would make me wake screaming. If I thought of the attack, it made me sick to my stomach and I would immediately vomit.

After calculating dates to figure out how long I had been at sea, my mind stubbornly refused to acknowledge the fact that my time of menstruation had not occurred yet. My hands shook as I carefully went through the numbers again. Cold sweat of sheer terror soaked through my bodice as the realization sunk in that I was pregnant. My mind raced back to the attack; I couldn't stop it.

***

The night they came for Til, Malcolm found me half in the gutter and half on the street. He closed his eyes and turned away so I couldn't see the horror on his face. Then he pulled off his coat, bundled me up, and carried me to a hospital where he knew a doctor.

"Where's Til?" he asked through clenched teeth before placing me on a gurney.

"She told me to run. I shouldn't have," I wept.

His eyes met the doctor's.

"I trust you, Joshua," Malcolm said in a voice so low the doctor leaned in to hear him. "She's been beaten and raped. I dare say by more than one man."

I drifted in and out of consciousness. I wanted to scream and never stop.

"No expense spared. Do you understand what I'm saying?" Malcolm demanded.

Joshua must have nodded because I didn't hear him say anything at all to that except, "I'll look after it."

***

Can I prove Lady Constance Carstairs ordered the attack? No, I cannot. My body doesn't care; my mind can't comprehend it.

Pregnant with my attacker's baby, my mind was fragmented with disbelief. The dates did not lie. Finally, I took another deep swig of laudanum and opened the letter.

September 30th, 1904

Dear Shannon,

It is with a heavy heart that I send this letter to you. Putting you on that ship with no one to assist you is one of the hardest things I've ever done. I wish we were right there with you. Someday we will all be together again. It's a promise.

In July, Til received a letter from a close friend, Lady Madeline Harper. She had asked Til to send a midwife to Oakland, Manitoba, Canada. At the time Til was going to say no, as you were already enrolled for the school year. In light of recent events, I have sent instruction that you are to be that midwife. I have already sent your qualifications, including your two years of training at the London School of Medicine for Women and date of arrival. Lord Harper has assured me the town constable has been retained to ensure you are protected at every step of this journey. You will have your own home, so you will have privacy to study and heal in the months ahead.

Til has been incarcerated on charges of abortion. Her trial date has not yet been set. I have established a legal team, and she will be exonerated in due time and with due process. Do not worry yourself for her. She has the finest legal minds at her disposal.

It is Til's wish that you are not here for this "circus" as she calls it. It is her sincere desire that you have a long and prestigious medical career. She is concerned that your reputation as a doctor would be muddied by this attack. It is her wish that you remain in Canada until we have this settled.

The clinic was burned to the ground at the time of attack, so there is no need to worry about who will care for the premises.

I know that you have been through a horrendous ordeal and I am so sorry, Shannon. I am hoping that Lady Harper will take care of you as you take care of her in her time of need. I will find the men who did this and I will deal with them to the fullest extent of the law.
Know that we love you and care for you. I will keep you apprised of all matters relating to your aunt. If you want for anything, do not hesitate to ask. I understand Lady Harper's husband is most reasonable and generous. I trust they will care for you, as you are so easy to love.

I'm so sorry about the interruption of your education. We will arrange for you to continue your studies next year after Lady Harper's baby is born.

I hope your travel has been as pleasant as possible. A letter will be ready for you when you arrive.

With Love,
Malcolm

Pain sliced through my heart. Right then, in that moment, I needed Malcolm. He was the only father I knew. I understood his whole life would revolve around Til's trial, and I couldn't help with that. Grudgingly, I saw the wisdom in getting me out of England.

I reread the letter, the part about how my attackers would be prosecuted to the fullest extent of the law. I wished that promise healed my heart.

***

I arrived in Brandon after traveling across Canada. I was weary and so thin my clothes didn't fit. Two long weeks ago, I had run out of nux vomica and I couldn't keep anything down. During the day, I refused to think about it. Only at night, when I had no control over my thoughts, the images came back. I desperately tried to push it out of my mind.

I sat, freezing to death in a train station, in what looked like the middle of a frozen wilderness. How could it be this cold? It was only the middle of November! I put my head between my legs since I worried I would throw up again. My throat was raw from the frequent vomiting. When my stomach finally settled, I got up and wandered to the window.

As I did so, a man approached. He was wearing a uniform and stood over six feet tall with broad shoulders. I hoped this wasn't the constable. The sheer size of him terrified me, until he smiled; his hazel eyes crinkled at the corners. He came closer, that smile genuine and warm. I tried to smile back, but instead I vomited. All over his shoes. I groaned with mortification and wished for the ground to open up and swallow me.

It didn't.

Available on Amazon

88911640R00249

Made in the USA
Lexington, KY
19 May 2018